Praise ....

"Stephenia McGee doesn't fail to delight lovers of historical romance and with some twists and turns, she engages the lore of old mystery in our hearts as well. Readers who love engaging characters and unique settings will devour McGee's stories! Run to your nearest bookstore now!"

- Jaime Jo Wright, ECPA Best-Selling Author of The Vanishing at Castle Moreau

"River pirates, gangsters, smugglers, and an unforgettable, vivacious heroine all set in the roaring twenties--this story has it all. McGee pens a unique and swashbuckling tale that submerses readers into the showboat world of a strong family of faith and the fish-out-of-water hero who brings trouble aboard. Readers looking for mystery, intrigue, adventure, and romance will not want to miss this entertaining read."

- Crystal Caudill, author of Counterfeit Faith

"Stephenia H. McGee delivers a riveting journey into the roaring 1920s in a delightful new setting—the showboat era! With its compelling characters, gripping plot, and immersive narrative, The River Queen stands as an unmissable delight for fans of historical romance and high-stakes adventure."

- Misty M. Beller, USA Today bestselling author of the Brothers of Sapphire Ranch series

The
River Queen

Books by Stephenia H. McGee

Ironwood Family Saga
The Whistle Walk
Heir of Hope
Missing Mercy

The Accidental Spy Series
*Previously published as The Liberator Series
An Accidental Spy
A Dangerous Performance
A Daring Pursuit

Stand Alone Titles
In His Eyes
Eternity Between Us
The Cedar Key
The Secrets of Emberwild
The Swindler's Daughter

Time Travel
Her Place in Time
(Stand alone, but ties to Rosswood from The Accidental Spy Series)
The Hope of Christmas Past
(Stand alone, but ties to Belmont from In His Eyes)
The Back Inn Time Series
(Stand alone books that can be read in any order)

Novellas
The Heart of Home
The Hope of Christmas Past

Buy direct from the author's online bookshop!
Support the author and find great deals.

https://shop.stepheniamcgee.com

The River Queen

River Romances Book One

Stephenia H. McGee

BY THE VINE PRESS

The River Queen
Published by: By The Vine Press, LLC
www.StepheniaMcGee.com

Printed in the United States of America

Cover design: Roseanna White Designs
Model photography: Period Stock, LLC
Cover Model: Daleigh Ramsey
Other images used under license.

Library of Congress Cataloging-in-Publication Data
Names: McGee, Stephenia H. (Stephenia H. McGee) 1983 –
Title: The River Queen / Stephenia H. McGee
Description: By The Vine Press digital eBook edition | By The Vine Press Trade paperback edition | Mississippi: By The Vine Press, 2023
Summary: River pirates, a stolen steamboat, and a deadly chase down the Mississippi—but falling in love might be the real adventure.
Identifiers: LCCN 2023938312 | ISBN-13: 978-1-63564-068-7 (paperback) | 978-1-63564-069-4 (ebook)
Subjects: Christian Historical Fiction | Novels

Now to him who is able to do immeasurably more than all we ask or imagine, according to his power that is at work within us, to him be glory in the church and in Christ Jesus throughout all generations, for ever and ever! Amen.

Ephesians 3:20–21

B lasted pirates. Dirty, filthy, rotten—

Emmett Carter concentrated on keeping his head above churning dark water. The Wicked River could swallow a man whole in a matter of moments. Faster in the dark. And he'd heard one too many stories of alligators as long as a man in these parts.

Kicking his legs, he forced his body toward the Mississippi's muddy shoreline. Pirates. Of all things. River pirates.

He spit out water and fought against the swirling current thick with sediment until his fingers brushed the shore. Digging, clawing, he struggled through the mire like a crawfish until he emerged on the bank as filthy as any backwater crustacean.

Jeers and laughter floated around the next bend before being swallowed by the raucous cacophony of bullfrogs and cicadas.

Heaving, he flopped onto his back. Mud clung to his hair, fingers, and shoes.

He breathed deep and sent forth a prayer for a thimble's worth of grace for the scallywags. He couldn't bring himself to give them a drop more. Overboard was better than dead, and cursing the rabble wouldn't get his boat back or save his sinking investment.

He'd only made it twenty-five miles downriver from St. Louis before disaster struck. He and Jacob should have never taken such a risk. What had possessed him to agree to help with one of his brother's schemes?

Emmett coughed, his expanding ribs sore from the hit he'd taken when they'd thrown him over the rail.

"Ho, there!"

He forced himself to his feet, fists at the ready.

"Mr. Carter? That you?"

Emmett released a breath and lowered his hands. The gray-haired engineer approached in the dusky light, his grin grating on Emmett's good manners. What right did this man have to smile while Emmett's entire livelihood slipped away down the Mighty Mississippi?

"They left the crew alive, sir. Only two are any worse for wear, and that's on the account of Lester and Leroy thinkin' they was strong enough to take on a gang of armed men on their own." Derwood snorted. "Boys. More bravado than brains, most of the time. Why, I ain't known a one of them two to—"

"They made it to shore?" The man could ramble at the most inopportune times.

"Well, now, about that." He scrubbed his beard. "All of the crew excepting me, you, and them two boys stayed on the boat." His lips twisted before he shrugged. "Looks to me like most of that crew you hired done went turncoat."

Meaning the crew went along to save their hides or they were in on the thievery? It didn't matter. Whoever had been plotting against them, they'd taken his inheritance downriver.

"Lester and Leroy. Are they hurt?"

"Nothin' but a bump on the head and a cut that's going to need a few stitches." Derwood studied the rippling eddies as the sun's final rays glistened on the churning silt. "Alive is fair enough, by my reckoning."

"I envy your outlook." Emmett fished out his soggy wallet. "Wish I could do more, but this should get you and those boys a dry room and a hot meal."

"Much appreciated." Derwood accepted the dollar bills with a smile. "Nearest town is just up the bank."

Emmett pointed to a hazy shape in the distance. "Is that a boat?"

Derwood followed his gaze as he tucked the money into his breast pocket. "Yes, sir."

"Friendly?"

Derwood lowered his brows. "One of them big showboats, so... yessir. Most likely. But they ain't the kind to take you on board. Not unless you're looking to buy a ticket and watch a show."

Emmett would spend his last dollar on a two-bit vaudeville act if it meant a way off this muddy riverbank and an opportunity to contact local law enforcement.

Electric lights flashed to life, illuminating a floating theater. Swells of gaudy music followed from what sounded like a steam-powered pipe organ.

"Best of luck to you, Mr. Carter." Derwood plopped a dripping hat over his long hair, unconcerned water rivulets streaked down his face.

"Wait. What about our contract?"

A sly grin revealed yellowed teeth. "This job's done, so I'm headin' back to be findin' the next." He turned out his palms. "Unless you got another boat up your sleeve and a new load of cargo that needs deliverin'."

When Emmett failed to answer, Derwood tipped his hat and marched up the bank. He disappeared into the shadowed embrace of a cottonwood cluster.

Emmett hesitated, judging the trek to town against the flashy boat. Derwood's way led to a dry room but maybe not to a law officer. Emmett lifted one shoe, dumped out the water, and did the same with the other.

The music drew swells of farming families from the nearby woods like rats to the Pied Piper. Likely everyone in town would come. Perhaps even a lawman.

Resisting the urge to shield his ears against the shrill whistles belting out a jaunty tune, he made his choice and trudged through the mud.

Better than the riverbank.

He repeated the line to himself as he trudged to the staked gangplank, but for some reason, unlike the sediment, the sentiment wouldn't stick. Town made more sense. So why did he keep sloshing toward the inviting lights like an addlepated moth?

Dressed in their Sunday best, the laughing swarm of townsfolk surged around him. No one took interest in the soggy man in a once-white suit as they hurried up the gangplank to a gleaming white boat. Two stories high, the showboat boasted porches all around its massive rectangle. People filled the bow as they waited to make their way inside, a festive flair sweetening the humid air. He'd never visited one of these floating theaters. Perhaps he could see the appeal for people far from big cities and their opera houses.

The music settled into a more reasonable volume, and the cheery notes accompanied the persistent slosh of his shoes as he shuffled up the walk. He stood in the line, ignoring a family who cast him curious glances.

Bold red letters at least three feet high marked the upper deck—*The River Queen.*

A flamboyant dash of peacock blue danced past the letters. He blinked, sure he'd swallowed too much muddy water.

A woman stepped up to the railing. Her blazing red hair hung in loose, thick ringlets down the back of her striking costume. Strands escaped from underneath a beaded headband and caught in the breeze, whipping around behind her like a dancing flame. Her brilliant-blue gown cascaded with peacock feathers matching the ones erupting from the sapphires set over her temple. Stunning.

"Welcome! Welcome!" The woman thrust her arms wide, grinning at the crowds.

Never had he seen a woman arrayed as though she'd stepped out of a tale from Italy's famed carnival. The electric lights danced off the shimmering gown that hugged every feminine curve. The voluminous skirt billowed in feathered waves along the deck railing.

"Sir? Could you move along?"

A woman's pinched voice behind him snapped Emmett from his stupor. He shook his head and hurried to fill the gap left ahead as the woman above him began to sing in a clear, strong voice.

"Welcome, welcome,
All my friends,
Welcome, welcome,
This is where the story begins,
Bring your sorrows,
Bring your joy,
Every man, woman, girl, and boy,
Welcome, welcome,
To *The River Queen*,
Where every moment is but a dream."

The fanciful lyrics followed him as he stepped beneath the upper deck and headed deeper onto the boat. He scanned the crowd to get his senses in order. He must locate a lawman. Perhaps best done by first finding a crew member.

No one other than the beautiful bird above seemed to be a part of this production, however, so he bustled along with the crowd until he passed inside a hallway and stopped in front of a ticket window.

"Welcome!" A woman in her elder years with sparkling blue eyes flourished a hand. "Do you already have a ticket, or will you be purchasing one?"

"I don't want a ticket. I need..." The word *help* stuck in his throat. He cleared it and tried again. "Do you know where I can find a member of the local law enforcement?"

The woman cocked her head like a confused parrot. "Sir, are you aware this is a showboat?"

Exceedingly.

Nodding to his state of disarray, she lifted a brow. "Fell into the river, did you?"

He clenched his teeth. "Something like that."

"I'm sorry for your misfortune." She brightened and flashed him a brilliant smile with perfect teeth. "Nothing cures a sorrowful day like a night at the play."

Emmett ignored the quip. He didn't have time to see a play. Of course, he now stood in line to do exactly that while people behind him grumbled with impatience. And he dripped water all over the floor.

He was about to murmur an apology and remove himself from the counter when the door behind the older woman opened and the lady from the balcony flounced inside.

Her presence filled the tiny space. "So excited to see the show you swam to the boat, did you?"

The laughter in her voice arrested all rational thought.

"Ah, poor dear." She patted the older woman on the shoulder. "Let's give him a pass, shall we?" Cobalt eyes focused on Emmett. "Not the best seat in the house, mind you, but I can't have you soaking one of my good seats. Now, can I?"

The other woman grumbled something and passed Emmett a ticket. He accepted the slip of paper and shambled away from the lady tsk-tsking behind him.

What had just happened?

The paper granted him standing room at the back of the theater. Perhaps he should let himself dry and rest a bit. The crowd pressed before and behind, ushering him down a sloping hallway to another set of large doors. A tall man with a gray mustache from another era motioned to see Emmett's ticket.

The man barked a laugh, then scanned Emmett from tousled hair to sodden foot. "Found her another stray, did she?" The words rumbled out of him with a touch of lilting Irish brogue. He pointed to a rear corner. "You can stand back there. I'll get Freddie to bring a towel."

"Appreciate that, sir." Emmett hesitated. "May I ask the favor of an announcement to request a lawman meet me after the show?"

The fellow blinked at him. "Why would I do that?"

"I assume the entire population of the nearest town is under your roof. My best hope of speaking to such a person is here."

The old man waved Emmett away. Did that mean he would make the announcement or not? Seeing no other option than to take his place, Emmett scooted behind a row of chairs and leaned up against the wall. Scents of popcorn and taffy caught in his nostrils, hinting at the time his mother had taken him to see a circus. A pleasant distraction from the musty smell wafting from his suit.

At the bottom of the sloping seating area, an orchestra pit stood in front of a grand stage lit at the edges by electric lights. Box seats swept along the narrow room's upper reaches, holding a single row of chairs almost all the way down to the stage itself.

Fine curtains hung alongside a backdrop depicting a window to a seaside scene. As people continued to file in, a juggler took the stage, tossing two, four, and then six red balls into the air, flinging them higher and higher until they nearly struck the ceiling. Children giggled while adults clapped.

"Here, mister." A boy of about twelve with a mop of brown hair thrust a rough white towel into his chest.

"Thank you." Before the boy could scurry off again, Emmett caught his elbow. "I've got a nickel if you'll do me a favor."

The boy's eyes rounded at the proffered coin. "What sort of favor?"

"I need you to make an announcement asking for a law officer to stay behind and speak with me."

He pinched his lips.

"After the show, of course. I don't want to cause any trouble."

The boy plucked the nickel from his fingers and disappeared into the crowd.

Hopefully that meant he'd accepted the job. Nothing to do now but wait. Unnoticed in the tucked-away corner, Emmett scrubbed his hair and then made a pitiful attempt at drying his jacket. Better to take it off and drop it to the floor behind him. Pride and propriety be hanged. He'd rather stand here in soggy shirtsleeves than a jacket he could swear had begun to steam.

Cooler, he tugged his collar loose and dabbed the towel over his ruined shirt. What would Jacob think? His brother probably would have fought the pirates and single-handedly saved the steamboat. He'd always been the risk-taker while Emmett stayed behind to handle the mundane responsibilities. Something he should be doing now instead of letting Jacob talk him into hauling a load of tobacco downriver.

Music flared to life from the orchestra pit, and the din increased as people hurried to their seats and settled in. The juggler took his final bow, and the lights dimmed before they brightened again.

A clear feminine voice rang out over the crowd. "*The River Queen* welcomes you to the 1923 season!" The flame-haired woman took center stage, her extravagant gown catching the light with a thousand sparkles. She dipped into a deep curtsy. "May your troubles be forgotten as you step into our dream." Her gaze found his while she rose, and a slow smile curved mischievous lips.

Troubles, indeed. This woman might well make him forget every logical thought he'd ever had.

For reasons he couldn't fathom, every care he'd had this night—his stolen steamboat, his scattered crew, his sodden clothes—drifted away. Transfixed, he could do nothing more than surrender to the spell of this strangely beautiful river queen.

Anola flourished a deep curtsy and winked at the dripping fellow in the back. She barely withheld a laugh during her final twirl for the crowd. Then she dashed back to the green room for the first costume change. Poor fellow. He looked a mess. A handsome one, though. About her age with dark hair, a firm jaw, and intelligent eyes that seemed to weigh and measure everything.

A tingle zipped over her arms. Nonsense. The man's appeal had nothing to do with her kindness.

She waved at Henry and Sue as the married couple helped one another backstage with their final costume touches. The first show of the season after they'd departed St. Louis always had everyone in their troupe buzzing. The four actors who supported the family in their productions had become like family themselves. Sue beamed, and Henry dipped a nod. Ben and Paul should be in place.

Perfect. Everything was running smoothly.

Lady Marie met her at the green room's doorway. "You're two minutes behind schedule." Her grandmother puckered her painted lips. "Watching that near-drowned fellow, weren't you?"

"Of course not." Well, the man *had* been handsome with his dark hair falling in waves atop a strong and masculine face, but that had nothing to do with it. Lady Marie merely saw romance wherever she could. Anola swiped the headband from her temples and ignored her grandmother's tented eyebrows.

She handed the peacock dress to Lady Marie and traded it for Mrs. Shuler's frock for the first act. She shimmied into the plain brown wool and tied the quick strings. She sure loved that about costumes. No difficult buttons or hard-to-reach places. All clothing should be as simple as their costumes. Of course, those flapper dresses she'd heard about seemed every bit as—

"Did you hear me?"

Anola tugged her long hair into a knot. "Forgive me. What did you say?"

Lady Marie huffed. "I said, don't let yourself get distracted. Remember what happened the last time."

How could she forget? Entranced with a romantic scene last summer, she'd made a mess of the production. In her defense, it was the first performance of the season, and her job tugging on the suspended rocker to release the fake snow across the window got monotonous. In her ardor, she'd not realized how hard she'd been tugging the line until the entire thing dumped on the actors' heads.

No one had let her forget it.

"I'll not be distracted." Anola wiggled her fingers for her bonnet. Still, she couldn't help but wonder. What was that fellow's story, anyway? In all her years on the showboat, she'd never once seen a person attend the feature soaked head to foot. Most would have taken their leave in favor of dry clothing. So, naturally, he made her curious. She'd do her part to be sure he got a good show.

Lady Marie shook her head in an amused sort of way and thrust the bonnet into Anola's waiting hand.

She placed a peck on Lady Marie's wrinkled cheek and dashed out the door. A shimmy past the scenery ropes and she was in the wings just as Paul spoke her cue from center stage.

"Keep your voice down! My wife will be here any moment."

Anola sucked in a breath and strode onto the hardwood. She peeled her shoulders back in righteous indignation and pointed at Paul, who played Mr. Shuler. "What's this I hear about a baby?"

The crowd gasped as she knew they would. As they would at this line in every town along *The River Queen*'s run down the Mississippi.

"You don't mean to say you think it's mine." Paul—Mr. Shuler—snorted. "Come now, Betty. You know this man is lying."

Anola couldn't help herself. She cut a glance across the crowd while Paul and Ben argued—Mr. Shuler and Mr. Holden—about who had fathered an illegitimate child.

The riverman, as she'd taken to calling him, stood in the far recesses under the balcony, and she couldn't make out his features. But he was enthralled, surely. How could he not be?

She stepped between the men, falling right into the scene without pause. "And Anna? What does she have to say on the matter?"

Mr. Holden snagged a ragged cap from his head. "Well, you see now, we can't trust her claims on account of—"

"I asked for *her say*, sir. Not yours. Shall I have the town council bring her before the hall and let her share her story there?"

The crowd murmured, caught up in the scandal. Paul looked properly stricken, as an accused husband should. The audience grumbled.

"She's claimed three men as the father, Betty. How can that be?" Mr. Shuler turned out his palms.

Anola pulled her bonnet from her head and sighed, placing a hand over her heart. "My own husband." She stifled a sob. "All

those nights you were out playing cards...were you...instead...?"
Her voice cracked, and the crowd leaned forward in their seats.

"Betty, you can't believe that." Mr. Shuler reached for her,
but Anola let out a strangled cry and dashed off stage.

She smiled and hurried over to the rigging to pull the next
scene into place. She'd given her finest performance and had
the crowd on the edges of their seats. When Mr. Shuler hung
his head and delivered his line about wishing he'd stayed home
with his family as a man ought, she tugged the lines to lift
the painted seascape and drop in the one that would portray
his office. There would be two more scenes before her next
appearance.

Her part in this season's feature was small, but she didn't
mind. She preferred welcoming and dismissing the crowds
anyway. There were always old friends she got to see but once
a year to wave to and new faces to greet. When she took the
stage, she had to play a part. But as spokeswoman for the Flynn
family, she had the chance to be herself.

The business scene drew to a close, and she let the main
curtain fall. A change of scenery while the cabin boy sold candy
and Ben performed his tap-dance and juggling combination.
Then she had one more scene to act out as Mr. and Mrs. Shuler
reunited before she returned to the green room to change.

This play, like all others performed by *The River Queen*,
carried a strong moral message. Mr. Shuler would have never
been suspected of fathering another woman's child had he
been home with his family and therefore above suspicion.
Every play Stephen Flynn produced would be true to his faith
and convictions, and what Da wanted, he brought into being.
Her grandfather, known to all as the captain, supported him.

Anola had no qualms about the choice, of course. Not that
she'd seen much of the world for herself, but Lady Marie had
told enough hair-raising tales about places like Natchez Under
the Hill for Anola to be glad she'd spent her life away from such
things.

12

She threw her heart into the touching reunion of Mrs. Shuler and her husband—as much as a woman of twenty-three who'd never had a serious suitor could, leastways—and then dashed back to the green room.

Lady Marie met her at the door once again, this time all smiles since Anola had returned on time. Matron of the showboat and self-proclaimed Lady of the Waters, Lady Marie kept every family member, actor, and crewman on task. Anola's grandmother helped her shimmy out of one dress and back into the other, then opened a tube of lip rouge and dabbed her pinkie in.

Anola dipped low enough to meet the other woman eye to eye, then waited as the red hue slipped over her lips and cheeks to refresh her features. The task finished, Anola placed an air kiss—one did not mess up her lips once painted—to Lady Marie's cheek and dashed out again.

She made it all the way to the wings before she remembered what she'd forgotten.

Oh my stars and sunrise.

Anola plucked pins from her hair and let the mass fall down her back. How had she been distracted to the point to forget her feathered headband? The accessory made the whole look come together. Not to mention the hours she'd put into it. She'd fashioned her ensemble after discovering a sack of assorted feathers in a curiosity shop somewhere in Missouri. Who knew who—or why, for that matter—had collected so many exotic feathers, but she'd been charmed.

The shop owner had said elaborate beadwork and headbands were all the rage. Without the added flair, she was simply another girl in a dress.

Oh well. Nothing for it now.

The final piano notes of Mam's "Sunshine and Moonbeams" washed over the theater, the cue their production came to an end. The expected hush settled for...one...two...

Anola lifted her hem just as the applause erupted and she slipped out onto the stage. The warm lights bathed her, and the same satisfaction she'd felt since she'd held her first role at four years of age welled in her center.

She dipped into a deep curtsy and motioned for the actors to join her on the stage. They completed their bows, their work of providing joy to another sleepy town completed. Anola ducked to the wings, a contented sigh on her lips, when Freddie snagged her arm.

"You gotta make an announcement."

Anola glanced over the crowd rising from their seats and beginning their exits. "Now? Why?"

He tugged her arm. "Please, 'Nola."

Poor lad. Those bright eyes did her in. She patted his head. "I shall do my best."

Anola hurried out to the center of the stage and tilted her head back. She knew of only one way to recapture a crowd's attention. She opened her mouth and began what Mam called "The Mermaid's Song" at the top of her lungs' capacity. The song had no lyrics, simply a rising and falling of pitch and melody, enrapturing of its own accord.

People paused, several plopping into their seats again for the unexpected performance while those who had already made it into the aisles turned back to watch. As the final note hung in the air, her chest tightened.

Oh no. She'd gained their attention, but she had no idea what she needed to announce.

Before the crowd could applaud and she lost them once more, she lifted her hands. "Thank you for joining us on *The River Queen* tonight!" A few started to clap, but she waved them down. "You have been one of the finest crowds I've seen, I dare say."

As unobtrusively as she could, she waved for Freddie to come out of the wings. When he didn't, she huffed and waved harder.

The crowd, thinking this to be a part of the show, started to chuckle.

Might as well flow with it.

In dramatic fashion, she placed her hands on her hips and said in a loud stage whisper, "They are waiting for you. Come on!"

Freddie peeked his head out from behind the curtain.

The crowd whistled and cheered. Freddie eased out further, his open mouth working the audience perfectly.

"My good people!" Anola gestured to the wide-eyed boy edging her way. "We have an announcement, if you please."

Freddie reached her side, and she leaned down to him. "What are we announcing?" Da had been known a time or two to conduct a surprise contest, much to the delight of their patrons.

"A lawman. Sheriff or somethin'."

The words didn't register. "What?" Anola frowned at him. "What in the stars are you talking about?"

Freddie glanced out at the crowd, who strained forward. The boy's face reddened. "That man, the one who done fell in the river, said he needed a man of the law." He produced a coin, but clutched it when she moved to examine it. "Gave me my own nickel for telling you."

Her stomach twisted as she straightened and scanned the crowd. The wet fellow—now damp best she could determine—stared at her with intense eyes.

Did the man know nothing of a production? Of the dream they brought to these people? He thought to ruin all they had accomplished by calling out for a lawman at the end of the show and thus causing the crowd undue worry?

Not if she had any say in it.

Anola grinned. "It seems we have a surprise for tonight! One lucky person has been chosen to join me on stage!"

The crowd murmured.

She stooped close to Freddie again, pretending to listen to something he had to say though the boy remained as still as a petrified mouse.

As an idea formed, she spun back to the crowd with a conspirator's wink. "Our winner will also take home a special prize!"

This gained a roar of approval. No matter she didn't *have* a special prize. "In this section. There. You in the back, against the wall!"

The riverman startled and pointed to himself, his widened eyes and opened mouth evident even from this distance.

"Yes, you." Anola chuckled and waved her arm. "What do you say, everyone? Should he join me on stage?"

The audience cheered, and as the fellow moved forward down the center aisle, more than one man clapped him on the shoulder. The man skirted the orchestra pit where Mam sat, fingers frozen over the piano keys.

He stepped onto the stage, wariness on his strong features. He was taller than she'd first thought.

"Are you ready for your prize, sir?"

The man stared at her.

He wasn't going to make this easy, was he? The crowd flooded the theater with their cacophony, cheering him on to whatever she had in store.

She hadn't a thing.

Float with the current.

With a grand smile and as much flamboyance as she'd ever employed, Anola grasped the man by his shoulder and planted the smack of a loud kiss on his cheek.

The man's jaw dropped, and the audience erupted in laughter.

Anola curtsied, then grabbed the stunned fellow by the hand, and led him offstage.

W hat had he gotten himself into? The river queen hauled him into another world. Men and women jostled ropes and lifted painted scenery boards. Jovial voices bounced off walls crowded with all manner of props and accessories. She kept a hold on him, weaving around the actors and through the staging area until they came to a small room nearly overflowing with clothing.

A costume room?

Two walls contained racks stuffed with clothing of every conceivable kind, many of the long hems hanging over the worn blue carpet underfoot. The other walls, having to bear the brunt of functionality, hosted two women's dressing sets, a table covered with hats and bonnets, a dresser, three chairs, and a stand mirror.

Occupying the center of the chaos stood the stout form of the older woman he'd spoken to in the ticket booth. One look at her stern features and he tried to pull free of the river queen's grip. But either she did not notice the cause of the matron's glower or she didn't care.

"Into the green room?" The dark-haired woman scoffed. "What's blossomed in that mind of yours now?"

The river queen released him, though no embarrassment tinged her pale cheeks. She laughed. "You should have seen his face. As wide-eyed as a first-day cabin boy and every bit as lost." She settled both hands on the curve of her hips and continued to speak as though he weren't there. "I had to think fast, seeing as he put me in quite the pickle."

Pickle? How had he done any such thing? *She* had drawn *him* onto the stage and embarrassed the life out of him. He best get this situation under control before...well, before it got any more out of hand than it already was.

The irony of the thought fell flat.

Emmett straightened himself as best he could. "Excuse me." He dipped his chin. "I must be going."

He made it no more than a half turn toward the door before she had hold of him again. "Without an escort?" Her snort somehow still managed to sound feminine. "I think not."

Escort? He—a man—needed this ethereal creature to be his escort? Then again, he would never find his way out of the bowels of this boat on his own. "I must find a lawman."

She crossed her arms over her bosom and cut a glance at the matron. "For this, he is here." Both women eyed him. "Freddie told me I had to announce that this man wanted a lawman. At the end of the show!"

She spoke the last line with such disbelief that Emmett drew back.

The matronly woman's eyes widened. "What sort of trouble have you brought us, young man?"

As he'd feared. The situation tumbled further out of control the longer the women went on. "My name is Emmett Carter. I was on my steamboat when we were assaulted by pirates. They dumped us into the river."

Both women stared at him, and the absurdity of his own words grated his already fraying nerves.

"I swam to shore near your gangplank. I boarded in hopes a sheriff might be present, seeing as how most of the nearby town had come to see the show."

The women exchanged a glance. Spoken aloud, his reasoning did seem odd.

"So you came on the boat, stood in the ticket line, procured a free pass from my granddaughter, and then told our cabin boy you needed a sheriff instead of walking the half mile into town and looking for said fellow at his place of employment?"

Heat clawed up his neck. "I asked the man looking at the tickets if he would make an announcement for a lawman to meet me after the show."

They exchanged another look.

"The captain knew about this?" The older woman, who had to be in her late sixties—though her hair had been dyed so deep a brown as to be nearly black—heaved a dramatic sigh. "And he let him remain?"

He didn't bother telling them the older man had ignored his request, prompting him to employ the boy.

"I'm sorry to have disturbed your production." That seemed to be the root of their ire, though for the life of him he couldn't fathom how his mere presence had done anything of the sort. "I'll take my leave now."

The river queen tapped a finger to her lips. "It's well past dark, and I'm sure everyone has retired for the evening. Why don't you stay for some dry clothes and refreshments? Do you like tea?"

The older woman's mouth gaped.

These were by far the oddest people he had ever encountered. Who served tea at this time of night? He nearly shook his head, but the prospect of a dry suit made him hesitate long enough for the woman to claim victory.

"Very good. Lady Marie, would you kindly find something for Mr. Carter to wear?" She raked her gaze over him. "He should be able to fit into one of Paul's outfits, don't you think?"

19

The other woman's eyebrows rose clean to her hairline. "You ask your da about this?"

A mischievous turn of her lips indicated she had not. Though rather than a reprimand, the older woman tittered.

"All right then. Off with you. I'll have him change and wait on the porch."

Emmett held up a hand. "Respectfully, I must decline. I need to find a lawman posthaste."

"You mean two hours or more after the incident, late enough into the evening that most people have already claimed their beds? So that, what? You can start a river race with rogues hours ahead of you through the dark of night?" The matron, Lady Marie, tilted her head, her mix of humor and exasperation once again leaving him speechless. "No, there's nothing for it now. You'll have to wait until morning."

"With that, I bid you adieu." The flame-haired woman dipped into a curtsy fit for a royal court, flashed him a coy grin, and then swept out of the room with a swish of blue silk.

The older woman sighed. "She'll have a time climbing the ladder to her room in that outfit."

She planned to climb a ladder? In a giant peacock dress?

"Let's see now..." The other woman fumbled through one of the racks. "There must be something..."

She continued to talk to herself as she rifled through clothing, but all he could manage to do was stare at the doorway the river queen had left behind.

Anola nearly burst into laughter. She managed to keep her composure all the way through the backstage area and to the ladder, the quickest way to the second deck. She hiked the layered skirt up to her knees and tucked the fabric under one arm, careful not to crush the cascade of hand-sewn feathers.

There. Easy enough. She scrambled up the ladder. Her room stood above the green room on the family hallway. Her grandparents occupied one suite of rooms to her left, while her parents claimed the suite across the hall. The small room over the green room had been hers ever since she'd been old enough to no longer sleep in her mother's steamer trunk.

Whistling to herself, she opened the door to her chamber and stepped inside. Now, what to wear for their customary night lunch with a handsome stranger? She laughed. The idea sounded like something out of one of their plays. No wonder Lady Marie had allowed it.

While Mam and Da proved more practical, Anola could always count on her grandmother to share in her sense of adventure. Unusual circumstances such as this were not to be dismissed. That man had a story, and she aimed to uncover it. Besides, he could use their help.

She crossed to the oil lamp and lit the wick. Since the show had ended and the showgoers had all gone home, the crew would shut down the generator, and they would exchange the electric lights for the simple flame of another era. As though on cue, the hum ended, and the lights outside her double windows flickered out.

She flung open her wardrobe and scanned the contents. A man dressed in such a suit—and owner of a steamboat, didn't he say?—would expect a lady. She fingered through each garment. She owned a work dress, a going-to-town dress, a few conservative dresses for Sundays, and of course her costumes for heralding in the showboat. She drummed her fingers on her chin. Too bad she couldn't have stayed in the green room. Clara Pickalow's walking gown from last season's production of *A Summer's Dance* would suit best.

Ah, well, nothing for it.

The old trousers and loose blouse she wore for comfortable family gatherings wouldn't do this night. But what did she wear to convey she was a nice lady who wasn't preoccupied with her appearance but concerned enough to make sure she dressed for the occasion?

She had no idea.

A knock saved her from making the decision alone.

Mam waited on the door's other side. "Anola. What are you thinking?"

She had a ready answer. "Is it not our Christian duty to help those in need?"

Mam hesitated. "Well, of course. But I hardly see how that applies to inviting a stranger into our private quarters for our family meal." Her tone fell flat. "At night."

"You saw him. The poor man has had quite the episode. Pirates taking his boat and throwing him into the Mississippi and all."

"What now?" Mam circled deeper into the room, taking in the disarray of Anola's wardrobe in one glance. "Did you say pirates?"

"Oh my, yes. The poor fellow was on his steamboat when out of nowhere pirates attacked!" She danced back, proffering a pretend sword and doing her best to thrust and parry in proper fashion.

"Pirates?" Mam snorted. "No such thing has been seen down these waters in years. The Wild River is far tamer than the old days the captain always talks about. And I daresay your grandfather's tales become more outlandish the older he gets."

Anola lifted one shoulder. "In any case, robbers relieved him of his boat and tossed the crew overboard. That's why he came to us soaking wet and looking for help." She offered Mam her most winning smile. "Hence, our Christian charity."

And perhaps assuaging her own curiosity about what must be an enthralling tale.

"I see." Mam inspected the wardrobe. "And I suppose we would do the same if this fellow resembled old Tom?"

Anola kept her face passive. Old Tom, their engineer, had thirty years and at least fifty pounds on the riverman. Besides, the appealing way God had designed Mr. Carter's face had nothing at all to do with her invitation. "Of course."

Mam arched a sculpted brow. "I know there aren't many eligible bachelors on the river, but there's no need to go to such lengths."

"What?" Anola's mouth dropped before she snapped it closed. "I have no wish for a suitor. Especially one who would not share our life." As she did not see Mr. Carter doing. He'd been far too stunned to be their type. That didn't mean she couldn't enjoy his company for an evening. "It will only be an actor for me. Same as for you and Lady Marie."

A sadness entered Mam's eyes but vanished as she refocused on the wardrobe. She likely felt bad they'd hired the same crew of actors season after season, hardly giving Anola the chance to create a romance of her own like when Mam had joined *Flynns' Floating Theater*.

Mam held out a green frock Anola had forgotten she'd shoved far back into a corner. "This will accentuate your blue-green eyes."

The long-sleeved dress fell to her midcalf, accentuated only by a belted low waist that hugged her hips. Boring, on the whole. But probably proper for such an outing. Mam would know better than she.

Anola grabbed the dress and wriggled out of her peacock costume, leaving it in a heap on the floor.

"You'll need stockings."

Stockings? She hated those things. They weren't practical, what with the ease with which they got runs. But she wouldn't consider arguing now. She plucked one of the two pairs she owned from her dresser and sat on the bed to slip them over her toes. After a few twists to get the seam in place up the back of her calf, she stood. At Mam's nod of approval, she pulled on the dress.

She inspected the mirror. "You're sure this one is the best?" She twisted a bit, and the little skirt swung around her legs. "It feels..."

"Plain?" Mam supplied.

"Exactly."

Mam chuckled. "That's because you're used to wearing feathered ball gowns." She gestured to Anola's reflection. "A pair of white lace gloves and my front-strap pumps will work nicely." She wiggled her fingers. "Come along. We don't want to leave that fellow with the captain and Lady Marie for too long."

Her grandparents would have the man's life story rooted out before he could count to twenty. And then Lady Marie would tell them all the sort of man she thought him to be. There were no secrets in the Flynn family. Not even those opinions one often kept to themselves in favor of politeness. At least, not where Lady Marie was concerned.

They entered her parents' apartment, and Anola braced for Da's questions. But he must be over on the steamboat with the crew setting course for their move to the next town downriver. Properly gloved and shod, she headed back out of the apartment.

"Oh. Your hair." Mam stopped her in the hallway. "We should put it up."

"Why? I've worn it down all evening except while playing the part of Mrs. Shuler. I see no reason to waste time on a style I'll only let down in an hour's time."

Conceding her point, Mam continued down the hall and they entered her grandparents' rooms without knocking, finding the trio already out on the wide porch.

The first part of the season allowed her grandparents to enjoy a river view on the portside of the boat, and Lady Marie took great pride in the abundance of plants she kept alive with drawn river water.

This late into the evening, the finches caged on the porch were subdued, their cheerful twittering calmed. Voices drifted through the open doorway.

"Are you a member of the peerage, ma'am?"

Peerage? What was the man talking about? She and Mam exchanged an amused glance as they passed through the apartment decorated with the odd array of mismatched furniture her grandparents had acquired. Vases from China, wicker chairs most people would have put outdoors, rugs from India, and a massive carved table that had taken half the crew to disassemble and bring inside. The store owner had regaled Lady Marie with a tale that the table had once belonged to George Washington—something none of the rest of them believed—and Lady Marie had to own it.

"Peerage, you say?" Lady Marie nodded her greeting but spoke to their guest. "There's no peerage in Ireland, lad."

Anola stopped stock-still. She covered her lips with her gloved hand. And here she'd been worried about wearing her comfortable clothes.

Poor man.

Lady Marie dressed this fellow in a mismatched costume—as if she'd taken two hundred years of history and mashed it all together.

He wore a pair of flight pants from that time they'd put on an airplane special, which fell three inches too short above a pair of boatman's shoes. As he stood to greet them, the billowy shirt from their medieval play hung past his waist and to midthigh, though he had pulled the laces at the neck up tight instead of leaving them open to reveal his upper chest as Paul had four summers prior.

His hair tumbled over his forehead in a charming disarray. Despite his appearance, however, his face remained serious. "Good evening."

"Good evening, Mr. Carter. So kind of you to join us." She turned her back to him and mouthed to Lady Marie, "What did you do?"

Anola should have known better, as any sort of secrecy did not exist for Lady Marie. She crossed her arms over her beaded dress with a neckline far too low for her age. "I did the best I could. That's what I did. He flat refused the Greek toga, though it would have been the best. Would have allowed for the quickest drying."

Mr. Carter made an oddly strangled noise. Perched in the chair next to his wife, the captain grinned. Anola lowered her eyebrows at her grandmother. This wasn't the time for one of her pranks. The fellow had been through enough. Was she testing him to see how he reacted to unfamiliar circumstances? Why?

"And there was that adorable aviator's suit we had, complete with the jacket. You remember that, don't you? Well, anyway, he rejected it as well, save the pants. Then the entire thing crumbled into finding the first dry thing he fit." She rubbed her temple and sighed. "There's nothing to be done with a man when he decides to be stubborn."

Over her shoulder, Anola regarded the mortified gentleman. "Ah, well. At least you are dry, yes?"

He returned to his chair, looking as uncomfortable as one of the crewmen might if they'd been asked to dance a jig in front of a full theater.

Anola settled into a rattan chair by a robust fern, right next to their guest, when Da stepped out to join them.

"So here is the man who wanted to cause a ruckus on my boat." Humor seeped into his voice. "One does not call for a law-man at a performance, lad. Makes the showgoers too anxious to purchase candy for the walk home."

Mr. Carter rose and extended a hand. "My apologies, sir. I am most grateful for your family's hospitality on what has proven to be a rather trying day."

"A bit of excitement does us all good now and again."

Poor Mr. Carter looked aghast, but Da planted his hands on his hips and rocked back on his heels the way he did when announcing the show to an audience. "Did any of you remember to make introductions?"

The captain shrugged. "I reckon he got the gist of it. But if you want it done proper-like, we'll oblige. I'm the captain of this operation." He gave a nod to Lady Marie. "My fair lady wife." He thrust his chin to Da, then Mam. "Our son and the piano player we expected to be a man who turned out to be a slip of a girl he married less than eight weeks later. And, of course, their daughter, the gem of *The River Queen*."

Anola beamed. She loved when her grandfather called her his gem.

Da chuckled and, with a flick to smooth his trousers, sat next to Mam. "If I may?"

The captain turned out his palms as though to say repetition was unnecessary, but Da could do as he wanted.

"I am Stephen Flynn. My father, known affectionately to all as the captain, bears the name Allister Flynn on a scrap of birth papers misplaced sometime during their journey to America. His wife, who will go by no other name than Lady Marie, though she has not a drop more of noble blood than the captain."

Anola's grandparents both held their heads high under such a declaration, undiminished by the ousting that they were neither an actual boat captain nor lady. In the world they had created, it hardly mattered. Though she could see how the pet name might be confusing to others.

"My dear wife"—Da grasped Mam's hand and kissed its back—"is Jocelyn and our daughter, Anola."

"So the river queen has a name." Mr. Carter's bangs swayed with a rueful shake.

The family exchanged glances. Didn't he know that was the showboat's name? Perhaps he'd swallowed too much silty river water. They should probably feed him.

27

"A unique name for a unique woman," Mr. Carter mumbled.

Did he mean her? No one else seemed to have heard him. Had she not been sitting so close, she might not have caught the words. Warmth gathered in her center. He found her unique, did he?

She caught his gaze and winked.

Just as she'd hoped, he turned the most charming shade of red.

This was becoming the most fun evening she'd had in quite some time.

T he low sound of a foghorn snatched Emmett from a deep sleep. He turned over on the hard bed. When would he ever get used to the quarters on this steamer? The entire ordeal of transporting the tobacco should have been left to his brother, who held a torch for such things as travel adventures and—

Pirates.

Emmett bolted upright, the previous day's events crashing through the lingering fog of sleep. The pirates. His steamer gone. Him tossed in the river. *The River Queen*.

The foghorn sounded again.

He leapt from his borrowed cot and shucked the bizarre outfit he'd worn last night. He tugged on his river-stained suit, now dry but still ruined. If he didn't hurry, he wouldn't make it out of this bunk on *The River Queen*'s tug before they pulled the gangplank.

The boat shifted, pitching him to one side. He scrambled for his boots and thrust his toes inside as the boat shuddered again. Surely they remembered he'd accepted their invitation to stay aboard last night. They wouldn't put out into the water without letting him disembark. But then, given what he'd learned about the Flynn family, they were just as likely to have forgotten he existed at all.

He snatched the door open and barreled out onto the hallway that split the middle of *Blue Belle*, the steamboat pushing the flat showboat down the river.

"Whoa!"

He bumped into a brawny man in a crewman's hat. His broad shoulders stretched a work-worn shirt.

The man took a step back. "Everything all right, fella?"

Emmett offered a thin apology and jogged down the narrow steps and onto the main deck, having to skirt three other crew members in his haste. He reached the tug's railing as a scrawny man leaped from the top of the showboat.

The fellow splashed into the river, then swam to the muddy bank. Why would he—?

Wait. The gangplank wasn't staked in the mud as it should be. Instead, it hung from the showboat.

He'd overslept. He'd better hurry. He pushed away from the rail but paused again as his stomach sank.

The man below tied a thick rope to an iron ring atop a man-sized pole sunk deep into the ground. Ground that hardly resembled the muddy bank he'd climbed out of yesterday.

Another man emerged from a room positioned on *The River Queen*'s roof and approached the edge, watching the commotion. Emmett drew a deep breath to calm his ire and headed in the fellow's direction. At the front of the steamboat, he cupped a hand to his mouth.

"Hello there! Mr. Flynn!"

The man turned, his hands in his trouser pockets. When his gaze landed on Emmett, his ruddy face broke into a smile that curved his mustache. "Good morning! Fine day, yes?" The lightly accented words drifted on the morning air, filled with friendliness.

"Have we moved?" Ridiculous question. But he couldn't remember the name of the town south of St. Louis where they'd been anchored yesterday, and this section of river grew fewer trees along the craggy rocks.

Mr. Flynn strode across the rooftop, then descended two ladders to reach the showboat's lower deck where it nestled against its tug.

Emmett met him as soon as his boots touched. "Excuse me, but I wasn't aware we would travel downriver when I accepted your invitation for a bed."

Exhausted, he'd been glad not to have to make the trudge into the nearest town. A decision he now regretted.

Mr. Flynn lifted his red-tinted eyebrows. "Best way to be sure we are ready to anchor first thing the next morning. Especially in these big towns."

"But your shows are at night."

"And now we have all day to gather supplies, pass out flyers for the performance, and be available for ticket sales." His attention remained focused on the goings-on below.

After a fair amount of grunting and shoving, a couple of the crew members secured the rope running to the showboat. The others still on board began pushing out the long gangplank.

Emmett gripped the rail. "How far are we from where we were yesterday?"

"What? Oh." Mr. Flynn jolted like he'd forgotten Emmett still stood there. He rubbed his hands. "This town here is Kimmswick." He nodded as though that was enough information.

Emmett clenched his jaw. Nothing for it now. He'd need to get off this boat and head into town. Yet, come to think about it, going further downriver might not be a bad thing. The pirates had gone this direction.

Grabbing onto the seed of hope, he stepped away from the railing.

"Headed off so soon?" Mr. Flynn matched Emmett's stride toward the gangplank. "Anola will be here any moment. She likes to hand out the flyers, and of course, I will be accompanying her and gathering supplies."

Did the man want him to join him and his daughter? Why? He had to admit Anola Flynn was a rather fascinating woman, but he had business to attend to. Besides, these people didn't know him from Adam. With a noncommittal nod, he continued toward the exit.

He should be able to find a policeman in this town and file a report. Then he needed to call Jacob and explain what had happened to their boat, cargo, and last hope of keeping the risky investment. If he failed, every shred of their inheritance would be sunk.

The thought soured his stomach.

By the time they reached the gangplank, the crewmen had hammered the stakes into place and secured the ropes. Emmett took the first step onto the wooden planks before he remembered his manners.

He offered a hand to Mr. Flynn. "Thank you for your hospitality, sir. I appreciate it."

Mr. Flynn responded with a firm shake. "We are always available for anyone in need who the Good Lord sends our way." He patted Emmett's shoulder. "Best of luck to you."

"Same to you."

Without a glance back at the showboat, Emmett hurried down the plank to the river's edge. What an interesting life these people led. Traveling from one town to the next each day.

A nomadic lifestyle foreign from his own. He'd lived in St. Louis his entire life. Where he had a stable home, responsibilities, and a job as an accountant in the prestigious Wainwright Building.

Well, he'd *had* a job. Jacob had deemed Emmett losing his position the week his brother had purchased a steamer to be nothing short of fortuitous. Finally, he'd said, they would get to embark on a venture together as brothers. Why had he let himself be talked into such nonsense?

If he ever got his money back for that ridiculous steamboat his brother had invested their entire inheritance into, he would refuse any more harebrained schemes and return home to a normal life.

A short trek up the bank and he entered a busy town. Far larger than the one upriver. His hopes buoyed. There would be a telephone and a police station here. He strode down the street past a barbershop, a general goods shop named "Old Ziegler Store," a restaurant, and a bakery.

Hadn't he heard something about this place before? Some kind of attraction? It would explain the number of men in fine suits with ladies dressed in calf-length skirts clinging to their arms. None of these people had the look of farmers.

Further down the road clogged with horses, carts, and motor-cars, he found something useful. The postmaster's office.

"Mr. Carter! Emmett!"

He paused at the musical voice. Miss Flynn. She wore a bright-blue dress with a sash of green slung across her hips. The outfit somewhat resembled what he'd seen other women wear, except for the feathers sprouting from her shoulders as though she'd decided on wings for sleeves. He couldn't tug his gaze from the way the iridescent feathers lay in perfect lines from the crest of her shoulder to midway down her upper arm. A chain of golden coins hung from her neck like something from a gypsy's tale.

When he caught her grinning at his open study of her, he regained a measure of his senses. He reached for the hat he'd lost in the river and had to drop his hand. "Good morning, Miss Flynn."

The woman smiled, ocean eyes twinkling. "Good morning, Mr. Carter."

Why did she seem amused with a proper greeting?

She held out a stack of pages. "I'm handing out flyers this morning. Mam says *The Cotton Bloom* and *Branson's Sensation* are both docked." She released a heavy sigh. "We'll have to outdo them. My, but it does get harder every year." A tinge of sadness hung on her words before she brightened again. "But there are always the tributaries, you know. The smaller towns who still find our coming to be the grandest event of the year."

How did one respond to that? He tipped his chin in lieu of his missing cap. No telling what sort of disarray his hair was in, seeing as he'd darted out the door without even an attempt at smoothing it, let alone applying any pomade. "I wish you the best with the show, Miss Flynn."

She neither moved from his path nor offered a reply.

"Uh, good day to you." Fool. He must sound absurd.

"Yes, it is indeed." An impish curve tipped her rosy lips.

Odd woman. He continued toward the post office. Miss Flynn fell in stride, her long legs keeping his pace even though she stood a few inches shorter than he.

Did she follow him on purpose, or were they simply going the same direction?

Given the odd late-night meal he'd shared with the family, he could only guess. He'd never met a more peculiar group. They'd asked him a myriad of questions about his episode on the river, but after he'd evaded most of them with vague replies, they'd settled into discussing the night's show, including him as though he belonged. They'd proven kind, if nothing else, but they were a curious group with undefinable motives.

At the post office, he held open the door for her, and she swept inside with the easy grace of a swan. No sooner had Anola Flynn entered the room than she owned it.

"Good morning!" Her clear voice rang over the small crowd gathered to mail out various parcels. "*The River Queen* invites you to an evening of wholesome family entertainment! Ten cents off for the hardworking local folk." She flourished a curtsy. "Lap children are free to attend, and the young men will get a chance to win ten dollars."

A murmur went through the crowd as Miss Flynn handed flyers to each person. How would she know who was a local and who wasn't? And why did that matter for the price of a ticket?

She handed a paper to each person and posted one near the door. When she finished, she placed a lacy glove on his arm. "I do hope to see you again, Emmett. I rather enjoyed your company." Without waiting for his response to her forward statement, she disappeared through the doorway.

Fascinating.

Chastising himself for forgetting his purpose once again, he waited in line for his turn with the postmaster.

"Where might I find the police station and make a telephone call?"

The postmaster, a thin man in his seventh decade, regarded Emmett from hooded eyes. "Sheriff's office is in Hillsboro. You can place a telephone call here."

"How far is Hillsboro?"

"'Bout twenty miles." He swept an assessing gaze over Emmett's rumpled suit. "Find yourself in a spot of trouble?"

"My steamboat was stolen, and I need to report the theft."

The old postmaster nodded. "Bad luck, that. I've heard tell of a band of miscreants making their way on these waters, bothering good folk." He snorted. "Best you find one of the deputies. They're always over at the park when the visitors are here."

Emmett thanked him for the information and on second thought requested a page to send a telegram. There would be no point attempting a phone call, as Jacob wouldn't be at home at this hour. He penned a simple message.

Boat stolen. Inform bank. Home soon.

Emmett handed over the paper and paid the fee—with bills he'd had to hang to dry last night—before stepping back outside. What would Jacob think about the disaster Emmett had allowed?

He followed the stream of well-dressed people to Montesano Springs Park, an amusement park owned by the Columbia Excursion Company. Right. He'd seen the advertisements in the St. Louis newspapers.

The park boasted a grand hotel, fourteen sulfur springs said to have healing properties, though they smelled foul, a restaurant, a dance pavilion, a boating lake, a merry-go-round, and a number of other attractions he'd forgotten. He had wanted to take Mother here on an excursion but had never gotten the chance.

Just past the entry sign, he spotted an officer in uniform. The dark-haired man had a nose with an uncanny resemblance to a halved parsnip.

"Good day, Deputy. Where might I file a report for a theft?"

"Deputy Olson." The officer raked his gaze down Emmett's suit, then tugged a notebook and a pencil from his shirt pocket. "Your name?"

"Emmett Carter. The steamer is the *Good Tidings*, owned by my brother, Jacob Carter, and myself." If the man noted the irony of the poor fortune of a boat named *Good Tidings*, nothing showed on his features.

"And it was stolen, you say?"

"By pirates."

He narrowed his eyes. "Pirates?"

Emmett squared his shoulders, refusing to feel foolish. "Or whatever else you wish to call a gang of men who ambushed a steamer with drawn weapons, tossed the crew into the river, and made off with the boat and its contents." Pirates, to his thinking.

The droll man lifted his pencil. "Any names? Descriptions?"

Emmett gave the details of the aging steamboat his brother had purchased. "I was in my cabin when the shouting started. Before I knew it, men grabbed me, hauled me outside, and threw me into the river."

He tried to swallow the shame boiling up from his center. What a coward he'd been. Unable to put up even a decent fight.

The deputy closed his book. "Yours isn't the first tale like it I've heard. Been reports all along the river since last summer about a gang bootlegging, carousing, and the like." He shook his head. "If this is the same crew, they murdered a man in

Clarksville last fall. A dip in the river is the least of what you could have gotten from the likes of Durkin and his gang."

The man had a point. "Yes, sir."

"I'll make the report and send word downriver. I suggest you stay in town the rest of the day, if you can. Meet me this afternoon at City Hall."

Emmett agreed, and the man strode off, his gait unhurried.

A river gang. Just his luck.

Guilt panged him. At least he was alive. He sent up a small prayer of thanks. He hadn't even wondered about Derwood and the rest of the crew. Had they found other work?

"Why, we meet again." Miss Flynn appeared at his side. "Imagine that."

Emmett rubbed his hand across the back of his neck, then held it out for a few of her flyers. She rewarded him with a sunny smile.

If he had to spend the day waiting in this town, he might as well be of some use.

This wasn't going well. Anola maintained a pleasant smile as one affluent person after another waved her off. She'd told her father they should skip Kimmswick this year and keep to the smaller towns. The people here had become too accustomed to playhouses and shows in St. Louis to be enamored with their showboat. To more sophisticated eyes, her family's production featured nothing but ragtag actors peddling melodrama.

Another woman in a stylish hat dismissed Anola with gloved fingers. She withheld a sigh, refusing to let her disappointment show. Last year, they'd waited all day at the river for ticket sales and hardly garnered a quarter theater. This year would be worse.

"Would you like to try somewhere other than the park?" Emmett appeared at her side, his stack of flyers still as full as her own. He hadn't baited any takers either.

"I suppose that would be best." Did her smile fall flat? She stretched it wide again. "The local people will be more to our liking anyway."

Emmett glanced at the well-dressed couples on their way to admire the bubbling springs or take their luncheon in one of the restaurants with outdoor seating. What must he think of her family now, knowing they couldn't bring in what he'd consider decent patrons?

"Why didn't you send a notice ahead so more people would know about the show?"

She veered toward an older gentleman and lifted a flyer. "Come see a show tonight on *The River Queen* and step into a dream."

The man tipped his hat but gave her a polite headshake.

Her fingers tightened on the paper as she fell back into step with Emmett. "We did. Hank runs the route three days ahead of us."

Emmett handed a little boy one of the flyers. "Ask your parents to bring you. There's a juggler and candy." He winked, and the little fellow grinned up at his mother, who gave Emmett a wry look.

Clever. He picked up on this game quickly.

"We had notices go out on the local postal route as well." Anola adjusted the papers rustling in the gentle breeze. "Da will pay the bill when he purchases our license and supplies."

As they ambled from the park grounds, Emmett frowned. "But I didn't see a notice in the post office until you brought one."

She hadn't either. Something she'd let Da know during their night lunch, but not right now. If the postmaster hadn't followed through on his deal, they could do little about it today. They'd have to mark this failure as a lesson learned for next year. Anola pushed cheer back into her voice. "The day is young. Plenty of people will still see it."

Good thing she and Mam had insisted they arrive early. Their chances of a full theater would have been thinner than a toad's hair if they'd arrived this afternoon.

"You normally don't travel at night?" Something odd grated through Emmett's tone, but she couldn't fathom why. He seemed almost irritated.

"Usually we take the river at sunrise, travel for a couple of hours, and reach our next stop by noon."

He stopped his casual pace and stared at her as though she'd started juggling a set of Cook's knives.

"Kimmswick is one of our longer distances." She continued walking. "And Mam and I wanted to tie up before another boat took our place."

Emmett sauntered down the street, mumbling something under his breath she didn't catch.

Oh.

She was used to actors and crewmen living on board, and she'd been distracted with their performance today. She hadn't even considered if Emmett wanted to travel with them. From the stiff set of his shoulders, arriving at a different town this morning had come as a surprise. Why hadn't Da told him when he'd offered the cabin?

She handed notices to four more passersby before he spoke again.

"I was rather surprised to find myself miles downriver this morning."

He regarded her, expecting a response. The only thing she could think to say was the obvious. "You didn't know?"

He lifted an eyebrow. "I suppose it turned out well enough since I've already spoken to a deputy. He's reporting the theft of our steamer and promised word this afternoon."

Anola resumed her pace down the town's main street, looking for anyone who might be a local farmer. "God's destination."

He cast her a sideways glance.

"A saying of Lady Marie's. It means we always end up in the destination God intended."

Emmett arched his eyebrows again. He must think her the oddest woman he'd ever known. He gestured toward the bakery. "How about asking the workers there?"

She veered in that direction. He might find her strange, but he proved helpful.

"If you don't mind my asking, Miss Flynn, why does your grandmother go by a title if she is not a member of the peerage?"

Anola shrugged. "She has a thespian's heart."

Emmett's expression said her answer wasn't an answer at all, but he didn't comment. He held the door open for her to enter the bakery. Delicious scents of bread and confections wrapped around her, and she savored them. If she had time to spare, this would be a wonderful spot to linger over sweets and conversation. Her mouth watered.

They passed out flyers, keeping their attention on the people clad in aprons dusted in flour. The promise of free passes for the baker's family if they handed the advertisements to their local friends had the pleasantly plump matron nodding.

After the bakery, they proceeded down the street. Anola spoke with the blacksmith, a candymaker, a bookshop owner, and an automobile mechanic before coming to the end of town.

Now all they could do was wait and see if they'd make enough in ticket sales to cover their coal costs. At least there were the added profits from candy and concessions to give them something in the money box. She shuddered at the thought of weeks of fish stew like they'd had to do last summer when supplies ran thin.

Anola pushed the thought aside. A worry for later. This early into the season, Cook still had a somewhat full kitchen.

She slipped her hand into the crook of Emmett's elbow and withheld a laugh when he startled. "Have you ever considered a showman's life, Mr. Carter?"

Emmett stumbled, but he caught his misstep quickly enough not to hinder the woman on his arm. He cleared his throat. "I'm an accountant, Miss Flynn. Not an actor."

Where had she come up with such an outlandish question?

"One familiar with boats and the Mississippi?" She turned those blue-green eyes on him. This close he could see flecks of gold floating in the cobalt depths. He'd never seen the like. When she smiled, he snapped his gaze forward. Blast. Caught staring again. She must think him a cad.

Where were they going? He had no idea where she wanted to visit next. "The boat was another of my brother's schemes to make a quick fortune."

"Oh dear. Then why were you the one on the steamer?" The sympathy pricked at his pride, but he did his best to squelch annoyance at a legitimate question.

"Because my brother is..." How did he best describe his brother's scheming—a trait inherited from their father—to a stranger? "He's the adventurous sort. He convinced me it would be better if he stayed behind and charmed other customers into using our services while I saw our first shipment safely downriver. Since I had recently been released from my accounting position when the company I worked for closed, I agreed."

A woman in a sensible dress approached with two boys bickering behind her. Miss Flynn captured their eye as she handed the woman an advertisement for the show. A tight-lipped smile said the mother wouldn't be attending, and Anola's eyes dimmed as the trio moved along.

He patted her fingers encouragingly and resumed his explanation as they passed a purring motorcar.

"In truth, I was less than forthcoming with my real motive. I thought if there was to be any hope of limiting further foolish notions, then I should be the one to accompany what I planned to be our one and only shipment to New Orleans. Then I would sell the boat, take back my portion of the inheritance, and return home."

"Hmm." Miss Flynn arched a brow. "I take it you did not approve of your brother's purchase?"

"He invested my portion of our inheritance without my consent. On my behalf, he'd said." Emmett poked a hand through his hopeless hair. "To be fair, this idea did seem to have more merit than his others. It isn't his fault river pirates muddled things. At least I purchased insurance."

They crossed the street and started up the other side. Perhaps they'd stroll back down to the park.

They passed several buildings before the vibrant woman on his arm spoke again. "My family knows plenty about the river, but the books are becoming a problem." A delicate crease formed between her golden-red brows. "When I was a girl, that kind of thing didn't matter. People flocked to the boat in droves, and we always had enough to purchase anything we needed along the way. I'm not sure how or when it happened, but it no longer seems so simple."

Emmett patted her hand. "All you likely need is a little budgeting. Does your father have a list of receipts and expenses? I'd be glad to offer some advice this afternoon if he is interested."

"I've never known him to be one who keeps bits of paper."

He didn't keep a record of expenses? "What about a tally of the earnings from ticket and concession sales?"

She turned out a palm.

No wonder they had expense problems if they didn't bother with accounting. "That would be your first order of business. You'll need a record of what you earn and what you spend."

Anola brushed a lock of hair swaying along the curve of her neck. "You must think us terribly backward. A band of hapless actors with no head for numbers." Before he could reply, she laughed. "Lady Marie says we are gypsies at heart. But then, she is whatever the mood strikes her to be."

What would it be like to live as free and open as these people? Going where the waters took them, living life day by day? "All well and good, Miss Flynn, but even gypsies need an accounting system if they hope to maintain their operation."

"I figured you'd say something like that."

She did?

"Which is why I'd like to hire you."

43

Emmett stopped short. "Pardon?"

The curve of her lips said she teased him, but her eyes remained serious. "You are without your steamboat, correct?"

"Well, yes, but..."

"And said steamboat is likely moving downriver, same as we are."

Or smuggled down a tributary or sunk. "Probably already gone."

Anola continued as though he hadn't spoken. "So as I see it, we can help one another. You need to continue downriver to find your boat and track the people who stole it from you. We happen to have a boat and a way of talking with hundreds of people all in one place." She lifted a finger in the air. "Tell me a better way to question that many river people. Traveling by land and stopping house to house?"

A subtle snort flared her nostrils. "Nonsense. We can give you access to all the information you'll need. Not to mention we have a steamboat crew of our own that, should we come upon your stolen property, would be ready and able to assist in its return."

Emmett could only stare. His lack of response must have come across as encouragement, because she took a breath and hurried on.

"So you see, it's a perfect trade. We'll give you a trip downriver with a bed at night and three meals in your stomach, and in exchange, you will teach me business."

"You?"

Her eyes flashed. "Yes, me. I am capable, I assure you."

Of that, he had no doubt. People skirted the strange pair of an excitable woman in a feathered dress and a confounded man in a stained and rumpled suit. What a spectacle they must make.

He offered his arm again. After a slight hesitation, she placed her fingers back in the crook of his elbow. "I meant no offense, Miss Flynn. I don't doubt your capabilities. I merely thought we were discussing your father's accounting practices. I do apologize."

"So you'd be willing to teach me?"

"I would, of course, but—"

"Excellent." She tugged his arm and steered him between a general store and a brick building. "We shall start right away."

He'd meant to say he would be willing to help her, but once he spoke to the deputy, he'd be returning home. Why did she think he was the type to take the law into his own hands and chase a band of ruffians all the way down the Mississippi?

She bounded along next to him, a contagious exuberance in her every move. He couldn't stop his smile. He had the day to wait before he could get a report, so what harm could come from lending a beautiful woman his aid?

6

Her and her big mouth. Anola knew better than to make such a proposition without having first brought the idea to a family meeting, but the urgency of the matter and the opportunity presented made a recipe for quick decisions.

She couldn't shake the feeling that Emmett could help them. While she didn't know anything about the man's skills—he could be a terrible businessman after all—she'd also learned long ago to trust her intuition. Lady Marie claimed all of God's children were gifted and Anola had been blessed with the gift of discernment. Maybe that was true and maybe not, but her intuition didn't often lead her astray.

Lord, change my mind if this isn't your will.

"Miss Flynn, I do think I should be clear."

Anola weaved through an alley and turned onto a pathway she'd used on her many visits here as a child. Back before the amusement park and the big-city tourists.

"What I mean to say is, I'm happy to offer any assistance I can, but I won't be joining your family on the showboat. I must return home."

Oh.

She patted his arm. "Of course you would have family and responsibilities to return to." How silly of her to think otherwise. "I sometimes forget others don't live as we do."

His features tightened. Had she said something wrong?

"I'm yours for the day, Miss Flynn."

Hers for the day. Why did the simple statement send her insides fluttering? She dismissed the sensation and pointed them toward the riverbank. Mam would expect her backstage helping with preparations and sweeping out the auditorium, but Freddie could handle her chores today. They wended their way to *The River Queen*'s gangplank, the familiar river scents washing over her and welcoming her home.

"Have you spoken to your father about this, Miss Flynn?" Emmett paused on the wooden ramp and frowned up at the boat.

"Are you going to call me 'Miss Flynn' every time you speak to me?"

Emmett startled, clearly not having caught her intended humor.

Oh my stars and sunrise, but this man is wound tighter than a coil spring.

She patted his arm again to soothe the redness creeping up his neck. It seemed to have the opposite effect. "Anola is fine, you know." She winked. "And I promise I haven't yet forgotten my own name, no matter how many others I've taken for the stage."

The fellow favored the color of a crawdad now.

"I... Well, that is to say..." He shook his head.

"Anola!" Lady Marie's voice fired from the upper porch. "Where is Jocelyn's suit?"

Anola shielded her eyes from the sun and located her grandmother. "She left it hanging in the kitchen to dry."

"It's not there." Lady Marie waved a hand. "Quick! Fetch it before this calliope busts a pipe."

"We don't even need that horrid instrument today." Anola hauled Emmett along. "I'll take you to the office to look at what little accounting Da has. Then I have to help find Mam's slick suit."

"Pardon? A slick suit?"

"Of course. Otherwise, the hot steam will scald her."

The man rubbed the whiskers sprouting on his cheek but allowed her to lead him through the showboat, up the main staircase, and to her father's office.

The room showcased none of Da's flashy personality but rather focused on serving as a gathering space for everyone to practice their lines before moving rehearsals to the stage. Only Da's simple desk and chair currently occupied the room since the floor pillows had all been stowed for the season. Inside the worn top drawer, she pulled out a leather-bound book.

"Anything we have will be written here."

"Miss Flynn, I don't think—" A crease formed between his brows.

Did he know he was a strikingly handsome man, or was he the type who walked through life without a clue as to why every woman from girls fresh out of pigtails to matrons applying wrinkle creams would bat their eyelashes at him?

"—Anola, if you prefer, I don't think that's wise. I'm not comfortable going through another man's books without his permission."

"Do you always have so many rules?" Without waiting for his answer, she stuck the book under her arm and hurried out of the office. Lady Marie would insist Mam play that confounded steam whistle, and the ensuing argument would get one or both of them hotter than a pepper sprout.

Emmett muttered something under his breath about confounding women. That was his fish to wrestle. Either the man would follow her or he wouldn't, but she didn't have time for a discussion right now.

She scurried down the hall, out onto the porch, and to the stern, Emmett keeping pace. Then she shimmied down the ladder and across to *Blue Belle*. This time she heard him remark on women in skirts climbing ladders, but she ignored him. She'd traipsed every inch of these boats since she could walk, and she wouldn't change anything now on account of one rather stiff gentleman. One who outfitted not only himself but also everyone else with a strict set of rules.

She had little use for frivolous rules.

She waltzed into the kitchen, Emmett on her heels.

The sturdy cook pointed a spoon at them, her Irish brogue thicker than her fish stew. "Now look here, lass. Yer man donna need to be in here." She shook the spoon, sending flecks of something splattering on the floor. She frowned at the mess.

"We're looking for Mam's suit. Have you seen it?" Anola pushed deeper into the crowded space, scanning walls covered with cast iron skillets and dented pots.

"Whe'r ye goin'?" The red-faced woman focused her attention on poor Emmett, who had followed Anola inside Cook's domain.

"He's helping me. We need that suit."

Cook glared at Emmett. "I donna allow no wet frocks in my kitchen, lass. Nor no moon-eyed boys. Best you be lookin' elsewhere."

Elsewhere turned out to be just outside the kitchen door leading to *Blue Belle*'s dining room. Anola snatched the heavy black coat from the hook. She waved to the boots and gloves on the floor. "Grab those."

Emmett obeyed, clutching the boots in one hand and the gloves in the other. They emerged onto the roof near the pilot-house to find the situation unfolding as Anola had expected.

"It isn't that bad." Lady Marie crossed her arms and tilted her nose in the air. "You're too delicate."

"If you think that, then why don't you press one of those keys?" Mam planted her fists on her hips.

"You just never liked playing it."

"Of course I never liked it. The thing is a terror."

Anola had to agree with Mam. The steam whistles could be heard from miles away, but the calliope was difficult to play and coated the musician in sprays of hot steam.

Best she diffuse this situation before these two spouted more steam than the pipes. "Is it necessary? I'm sure the people already know we're here. That thing is better for finding farmers in the fields than ladies and gentlemen in an amusement park."

Lady Marie huffed. "Another of my family brushing aside tradition as though it means nothing." She slapped the back of her hand to her forehead and closed her eyes. "My own flesh and blood, disregarding the legacy brought before her."

Anola glanced toward the heavens. "I hardly think this marks the end of tradition... Grandmother."

That last word garnered the desired effect, and Lady Marie's eyelids popped open.

Emmett laughed. An odd sort of strangled sound in his throat. All three women looked at him. Mam with a thoughtful expression, and Lady Marie aghast.

Anola could only grin. "How about we save legacy for the next town and focus on the problem of today."

The statement stopped whatever the other Flynn women had opened their mouths to say. They exchanged a loaded glance. Then Mam noticed what Anola still carried under her arm.

"Why do you have the ledger?"

Anola tipped her head toward Emmett. "He's a businessman and offered to help us with our bookkeeping."

"Ledger?" Lady Marie scoffed. "My son couldn't keep a ledger if his life—"

"That's hardly necessary." Mam said at the same time. "We are—"

The women frowned at each other.

Anola took advantage of the cease-fire. "I suspect ticket sales will be even lower than last year, and we need to keep a record of expenses and our profits. Emmett can help us, in exchange for a bed and meals."

"I said for the day, Miss...uh, Anola."

She turned out her hand. "Did you not sleep in one of our beds last night?"

"Well, yes, but—"

"And we will also give you dinner and supper. Even night lunch, if you wish." She focused on Mam. "He can help. I'm sure of it. What's the harm?"

After Mam and Lady Marie exchanged another weighted glance, Mam released a slow breath. "No, it can't hurt, my gem."

Anola pressed her lips together. Their situation must be worse than she'd thought. Mam hadn't used the childhood pet name in years.

Lady Marie announced they didn't need the calliope today and her presence was required in the kitchen. She marched away with her usual fanfare.

Mam straightened her blouse and motioned toward the ladder. "Shall we?"

He *had* asked for her father to be apprised. Emmett tugged at his collar. But he hadn't expected the request to garner a family meeting. He flipped another page, then thumbed through to the end. The book held little more than notes on which merchants traded goods for tickets, who had been loyal in bringing friends to the show, and which towns charged more for the required license.

He rubbed his temples. He scanned the family members gathered on the porch belonging to the elder Flynn gentleman, the man whom everyone only ever called "the captain." They had enjoyed a simple luncheon of Irish potato hash and had now set aside their plates, ready to learn.

How could he teach what had taken him years to master in the span of one afternoon? Emmett folded his hands. "The first thing I recommend is keeping a detailed list of receipts and sales. Do you also have other sources of income in addition to tickets?"

"We sell prize candy and concessions." Jocelyn included Lady Marie with a glance.

"You'll need a detailed record of how much you spend on supplies and how much money you make each night for the candy and concessions."

The captain puffed on a long-stemmed pipe, though no smoke rose from the end. Perhaps he'd forgotten to light it. "What for? If there's money in the box, we use it for what we need. If there's not, then we tighten our belts. Been doing it that way for forty years."

Lady Marie nodded regally. "I don't see how writing it all down makes any difference. Things cost what they cost."

"Yes, ma'am. But do you know how much, exactly, they cost? Do you know if you are making a good profit on your sales? What if you discover you've been spending more on supplies than you thought and, with your current pricing, you aren't making any profit?"

The family exchanged glances. All except for Anola, who watched him intently.

"If, for example," he continued, "you know you are spending three dollars on candy, but then you tally your sales for the night and see you have sold all that candy for only three dollars and ten cents. Is that worth the effort? Should you raise your price?"

The captain snorted. "Fair point, lad. Fair point." He pointed his pipe at Stephen. "How much have you been spending on candy?"

Stephen shrugged. "I'll ask for receipts, and you can write it all down."

"Me?" The captain shook his head. "I don't have time for that."

"And I do?"

"I'll do it." Anola held Emmett's gaze. "I don't mind. I'll trade sweeping the auditorium for writing down numbers each day."

This caused a discussion, but they conceded Anola would keep the books. Did they debate everything this way? How did they ever get anything done?

"Since we've settled that, we need to discuss the menu." Lady Marie poked a crust of bread through the wires on her birdcage, and a finch plucked it from her fingers. "What did you bring me to work with?"

"Ham wasn't an option." Stephen stroked the long ends of his mustache. "But I managed to get a few chickens."

"Chickens?" She placed a hand over her heart. "How am I to feed an entire cast and crew"—she jutted her chin at Emmett—"and guest with a few chickens?"

"Chicken and dumplings, perhaps?" Anola tossed her another piece of crust for the birds. "At least it's not fish again."

Turned out they did discuss everything. Emmett waited as the family debated over a menu, what to do about a postmaster who didn't keep his word, the missing fellow who should have scouted ahead to spread the word the boat was coming. Then came a prolonged conversation over whether one of the actors needed a new costume.

Fascinating people.

Finally, the meeting drew to a close as each member received their daily assignments from Stephen and rose to leave.

Stephen extended a hand to Emmett. "I appreciate any peace of mind you can give my daughter." A firm pump. "And I do apologize for bringing you downriver without warning. I trust you found what you needed in Kimmswick?"

"I'll speak to the deputy again this afternoon. Then I'll be heading back to St. Louis."

Stephen patted his shoulder and released Emmett's hand. "A pleasure knowing you. We wish you God's grace and a safe journey."

"Thank you, sir. Same to you and your family." He turned to Anola with a slight bow. "It was a pleasure making your acquaintance."

Anola smiled, but something flickered in her expression.

Why did he have the oddest sense of reluctance pulling at his center? Shoving the sensation aside, he finished his goodbyes to the rest of the Flynn family and took his leave.

I llogical. Emmett scolded himself and pivoted toward the park. What was he thinking? His feet had tried to march him right back to *The River Queen*. What was it about the boat—or the family aboard—that had him acting irrationally?

After a trip to the local bank to wire funds from his private account, which he thankfully didn't share with his brother, and a stop at the general store to purchase a few poor-fitting pants and shirts to stuff into a cheap duffle, he'd returned to the post office to send another telegram. Since he'd informed the bank and the insurance company of the loss, he'd run out of productive things to accomplish.

He strolled through the town and to the amusement park to wait out the afternoon until he could speak with the deputy. The Flynn family hardly resembled any group of people he'd ever encountered. They were boisterous, flighty, and ungrounded in normal society.

And Anola.

Never had he met her match. He nodded to a pair of older women and gestured for them to enter the park ahead of him. The narrow-faced one offered a thankful tilt of her head, but the other raked her blue gaze down him with a nose wrinkled like she'd smelled something rotten.

Ignoring them, he approached one of the springs. The air misted from the water, cooling his face. Though it carried a sulfurous odor, the tinge didn't detract from the park's beauty. He found an unoccupied bench and took a seat and focused on the tasks at hand. He would need to get home and file insurance papers, as well as have a meeting with the bank. Would they call his loan with the steamboat gone? He rubbed his temples.

Nervous energy pulsed through him, and he gained his feet once more. He couldn't sit here all day. A brisk walk put him at the deputy's office two hours early. The elderly man at the front desk said Deputy Olsen had stepped out and to check back later. Emmett ambled down the main street for what had to be the fourth time today and entered the post office to make sure the flyer was still posted. A telegram waited.

Call home

Must talk

Extremely urgent

Clutching the paper in his fist, he addressed the postmaster. "Do you have a telephone?"

The man thumbed toward a nook in the corner. "Ten cents to make a call."

Emmett slid the coin to the man and followed his directions to a candlestick phone. He lifted the receiver and waited for the operator. "St. Louis East, number 214, please."

The pleasant female voice wished him a good day before connecting the line. It rang only once before Jacob connected.

"Carter residence."

"Jacob."

A huff of air rattled the line. He could feel his brother's relief. Had he been that worried?

"Tell me you haven't contacted the police."

Emmett gripped the phone receiver. A tingle wormed through his center. "The boat was stolen."

A moan. "What did you tell the cops?"

"I told them how I was assaulted and thrown overboard to drown." He hadn't meant for his voice to rise or for his words to snap. People in the post office stared at him. Emmett turned his back to them and lowered his voice. "What's going on?"

A pause. "I need you to trust me."

Not a good sign. "What did you do?"

"Just trust me, will you? I'll meet you in Memphis and explain everything."

"Memphis! That's over two hundred miles. Have you taken leave of your senses? I'm coming home."

"I won't be here. You don't need to come home. Promise me you won't."

Heat leached from his face. "Whatever trouble you're in, we can—"

"Please, brother." The desperation in Jacob's voice stole any words of encouragement.

"Then I'll need to—"

"I'm sorry for spending all of our inheritance. But you have plenty of other funds, right? You'll be good until we can meet up." A noise sounded over the line. Was someone else in the house? "We have to get that boat back. Before it gets to New Orleans."

"Why?" Emmett bit the words off. "Explain. Now."

"I can't." Muffled voices came from somewhere in the room. "Who's there?"

"Don't come home." Jacob's voice strained thinner than a taut wire. "Please. Go to Memphis. I'll meet you at the Blind Bat."

"Is that a gin joint?"

"Tell them Scissors sent you to talk about church on Sunday."

"Scissors? What in the heavens are you talking about?"

"Two weeks." More voices sounded in the background. An angry shout. "Promise me, brother. Two weeks. Scissors. The Blind Bat. I need you to—"

The line went dead.

Emmett stared at the phone, unable to form a single coherent thought.

"Hello? Hello, would you like to place another call?"

The female operator's voice jarred his senses. He replaced the receiver.

God help him. What had his brother gotten them into now?

Anola tapped her finger on her chin and scowled at the numbers scrawled in the ledger. How hard could it be? She'd learned to fish, dig up crawdads, juggle, act, sing, run the ticket booth, and...well, a host of other things she suspected most young women never did. Surely she could figure out accounting.

First, she needed to conduct an inventory. Write down everything Da had purchased and compile a list of expenses. Satisfied with her plan, she tucked the book under her arm and whistled a tune from this season's show as she clambered from the showboat over to the steamboat.

Cook made a perfunctory complaint about all of Anola's digging and poking about, but mostly let her be. In short order, she'd compiled an account of all their supplies and yielded to Cook's insistence she make a list of items Lady Marie never let them buy.

Anola filled three pages with foodstuffs, concessions, a count of the coal loads, and a list of the complimentary tickets they'd given out in town. She brushed a lock of damp hair from her face. Only one place left to look.

Sometimes when the crew went ashore, they asked for a stipend to purchase supplies. Cleaners, ropes, and other odds and ends they needed to keep the steamboat running. Da would say a detailed list of those items was unnecessary, but according to Emmett, they needed to know how much Da allowed and what that amount could purchase.

Near the boiler room, she located the closet where the crew stashed anything that didn't have somewhere else to go.

"Gracious sakes." She fisted a hand to her hip as she surveyed the space. Not a single crew member stood nearby to hear her thoughts on their lack of organization.

Grunting, she scooted around a haphazard stack of mops, counted three cans of kerosene, and poked through two piles of what could only be called junk. Why did they keep broken pulleys, frayed ropes, and a jumble of some kind of metal she couldn't identify?

She'd need to tell Da to get these men in here to clean—

What was that over in the far corner, half hidden beneath a stack of oily rags? She moved closer, and the shape of a squat wooden crate took form. She harrumphed as she shoved the rags aside. They probably had plenty of supplies right here they'd forgotten.

The top of the crate refused to budge under her fingertips. No matter. She located a long-handled screwdriver, and after her prying and a few jumps to gain leverage, the top groaned against the nails holding it secure.

By the time she released the top, sweat beaded on her brow, and she'd lost three feathers from her dress. No wonder this thing had been shoved back here. Someone got tired of trying to open it. But such thoughtlessness wouldn't do. She leaned closer to see better in the dim light.

Neatly stacked cloth bags filled the box.

What in the heavens? She plucked one from the pile. Larger than her palm, the rectangular sack made a crinkling sound as she handled the fabric. Odd. She released the drawstring, revealing the interior stuffed with sweet-smelling dried leaves.

She shook her head and pocketed the herbs. Da must have purchased the spices in bulk, and the crew delivered them to this closet instead of to Cook. He'd likely forgotten, and she hadn't known to ask. No telling how long they'd been sitting in here, but they still smelled fresh. This crate would last at least the entire season. If not all of the next as well. Good thing she'd poked around in here.

She'd take this bag by the kitchen and have Cook send one of the fellows after the rest. The sun slanted low across the western sky. She needed to hurry if she was going to be ready for tonight's show.

Back on the showboat deck, she caught sight of their first customer nearing the gangplank. Either this fellow came early or she had spent more time looking for inventory than she'd thought. The figure stepped a foot on the walkway, carrying a traveling bag at his side.

Emmett?

She hurried to meet him at the railing. "Decide to come see the show after all? I can't promise you another backstage tour again, you know. Things like that can't become a habit...." Her teasing drifted away as he lifted his face. "Are you all right?"

His mouth pressed into a tight line. "I need to speak to your father."

"What's wrong?"

He hesitated. "I'd like to ask him for a job."

They could scarcely afford the men they had now.

Of their own accord, her lips twisted into a smile and let forth words she hadn't had time to consider. "Of course we'll hire you. Welcome to the family."

He blinked, and the redness creeping into his cheeks paled. Poor fellow. He did seem to be the nervous sort.

Saving him from a response, she took him by the hand and led him toward her father's office.

Surely they had room for one more.

Wow. Emmett leaned away from the theater's rear wall. He slid into one of the many empty seats no one would claim this deep into the performance.

Anola commanded attention in her flamboyant peacock costume, her clear voice resonating in the near-empty theater and her hair glimmering like liquid fire. If she noticed the lack of patrons, she gave no sign. She must put her entire heart into every performance. When the song ended, she sashayed across the stage and disappeared into the wings, breaking the spell.

"Come with me." The gruff voice startled him from the edge of the seat.

The captain grinned around the stem of an unlit pipe. "You'll sell the prize candy."

He followed as the older man zipped behind the seats and darted through the door. When he'd asked for a job, he should've suspected he'd be asked to do any number of strange tasks.

Once in the ticket booth outside of the auditorium, the captain hefted a flat tray with a leather strap attached to each side. "It's simple, see. All you do is sell the candy. Some of the bags have a prize." His face scrunched. "Better add more prize bags so at least someone gets one."

Emmett accepted the tray topped with bags of caramel corn and assorted confections. "But how do I know which ones have a prize?"

"You don't, of course. That would defeat the purpose."

He stopped short of asking after said purpose as the captain launched into a rapid succession of instructions about selling and prices Emmett struggled to catch.

"Good now. Off you go, lad." But the man stopped him again before Emmett took three steps. "And see if you can't get any of them to come back tomorrow."

Before Emmett could ask more, the old man scuttled away.

Emmett withheld a sigh. Selling candy he could do. But hadn't Anola said they'd be on their way first thing tomorrow? Why would any of these people return for a second night? As the lights brightened, he plastered on a smile and reentered the auditorium.

The patrons looked bored, and several waved him away before he could get three sentences into his salesman's speech. On the theater's opposite side, two couples rose to leave. Disheartened for the Flynn family, Emmett let his shoulders droop.

The baker he recognized from town bought a bag of sweets for each of his four children so at least the Flynn family would get something even though the tickets had been free. Emmett completed his round as the man juggling and attempting to get the audience to laugh finished his act and left the stage.

With no sign of the captain or Lady Marie, Emmett entered the rear door to the ticket booth and unhooked the strap from around his neck. He lowered the display tray onto the ticket counter. He was about to exit when a figure approached and tapped the window.

Tall and dour as he remembered, Deputy Olsen regarded Emmett. He slid the window open. Would the man be suspicious he never returned? He worked moisture into his mouth.

"Forget to come by?" the officer deadpanned.

He hadn't forgotten. He'd *decided* to walk the irresponsible path of protecting his brother. Whatever the fool had landed himself in, he'd been clear about not going to the police. Until they met up in Memphis, Emmett had little choice. Rather than lie, he turned out his palms.

The deputy grunted and cocked an eyebrow toward the theater doors. "You some kind of actor?"

One who wasn't in the show? "Just helping the family."

The deputy regarded him. "Thought about seeing it myself, but duty keeps a man busy."

So had he come to find Emmett or see the show? "There's plenty of seats if you want to take one. On the house." They could take the cost out of his payment. Assuming he got one.

Deputy Olsen's eyes narrowed into slits. "I sent word downriver about your missing boat. Seems no one's seen a vessel matching that description."

"That's impossible." When the deputy didn't respond, Emmett leaned closer. "It's a steamboat. Yes, there are a lot of them on the river, but it couldn't have... what, *disappeared?*"

"I'll send word if we hear anything more." Deputy Olsen tapped a finger on the worn counter. "Are you staying in these parts?"

Reluctant to let this man know about his new position on the showboat, Emmett scoured the area for a writing utensil. "I live in St. Louis." He scribbled the address on a strip of paper and passed it across the counter. "If you could send word here, I'd appreciate it."

They would need information to take to the insurance company. No matter what Jacob said about police, they had to have the money from that policy. It wasn't as though this man was going to travel to St. Louis and visit Jacob.

The deputy pocketed the paper and looked toward the theater where sounds of the show seeped past their confines.

Emmett scrambled out of the ticket booth and around to meet the man, then held the door open for him. "You can catch the end, if you'd like."

The deputy slipped inside and chose a seat at the back. Emmett released a breath and closed the latch.

"Giving out free tickets now?"

Emmett jumped. "Where did you come from?"

The captain smirked. "This is my boat, lad." He winked and entered the ticket booth. "Never know where I'll turn up."

"You can deduct his ticket from my pay." Emmett rubbed the back of his neck, which had grown tense, and peered at the old man through the window.

He didn't even glance up from what he was writing. "After the show, you get to sweep the aisles. Seeing as how you're still here and were the one to give Anola a new hobby, seems fitting."

How was he supposed to respond to that?

The captain didn't appear to require a response. He finished writing, set down the pen, and stretched his back. "We'll have our night lunch on the porch after the show again. You're welcome to join us, or you can settle with the rest of the crew on the *Belle*. That lot goes to bed early, mind you, on account of them having to get up early." He twisted his gray mustache. "You trying to get on the steamboat crew or in with the actors?"

"I'm not sure as I have an actual position yet."

"My son didn't say?" His eyebrows worked like two gray caterpillars trying to escape his face.

"Well, see, Anola said I could have a position."

The man leaned back and laughed. "Of course she did." He sobered as quickly as the humor had overtaken him. "Best you come to lunch with us, then. Looks like we have plenty to discuss. Broom is in the closet at the back of the theater. Don't take too long, lad, or my lady wife won't save a crumb for you. She likes punctuality, my Lady Marie."

Without bothering to tell Emmett when that time might be, he exited the ticket booth and disappeared around the corner.

Emmett stood in the hallway, half expecting another member of the Flynn family to pop out of the wood paneling.

Applause announced the end of the show, and the doors opened to a meager stream of showgoers who dispersed. Deputy Olsen didn't spare him a glance. Had the man enjoyed the performance? After the last family slipped out, Emmett found Anola sitting on the edge of the stage, chin propped on her hand and feet kicking a glum rhythm.

She looked up as he neared and let out a long sigh. "That was even worse than I'd feared."

"The baker and his family had a good time." He eyed the orchestra pit and skirted the side to a set of stairs.

Anola watched his progress. "I'm glad for it—I truly am. But I don't think anyone came other than the people we gave free tickets to attend." She shook her head, sending the long peacock feathers waving. "What do the other shows have that we don't?"

He had no idea. Emmett lowered himself to sit a respectable distance from her and swung his legs over the edge. They settled into silence before she spoke again.

"The time has come for us to leave the Mississippi, I think."

"You aren't going to do shows anymore?" The idea unfurled a sadness in him. He couldn't imagine Anola settling for any kind of regular life.

She snorted a laugh. "Don't be silly. What else would we do?" She scooted closer and bumped his shoulder with hers in a friendly yet familiar fashion. "But these big cities have so much more to offer. They have theaters and restaurants and...and well, lots of things. The small farming and mining towns are filled with simple people. That's where we need to go. The tributaries. The forgotten lands."

The woman's fanciful way of speaking drew him into her world. "Makes sense, I suppose. Does that mean you won't go down to Memphis?"

She eyed him as though she knew his question held more than simple curiosity. "We will finish the season as scheduled. But they are going to have to listen to me about next year. We need to find a new route. Maybe even a new place to dock instead of St. Louis."

"You dock in St. Louis?" The thought of her so close to his home intrigued him for reasons he couldn't piece together.

"Usually. My mother has cousins there. My grandparents would prefer we spend the winter somewhere warmer, but family is family."

Family was family. A sentiment he understood. He pushed himself up and offered a hand to help her. "The captain said to sweep the aisles and then I needed to be at lunch on time or Lady Marie won't leave me any crumbs." When Anola accepted his hand, he helped her stand. "Trouble is he didn't explain why you had lunch at night or what time that meal is supposed to be."

Anola grinned, her somber mood dissipating under what he expected was a persistent enthusiasm. "That's easy. Actors eat another meal because we work at night. Crew breakfast is at four-thirty, but Cook keeps it until ten for the actors because we don't rise that early—well, except Da, but never mind that. Dinner is at noon, and supper is at five. But we get hungry again after a show. We call it night lunch, not to be confused with dinner, of course." She lifted feathered shoulders as though Emmett should understand something so simple—but even their eating habits felt foreign.

"Some people call it a night snack, I think." She smoothed the edge of a rumpled peacock feather sticking out from underneath her. "But lunch is what we've always called it here. My grandmother will serve her meal one hour after the show, fifteen minutes after the lights go out."

Remembering the last time someone had cut off the big generator and the electric lights had ceased, leaving him in darkness, he nodded. "Best I get to sweeping, then." At least when the lights went out, he'd know it was time to feel his way through the dark.

"Do you remember how to get to my grandparents' apartment?"

In the dark, likely not.

She waved, not waiting for him to answer. "I'll come get you." She tipped her chin toward a door tucked at the edge of the stage. "Broom's in there."

He'd just dumped the last pan of discarded popcorn bags and dust when the lights flickered. He replaced the broom and hurried toward the exit. Darkness surrounded him as he reached the auditorium doors.

Hand outstretched, he inched forward.

Light erupted in his vision, and he stumbled.

"Oh!" A hand snaked around his waist. "Easy there. I have you." Anola shifted her light away from him, her body pressed into his side. "You are a bit of a clumsy fellow, aren't you?"

He wasn't clumsy. Merely unaccustomed to wandering around strange places in the dark. Not that he could think to say any of that with her so close. She smelled of clean soap and something akin to peaches.

She snickered and stepped away from him, leaving a coldness at his side. Dressed in a slim pair of trousers and a loose blouse, she somehow still seemed the pinnacle of femininity despite the lack of what his mother would have called "proper attire."

"Come now. We need to explain your circumstances to my father. And of course, you'll need to come up with a compelling reason for your employment."

In addition to teaching her bookkeeping and doing odd jobs?

She smiled. "But I'm sure that won't be any trouble, will it? Can you act? It would be helpful if you could. We can find a place for you to fill in and give one of the others a rest if he's sick or something. Oh, I don't suppose you play an instrument?" At his goggle-eyed headshake, she sighed. "Ah, well, I might have known. Hurry up now."

She swayed down the hall, leaving him no choice but to follow. At least she didn't take him to a ladder.

"I'm an accountant." Not a great one at that, but he didn't know what else to say. "Not an actor. Or a boatman." Which didn't give them a compelling case to keep him.

"No other skills?"

"Well...no, never mind."

Anola stopped and swung the lantern his way. "What?"

He jerked back as she thrust the thing up by his face. One hand shielded his eyes. "I haven't done it since I was a child, and only then because my mother insisted. At least until I got old enough to stop."

"Stop what?"

"Tap dancing."

Her eyes rounded. "You tap dance?"

"No."

"But you said—"

"I couldn't do it now. I don't know why I even brought it up."

A twinkle entered her eyes, and he shivered with the sneaking feeling that gleam portended mischief.

"Emmett is a dancer," Anola boasted the moment they reached the porch.

All eyes turned to him, and his face reddened.

"He's out of practice, but that is easily remedied." She selected a sandwich from the tray and three slices of apple. "He doesn't mind helping wherever else he is needed."

Her grandfather grunted a laugh and pointed his pipe at Da. "This little gal has gone and hired us a new fellow."

While Mam lifted a hand to her throat, gawking at Da, then her, Anola shrugged. "He needs to get to Memphis and offered to work for his ride. No harm in that, right?"

Her parents remained quiet.

"Dance, you say?" Lady Marie eyed Emmett as though he had two left feet. "What type of dance?"

Emmett opened his mouth, but no words came out.

Anola rescued him. "His mother taught him to tap dance. Isn't that lovely?"

The others gave Emmett approving smiles. One thing they understood was a parent passing talents to their children.

"Perhaps we can let you perform a number or two during the vaudeville." Da bit into his apple, probably already sketching out the act in his mind.

"No, sir." Emmett jerked his head with far more vehemence than necessary. "I don't think that's a good idea."

"He needs practice. I'll help him." All three men eyed her now. Anola raised her chin. "And he's going to help me with that accounting." The word popped out with more disgust than she'd intended. She *would* get control of that book. "A decent trade."

Another thing her father and grandfather held in high regard was the ability to garner a good trade.

Mentioning the accounting reminded her of something, so she switched topics before Emmett could let his shyness rob him of a good opportunity. "I found an entire crate of herbs in the storage closet someone forgot to take to Cook." She arched an eyebrow at her father. "This is why we need an inventory system. He was right about that."

"Herbs?" Lady Marie poked a piece of bread through the wires for her birds. "When did you get herbs?"

Da tilted his head. "I don't recall."

"Looks like they were there for some time."

"You can't recall?" Lady Marie ignored Anola and focused on her son. "How many times have I told you I need to know what happens with my kitchen?"

Lady Marie insisted the kitchen, like all other areas of the boat, was hers to command. An area the men generally left to her. Except when it came to purchasing supplies.

Da finished his bite and sipped his water. "Maybe it was from that peddler at the end of last season. I don't remember any herbs, but we did get several crates from him when his store flooded."

Who could forget the shelves full of canned goods without labels? Cook had groused about that for months and said not a one of them could complain that they'd had peaches with their fish stew or hominy for dessert. Not her fault she didn't know what a can contained until it was open.

"I'm not a dancer," Emmett announced when silence settled. "I'm not going to dance."

Poor man seemed panicked.

"Memphis, you say?" The captain chewed his pipe stem. "What's in Memphis?"

Emmett's shoulders lowered from where they had gathered up near his ears. "My brother."

"I thought you lived in St. Louis."

"I do." He shifted his gaze her way. "But I need to meet him in Memphis in two weeks."

"About how long it will take us to reach there." She cast a knowing look to Mam. "Once again, it seems God's plan includes Emmett."

If she'd thought the man had paled before, he looked ghostly now.

What had she said wrong?

A nola awoke before dawn to the familiar sounds of shouted orders, running feet, and the creaks and groans of the gangplank being hauled aboard. She rolled from her bed and stretched. What would this fourth day with Emmett Carter in their midst hold? She splashed her face with tepid water from the basin and pulled on a pair of work trousers, sturdy boots, and a knit blouse Lady Marie had made to counteract the Mississippi's predawn breeze.

Air heavy with the scents of life filled her lungs as she scurried from her room on the showboat and over to *Blue Belle*, where Cook already had a hot buttered biscuit and Da's coffee ready. Eating the flaky delicacy as she walked, Anola skirted the guardrail along the full length of the boat. She shoved the rest of her breakfast in her mouth and secured Da's coffee with one hand so she could climb the ladder leading from the showboat's second floor to the roof.

There she would find her father in his kingdom—the small box atop their world where he'd direct the fates of all who followed his lead. The pilothouse sat close to the bow, and the one-hundred-twenty-foot walk always exhilarated her, even though her feet had tread this path since she'd been old enough to slip from Mam's grasp. Keeping to the middle, she cut a direct route to Da at the wheel.

Sensing her approach in his uncanny way, he turned and waved her up the four steps into the pilothouse. Then he secured the rudder by slipping an anchored loop of rope onto one of the wheel spokes and tying it in place.

"Thank you, my dear." He accepted the coffee and closed his eyes as he enjoyed the first sip.

Light glimmered on the water, awakening the river with colors of pink and orange. They said this could be a wicked river, but it could be a beautiful one too.

"Keep her nose on that point." Da nodded toward the wheel.

Anola gripped the spokes, the same thrill she'd felt as a girl tingling over her. She should come here more often.

Da leaned closer. "Don't let her drift, now. Pull right."

She lined the jack staff—a whip-thin pole situated on *The River Queen*'s starboard front corner—with a graceful oak on the bank and kept the wheel steady.

"What brings you up here this early?" Da drew another sip. "Not that I mind getting my coffee sooner. Though you could have thought to bring me a biscuit."

The humor in his voice drew a laugh. "And have Mam admonish me for ruining her scheduled breakfast with you? I think not."

Da adjusted the wheel, his keen eye picking up some eddy or swirl in the Mississippi Anola didn't see.

"I woke up early is all." She counted two buoys and tried to remember how many more it would take to get to Rockwood. A tiny community far better to her liking than the larger cities they were leaving behind.

"Any luck finding those missing herbs?"

She twisted the wheel a touch to her left to keep the jack staff on the approaching oak. "It's the oddest thing. I can't find that crate anywhere. I asked Billy, George, and half the crew, but no one remembers a thing about it."

"And Cook didn't take it?"

"She says she's not seen 'a hide nor hair of no cookin' spice' other than the one bag I gave her, and she shooed me away when I asked her a second time."

Da grunted. "Lady Marie might have been in a tiff over the entire affair and dropped the lot of it overboard."

"She'd do no such thing!" Especially knowing their financial condition.

"You don't know your grandmother as well as I do." The twinkle in his gaze belied the accusation. "The woman can turn to trouble if the notion suits, and the entire time, she'll let you think she's never harbored a mischievous thought."

"I can't imagine she'd have a to-do over some herbs. But I'll ask if she's seen them."

Da shrugged and adjusted the wheel a fraction. "Did you manage to get young Mr. Carter to dance?"

Anola scrunched her nose. "I don't understand it. He is adamantly against the notion."

"Maybe he has stage fright." Da sipped his coffee as his gaze trailed a sandhill crane's graceful swoop toward the bank. "Let it be. You have a few of your grandmother's tendencies yourself."

She'd hardly say prompting a man to practice a talent—as those needed polishing to be of use—had any similarities to dumping perfectly good cooking supplies. Obviously, Emmett needed the reminder.

"He doesn't seem to be much of a deckhand, and he's uncomfortable with the stage."

The censure in Da's voice had her hurrying to Emmett's defense. "But he is a hard worker. Smart too. He's already taught me a lot about finances."

Da was quiet as she handed the wheel back into his expert care. He settled his calloused hands over the spokes. "You like him, don't you?"

"Of course I do. He's a nice man. I see no reason why anyone wouldn't."

He tilted his captain's hat back on his forehead, the gesture and the renewed twinkle in his eye saying he knew Anola understood he'd meant more.

She puffed her cheeks and blew out a breath. "Mam says it's because I haven't been around enough young men. That's nonsense. I've seen hundreds of young men on this boat." Of course, that hadn't been what Mam meant either. But seeing as how the three of them could communicate with such half-spoken implications and still understand one another perfectly...well, then some things were left unsaid.

"The moment your mother came aboard, I knew she was meant for me."

She'd heard the story a hundred times, but she still pulled the stool close to the wheel and settled next to her father as he recounted meeting the love of his life.

"We had just traded the captain's first showboat—"

"*Flynns' Floating Theater.*"

"Exactly. She only seated a hundred and forty people, but she'd served the captain and Lady Marie well for many years."

"And then you were able to buy *The River Queen.*"

Da chuckled as he navigated a bend. "Do you want to tell it or shall I?" After Anola rolled her eyes, he slipped into his stage voice, eyes growing distant. "*The River Queen*, we called her. She was the jewel of the water and no one could resist her charm."

His wistfulness had her aching to restore the grandeur that far outweighed their pitiful showing in Kimmswick.

He adjusted the wheel and navigated a shallow bank in the turn. "By the second year, Lady Marie insisted we needed a pianist who could also play her new calliope. The calliope would bring the people from near and far, she'd said, and of course, the captain surrendered to her wisdom. He placed an ad in the *Billboard* and in response received a telegram from one Joe Costello."

Anola couldn't help but chuckle, knowing where the story headed. She'd often wondered what expression Lady Marie had worn that day.

"The telegram read, 'Experienced Pianist. Salary your limit. Can join at once.' Lady Marie, well, she got a notion in her head. Costello, she said, had to be an Italian name. And everyone knew Italian men were musical. Therefore, without having ever met the man, the captain wired confirmation to Joe Costello."

Anola shook her head with mock ruefulness.

"When our new pianist arrived, we were all rather surprised to discover Lady Marie had hired a lovely young Irish woman who looked nothing at all like the Italian man she'd expected." Da winked.

Anola laughed. "She probably said something along the lines that the Irish were better musicians anyway."

Da tapped the end of his nose. "And why wouldn't she? Given we are an Irish lot. Your mother never did understand why Lady Marie mistook Jocelyn Coslow for Joe Costello."

And if Mam had addressed the telegram that way on purpose, she'd never tell a soul.

"She joined our cast and took to the river life like she was born for it."

"You married her eight weeks later."

"And you came along soon after." He eased the wheel and nodded toward the riverbank. "Getting close to our landing. You want to bring her in?"

"Best you do it." She enjoyed steering their four-cornered swan down the river, but she'd never trust her skills at bringing such a vessel to dock.

Da maneuvered the boat to the muddy bank where the crew would wade over to anchor them down. They'd secure a buried deadman in the loose soil if needed or use thick ropes and trees if the water remained gentle and the banks solid.

"Do you think it will ever be that way for me?" She hadn't meant to say the words. They marched right between her lips of their own accord.

Da didn't seem surprised. "None of us knows what God's plans will be until we're standing at the start of the path."

That hardly answered her question.

"The river isn't a usual life, my gem. Not many people are drawn to our ways." His tone sad, he kept his focus on the shore. "Someday you may find a different journey waits for you."

The words drifted between them but could find no anchor in her heart. No matter what she had to do or how she had to work the numbers to keep them afloat, she knew one thing with certainty.

She belonged on the river.

Emmett accepted a buttered biscuit from Cook and settled in the dining room with the rest of the crew. Hopefully the simple meal would settle his stomach.

The dining hall, a long room with tables and benches, connected to Cook's domain. The whitewashed walls and scuffed floors reflected little of *The River Queen*'s grandeur, but the simple function suited. The men here were rough around the edges, and the shine of the theater on the connecting boat may as well have been miles away.

Here, the steamboat crew lived a far different life. One filled with boisterous conversations that started well before dawn, unusual meals, and worst of all, the constant swaying of the floor. He chewed slowly, savoring Cook's handiwork. A far cry better than the boiled mudbugs she'd served him last night. It had taken him far too long to peel the critters, and the tiny amount of meat he'd gotten for the effort hadn't done much to ease his hunger. What he *had* eaten had been so spicy his stomach rebelled this morning after a night of pitching and heaving as the Mississippi River surged beneath them.

He'd been too exhausted his first night aboard to notice the way the inconsistent movement robbed a man of a good night's rest, but the past few nights he'd snatched sleep in fits and starts.

"Mornin'." A beefy man with a barrel chest and jowls fit for a bulldog slapped Emmett's shoulder.

He grunted at the impact.

Billy lowered himself onto the bench. "You a good swimmer?"

"Not particularly."

He stroked his chin and eyed Emmett as though he thought him a liar. "Know how to handle a shovel?"

What man didn't? "Yes." He withheld a wince. He had no desire to spend the day shoveling coal. He'd been assigned that task two days ago and still imagined coal dust in his nostrils.

"And you don't mind heights, right?"

"Heights?"

The burly man shrugged. "George generally jumps right off the roof. He ain't feeling good today, so we thought we'd ask the new fellow if he wanted to give it a go."

"Give what a go?" Already regretting asking, Emmett accidentally crushed the rest of his biscuit. The crumbs littered the table. "What roof?"

Billy jostled his shoulder again. "We need the deadman." He glanced at Emmett's empty plate. "Since you're finished, let's get to it. Aye?"

Seeing no other choice, Emmett stepped out of the room just as *Blue Belle* eased *The River Queen* to the bank and nestled her up next to the shore. Yesterday, one of the crew had told him Stephen Flynn could steer both boats from his little house atop the showboat using the long lines connected to the steamboat's rudders. He and the steamboat engineer communicated with a series of whistles when needed, but mostly they worked so well together they moved in tandem.

Billy stopped on the steamboat's upper deck and gestured to the bank, still a good thirty feet away. "You can jump off here and swim to the shore. Then we'll need to get one of those logs there." He pointed to a tree as big around as Emmett's waist. "We'll tie ropes around that there and then bury her in the mud so as to create a solid anchor."

Emmett leaned over the rail to gauge the depths of this fellow's lunacy. "What does any of that have to do with jumping out of the boat?" Memories of scoundrels tossing him into the muddy water surfaced. He took a step back. "I can go ashore to dig the hole."

Billy howled with laughter. "How you planning on getting there? Are you Saint Peter? Goin' to go walkin' on the water?"

"Now you leave him be Billy Brunswick before I get Cook to smack you with her paddle." The fiery redhead approached, and the fierce arch of her brows said she hadn't been joking. "I won't have you taking advantage of the man because he's too green to know better."

Billy ducked his head, properly chastised. "Ain't making fun, miss. George do always jump from here."

"But why does that mean Emmett has to?"

White-hot pride swelled in him for reasons he couldn't fathom, and his chest puffed out. Words no sane man should have spoken popped from his mouth. "I can jump if I need to jump."

Anola wrinkled her nose. "Nonsense. You aren't capable of—"

"You don't know me well enough to say what I am not capable of, Miss Flynn."

Her eyes flashed. "That so?" She waved to the churning water below. "Then, by all means, tell me where the safest landing spot will be so you won't break your neck."

He dared a glance over the railing again, all false bravado disintegrating. Before he could succumb to his shame, however, Anola had him by the hand.

"Lucky for you, I am most excellent at reading the river and know where we shall jump."

His throat constricted. "We?"

The grin she flashed had just enough time to land a cannon-ball of dread in his gut before she snatched him forward.

This woman was going to be the death of him.

10

Exhilaration swept through Anola like a storm as her body became weightless. Emmett gripped her hand so tightly her fingers might break, but he took the leap with her. For one glorious instant, they were falling together, the wind rushing past them and tangling in their hair. Above, people shouted. Below, the muddy water reached up.

They entered the Mississippi's silty embrace, the churning water grabbing them and trying to tear their fingers apart. She let go so she could right herself, then kicked her legs toward the shore. She'd gauged the landing perfectly, and with only a few pumps of her legs, her feet touched the bank.

Too bad she hadn't taken the time to remove her shoes.

She stood in the chest-high water and wiped it from her face. After making sure Emmett surfaced, she swashed toward the shore. The mud sucked at her feet and threatened to take her boots into the mire. Struggling, she churned her way forward.

Emmett's arm wrapped around her waist and held her close. Then he hauled her right up the side of the bank and set her down under the shade of a towering oak.

But he didn't release her.

His breath came in rapid succession, and the eyes staring down into hers almost made her breathing cease. He tugged her closer, their wet clothing mashed between them. This felt like something out of one of their plays. A romantic interlude where the hero and heroine realized they were meant for one another and—

"Are you out of your mind?" Emmett's eyes bulged.

She blinked. *Oh.*

The man crushing her against him looked more angry than enchanted. She sputtered for an answer, but none came.

"What if you had hit your head? Or the water had sucked you under?"

"I know these waters—"

"What if I couldn't have saved you?"

Her words stuttered to a halt. Why in the heavens did he think she needed saving?

He shoved a hand into his dripping hair, yet he still held her tight with the other arm. As though he feared she might disappear into the river if he loosened his grip.

"I can't—" He shook his head. "I don't—"

The man was rather attractive, dripping wet and spluttering. And the way he held her had all kinds of charming notions firing through her. His mouth twisted into what he probably meant to be a grimace, but it looked more like lips that needed help smoothing out.

Before she could tell herself better, she pushed up on her toes and let her lips hover near his. An invitation.

He stopped sputtering.

Her lips curved. "But wasn't it exhilarating?" Her words came out breathy. "I suspect few other things give a person such a thrill." Her lids fell to half closed. "Don't you think?"

His gaze trailed down to her mouth.

Would he...?

Her breath caught. He bent forward, and the world slowed. Achingly gentle, his lips brushed against hers. Soft. Sweet.

Tempting. She pressed closer to him, wanting more. Then the intoxicating sensation ceased. He leaned back.

His gaze captured hers as her lids fluttered open. "You gave me a terrible fright."

"I didn't mean to."

He pulled in a breath, held it, then released it. He smelled of lye soap and river water. And he stirred her like nothing she'd ever known. Perhaps, if she leaned in again, she might get him to go back to kissing her. It seemed they'd hardly started, and she wanted to explore the sensation further.

"Anola Flynn!"

Da's voice snatched her from her stupor. Emmett must have been jostled from this most delightful moment as well because she found herself without his support. She stumbled, and he caught her elbow to right her. Once her legs steadied, he released his hold.

Up on the porch of *Blue Belle*, her father, mother, grandfather, grandmother, and at least half of the actors stared down at them. The crew kept elbowing one another and grinning. Lady Marie and the captain each bore an amused smirk.

But Da...

Anola twisted her fingers together and risked a glance at Emmett. Poor man had turned as red as a crawdad. She lifted her hand, waved to the boat, then took a deep bow. "We have succeeded in our jump! Will someone toss us a shovel?"

The men on board hooted in laughter. Then a shovel flew through the air. It landed with a wet slap a couple of feet from Emmett's shoes. When she looked back up at the railing, Da was gone.

From the look on his face, Emmett had noticed as well.

He'd been right. One way or another this fiery bird would be the death of him. Now her father marched toward him, and Emmett steeled himself for the encounter. What had he been thinking, letting himself kiss her?

He hadn't, and that had been the problem. She'd terrified him when she'd leapt from the second story, and he'd fought a debilitating panic when he'd lost his grip on her as they hit the water. A miracle one or both of them hadn't broken a leg or gotten sucked beneath the unpredictable currents.

They didn't call this the Wicked River for nothing.

"Decided to be a bit adventurous, did you?" Stephen Flynn stopped a pace from Emmett and eyed the length of him. "Didn't take you for the type."

What type? The kind who jumped into dangerous waters or who took liberties with daughters? He no doubt meant the second. "Forgive me, sir. It won't happen again."

One blondish red eyebrow ticked toward the hat perched on the man's head and the tips of his mustache twitched.

He'd gone and done it now.

"Da, I'm the one who made the leap." Anola stood next to him, water dripping from her clothes.

"I have no doubt." Stephen huffed. "And what of the other?"

"Other?" The squeak in her voice gave away her attempt at playing innocent.

"Entirely my fault, sir." Emmett strode a half step forward, tucking Anola behind him. "It won't happen again."

A weight dropped into his center. But it was the right thing to say. He shouldn't take such liberties when they'd soon be parting for good.

Stephen darted a gaze between Emmett and his daughter. "That so?" He grunted. After an uncomfortable pause for what had to be a rhetorical question, he gestured toward the water. "What think you of the river, lad?"

"The river?"

Stephen didn't repeat himself. He stood there eyeing Emmett as though whatever answer he said would determine the fate of the world.

It could determine his. "Can't say as I know enough about the river to have much of an opinion. My brother acquired a steamboat without my consent. He left me no option but to see the venture through, despite my inexperience shipping or boating. On my first voyage, thieves relieved me of the boat." Pitiful as it might be, he'd left nothing out.

"What do you think of the river now?"

It felt like a weighted question. He cut a glance at Anola, who seemed to be speaking volumes to her father through her eyes, though he couldn't decode a word of it.

"I've found it...fascinating."

That earned another grunt from the older man. What that could mean, Emmett couldn't fathom. He clasped his hands behind his back and waited.

The man studied him, then bobbed a nod as though coming to some decision. "What are you standing around for, lad? Aren't you meant to be digging the deadman? I haven't got all day to wait for this boat to be anchored."

He spun and marched forward with as much purpose as when he'd first walked Emmett's way.

"Emmett, I—"

Whatever Anola had been about to say was cut short by Stephen's call.

She flashed him what almost could be a shy smile and darted after her father. Emmett stood there dumbfounded until they reached the lowering gangplank.

He picked up the shovel. A crazy dive into the river. Mud everywhere. A hole that would take him ages to dig and a tree he had no hope of burying on his own. On all accounts, a rather disastrous morning.

Yet he couldn't stop grinning.

11

O h no. Anola knew that look. "Lady Marie. It's a simple question."

Her grandmother snorted. "Have you lost your senses?" Instead of an indignant frown, however, she tilted her lips into a sly smile. "Whatever gave you such a notion?"

Anola tugged on a pair of long white gloves to go with this evening's costume. "I was thinking you are the mischievous type."

A puff of perfume enveloped Lady Marie in a cloud of sweetness that would likely suffocate Henry before he could say his lines. "Fiddle-faddle. I'm nothing of the sort." She dusted her face with rice powder and poked at the persistent lines around the corners of her eyes. "And even if I was"—she pointed a finger at Anola's raised eyebrows—"which I am not, I'm far too frugal to waste perfectly good ingredients out of annoyance with your father."

She did have a point.

"I've asked everyone on this boat. It's become a mystery."

And Anola did enjoy a good mystery. Like the time she'd been the one to discover the cause of the strange noises they kept hearing at the most inopportune times during performances. The screeching and grunting had come from a stranded possum tucked behind the orchestra pit.

Despite the allure of some sleuthing, a tightness settled in her chest. "Something isn't right."

Lady Marie shrugged. "You're turning this into more than it is." She swiped a vibrant purple from the tube and lined her eyes. "What is not a mystery is how you've captured the attention of one Mr. Emmett Carter."

The aquamarine dress Anola had chosen for tonight accentuated her eyes perfectly, and she had to admit she'd picked the gown in hopes he might like it. "It's been three days."

Three days since they'd kissed and he'd been as scarce as a rabbit in a den of foxes.

"Your father did get a touch hot under the collar with that spectacle." Lady Marie flashed a smile. "I, of course, found the show amusing."

Anola laughed. "So did the entire cast and crew." She'd had little choice but to embrace their display of wiggling eyebrows and knowing grins.

"I'm sure his avoiding you has more to do with consequences from Stephen than any objection to you."

"Da didn't give him any consequences."

"That you know of."

Da wouldn't do any such thing. Would he? He hadn't seemed all that angry. "Da says he's not the type for the river." She pulled the fabric over her waist and turned her back to Lady Marie to secure the buttons. "But when Da asked him, he said he found the river fascinating."

"The river, or you?"

How did her grandmother know she'd also sensed a double meaning to Da's question?

"Both, I think." She dabbed her pinkie in the rouge and applied a touch to her lips.

"God often gives us our opposite so we can smooth out one another's rough places."

Doubtful. The captain and Lady Marie were most certainly cut from the same cloth. "Da and Mam aren't opposites."

"Aren't they, though?" She hummed to herself as she pinned a lock of dyed hair. "You probably don't see it because they've worn off on each other over the years. But when Jocelyn first came to this boat, she could be as stiff and determined as your Emmett."

Anola couldn't imagine Mam as uptight as Emmett. But perhaps life on the river changed a person.

What if Emmett stayed for the season and gave whatever sparked between them a chance to grow? "I do like him."

"Obviously." Lady Marie secured a stole around her shoulders. "But don't go letting fanciful notions distract you from what's in front of you. Your heart is a precious thing, lass. Don't give it away too easily."

Anola placed a feather-light kiss on her grandmother's cheek and darted out the door before she could think too much about her growing attraction to Emmett. Lady Marie had a point. Emmett had to prove his love for the river before she could consider letting her heart set a course for him.

If she showed him all the ways the Mississippi could be charming, then he would surely become enchanted.

How could he not?

He hated this river. Emmett dumped silty water out of his shoe. If Stephen hadn't made a point to state otherwise, he would think making him set the gangplank every morning was a strange form of punishment. Especially since Emmett never got the job right and had to reset the stakes before the performance even started.

Not that anyone ever told him the proper way and saved him the trouble.

He tugged the shoe over his sodden sock and grimaced as his feet squished back toward the boat.

Anola's musical voice rang out from above. "Figured it out yet?"

His fists clenched. "How should I know? Nothing I try works."

Her laughter shredded his good manners, and he glowered. They must all find his mortification amusing. Perhaps that's what they discussed during the night lunches he'd declined to join.

Clad in an ensemble as dazzling as the peacock gown, the river queen stood on the deck waiting. Hundreds of sparkling beads caught the last rays of the day's light. Fringes fell in three layers from her hips to the floor, shifting in shimmering waves each time she moved. Around her temples glimmered a matching headband with crystals and blue and gold feathers.

If he'd been faced with a mythological Irish fairy, he wouldn't have been surprised.

"I need your help solving a mystery," she announced the moment he neared.

Emmett gestured to his shoes. "And I need proper instructions."

She thrust out a gloved hand. "Deal."

He should have known she'd meet his gruffness with buoyant enthusiasm. A chuckle lodged in his throat.

He wiped his hand on his pants in an effort to remove the sludge, but Anola didn't seem to care. He gave her gloved fingers a professional pump. "Deal."

"You aren't getting the stakes deep enough. The mud shifts, and the water will wriggle them free if you haven't gotten beneath the silt." She pointed to where he'd reset the stakes. "You did better this time, moving that last set past the end of the planks."

Something he'd learned by trial and error. Must every task on the water render him an incompetent fool? Her explanation couldn't be any simpler. "I'll remember that."

"It's the same concept as the deadman. We have to get beneath the silt and create an anchor that won't shift." She flashed a brilliant smile. "Now, about that mystery."

Emmett followed her onto the main deck and underneath the shade of the upper porch.

"Remember the crate of herbs I told you about? It's gone missing."

Hardly a mystery that required sleuthing. "Cook probably used it last night." There'd been enough spices in that stew to set a phoenix on fire.

"An entire crate's worth?" She clucked her tongue. "Besides, she says she hasn't seen it. Nor has anyone else on this boat. But someone had to have moved it, or it would still be in the closet. Da claims Lady Marie tossed it overboard in a tiff, but of course, I don't believe it. And before you ask, I did tell her what he said, and she denies such foolishness. She says her frugalness when it comes to ingredients outweighs her mischievousness, a sentiment I believe."

The torrent of words trickled to an end, and she stared expectantly.

"I haven't seen the spices."

"I wasn't implying you have." She waved the statement away. "I wanted your help solving the mystery."

"Why?"

She scoffed. "Because I want to know what happened and why anyone would keep such a thing a secret. A few herbs aren't worth being untruthful for."

A seed took hold in Emmett's mind and sprouted a sour feeling in his stomach. "What type of herbs did you find?"

"Several little bags of the thing. Dried green herbs that smelled sweet."

"And you're sure they were herbs?"

A crease formed between her brows. "What else could they be?"

The suspicion rooted. "And now they are missing, and no one will admit to moving them?"

She lowered her chin while her brows hiked the opposite direction.

"Anola, I don't think those were herbs."

Her expression shifted to a frown. "Then what are they?"

"I've heard about a plant people have been smoking that has similar effects to opium. Have you heard of opium dens?"

A flicker flashed in her eyes before settling. "Mam said a lot of the soldiers succumbed to that after returning from the Great War. They thought it might help with the mental and physical effects of the trauma, but Mam said the empty release only introduced another type of prison. The effects are similar to when men drink too much whiskey, but in this case, their drunkenness comes from smoking a certain type of pipe."

Her eyes widened. "Not like the pipe the captain has. He used only tobacco in that and hasn't even packed the bowl in..." Her lips compressed. "Four months, I think. I'm not sure why." Her head tilted in an adorable way as she answered her question. "Likely because Lady Marie mentioned she didn't care for breathing the smoke from a pipe she didn't light."

Emmett clawed through his memory. What had Jacob said that time about... What was it? Mutton heads? No...muggles. Muggleheads. "Could any of your crew be smuggling those bags downriver?"

Anola pulled back as though he'd struck her. "Nonsense. We are all family. What you're implying sounds sneaky at best and immoral at worst." She shook her head, sending styled curls frolicking over her shoulder. "None of our people would do anything like that. There must be another explanation."

Noise behind them saved Emmett from having to point out the holes in her theory.

She straightened her shoulders. "I must greet them." She whirled around and dashed up the stairs.

A moment later, her enchanting voice rang out over the evening air.

"Welcome, welcome,
All my friends,
Welcome, welcome,
This is where the story begins,
Bring your sorrows,
Bring your joy,
Every man, woman, girl, and boy,
Welcome, welcome,
To *The River Queen*,
Where every moment is but a dream."

A farmer and his family grinned up at Anola as they boarded, and Emmett waved an arm toward the ticket booth to guide them before retreating around to the boat's other side.

He scoured his mind for more memories of what Jacob had mentioned about the plant the newspapers had likened to opium. Something about New Orleans and...

Daggers of ice knifed through his center.

Their steamboat had been heading to New Orleans. His brother's panicked voice echoed through his mind.

"Tell me you haven't contacted the police."

"We have to get that boat back. Before it gets to New Orleans."

"Don't come home."

Could whatever Jacob had gotten wrapped up in and Anola's missing herbs be connected?

"I 'll kill you for messin' with my wife!"

The bellowed words cut into Anola's second round of the welcome song. At the tree line a few dozen paces from the river's edge, a farmer with shoulders wide enough to pull his own plow waved a pistol in the air.

"Where are ya, you cur? Come here and face me like a man!" He lowered the barrel toward the swarm of people headed to fill her theater.

Anola gripped the rail. Surely he didn't mean to shoot anyone.

The man barreled closer, the flop hat covering long muddy-brown hair bouncing with each step. Women squeaked and pulled children behind their skirts. If she didn't do something, he'd scare away her audience. She hurried down the stairs and past people pushing their way on board.

Just as she reached the gangplank, an arm scooped around her waist and arrested her forward momentum.

"Oh no you don't."

Emmett! She twisted her head to glare at him. "Release me. I need to do something about that man before he causes a fuss."

"He's already caused a fuss. And what is an unarmed lady going to do about a brute with a gun?"

"Speak reason to him."

Emmett fell silent at her revelation, but he didn't release her.

"Death of me for certain." With that confusing statement, he tucked her behind him. "Stay here. I'll deal with him."

He swam through the encroaching crowd so quickly she lost him and had to plant her feet to keep from being pushed in the opposite direction. Perhaps she could be of a different use.

She lifted her hands and her voice. "Good people, enter straight into the theater! We'll collect your ticket money once you take your seats. Yes, move along here, please."

She pointed to a skittish fellow with ears that clung to the side of his head like two rumpled butterflies. "You, sir, this way!" He eyed the press of the crowd blocking what he likely considered escape and turned toward the theater.

The line moved forward, releasing the dam and allowing them to flow inside and gather up stragglers in the current. More people hurried to the boat while the man with the gun bellowed from the shore.

Without bothering to explain to Mam, Anola hustled the people past the ticket booth and through the double doors. After more smiles and shooing motions, she could reach the ticket window.

"What's happening?" Mam rose and pushed herself up next to the window, though no amount of craning her neck would give her a view of the riverbank.

"Just a touch of drama. Emmett is handling it."

"What drama?" Lady Marie swept out of the theater in a hurricane of feathers and silk. "And why do none of these people have tickets?"

"We'll need to get Freddie and the captain to sell the tickets to them from their seats. Emmett can help once he finishes with the gunman."

"Gunman!"

"Gunman!"

The two women spoke at the same instant, locked eyes, and a heartbeat later scrambled toward the main deck. Despite having farther to go, Mam beat Lady Marie to the main deck.

Anola followed, tripping only once on her gown in her haste.

"Get out of the way!" Emmett's voice rang out, his clear baritone heavy with authority.

He couldn't be talking to—

A gunshot split the air.

Her chest ceased. Mam shouted.

Silence.

Then chaos erupted. People screamed. Footsteps pounded past her.

Anola blinked. Twice more.

Her senses returned, and she broke out into a run, barreling down the gangplank and toward the form in the mud.

Someone shouted her name.

A hand tried to grab her.

She ignored everything but the man in a crumpled heap. She shouldn't have let him go without her. Men and their tempers. Things like this were best handled by a woman's cool head and delicate touch.

She plunked onto her knees and reached for—

Not Emmett.

Relief surged through her like swollen floodwaters, and she gulped for air. *Not* Emmett. Emmett was safe and... Guilt tugged her from the torrent. This man was not.

Forcing herself to think, she scanned the riverbank for the broad man with the gun but found no one. She dropped her gaze to the man before her.

A pair of blue eyes stared back up at her, wide and frightened.

"Are you harmed?"

"He tried to kill me!"

"Yes, but are you harmed?"

The man wailed, and Anola moved her gaze from his cleanly shaven face, down the length of a simple brown jacket to the place where he clutched his thigh.

No blood seeped between his fingers that she could see. A good sign.

"Is he dead? Oh, God above, help us if that man is dead!" Lady Marie's screech found Anola before the woman herself. "He's dead. I knew he'd be…" She came to a halt where Anola knelt in the mud.

"He was shot. There, I'd reckon." Anola jutted her chin to indicate where the man grasped his leg.

"Move, before you faint and leave me with two patients." Mam shooed Lady Marie out of her way. The elder cast Anola one fleeting look before fluttering back to the safety of the boat.

"Move those fingers, sir, so I can see." Mam spoke in her no-nonsense way, but the man only stared at her.

"He shot me!"

"I know." The words held no gentleness.

Anola shifted so Mam could attend the wound. She grabbed one of his fingers and tugged, then applied more pressure until the fellow gasped and pulled his hand back. Anola leaned over for a better look.

She blew out a breath and moved back.

The bullet had grazed him just enough to open a gash in his trousers and leave a scorched trail. He wouldn't even need stitches.

Now that she knew he wouldn't be dying anytime soon unless God had some unusual plans in store, she gained her feet and searched the bank for Emmett. "Did he shoot anyone else?"

"What?" The man snatched his gaze away from where Mam poked at his leg. "He ran off after he shot me, and some other fellow—Ya! That hurts!"

Anola trailed her gaze along the bank. Still, no sign of Emmett.

"Why did he shoot?" Mam asked, likely to keep the man's attention focused somewhere else.

He bit back a yelp. "Says I was messin' with his wife."

"Were you?"

"How should I know?"

Mam growled and rose. "You'll be fine. Clean it and put a bandage on it. And I suggest you find out if a woman is married *before* you court her."

The lanky man struggled to his feet and grasped Mam's arm. "What if he's waiting for me?"

She lifted her brows at his hand until he released her. Then she spoke to Anola. "I'll take him on board until he regains control of himself, and then Billy will escort him to town. Alerting the law will be up to him. I'd tell you not to go looking for Emmett, but we both know it won't do any good. Will you at least fetch your father first and take him with you?"

A sensible suggestion. Anola helped her mother guide the distraught man into the ticket booth and placed him under Billy's watchful eye. The sooner they got him off their boat, the better.

The first strains of the opening music reached her ears as she darted into the green room. They didn't have much time.

She found Da finishing the last twist of a cravat to complete the costume for his role of the fanciful comic, which thankfully wouldn't begin until the second act.

"I need your help." She snagged his elbow and pulled him toward the door. "Some farmer shot a man for cheating with his wife, and now he and Emmett have disappeared. Mam says I shouldn't go looking for Emmett without you. We do need to hurry, or we will miss our cues."

Da sputtered something incoherent but never slowed his steps. They scurried through the back passages and down the gangplank. Stragglers meandered their way toward the boat.

No sign of Emmett anywhere.

"Emmett!" Only the lap of the water and the hoot of an owl responded. Her throat tightened. "Da, you go that way, and I'll take the other."

He gripped her wrist before she could take a step. "We stay together. Don't worry. We'll find him."

She prayed he was right. But the farther they got from the boat, the more her hope faltered.

His lungs heaved. Emmett cut left once more, dodging through the trees and under a low-hanging branch. He'd lost all sense of direction. Not that it mattered as long as the bull after him did the same.

"You!"

The bellowed shout gave Emmett enough warning to dart out of the way of a meaty hand jutting from the shadows to his right.

"I don't know your wife!" Emmett shouted the truth again and scrambled out of reach. Logic did nothing to stop his pursuer.

A towering pine ahead might offer a reprieve. He forced his aching legs to move faster, slipping from shadow to shadow in an attempt to stay hidden. He grabbed the rough bark and slid behind the ancient tree. His palm burned as he rested his back against the trunk and pulled in heaving breaths.

Boots stomped behind him, snapping twigs like those paws would his neck.

"Man that sins with another man's wife deserves what's comin' to 'em." Each slurred word ground out a death sentence.

How much longer could he outrun a jealous husband? Lord help him. This was not a situation he ever expected to experience.

"Gotcha!" Fingers latched onto his shoulder like a vise.

He twisted and surged. But the other man outweighed him by at least fifty pounds, and the hand holding him could crush bone. Emmett stilled and held the other man's gaze, praying logic and truth would win out.

"I came on the boat. Never set foot in this town before in my life."

The deep-set eyes narrowed, scouring Emmett's face. The sour stench of liquor washed over him.

"You have the wrong man." He accentuated each word. "I stopped Anola from coming instead. That's the only reason I left the boat."

The man leaned closer, his head filling Emmett's vision. "Who's that?"

"Anola? She lives on the showboat. She was the pretty girl singing."

"That your girl?"

He wanted her to be. Emmett shoved the unexpected revelation aside and focused on getting this drunken brute to listen to reason. He might not survive otherwise. "I work for her father. We are friends. And I haven't been with any women. I live in St. Louis. I'm headed to Memphis. I promise, on my honor, I have never dallied with anyone's wife."

The man burped and narrowed his glassy gaze. "How do I know you aren't lyin' to save your skin?"

Emmett scrambled for an answer but came up short. "Do I match the description you've had of this adulterer?" Surely the man must know something about who he'd come to murder.

The brute eased him back to arm's length and seemed to see Emmett for the first time. He snorted. "Too short."

Emmett latched onto the seed of doubt. "If you want to go back, you can ask anyone on the crew. I've never left the boat, so I couldn't be the man you're looking for."

The man grunted and hauled Emmett away from the tree. "We'll see. Might be I can find that cur yet."

Had he sentenced another man to death?

"You don't try scamperin' off, ya hear? Just 'cause my gun jammed don't mean I can't still kill you."

He had no doubt.

They marched through the deepening shadows back in the direction they'd come. Hopefully. How could this man know where they were? He didn't have to wonder for long. *The River Queen*'s shimmering lights beckoned through the trees.

A voice called like a siren through the darkness. Anola?

"Emmett! Where are you?"

"That your pretty lady from the boat?" The bear growled in his ear, voice low and menacing.

Emmett nodded.

"You don't say a thing." He shook Emmett for good measure. "You hear?"

Heat pooled in his stomach and stiffened his spine. No matter what it took, he'd find a way to keep this blackguard from harming Anola.

"Emmett!"

Stephen?

At least now he had backup. Had Stephen brought a gun? "Here!"

The madman behind him growled and shoved Emmett forward. They burst through the trees and onto the riverbank. *The River Queen* held court at least a hundred yards away. He'd been running for what felt like an hour. Had he gone in circles?

Stephen and his daughter both turned at their approach, but the shadows had deepened too much for Emmett to make out their expressions. Anola rushed forward, the fringe on her gown swinging. Her father grabbed her arm as they neared.

"Stop!" The bear shook Emmett so hard his teeth rattled. "You want me to let this man go, you answer me first. And don't you lie!"

Anola halted paces away and squared her shoulders into a regal bearing. "I never lie, thank you." Her brow crinkled. "Well, except one time when I hid a kitten from Mam, but only because—"

"Enough!" The man marched Emmett closer so Stephen and Anola could see the full revelation of his shameful circumstances. "This your man?"

"He works for me, yes," Stephen answered, his stance wide and expression wary. No sign of a gun.

"Has he been on your boat?" The man swayed but used Emmett to regain his balance.

"Hasn't left it except to tie anchor on the banks for over a week now. Whatever you think he may have done, I can promise on my good name as captain of *The River Queen* that this man has not been out of sight of me or mine since he came aboard just south of St. Louis."

How closely had they been watching him?

The brute grunted again, and some pressure released from Emmett's shoulder. His bones groaned in relief. The bruise would last for weeks. Assuming he lived long enough.

"You, pretty lady. This your fellow?" He shook Emmett again as though she couldn't see him. He felt like a puppy being held out for inspection.

Anola sucked in a breath, and Emmett cringed.

"We are friends, and he works on my father's boat. But..." She hesitated, a slight quiver in her voice. "I am not opposed to seeing if he might be the man God has planned for me."

Silence settled, and something odd skipped through Emmett's stomach.

"And if you found out your man was with another woman, what would you do?"

Even the dim light revealed Anola's arched brows and Stephen's smirk.

"My girl would skin him alive, just as her father taught her." Despite the gravity of his situation, Stephen's words carried a hint of laughter. Still, Emmett didn't doubt the sentiment. The Flynn family seemed the type to protect their own fiercely.

The claws holding his shoulder released. "Reckon you can have him back, then. But I'm coming on that boat. That no-good cur ain't escaping his due."

Emmett stalked toward Stephen with as much dignity as he could muster.

"Would this cur be a leggy fellow about so tall?" Anola lifted her hand well above her head, several inches taller than what Emmett stood. "With blue eyes, a thin nose, and hair the color of summer wheat?"

The brute's voice darkened. "That's the one."

"You shot him." She spread her hands. "My mother tended to him, but there was nothing she could do. He's gone now."

The big man sneered. "I want to see the body."

"I'm afraid you'll have to ask in town for that."

His gaze slid off Anola's confident stance and landed on her father. "She best be tellin' the truth."

Stephen inclined his head in a diplomatic fashion. "That man is not on my boat. And I would kindly ask you to keep your personal affairs off my property. Otherwise, we'll need to bring in the law. I'm sure you understand."

If the man had any hope of escaping murder charges, he should be making himself scarce.

Stephen didn't wait any longer. He hooked Anola through the elbow and turned toward *The River Queen*. None of them dared look back until they reached the deck. Nothing but shadows and bullfrogs remained on the shore.

Brittle laughter leaked from Anola. "My, wasn't that an adventure?"

Stephen pulled a watch from the pocket of a Victorian-era costume, neither seeming concerned that a man had been murdered.

"If I hurry, they won't be forced to make Ben play double." He stabbed Emmett with a concerned look but hurried toward the theater.

Anola grabbed his sleeves. "What happened? Why did you run? We thought you were the man shot, but then of course you weren't. Still, we couldn't find you anywhere, and I'll admit, I thought the worst."

The thought of Anola Flynn scouring the woods for him in that outfit tugged his lips into a wayward smile.

"Did you miss your show?" Why did he say that instead of answering any of the questions she'd flung at him?

"Obviously." She fluttered a hand toward the music wafting from the theater. "But I'm sure Lady Marie had no trouble taking my place between acts."

They stared at one another, something earnest in Anola's expression, but he couldn't decide what it meant.

"Well," she said, "do you intend to keep me in suspense all night?"

"He fired off a shot, but then the gun jammed. I thought I could get it from him."

"You charged a man with a gun?"

The bright lights hid none of her admiration, and his pulse thrummed. He hated to dash her heroic vision of him. "I thought I might distract him enough to keep him from getting off another shot, but he threw the gun in the river and turned his rage on me."

Shame soured in his mouth. "I ran."

"Of course you did." Not the slightest hint of disappointment or condemnation tainted her voice. She patted his arm. "Any sane man would have. You did well getting him away from the boat and keeping my audience intact. Thank you."

Keeping her audience from dispersing hadn't crossed his mind, not that he wanted to admit such. He settled for a nod. Then he stood there, struggling with how to ask the question on his tongue. "How did... What did you do with the body?"

She threw her head back and laughed. "I said he shot the man. I never said he killed him." She winked. "People hear what they want to hear. See what they want to see."

103

The notion unsettled him. "So he's not dead?"

She snorted. "Barely grazed. Though you'd think he'd suffered immensely the way he carried on. Mam said she'd let him sit in the ticket booth and then have Billy take him back home. Like I said, that man will need to make his own inquiries in town."

"Clever." He eyed her. "I suppose I shouldn't expect anything different from an actress."

Red eyebrows climbed toward her forehead, one arching higher than the other. "What do you mean?"

She had turned the truth rather easily. Played a part. Did she do the same with him?

Something tightened her expression and caused an unease in his chest he couldn't dislodge.

The music shifted, and her eyes widened. "Oh!" She snatched up the fringed edges of her skirt, not noticing the twigs and leaves caught in the shimmering fabric. "I have to go."

Before he could move, she darted away.

Emmett stared after her, unable to untangle the thoughts pounding through his head. God help him. Never mind what unknown dangers awaited him in Memphis. He might not survive the journey there to find out.

A nola stood on her grandparents' porch and stared at the swirling eddies in the muddy water, contemplating what to do next. Emmett did not match the hero in any story she'd heard before. Weren't they supposed to come sweep their princess off her feet and carry her away into the sunset? She'd made her interest in the man clear, yet in the three days since, he'd not declared his ardor.

Did he find her lacking?

She'd always been different from other girls. Probably because she'd grown up as the only child on a showboat. But did that make her more undesirable than she'd realized?

"Well, just who does he think he is, anyway? No one can tell me I'm not good enough." She frowned at her undulating reflection, the water roiling with as many emotions as her heart.

"Good enough for what?"

Anola yelped and dropped the rope. The bucket on the other end splashed into the river and disappeared. She whirled around to face Lady Marie, who stood next to Mam on her grandparents' porch, both eyeing her like a pair of herring gulls who'd spotted a fat crab.

STEPHENIA H. MCGEE

Mam plopped her hands onto the hips of her green trousers. "Who said you weren't good enough?"

"It wasn't that shy boy you plucked out of the river, was it?" Lady Marie sniffed. "I'd thought he had better sense."

Anola notched her chin a fraction. "He didn't say it. But he must think it."

"And why have you gone and set your cap for him anyhow?" Lady Marie patted her coifed hair. "Just because he's the first fellow your age to stay on board for longer than an evening since that Jack boy doesn't mean he's your only option." She let out a dramatic sigh. "Flynn women have nothing if not a myriad of options."

Jack had been a boy from St. Louis who had captured her fourteen-year-old heart. They'd been the greatest of friends for all of two weeks before the season started and *The River Queen* left town for the summer. By the time they returned, his family had gone to some mining town.

Emmett Carter was nothing like Jack. Something both women knew well, so Anola denied them the satisfaction of hearing her say it.

The late-night breeze played across the family porch, bringing with it the smells of water, trees, and life. The night creatures plied their song to the heavens, greeting the cooler temperatures after the sun's final bow.

"Options for what?" The captain swept out onto the porch with a tray of Lady Marie's sandwiches and set them on the table. "Do we have a new script?"

"Hush, you. This is women's talk." Lady Marie dismissed her husband with a shooing motion softened with a kissing noise.

"Since when are new scripts women's talk?" He harrumphed and plucked his pipe from his pocket.

Anola resigned the water bucket to its fate and whispered an apology to the birds who wouldn't get a refill on their bath tonight. "We were discussing Mr. Carter, not scripts."

That earned a grunt. "Seems to me talking 'bout men should be men's talk. Not women's."

All three women gaped.

He laughed. "Said it *should* be. Not that it was."

"Should be what?" Da closed the door behind him and placed a basket of grapes next to the sandwiches.

"These womenfolk," the captain said around his pipe, "were having men-talk they call women-talk."

"Oh, for heaven's sake." Mam snagged a plate and rolled her eyes at her father-in-law. "We were discussing Emmett and something unkind he said to Anola."

Da's eyes flashed. "What now?"

This situation was getting out of hand. "Emmett said nothing unkind to me."

"You said he thought you weren't good enough." Lady Marie plucked three grapes from the stem and plunked them on top of half a sandwich.

"Good enough for what?" Da's brows tipped toward his nose.

"That's what I said." The captain gestured toward Mam and Lady Marie. "Then I was told to hush because it was women's talk."

Anola groaned. She loved her family. But sometimes... She shook her head. "He didn't say anything of the sort." Unable to keep her father's curious gaze, she studied the deck. "I merely wondered if he thought it, seeing as how he doesn't seem to share my...interest."

No one spoke. She couldn't help but lift her gaze to see what had rendered her boisterous family mute. They all gawked.

Heat churned in her stomach and flowed up to her neck.

"Did you tell that man you were interested in him?" Da regarded her as though she was still seven years old and hadn't thought through the consequences of bringing her new pet lizard to bed.

"You were there." The heat intensified, creating an itching path all the way up her neck to her face. She resisted the urge to rub it away. How had he forgotten she'd told Emmett she wanted to see if he was the man God had for her?

The captain plucked the unlit pipe from between his lips. "She told that boy she was smitten with him right in front of you?" He howled with laughter. "I hate I missed it!"

Da snorted. "She said she was *not opposed* to him. Not that she was smitten." He lifted a hand to stay more laughter. "At which point, we also discussed how she would gut him like a fish were he ever to harm her."

Anola remembered the conversation differently. More like Da had said something about skinning him if he dallied with another woman. Come to think of it, perhaps Emmett's avoiding her sat on Da's shoulders.

"This is your fault, you know." Lady Marie plopped her sandwich back on its delicate plate. One of the grapes rolled free and skittered onto her lap before she gripped it between her fingers and pointed at Da with it. "You're the one always telling her about how Jo Costello wasn't a Jo but a Jocelyn and you married her straightaway. What else is she supposed to think?"

Da paled. "Well, now, I didn't..." He sputtered. "That's different."

"Why?" Lady Marie pinned him with a look conveying more meaning than Anola could decipher. "What other examples does she have than a whirlwind romance and a bunch of glorified productions? What does our gem know of the real world?"

Even the frogs seemed to fall silent as a mood Anola had never experienced before descended on the porch. The sensation unsettled her.

"You should tell her." Mam sighed and put down the plate she hadn't even filled. "She needs to know."

His face pinched, and he seemed to age a score of years.

Anola's heart thrashed like a walleye caught in a net. "Tell me what?"

He rubbed the back of his neck. "We wanted to tell you after the season."

Her family looked everywhere but at her. The silence stretched thin, plucking at her nerves.

"Tell me what?" She hated repeating herself. But it didn't seem anyone would talk otherwise.

The captain rose like a general delivering orders. He squared his shoulders and met her eye. "This is our last season. We are taking to the shore and selling the boat once we reach New Orleans."

"To shore!" The words tore through her throat. The rest of what her grandfather had declared refused to find purchase in her floundering heart.

"Things aren't what they used to be," Mam said. "We thought it would get better after the Great War ended, but they've only gotten harder. People don't care for the showboats like they did when you were a girl. We can scarcely survive, and that isn't the life we want for you."

"What about the life I want?" She took a step back, betrayal leaving an ugly scorch through her center. "You can't sell *The River Queen*. Our home. You can't take everything away from me." She stepped back further and hit the wall. "And you weren't even going to tell me? To give me a chance?"

She hurled daggered glances at each of them, but not one would meet her eyes. She refused to let her voice waver. "I won't accept it."

Anola spun on her heel, flung open the door, and left her dearly loved traitors.

Emmett shoved his hand through his damp hair and filled his lungs. The night air tasted of an earthiness he'd not experienced in the city. Clean, yet filled with hundreds of faint scents all portraying a unique world. Life on the river differed from anything he'd experienced. He rested his forearms on the rail of the *Blue Belle* and stared at the pattern the starlight created on the rippling water.

He tried to pray, but the words eluded him. Worries over his brother and both their futures tangled in a writhing knot and threatened to choke him. One of his best memories of Mother had been her steady hand resting on his shoulder as she'd prayed over him. Told him God would grant peace.

What he wouldn't give for her presence now.

After the debacle with the gunman, Billy had seen to it that Emmett had something of use to occupy his every waking moment from before first light until well after the rumbling generator sputtered to sleep. He'd once found the man waiting on him to finish his private business. After three days of relentless labor and falling into his cot each night into the embrace of sleep, he'd been able to extract himself from Billy's overbearing presence.

That should have brought a measure of the peace he sought.

Pounding footsteps drew his attention across the short distance separating the mighty theater from her humble tug, a queen's carriage hitched to a scraggly nag. A form moved across the upper deck. The full moon cast silvery light that caught on shimmering red hair and set it aflame. Even from here, he could hear Anola's heated words, though he couldn't see anyone in her company. Curious, he watched her stalk like a caged lioness along the rail, making a full circle around the upper deck. Each time she came close enough, he caught snippets of her words.

"...like they thought I wouldn't find out. How could they even think..."

She disappeared around the back of the boat and, moments later, came down the stretch toward him again.

"...there's a way, of course. There's always a way. I just need you to show me so I can..."

This time Emmett pushed from the railing and crossed over to the other boat. Anola rounded the far end and headed his direction, still mumbling. She was nearly upon him before she drew up short.

"Emmett."

Not sure what else to do, he offered his arm, so she might walk with him. She hesitated long enough that he lowered his elbow. He shouldn't have assumed she'd want his company. He started to bid her a good night and leave her to her contemplations when her words stopped him.

"They are going to take my home from me."

"What? Who?"

She clenched her hands and stalked off, leaving him without an answer. If she hadn't spoken his name, he might think she'd not noticed him at all. He fell into step next to her, but her previous tumble of words had ceased.

By the time they made a full lap around the boat, his concern over her silence outweighed the awkwardness. "Who wants to take your home?"

"I'll need you to help me save it." She let out a sigh and mumbled something he almost didn't catch. His brain worked out the words until the meaning caught. "Even if you do find me lacking."

He didn't find Anola Flynn lacking in any manner. The only meaning he could puzzle out must have something to do with the bookkeeping. She'd claimed she didn't have the head for numbers, but he'd seen her quick intelligence.

"What do you need me to do?" he asked.

She glanced at him as though she'd forgotten he stood next to her. Then she unlatched hands that had been worrying one edge of her white blouse. "They think I would want a different life. I have never wanted anything else. This is my home, and I intend to keep it." She flashed her eyes at him. "I refuse to let someone tell me keeping my home is too difficult. There must be another way."

He worked the statement over, turning it and fitting her vehemence with what he'd pieced together about the Flynn family.

"Your father believes you are not selling enough tickets to keep the boat going, so he wants to sell it?"

Anola made an annoyed sound somewhere between a strangled cry and a growl. "And they weren't even going to tell me until after we got to New Orleans, where I can only assume they have a buyer lined up." She flung out her hands. "What do they expect me to do? Become a laundress?"

What did being a laundress have to do with selling a show-boat?

"I will not stand for it. I won't." She fumed, her pace gaining momentum as she barreled toward the stern once more. "We need a new route. To stick to the smaller towns. We can live simply, no matter what Lady Marie says. And they can go to shore. They can, if that's what they are ready for. It doesn't mean I must."

Who could help but admire the fiery passion sparking through this woman? He'd never felt so adamant about anything. So sure of what he wanted from life. "Did you tell your family that?"

"No." Her shoulders drooped, and she slowed her steps. "I was praying through it first."

Had that been what she was doing walking around the deck?

"I'm sure it will work out." Not that he could know or even that it was his place to make such statements, but he couldn't think of anything else to say.

She regarded him, something dancing over her features and settling into a set mouth. "I'll not be toyed with, Emmett Carter. I'll have you know that. And just because I know my own mind and I am not afraid to say so doesn't make me lesser than anyone else."

Lesser? Whatever had given her that idea? "I'm not sure I understand what you mean."

"You don't have to like me. But you can give me the courtesy of saying so to my face rather than ignoring me. I will not be ignored."

Of that, he had no doubt. "I haven't ignored you." Fire coiled in his chest. "And I never said I didn't like you." If anything, that kiss said the opposite.

She regarded him as though he'd stuffed fish guts in his pockets. "Da always said you could tell everything you needed to know about a man by his actions. Words are easy. But what a man does shows his true self."

The truth of the statement settled deep into a tender place inside he hadn't realized existed. Had he offended her?

She took his lack of response as confirmation of whatever she had decided about him. She sniffed, and her features may as well have been carved from ivory. Beautiful, but unyielding. "Will you still help me script a plan to keep *The River Queen* afloat?" She thrust out her hand, nearly jabbing her fingers into his stomach.

Hadn't he been doing that already? He grasped her fingers, and she gave his hand a firm shake.

"Now, if you will excuse me, Mr. Carter, I have much to consider."

Without waiting for his response, she stalked away, once again leaving him with nothing to do but stare after her.

14

"**Y**ou are going to dance."

At the familiar feminine voice, Emmett looked up from the steaming mug of coffee he'd been nursing—in an effort to avoid Billy longer—to heel-clad feet, one of which tapped out an annoyed rhythm. Dare he argue with a woman in a temper so early in the morning?

He braved a brief headshake.

Anola scoffed. "You will dance, Emmett Carter, and I'll not hear another word on it."

When had he spoken? Behind him, members of the crew chuckled. Emmett let his gaze travel from the tapping shoe to stockinged calves, a flowy yellow skirt, and hands planted on the curve of hips.

"A skill learned is not hard to remember. You simply need practice. Ben sprained his ankle when he tripped over a discarded bucket backstage. You can replace him until he recovers."

Emmett's roaming gaze met her eyes, only to find their depths still filled with the same fire that had scorched him two nights prior. Then he noticed the rest of her. Had the woman already dressed in costume, or had she decided a gypsy's cape should be normal attire?

"Come on, then. Let's get to it. I've already told Billy you'll not be working for him today."

His sore muscles rejoiced despite the logic telling him a day with Anola Flynn might prove more difficult. "I haven't danced since I was twelve years old. I'll not do so now in front of several hundred people." He rose. "Besides, we've nearly reached Memphis."

Hurt flashed in those cobalt depths, and he could have punched his stupid mouth. Why had he said that? He shoved a hand through his hair. "I'm sorry. I didn't mean that like it sounded. I've been worried about my brother and with the food and the sloshing and..." He shook his head. His sleepless nights were no excuse for meanness. "Never mind. I'm sorry. I never meant to imply I wished to be rid of your company."

She eyed him as though seeking to measure his sincerity. Then she gave a curt nod. "You'll make it up to me by performing a tap dance."

"I will not."

They locked gazes in a stalemate. One breath. Three more. A breath from losing his ground to the charms of a woman beautiful enough to make a blind man stare, Anola surrendered first and flung out her hands.

"Why? Is it stage fright? You forget the people are there. It can't be because of a lack of practice, as such a thing is easily remedied. Can't be because you have to work with Billy, because, as I already said, I took care of that. And if it is to avoid me or because you want to wield a man's obstinacy against me in order to win some kind of battle, then you best go ahead and say so."

What? The woman volleyed so many words at him he might as well be standing in front of a firing squad. And less than half of her bullets made any sense.

"Lady Marie warned me you would use such a tactic. So I came prepared with a barter." Anola scrunched her face. "A new suit. To replace the one you ruined."

An odd sensation bubbled in his stomach, lurched up his throat, and burst forth in the most absurd bout of laughter.

Red bright enough to match her hair scorched her face until she appeared to be on the verge of catching fire. Her lips parted.

Emmett held up a hand to stay whatever would come out of her mouth. "No. I'm sorry. Don't." He sucked a breath. "That's kind of you."

He blinked back moisture from his eyes. Had he gone mad?

From the look on her face, apparently.

"I don't understand."

Forcing himself to gain control, he glanced around the now-empty dining hall, thankful the others had gone about their tasks and hadn't witnessed his mad cackling.

He cleared his throat. "You put me off my guard, keeping me on my toes and making me feel like I'm ten feet under water and don't know which way is up."

She gaped at him.

"Now you want me to dance, and even though I have made my wishes not to do so known, you insist a new suit will erase years of humiliation and send me running to the stage." Another strange mad laugh bubbled out. "Funny thing is, though, you would be the one person to make me want to do it anyway, if for no other reason than to see you smile. But for reasons I cannot fathom, I have become what appears to be your enemy."

Anola opened her mouth, closed it, frowned, and opened it again. A sigh released the tension from her shoulders. "Thank you."

She *thanked* him?

Of all the things he might have expected to shoot from an angry woman's mouth, it hadn't been that.

"I do appreciate your honesty. It is not my intention to humiliate you. Nor do I consider you my enemy. You've"—she

116

gestured with her hands in a random sort of way until she settled on—"flustered me, and I'm not sure what to make of you."

That made two of them.

Anola straightened herself and smoothed her vibrant yellow skirt. "I need your assistance. Our actor is injured, and we must put on a show for tonight. Tomorrow we can switch scenery and do the return production early, but we can't make that happen today. And Da can't do the tap dance."

"Do you have to have a dance?"

Her lips flattened. "The scene is about a man following his dreams to dance in a moving picture."

"I thought the play was about a man who spent too much time playing cards and his wife suspects him of being the father of another woman's baby."

"Well, that's part of it, yes. But he dreams of being in a picture." She waved her hands. "It's only one dance. And only for one day." Her big eyes pooled into liquid pleading. "Please, Emmett. I have no one else."

What about this woman made him want to forget himself and give in to her whims? "You expect me to act too?"

"No." She scrunched her nose. "Oh. I see your point. It would be odd for one man to dance and another to play the role. I'll have to think about how we'll work that out. I'm sure Da will help."

Thunder cracked overhead, and then rain pounded the hull as though desperate to breach inside.

Anola groaned. "Not today!"

"Is today a bad day for rain?"

She shook her head as though he should understand something simple. "This is our last stop before Memphis."

He had to think before the meaning settled. "Where the town is too big and so you think the crowds will be too small."

"Exactly."

"And if it's raining, fewer people will come tonight."

Anola groaned. "We will stay in Memphis for a few days, but I had hoped to earn enough for more supplies before we got there."

"What do you usually do on stormy days?" He stuck his hands in his pockets and watched thoughts gallop across her features, one right after another.

"Anchor down and stay in our rooms." She puckered her rosy lips. "Something I cannot afford right now."

"What if we use this time to work on the books?" Encouraged by a ghost of a smile, he continued, "and if there's time...maybe I'll see how much of my mother's dance I remember."

Now why had he gone and said *that*?

The smile erupted on her face and showered the room in light.

That was why.

She hooked her arm through his elbow and guided him toward the door. He sank in his heels. "We'll get soaked."

Her laugh tugged him along as surely as her fingers, and then they stood on *Blue Belle*'s deck. Rain fell in sheets, making a waterfall beyond the railing. At least they had the upper deck for cover. Anola flourished her cape and settled it around her shoulders, creating a shield for the mist. Perhaps the woman could be more practical than he'd assumed.

They raced down the walkway, mist and rain coating their hair. Her delicate hand nestled in his, urging him to keep moving. Water droplets glistened around them, accompanied by the beating percussion of thunder. Even the most inconvenient things became an adventure with Anola. He ducked his head and hurried forward with her through the tunnel of water and whimsy, lost in the magic of her. Too soon, they reached the end of the boat.

Anola ducked her head and surged forward.

"Wait! What about the—" He didn't have time to finish before they entered the deluge cascading between *Blue Belle* and *The River Queen*. Icy water awakened his senses and slithered down

118

his shirt. In the second it took them to scurry from one boat onto the next, they were drenched.

Laughing, Anola hauled him underneath *The River Queen*'s upper porch. They heaved breaths as though they'd run a mile. Water streamed down her face, pulling some of the black eye makeup she wore down with it. He cupped her cheek to wipe the smudge, and she stilled.

He should move. He shouldn't be standing here, soaking wet, touching her like—

"Are you going to kiss me?"

Was that an invitation or an admonishment? She spoke with such frankness, he couldn't think of anything to say.

Honesty pushed free. "I want to."

"Why?" The question held a hundred more.

"Because you fascinate me. Make me feel...I don't know. Alive. You're freedom and joy and beauty. Fierce and—"

Whatever other fitting descriptions he might have come up with were smothered under the intoxicating sensation of her lips on his. He clutched her closer, unable to help himself. Anola Flynn was rain to the desert. Sunshine to the flower. A vibrant source of light and goodness.

If she wanted him to dance, he'd dance. He might do anything at all for her. Especially if she kept kissing him with this unfettered abandon. A nagging sense in the back of his mind cautioned he best not let himself get carried away. Slowly, reluctantly, he eased the fervor into gentleness and let himself caress the softness of her lips a moment longer, then rested his forehead against hers.

"Have you kissed many women, Emmett?"

The question punched through the warm haze surrounding him. He blinked. "What?"

"I'm not overly experienced, having only sneaked behind a gum tree a few times as a girl, but I dare say you possess a fair measure of skill in kissing."

"I, um, well." He cleared his throat. "Thank you. I have kissed a couple of women, yes. But not..." He closed his eyes and exhaled. "Not like that."

Anola awakened something in him that dug deeper than attraction. The sensation scared him. But in the thrilling manner jumping from the boat into the river had.

"Good to know." She teased him with one more feather-light brush of her lips, then eased away. "We should get dry clothes on."

Dizzy, he followed along as she chattered about which outfits they had in the green room. The encounter mustn't have muddled her senses in the way it had his.

Without paying much heed to their route, he found himself in the overstuffed costume room.

And under the hawkish gaze of Lady Marie.

Her gaze swept from Anola to him and back to her granddaughter. One arched brow rose. Then a mischievous grin toyed with her mouth.

Did she know?

He resisted the urge to touch his face. Had Anola been wearing lip rouge?

"Tell me, Mr. Carter. What think you of our river life?"

"Lady Marie." Anola's words through clenched teeth spoke of warning.

Without allowing his gaze to wander to Anola and give away too much, he drew himself to his full height. "I think you have a charming life here. You see new people and places, enjoy a tight-knit family, and seem happy. I can see the appeal and imagine anyone would be reluctant to leave such an enchanting existence."

If Jacob had been around to hear his speech, he'd wonder who had taken his brother captive and masqueraded in the quiet accountant's stead.

Anola made a strange squeaking noise. Her eyes glistened, and the smile she sent him indicated he'd said the most perfect thing imaginable.

Lady Marie chuckled. "Well, isn't that something." Waving away the strange mood in the air, she nodded toward the clothing racks. "Come for something dry? Not that you both don't have wardrobes of your own, mind."

Having nothing to say, they waited as Lady Marie riffled through clothing, coming up with a long-hemmed ivory frock for Anola and a brown suit that might actually fit for Emmett. Where had that been his first night here?

At least she didn't suggest the toga again.

"There's no one backstage right now, so you can change there, young man." Lady Marie shooed him toward the door.

With a glance at Anola—which earned him a wink—he scuttled out the door.

The backstage stood dark and quiet, the actors having all found other places to be for the day. He made quick work of changing and shook water droplets out of his work pants and shirt. He draped both over a coatrack likely used as a prop in one of their scenes and then made his way back to the green room.

He knocked.

"One moment, boy. Takes women at mite longer." Lady Marie groused.

Apparently not too long, as the door opened soon after.

Anola sat at the dressing table, tugging a comb through her long hair.

Lady Marie caught him staring. "Do you know why we named her Anola?"

His gaze snapped back to the other woman's face, but she didn't wait for him to answer.

"It's for the singing river." She patted his arm. "Have you ever heard of anything more fitting?"

He wasn't sure he understood, but he nodded anyway. Lady Marie directed him to a chair and then settled at the other dressing table to face him. She laced her fingers in her lap, and he felt like a boy again, sitting at his mother's feet and waiting for a story.

"Anola was a princess of the Biloxi tribe. The Biloxi and their neighboring tribe, the Pascagoula, clashed with each other for many years. Anola was supposed to be married to the chief of the Biloxi tribe, but she fell in love with the prince of the Pascagoula tribe."

Anola shifted in her seat to watch her grandmother. Or perhaps watch Emmett as he listened.

"The Biloxi tribe became angry. As I'm sure you can imagine." Lady Marie wiggled fingers that each contained a paste jewel ring. "Families do have a way of making plans for their children that they think are best. Anyway, the tribe didn't want Anola to marry Alatama, that prince from the other tribe, so the Biloxi attacked the Pascagoula. They killed some and enslaved others—including the prince Anola loved."

Anola grunted.

"The Pascagoula chief, well, he was a strong man like my Stephen. He wouldn't leave his family without a fight. He rescued his people and his son and took Princess Anola. They escaped. But the Biloxi caught up to them, and the Pascagoula had nowhere to go. They were trapped."

Emmett caught himself leaning forward as Lady Marie drew out a pause.

"The Pascagoula could not outrun the Biloxi, and they were outnumbered. The women reminded the chief of the old stories. Of the singing river. Of the sirens that ruled the depths. The Pascagoula didn't want to die at the hands of the Biloxi, they didn't want to be slaves, and Anola didn't want to marry the Biloxi chief. She was strong like that. Like our gem here."

Emmett couldn't help himself. "What happened to them?"

Anola lifted her chin. "They joined hands and sang a song of their ancestors." She rose from her chair. "It's just an old myth."

"But what happened to them? Did they escape again?"

Lady Marie threaded her slim fingers. "They chose their own way, so they joined hands and walked into the river to let the river sirens take them."

Emmett rocked back in his chair. So they all died? "How horrible." What sort of people named a child after something like that?

Anola gave her grandmother a meaningful look, clearly having read Emmett's thoughts. "My family is known to have an odd way about them. No one else names their child after a drowned princess."

"You missed the point." Lady Marie huffed and brushed at her embroidered purple skirt. "The story is about the singing river. The story is that the Pascagoula could hear the sirens sing, giving the Pascagoula River the nickname the Singing River. Which is the reason the Pascagoula people chose to enter into the water."

How did that explain anything?

She crossed her arms over a yellow blouse studded with more paste gems. "They were a strong and brave people who took their fate into their own hands. Anola was a beautiful princess who chose love over everything else."

Why did he get the feeling there were more layers to this story than he could grasp? He cast a glance between both women, but neither elaborated.

Anola rose. "Enough with creepy old stories, *Grandmother*." She bit out the word like some kind of insult, and the other woman gave a haughty sniff. "We need to practice. Emmett is going to dance."

Dread settled in his stomach as Lady Marie clapped.

"I knew you would convince him."

A smile tugged Anola's lips into a sly grin.

He could only chuckle. Whatever game she'd played, it had been worth it.

15

Why wouldn't he listen to reason? Anola kept her expression passive even though Da had yet to turn his contemplative gaze her way.

"That's ridiculous." Da stared out of his living room window at rain that had not bothered to lessen in more than a day. The weather had turned so foul they'd canceled last night's show and probably would tonight's as well. The river churned too dangerously to risk navigating, so they were stationary.

"But this is the perfect opportunity to let him get in some practice." She plucked at a stray thread on one of Mam's afghans.

"Or for us to change productions, which we are already in the middle of doing." He hooked a thumb through his suspender and faced her. "You know he can't do Ben's part for the entire production, so there's no point."

She shrugged. Fine. They both had a fair point, he and Emmett, but still. She wanted to see Emmett dance.

"Why are you so intent on making the poor man perform?"

Had Da read her thoughts? "Why not? Might loosen him up."

"Hmm." Da returned his focus to the window. She waited for him to collect his thoughts, but when he spoke again, the subject took a turn. "How long are we going to avoid talking about it?"

It.

Da didn't mean Emmett's dancing she'd tried to distract herself with or changing sets or the weather. She grabbed the back of her mother's favorite chair to steady herself. "I'm not meant to be a laundress."

"What?" Da's brows plummeted. "A laundress?"

"Or whatever else normal women do." Despite herself, her upper lip curled. "Maids. That sort of thing. Staying in one place all the time."

She shook her head, heat pooling in her eyes. "No singing. No beautiful dresses. No new places to see or people to bring joy and magic." The heat dripped down her cheeks. "What will I do without the magic, Da?"

His strong shoulders rounded. "I fear the era of the showboat is coming to an end. They don't..." He drew a deep breath. "They don't come like they once did. Smile like we've brought them Christmas. We have become mundane."

Mundane? They could never be that. "We need to abandon the big river. Go to the tributaries, to the small towns and the quiet folk who still want the magic we can bring them. The story we can tell."

"With the money we make from selling this boat"—his voice wavered, pain akin to hers seemingly clawing up his throat to cut off his words—"I–I can buy us a house. A nice one. Anywhere you'd like."

Were they worse off than she'd thought? Had she let her desires overshadow what her family wanted? Or needed? They'd spent their years on the river. She couldn't settle for the mundane. Not yet. "There must be another way."

"If we can find one, my gem, we will look for it."

125

For now, she couldn't ask for more. Swallowing the thickness in her throat, she shifted the topic back to more solid ground. "We will be in Memphis soon, and Emmett will leave us."

Da nodded. "Did he teach you everything you needed to know about those books?"

"I suppose. The concept is simple. Keep track of what we earn and what we spend. Try to make sure there's more of the first than the second." Maintaining said records, however, proved tedious. She still felt as though everything she knew about bookkeeping could be shoved into a thimble and still leave room for her thumb.

"I cannot understand how he can get excited about showing me stuffy numbers. His eyes light up when we're discussing inventory systems, but ask him to dance and the man turns rigid." She plucked a wilted petal from a rose on the side table and rolled it between her fingers. "Upside down entirely."

Da chuckled. "What would the world be if all of us loved singing? I reckon there would be many a folk miserable with their lot in life when they had to be bakers or tailors or...accountants." His eyes twinkled. He moved from his place at the window and rested a warm hand on her shoulder. "You will find your path. As will Emmett." He gave a gentle squeeze. "Now, let's get to the stage and give the actors a hand before Lady Marie has Freddie coming after us."

Anola followed him from her parents' apartment, every lovingly worn piece of furniture and every recognizable scuff on the floor speaking of life and home.

She would find a way to keep *The River Queen*.

She had to.

He had to get off this boat. Emmett scowled at the steady drizzle. They'd wasted two days because of the downpour. He'd feared Stephen would want to wait an additional day to cover the performance they'd missed, but they'd taken to the swollen river this morning.

The worry in his brother's voice lacerated his ear again and tightened his chest. What if he was in serious trouble and Emmett was too late?

Through the gloom, he could spot the shoreline. At least in Memphis, no one had to jump off the boat or bury a deadman. The harbor would be wide and the berths ready to hold the showboat for days.

Water misted in the air, and his thoughts wandered to Anola and the last time he'd been in the rain with her. He gripped the railing, breathed deep, and made his decision.

He found her in the theater, eyeing the new backdrops. The actors had transformed the stage into the interior of a homey cabin, with a window overlooking grasslands. What character would Anola play this time?

She spotted him and gifted him with one of her dazzling smiles. "Looks great, doesn't it?" She heaved a dramatic sigh. "Though I will admit, I hate I won't get to see you dance."

"Set looks good." He stuffed his hands in his pockets, awkward now that the time had come to voice his question.

"Will you tell me one thing?" She placed both hands on her hips, her expression a blend of mischief and exasperation.

"Why I don't want to dance?"

She motioned toward the nearest row of seating and scooted in, leaving the aisle seat for him. "Yes, that. And if you despise it, why did you learn in the first place?"

127

He eased into the chair and focused on the stage, his mind's eye wandering back to the past. "I learned because my mother wanted me to. She always did love the theater."

He could still see her twirling circles in the garden when she thought no one was looking. "Mother thought I should know music and dance should I ever want to pursue the arts like she'd once dreamed. Or, she'd said, I would be prepared as a cultured gentleman should I ever find myself in upper society."

Anola shifted in her seat to face him fully, her chin resting in her hand and eyes bright. He expected questions, but she remained silent.

He cleared his throat and unhooked his gaze from those distracting ocean depths. "Unfortunately for her, I showed talent for numbers, not the arts. Math made sense to me. Numbers didn't require opinion or interpretation to be right. They just are what they are. Clean."

Somewhere behind the backdrop, one of the actors laughed. Something scuffed across the floor as someone moved furniture.

"My father and my older brother were cut from the same cloth." He settled against the cushion and closed his eyes. "Adventurous. Always going from one new idea to the next. I'd suffered from pneumonia as a child, and my mother thought I was sickly and should stay home while they left for months at a time. I think she liked having someone in her family around. I spent the majority of my time with her while my brother lived at my father's side."

He drew a long breath and let it out. He'd never shared this with anyone, but it now welled inside him and begged for release. "Mother became sick, and within months, the vibrant woman I had known withered. Then she was gone. In my childish delusions, I thought dancing would make my father smile, as it had my mother. It never occurred to me that he'd never seen me dance before nor that he didn't know she'd taught me."

Anola made a little noise, and fabric rustled beside him.

He didn't open his eyes. Now that he'd started, he had to finish.

Images of his father's shocked face, followed by angered mortification, assailed him as though he still stood in the parlor as a twelve-year-old boy.

Anola placed her warm palm against his forearm.

He opened his eyes and tilted his chin toward her. The liquid warmth in her gaze melted some of the ice in his chest.

"Your father didn't like you dancing, and your mother was gone. So you never danced again, and the memories bring you pain." She nuzzled his shoulder. "I'm so sorry I pushed you."

He rested his cheek against her fiery hair. "You didn't know." He breathed in the fresh floral scent of her, savoring her tender nearness, then cleared his throat. "I'd like to ask you something."

She shifted once again so she could look at him.

"As you know, I'm departing today to meet my brother."

Her eyes dimmed, but she nodded. She must be accustomed to people coming in and out of her life.

He hated being one of those people. "My brother is in some kind of trouble, and he needs my help." Why had he let that slip?

"What kind of help?" She straightened. "Anything we can do?"

Bless her compassionate heart. Emmett shook his head. "I'll find out soon, but I'm sure it only pertains to our losing the *Good Tidings* and the financial troubles of our business." The worry eased from her face. "Once it's cleared up, I'd planned on returning to St. Louis. But seeing as how I no longer have employment there and left to join Jacob on one of his schemes..." No reason to follow that tangent. "Anyway, what I mean to say is—"

"You want to stay with us?"

"Well, I was going to say—"

She scrunched her face. "I won't make you dance. I promise."

He laughed. "Are you going to let me finish a sentence?"

She wiggled her eyebrows.

"I would like to court you."

Her jaw dropped before she jerked it shut. She opened and closed her mouth twice more, sending his pulse into an erratic rhythm. "You want to court me?"

Were his palms sweating? He discreetly wiped them down his pants.

"Anola? Are you in here?" Jocelyn's voice came from behind them, followed by footsteps.

These people had the uncanny ability to appear out of thin air. He withheld a groan.

Anola launched herself from her seat and crawled over him before he could rise. "Emmett has just asked me to court him." She clasped her hands and grinned. "Isn't that wonderful?"

He rose and met Jocelyn's eyes.

She regarded him with pursed lips. "I take it you have decided to join us on the river?"

Without awaiting his answer, she faced her daughter. "You did tell him this is our last season, didn't you? I thought he had a family in St. Louis."

Her focus shot back to him. "We only dock there because of the cousins, and I don't think the captain and Lady Marie wish to buy our new house there. Have you considered New Orleans?"

He tugged on his collar. Which question did she want him to address?

Anola came to his rescue. "We've not had a chance to discuss those details, Mam, as he's only asked me just now."

She turned expectant eyes on him. Not a rescue after all.

Emmett cleared his throat. He had proposed courtship, not marriage, hadn't he? The way they looked at him, he doubted himself. "I need to meet my brother in Memphis and handle some business details. I had thought perhaps when you return to St. Louis at the end of the season I might be able to court Anola."

Jocelyn's forehead scrunched. She tucked a loose strand of dark hair underneath a green headband. "You didn't tell him about New Orleans."

"I did tell him." Anola tipped her head at him quizzically. "You only want to court if I return to St. Louis? I'm not sure how that will work since Da wants me to be a laundress in New Orleans."

Jocelyn threw up her hands. "Will you stop with that?" She blew out a breath. "No one said you were going to be a laundress, Anola."

His gaze bounced between the two women.

"I suppose, once he finishes his business in Memphis, he can stay on until we reach New Orleans." Jocelyn eyed him. "We'll all need to discuss this, of course. But by the time we arrive, you'll have concluded if a courtship worked."

He blinked under their steady appraisal.

"I'm...um." He tugged his collar again. "So we are all clear—you plan to discuss with the family if I will be allowed to court Anola. But only while we are on the river on the way to New Orleans. And at the end of that time in New Orleans..."

Jocelyn nodded like a teacher who had a slow student. "Exactly. That's weeks from now. By then, you two will know whether you want to wed, and Anola can decide if she wants to live in St. Louis with you or in New Orleans with us."

The color drained from Anola's face.

Emmett couldn't utter a word.

What had he gotten himself into?

16

"Soaked from head to toe." Emmett groaned. And now he'd started talking to himself. Water collected on his hat brim and slithered underneath his collar to roll down his back. After two hours of walking, he still hadn't found an establishment called the Blind Bat. How ironic, seeing as he was feeling like a blind bat wandering the streets.

He glanced over his shoulder once more to be certain no one followed him. Not that anyone had cause to, but the people he'd encountered in the narrow alleyways here didn't seem the sort to be up to anything good. He took a turn at the next street.

Why hadn't Jacob given him better directions? Frustration churned in Emmett's chest. He'd stopped three times to inquire where to find this establishment, only to be met with suspicious looks from two hotel clerks and a grocer. The last man had at least pointed him to this part of town.

The shops and buildings lining the road gave subtle signs of wear. A sagging shutter. Paint a season or two past needing a fresh coat. The area seemed neither prosperous nor poor, but clung to the middle ground in a desperate attempt not to slip into the kind of place no one wanted to walk at night. At least not decent folks, anyway.

People in heavy coats hurried from one doorway to the next, most trying to avoid the despondent weather. Once in a while, an automobile rumbled past, looking just enough out of place to draw attention. Most disturbing, however, was the lack of any kind of signage. Not that a place selling illegal liquor would advertise their whereabouts, but if the reputable shops announced their businesses, he could try to figure out whom to ask.

Spotting a scruffy man with a broom trying to push water away from the front of his unnamed shop, Emmett crossed the street.

"Excuse me, sir?"

The stout fellow paused his futile sweeping. "Nasty weather." He tapped the bristles in the water and scowled. He barely spared Emmett a glance.

Asking about the Blind Bat hadn't gotten him far, so Emmett tried another tactic. "Can you help me? I'm searching for my brother."

The man grunted and kicked at a puddle that returned to the wallow in the ground.

"I believe he's found a spot of trouble."

The man stopped and looked at Emmett for the first time, his gaze roaming Emmett from boot to hat. "That so? And you think he's 'round here?"

"I'm supposed to meet him in Memphis." Words rushed out as the man started to turn back to his door. "Our steamboat was stolen. He said to meet him at some inn called the Blind Bat, but I can't find anyone who knows where it is."

The man pushed the water again, sending droplets Emmett's way. "That's 'cause the Blind Bat ain't no inn. Though I reckon you already knew that."

"I had my suspicions, yes." Emmett stepped back to avoid the tiny waves lapping his shoes.

"Not a cop, are you?"

Emmett drew back. "No, sir. Though I am a law-abiding citizen." He had no idea if the admission would help or hurt him.

The man chuckled. "No doubt." He gestured Emmett closer. "You didn't get this from me, you hear? You get your brother out of there and talk sense into him."

"That is my sincere intention, sir. You have my word."

"Two blocks thataway." He jutted his chin east. "There's an alley between the seventh and eighth streetlamp. Door's on your left. Gettin' in is up to you." Without waiting for a response, the man shuffled inside his unmarked shop and shut the door.

At least now Emmett knew where to go. He shrugged his coat up to his ears and shivered. The day started to grow late. Already he wanted nothing more than a set of dry clothes. And perhaps the warming company of one rather cheerful redhead.

He counted streetlamps along the road, coming to the alley the man had indicated. Jacob and his foolish plans. This debacle would see one or both of them on the wrong side of the law.

Taking a deep breath, Emmett ducked into the alleyway. Gloom settled in the narrowed space, making the day feel much older than it should. Unease tingled along his senses, though nothing but a stray cat moved among discarded garbage. He did his best to ignore the smell.

Near the back of the building on the left, he located a door. This must be it. He tried the handle. Locked. Maybe he'd not come to the right place.

That or they didn't let anyone walk in off the street. He knocked three times. Now what had Jacob said to say—?

The door swung open, and the largest man he'd ever seen filled the frame. His arms had to be as thick as Emmett's thighs, and he crossed them over an imposing chest. The man stared down at him, scars crisscrossing his dusky complexion. "Ain't buying whatever you're selling. Be movin' on." He started to close the door.

"Wait! Scissors sent me."

The man stopped, probing eyes narrowing. How stupid. Jacob must have been playing with him. Setting him up.

But the fear in his brother's voice had been real. "He, uh…" Emmett cleared his throat. "He said to talk to you about church on Sunday."

The man didn't move. Should he mention he knew this was the Blind Bat?

The giant sneered and stepped back from the doorway. Emmett entered a hallway no brighter than the alleyway he'd exited. The door clicked behind him. He waited, but the guard turned back to his post, arms folded.

Emmett opened his mouth to ask where to go but thought better of it. Shoving his hands in his pockets to keep from clenching them, he crept forward. The deeper he went, the more light filled the area. Bricks took shape along the hallway, and soon decorative sconces dotted the walls. Jovial voices sounded from ahead. Male and female laughter twirled along the walls and beckoned him closer.

He exited the dim hallway into another world. A cavernous room vibrated with dozens of conversations and the mellow tones of a saxophone. Even on a Saturday afternoon, men in expensive suits twirled women in glittering dresses across the dance floor. Electric lights glowed overhead, catching the women's jewels and sending sparkling prisms over the men's faces.

Behind a carved bar top, the mirrored back wall reflected dozens of liquor bottles. Before it, men held glasses of whiskey and bourbon as they talked, gesturing with smoking cigars.

Low and sultry, a voice from the stage poured like an airy liquor around the easy conversations and relaxed laughter. Anola would have adored her silver gown, its layers of fringe swaying as she moved. A band of clear crystals encircled her black hair, and gloved hands gripped the mic.

"Can I get you something, luv?" A golden-haired woman with poppy-red lip rouge smiled at him. She'd cut her hair short, and the ends grazed just below her chin.

"What? No. Thank you."

She waggled her eyebrows. "Haven't seen you here before. Need a recommendation?" She moved closer, brushing her arm against him. "Whiskey will help you relax."

"I'm looking for my brother." He stepped back. "Have you seen him?"

"Could be." She pursed those bright lips. "What's his name?"

"Ja—" Emmett swallowed the word. Had there been a reason Jacob hadn't said to use his name? "Um, he likes to go by Scissors." Stupid name.

If the woman recognized the name or found it ridiculous, she gave no indication. With another sultry smile, she pointed toward the bar. "Why don't you go see Charlie? He'll get you what you need."

She swayed past him, gliding in a way that said she intended to accentuate her feminine assets. Only one man stood behind the bar, wiping out glasses. Emmett crossed the crowded room, drawing attention. Lady Marie had given him a new suit as promised, but the cut was off and the style out of fashion. He didn't blend in with the quality here.

He slipped past two men holding an animated conversation about a horse race and raised his hand for the bartender.

The man neared. "What'll it be?"

"I don't want a drink, thanks. I'm looking for my brother."

A scowl creased the bartender's cold face. Three seconds passed. Right. Probably wouldn't get any information without paying for something. Emmett grabbed his wallet and pulled out a dollar bill. "Ginger ale."

"With rum or whiskey?" The glint in his dark eyes hinted that saying neither wouldn't be an acceptable answer.

"Rum."

The man nodded, his countenance relaxing. He gathered the ingredients and filled Emmett's glass.

Drink in hand, Emmett tried again. "I'm looking for my brother. He likes to go by Scissors. My height, dark hair. Few years older. Have you seen him?"

The man the sultry woman had called Charlie stretched his lips wide. "Brother, huh?" A dark chuckle rumbled from his throat. "You're a few hours early, *brother*. Scissors don't come in until Stella starts her show."

"What time is that?"

The man shrugged. "Night show."

That wasn't helpful. With nothing else to do, Emmett gripped the cold glass to soothe his sweating palms and waited.

A knock pounded on the door, interrupting the family's supper around her grandmother's prized table. Anola started to rise, thinking it must be Emmett, but Da waved her down and went to answer.

"The boy's ears must have been burning." Lady Marie tittered. "Maybe he heard us talking about him all the way from shore."

Anola would have preferred Emmett to be present for this discussion about their pending courtship. But he'd had important business with his brother, and it must be taking longer than expected. He'd even missed out on Lady Marie's smothered pork, something she saved for special occasions. Anola lifted her chin a notch, refusing to let them cause her embarrassment. The gesture only earned another snicker from Lady Marie and a wry smile from Mam.

"Cook poisoned the crew!" Freddie's panicked voice volleyed into her grandparents' apartment and brought a halt to their conversation.

Anola dropped her fork. "Did Freddie say Cook poisoned the crew?"

Lady Marie put a hand to her throat and leaned back to glimpse Da at the door. "The boy's exaggerating."

"She probably found an old can 'o something and tossed it in the stew." The captain tilted his chair, looking far more amused than the situation warranted. "Gave them all a need to get to the privy all at once."

Lady Marie sniffed. "That's not something we talk about at George Washington's table." Whenever her grandmother didn't care for a topic of conversation, she pointed out that they sat around George Washington's table.

"You only say that because you're the one who bought meat on sale again." Mam eyed her plate with open suspicion.

Lady Marie gasped. "Why, I'll have you know—"

Da shut the door. The concerned crease between his eyebrows brought immediate silence to whatever retort Lady Marie readied to hurl at Mam.

Mam rose. "What's wrong?"

"Freddie said the crew have all gone mad." Da pressed his lips tight, the droopy mustache limp above them. He rubbed the pinched space between his brows. "He claims she poisoned them, but of course, that's nothing but a boy's nonsense."

"He didn't eat?" The captain studied the little left on his own plate.

"Suppose not."

"Mad?" Mam rounded the table and touched Da's arm, her grip crinkling his linen shirtsleeve. "What do you mean?"

"Must have fed them something spoiled, but the thing is, this isn't the normal type of stomach problem. Freddie says some's acting like they have fever. Seeing things and the like. Others are breathing like they've run a mile."

Lady Marie turned clinical. "Stomach cramps and vomiting?" She motioned to the captain. "Where's the elixir we got from that traveling salesman?"

"Now you know that wasn't nothing but syrup, rum, and cinnamon."

"Always made you feel better."

The captain grunted.

"We should go see what's happening so we can decide for ourselves." Anola tossed her napkin on the table and started toward the door.

The action sent the rest of the family into a flurry. Soon, they left their half-eaten meal—one Anola was now quite glad had been prepared by Lady Marie especially for the family to celebrate Anola's courtship—behind to scurry into the hallway. After reaching the damp decks, they crossed over onto the *Blue Belle* with Lady Marie insisting the entire time someone was playing a trick on them to get them out in this horrid weather.

They entered the dining area to a scene unlike any Anola had ever witnessed.

What in the stars was going on?

17

"There you are!" Emmett pushed away from the bar as the man who looked very much like their father casually crossed the room.

Jacob waved him down with a flick of his wrist and a slight headshake. Dressed in a stylish suit with his dark hair pomade slick, his brother didn't appear to be a man in trouble. He greeted everyone he passed as he moved deeper into the room—a space that had become livelier in the three hours Emmett had been waiting.

Tendrils of smoke drifted in the air, creating a haze. Emmett sat back in his seat as Jacob inched closer, his tailored dark-gray suit a sore contrast to the shabby version hanging on Emmett's frame. A gold chain dangled from Jacob's vest pocket, and the bright-red—was that silk?—tie gave him a debonair charm. A smile creased his cheeks, but his eyes told a different story. Those wary eyes examined every couple and noted every detail with shrewd intensity. The juxtaposition made Emmett uneasy.

After stopping to talk to three more men, Jacob reached the bar and spared only a polite nod to Emmett before calling Charlie over. Emmett clenched his jaw to keep a dozen questions from spitting between his lips. Something had changed in his brother's eyes. Something that had Emmett's senses on edge.

The bartender neared, asking if Jacob wanted the usual like he was a staple in this hidden gin joint and a well-paying one at that. As Charlie handed over a glass with dark amber liquid, he jutted his chin toward Emmett. "Fellow here says he's your brother."

Was that skepticism or accusation?

Jacob chuckled and slapped Emmett too hard on the back. "We're all brothers of a sort in this life, wouldn't you say?"

Charlie grunted but seemed to relax. "Of a sort. Still, don't think I'd go about claiming you unless I had to."

The insincere laughter rang false. Jacob threw the glass back, gulped the contents in three swallows, and then motioned for Charlie to give him another.

Refilled glass in hand, he tossed a few bills on the bar and motioned to Emmett. "Let's get a table to watch the show."

Emmett held the warm glass he'd been clutching all evening and followed his brother to a table in a dark corner. The small round top with two stools made it possible for him to sit close.

"What's going on?" The harsh whisper snaked out to bite his brother as soon as Jacob settled his well-dressed form onto the stool with far too much casual ease.

"There's a lot you don't know, baby brother." Jacob kept the smile in place as he nodded to a stocky man in an even more expensive suit. The fellow's sharp eyes took the brothers in an assessing glance before moving on.

"I'd say so." He hated when Jacob called him baby brother. With only five years between them, he hardly thought the name fit. "When I talked to you on the phone—"

"Look, have you found the boat yet?"

Jacob's desperation drew Emmett up short. "No. You said not to go to the police."

Breath leaked out between his lips. "So you didn't. Good. But you've been on the river for weeks, right? Surely you've heard something? Anything...unusual?"

What did that mean? "There are a lot of boats on the river. I'm neither a detective nor a boat captain." He rested his elbows on the table. "We need to file with the insurance company if we have any hope of saving the business."

"The business is gone. So's the house."

The flat words raked across Emmett's ears but didn't find purchase. "What are you talking about?"

"There were...debts. But don't worry, baby brother. I've got it handled." Jacob knocked back another swig. "But we aren't going back to St. Louis."

Not going...? Had Jacob lost his mind?

He sipped his second glass of bootleg liquor.

"Our *house*." Emmett ground out. "The one our father left to the both of us." The one where Mother died. The only home Emmett had ever known. "What do you mean it's *gone*?"

Jacob's gaze stopped roaming the room and settled on Emmett. "Don't worry. I have a plan. Everything will be fine."

"Everything is not fine." A sensation akin to riled hornets swarmed through his center and prickled along his skin. "You invested our entire inheritance, without my consent no less, into a boat that is now gone. One which for some unfathomable reason you refuse to inform the insurance company about, and now you're telling me I no longer have my *home*?"

His hands fisted. "How much more have you stolen from me?"

They locked gazes, Jacob's filled with an usual combination of fire and ice. Emmett refused to look away first, no matter how much the childhood version of him still longed for his brother's approval.

Jacob lowered his gaze to watch melting ice swirl in his glass. "I'll make it right. I promise."

Emmett unclenched his jaw. "You always say that. Father did too. All it means is you've cooked up another scheme. One that won't work out any better than the one that got you into trouble." He pushed away from the table. "I'll have none of it."

"Sit." Jacob locked his arm in an iron vise. "If you have any care for your life, sit. Now."

Emmett started to pull away, but men around the room stood watching them. He ground his teeth, regained his seat, and lowered his voice. "How much trouble are you in?"

"Enough." Jacob relaxed against the back of his chair and clapped when a woman in a slinky dress took the stage. Barely audible under the erupting cheers, he said, "This time I'm in deep. I need you."

Jacob had never claimed to need him before.

"How?" His brother shot him a glance so filled with gratitude that Emmett's stomach turned. "What do you want me to do?"

Jacob shifted his body so his back faced the rest of the room, huddling them closer together. "You've been on a riverboat the last couple of weeks, right? Got a job or something?"

How did he know?

"All I need you to do is sneak a few crates on board for me. Make sure they stay hidden until you get to New Orleans. I'll meet you there, and I promise, it'll be worth it. You just have to trust me."

Emmett was already shaking his head. "I'm not going to use Anola's boat for smuggling whatever illegal thing you are doing."

"You have to."

Stubbornness set in. "No, I don't."

Jacob turned up the cup and swallowed the last of the watered-down alcohol. His mouth twisted into a weary smile. "You do if you don't want to be the last Carter left living."

She'd walked into a nightmare. Anola clutched Mam's arm. "What's wrong with them?"

"I have no idea." Mam fingered the beaded necklace hanging against the cream dress she'd worn for their special evening.

The family had entered the dining hall but scarcely made it past crowding in the doorway. Big Billy was lying on his back on the floor, arms and legs moving like he was swimming. Pat and John were sitting at the table, both gawking at the wall. Old Tom leaned against one wall, fist poised as though ready for a fight. Three others were caught in a bout of uncontrolled laughter. Anola had never seen the like.

"Hey now!" Da shouted. "What's going on in here?"

Only George noticed them. He grinned and wandered over, his long legs wobbly. Had he found alcohol? He slapped Da on the shoulder and laughed. His eyes glazed as he spoke, red lines snaking over the whites.

"Wind's a beauty today, ain't it?"

Da studied the normally quiet man. "Are you all right?"

"Fine as frog's hair!" He jostled Da's shoulder again. "Oh, and lookahere. You brought a gal." He bowed to Anola. "Want to dance? That fiddler's right good."

Before Anola could respond, Da stepped between them. "Why don't you go ask that lady over there instead?"

Though the question didn't make the first bit of sense, George bowed again and sauntered off to find the fictional woman. Da wove through the crew, scrutinizing each one before moving toward the kitchen.

Lady Marie and the captain ducked their heads together, words flying between them in rapid succession.

"...like the opium den." Mam muttered under her breath.

The final words caught in Anola's ears. "What was that? Did you say opium den?" She pulled her gaze from where Billy still tried to swim across the floor. "When have you ever been in an opium den?"

Mam waved the question away. "Let's go with your da. Maybe Cook knows what's happening."

Frowning, Anola followed her mother. What sort of adventures had Mam had before coming to the river? Now that she thought of it, she'd heard few stories of Mam's life before Da. She'd have to ask. But those were questions for another time.

They found Da in the kitchen, his hand on Cook's shoulder. She smiled up at him, her Irish brogue thicker than Anola had ever heard it before. "Won' a go throwin' no good food in the river, lad. 'Ave ya done a-lost yer mind?"

"It's made you all sick," Da soothed. "I need you to tell me what's in it."

"What's in the stew, ya say?" Cook snatched a bowl from the table and thrust it toward him, sloshing some over the side. "Ya know what I put in me stew, lad. 'Tis one of yer favorites."

"Yes, it is. Why don't you remind me of all the ingredients?"

Cook beamed. "Carrots and potatoes. Mutton I cooked down all day so it's good-n-tender. But I won' a go tellin' you my secret to the sauce, lad. That's Gram's own, and it ain't my secret to be sharin'."

"Of course." Da turned out his hands when Cook frowned. "Mind if I look around the kitchen?"

She roared with laughter, her cheeks redder than usual. "'Course you can, lad. Go right ahead. Then you can be awashin' some of those dishes while you be in here."

Cook reached for the bowl again, but Anola hurried forward and grabbed it. "I haven't had any yet. May I?"

"What? Oh. 'Course, lass." Cook let go of the bowl. "I'm just goin' to rest my eyes a minute while you eat." She crossed her arms on the table and laid her head down.

Mam caught her wrist. "Don't eat that!"

Anola rolled her eyes and put the bowl back on the table. "I wasn't. I just didn't want her to."

Mam bustled over to Da, who had found something on the counter. He lifted a burlap pouch and sniffed the contents. A furrow creased his brow.

"Anola?" He waggled the sack in her direction. "Are these the herbs you were missing?"

She'd forgotten about the bag she'd taken. "Oh. Yes. I brought it to the kitchen before the rest disappeared." Her stomach knotted. "Are they bad? Is that what made everyone sick?"

Mam and Da exchanged a look. "They aren't sick. Not really." He cinched the drawstring and tucked the sachet into his pocket. "Should wear off in a couple of hours."

"What should wear off?"

Da continued as though he hadn't heard her. "First thing in the morning, we are calling a meeting. I need to know where this came from and who brought it on board." While Mam wrung her hands and nodded along, Da stepped closer to Anola, his shadow falling over her. "And there was an entire crate of bags like these?"

"Yes."

Cook had started snoring.

Anola shivered and rubbed at goose bumps. "Are they going to be all right?"

"It's going to be a long night. Go tell the captain to man the door. No one leaves this room until morning."

"What about the actors?" Mam tugged the lapel of his tweed jacket. "Do you think they got any for their supper?"

Da paled. "Tell the captain to gather them all and bring them in here if he can. I'll be out soon to help him. I need you to keep everyone else confined here."

"But why, Da? What is it? What did it do to them?"

"We think it's a substance like opium," Mam answered. "Usually people smoke it in a pipe. It will do strange things to their minds. Make them see what isn't there." She shook her head.

"I don't think you are supposed to eat it. Maybe it makes the effects worse."

"I'm so sorry." Anola's throat constricted. "I didn't know."

"They will be fine come morning."

"And come morning"—Da's voice hardened—"we are going to find out which of our crew betrayed us."

Her mouth went dry. "Betrayed?"

"Someone on this boat brought this substance aboard and tried to hide it. I intend to find out why."

In a flurry of anxious activity, the family retrieved sleeping blankets, pillows, and fresh water. Within the hour, they'd converted the dining room into a makeshift camp.

"Are you sure this is a good idea?" Mam frowned at Nicolas, a new crew member they'd hired this season, as he argued with Billy over who would take which bedroll. "What if they get out of hand?"

Da grunted. "I won't play nursemaid, but neither will I let any of them wander outside and fall off the side of the boat. This is no worse than leaving a drunk to sleep it off."

After making sure their inebriated crew was as safe and comfortable as possible, the family removed the oil lamps and matches, leaving the men in the dark. They stepped outside into the damp night shrouded in a somber mood. The captain brought one of the boards they used to secure the plank, and they locked the crew inside.

18

This couldn't get any worse. Emmett clutched the still-full glass so hard it should have cracked.

Jacob watched the girl on the stage with a smile that didn't match his eyes or his tone. "Could be there won't be any of us left. Including that nice family on the boat you've grown so fond of. A few crates aren't worth it, baby brother."

He delivered the threat of murder with as much concern as if he'd told Emmett there would be more rain tomorrow.

Emmett thumbed open the top button of his shirt to ease the suffocating feeling gathered in his throat. It didn't help. "Find someone else. Leave the Flynn family out of this."

"The Flynns." Jacob cut a glance at him. "Wouldn't be the people on *The River Queen*, would it?"

Didn't he already know? Seemed like he knew way more than he should. Was this some kind of a test? For what purpose? Emmett glowered.

"I thought so, but needed to be sure." Jacob barked a humorless laugh. "They have words for things like this, you know. Luck. Fortune. Some kind of Eastern mysticism about karma or some such." He laughed again, his gaze never leaving the woman on the stage. "Regardless, I'd say fate has handed us a boon, baby brother."

Emmett's teeth ground together so hard his jaw hurt. He forced his focus to the singer to give himself a moment. If he looked at Jacob any longer or got called "baby brother" one more time, he might punch the smile right off Jacob's face. Deep breath in. Hold. Release. An exercise his mother had taught him when he'd become overwhelmed as a child. He hadn't needed it in years.

The soloist lifted one hand as she sang, her clear voice sweet and inviting. Raven hair cut in the new fashion grazed her chin and swayed as she moved with the piano's sultry sounds. After two more stanzas, he was able to speak again. He kept his focus ahead and his tone even. "Explain."

"Just lucky, is all," Jacob replied, seeming not to notice Emmett's dark mood. "Extra lucky for us that we already have a man on the boat." He swigged the last of his liquor. "Makes it easier."

"Who?"

Rather than answering, Jacob popped from his seat and sauntered back to the bar to refill his glass for the third time. He returned with a drink in each hand. Emmett shook his head, but Jacob placed the glass in front of him anyway. "Your ice melted." He eyed the wasted liquor with more concern than he'd shown when predicting their demise.

Emmett pushed the glass to the center of the table. Jacob downed his own, then reached for the other.

"Who?" Emmett hated repeating himself.

"No one important." Jacob slapped Emmett's shoulder. "Wait here."

He was gone again before Emmett could protest. Minutes later, Jacob appeared through the smoky haze with a stout gentleman in a white suit and an emerald tie. The fingers clutching his glass were decked with three thick gold rings.

"I told you I'd make it right." Jacob nodded toward Emmett. "This here's Joe. He's got us a fix for our little problem. *The River Queen.*"

The man Jacob hadn't introduced eyed Emmett. "That so? How oddly convenient." He shrugged brawny shoulders. "But that horse has already left the barn. This is their last river run. Don't know who we'll have to hitch to next."

How did this man know anything about this being *The River Queen*'s last season? The notion left Emmett cold. And what did he mean about "hitch to next"?

Jacob grinned. "Joe here is in with the family." His eyes bore into Emmett's. "He'll be able to solve the issue."

He couldn't mean any of that. Maybe Jacob only said what he had to in order to get himself out of this current situation. Emmett barely kept a snarl from his voice. "No promises."

"That so?" The man chuffed air past his full lips, and his florid cheeks jiggled. "Well now. Brave one you found here, Scissors."

Jacob shifted his stance. A small tell, but enough of one to prove Jacob's nerves sat on edge. Still, Emmett wouldn't promise something he most certainly would never do.

After a tense moment, the man laughed. "Fine, fine. You cut a good bargain." He tipped his head to Emmett, scrunching his double chin. "Do a good job, and I'll get you a position with old Scissors here."

He fixed his emerald-studded cuff links and traced the line of one as if speaking to it. "There's no replacing what Durkin took. You know that, of course."

Durkin. Where had Emmett heard that name before? Something about...? The memory returned. The gang the deputy had mentioned. The one causing trouble on the Mississippi. Were they connected to these people or a rival?

"I'll make good on this. I swear it."

The man's lips twitched at Jacob's desperation. Had Emmett seen him in a different environment under other circumstances, he might consider him jovial. "You do that, and we'll call what's between us even."

What was between them? It must have something to do with the *Good Tidings*, but how did it connect to *The River Queen*?

The Adam's apple in Jacob's throat bobbed. "Thank you, sir."

The man spared another assessing glance at Emmett and then wandered away.

Jacob melted back onto his stool.

"Who was that?" Emmett hissed. "And what were you talking about? You know I won't put that family in danger or lock them into some kind of ongoing scam. I won't."

When his brother gulped the booze, ignoring him, Emmett plucked the glass from his fingers and thrust it across the table. It skidded, almost toppling off the other edge.

"Easy, brother." Jacob held up a hand. "I have a plan. Trust me."

"Find some other boat."

"Can't. They already know I promised this one."

How dare he—

Emmett smothered the burning urge to clobber him. Instead, he drew in another long breath and released it. It didn't help. "I'm not going along with this."

"Then you've sentenced us all. This has to be handled just right, or it will never work. Mickey won't just hunt us down. He'll wipe out everyone you ever cared about first. Make you watch while he takes his time about it." Jacob shuddered. "We can't risk it. Do this one thing, baby brother. One thing. Then I promise I'm done with all of this. I promise we'll be able to start over somewhere else. Just you and me."

Emmett leaned his head back and closed his eyes.

God help me.

Anola pulled a soft blanket up around her, more for comfort than warmth. It smelled of the captain's aftershave. She snuggled deeper into the couch and watched her family's serious faces.

"It isn't going to work." Lady Marie lit another candle and shook out the match. "If someone did something sneaky, then asking each one of them if they did it won't get you anywhere."

Da sat in one of the wingback chairs, his elbows resting on his thighs. The captain occupied the other, chewing on his pipe. Lady Marie fidgeted around the living space, the ends of her gypsy skirt tickling the carpet as she fluttered. Mam took up some yarn and tried her hand again at knitting. She hadn't improved any, judging by the crooked lines that kept unraveling.

"Then what do you suggest?" Da watched his mother make a trip around the room without finding anything else to do. He rubbed his temples. "We can't leave them barricaded in the dining room forever. I just hope they all stay asleep and no one gets worse through the night."

"There should be an investigation for certain, lad," the captain said. "I donna want none of that kind on me boat." He grunted and chewed on the pipe stem with vigor.

Anola hadn't heard his Irish brogue so pronounced in years. He'd worked hard to even it out. Blending in with the local folk, he'd said. Something he passed to his wife and son. The captain only spoke that way when he'd been startled or was very upset.

Lady Marie grabbed a dust rag and started to work on the already clean table. "Something must be done. We agree on that much."

None of them seemed to know what that something might be. They sat in silence until a knock came at the door.

The captain sprang to his shoeless feet. "Who could that be at this hour? It has to be nigh on eleven." He checked the clock mounted on the wall and huffed.

Just past eleven thirty.

"Emmett." Anola untangled herself from the blanket. "Something must be wrong." Why else would he have missed their special supper? She had so much to tell him.

Da opened the door, and Emmett stepped inside, followed by another man. Emmett's shoulders stood rigid, and from his uncomfortable expression, he wasn't pleased by the newcomer's presence.

He cleared his throat. "Sir, this is my brother, Jacob."

Anola moved closer, hunting the resemblance in the shape of his brown eyes and the color of their hair. The similarities ended there. Jacob's face seemed harder somehow. Less...*open* than Emmett's.

A man with secrets. How interesting. She scooted closer so Da would introduce her, but he merely crossed his arms over his chest.

"He smells like liquor." The statement hung in the air.

Emmett winced. "Yes, sir. I hate to impose on you for help but—"

Da cut a glance over his shoulder, frowned at Anola, and then ushered the men out the door. It clicked behind the three of them.

She notched her hands on her hips. "Do you think Emmett has been out drinking? That's why he missed our supper?"

Mam harrumphed. "That boy doesn't look like he ventured a sip. Probably had to half drag his brother on board."

Lady Marie grunted her agreement.

The captain plucked his pipe from between his teeth, set it on the end table, and brushed his hands over his linen shirt.

"Where are you going?" Lady Marie stopped dusting.

"Better go and help."

Lady Marie didn't argue, and the women watched him exit. Anola glimpsed Emmett when the door opened. She couldn't see his face, but the tension in his shoulders seemed to have doubled.

"What do you think they are talking about?" She settled onto the couch and pulled the blanket over her legs again.

"He'll give the boy a cup of coffee and send him to a cot." Mam sighed. "But since Cook is..." She shook her head. "Coffee will have to wait, I suppose."

"I can go down and brew it." Lady Marie threw the rag down and hurried to the door.

Mam's voice stopped her. "You want to barge into the kitchen while Cook is in a state?"

Lady Marie eyed the door, clearly debating whether it was worse to admit Mam was right or to face Cook. "The lesson of a sour stomach might do him well anyway." She settled in the chair her husband had vacated and leaned her head back, placing her forearm over her eyes. "My, but it has been a trying day."

Indeed. Proposed courtship, herb-induced madness, and now this. She hadn't had a day this strange since...well, ever. After nearly a quarter hour—she knew since she kept an eye on the clock—Da returned. Without Emmett and his brother.

"Bed, Anola."

She tilted her head. "But we aren't finished with our discussions. What happened with Emmett and—"

He gave a sharp shake of his head, and her mouth snapped closed. Da never cut her off. "We'll discuss it later."

Blinking back her surprise, she rose, folded the blanket, and walked over to kiss his cheek. "Good night, Da."

"Good night, my gem." His face softened. "We'll talk more tomorrow."

She said her good nights to her mother and grandmother, then made her way to her room.

Sleep wouldn't come easy tonight.

19

The captain glowered at him. Emmett kept his gaze. Looking away would diminish him in this man's sight. After another moment, Emmett was rewarded with a jerk of the man's chin.

He thumbed toward the room where they'd stashed Jacob. "He makes things a mite more complicated, lad."

Rather than putting him on a cot with the crew where they slept together on *Blue Belle*'s main deck, they'd given Jacob a tiny cabin on the same level they'd given Emmett. Rooms only the actors used since the family lived on the showboat. He was glad for it since it would keep Jacob more contained.

"Yes, sir," Emmett replied. "But I couldn't leave him. He was in trouble." Bringing trouble here churned his stomach, but what else could he do?

"Family is family. I know that well enough. So you understand that I want to keep trouble from me and mine."

"Yes, sir."

"Lord knows we have enough trouble tonight." The mumbled words barely reached Emmett's ears.

Sweat trickled down his neck. Mickey, whom he could only assume was the boss of the operation Jacob worked for, had said they had a man on this boat. Emmett motioned toward the rear of the steamboat. "Stephen said something about you locking the entire crew in the dining room?" Had they discovered the criminal on board?

The captain waved to shoo the question away. "Ate something bad."

Who would lock people with upset stomachs together in the same room with nowhere else to go? Emmett opened his mouth to suggest they let the poor people go ashore, but the captain changed the subject.

"Is your brother's condition why you missed Anola's special supper?"

"I didn't plan on my errand taking so long." Emmett couldn't hide his cringe this time. "Or on finding my brother in such a state."

He could barely make out the captain's features in the gloom, but he sensed the man's agreement. "Lucky for you, she forgives easily. A trait a man would be wise not to take advantage of."

"That would never be my intention." They started walking back toward *Blue Belle*'s bow. Emmett fidgeted until he mustered the courage to ask what was on his mind. "Did Anola tell you I asked to court her?" Something he should have consulted her father about first, but the idea had so overwhelmed him that he hadn't thought through the planning.

The captain snorted. "What do you think the special supper was for?"

Now he felt worse about it. "I'm not sure... What I mean to say is..." He cleared his throat.

"You asked about courting, and Jocelyn turned it into a marriage proposal?" The man's humor relieved some of Emmett's tension. "I understand your hesitation, but I also see what Jocelyn means. Her suggestion makes logical sense, lad."

Of course they'd all had this discussion. Probably at length. He let out a long breath. Could he consider building a relationship right now?

The captain must have taken his silence for disagreement. "Think about it. No sense in courting a woman if you aren't thinking of marrying her. And this life isn't like any other." He turned out his palms, then rested them on the rail as they stopped at the prow. "If you aren't willing to marry the river as well as the girl..."

"I thought Stephen said you'd sell the boat once you reached New Orleans." Without the boat, the Flynns couldn't be forced into whatever schemes Jacob had concocted.

The captain leaned against the rail, his answer slow in coming. "My lady wife and I are ready to find a quieter life. This one has been an adventure we've loved, but one we've been on for nearly forty years. We'd like to stay in one place for a spell. Stephen and Jocelyn still have adventuring years in them, I think, but Stephen worries about feeding his people."

Understandable. "Anola wants to go to the tributaries and the smaller towns. Do you think that will sustain the show?"

The captain sucked his teeth. "Might. She doesn't want to leave this life because it's all she's known. But could be she would find a new adventure in a home on land with children at her skirts."

Somehow, Emmett couldn't picture it. Not the children part. He merely pictured her dressing them in costumes and parading them on stage or teaching them to swim as fearlessly as their mother instead of watching them run around in a yard. The thought made him smile. "Seems like a lot to consider."

"It is. Good Book says a man must put his wife and her needs ahead of his own. So if you are thinking you might want my gem to take your name, you'll need to first decide what you want to do about the river."

"I could never take her dream from her." The words slipped out before he could consider them, but they held the weight of truth. Could he be a husband to such a passionate and adventuresome woman? "But I'm just an accountant."

"No man is ever *just* one thing, lad." The captain clapped him on the shoulder. "Why don't you try your hand at a few different jobs around here? See if something sticks. Lord knows we already needed someone with a head for numbers and you've been the answer to that. Maybe you'll discover you're good at something else as well."

An intriguing idea.

The captain yawned. "I'm going to bed. I'm sure my family is still in my living room, but it's past time they get to their own blankets. I suggest you do the same." He squeezed Emmett's shoulder. "Sleep gives men clarity. You'll know what to do with your brother in the morning."

Emmett doubted it, but he bid the man good night and watched him make his way over the connecting planks to the showboat. When no other sounds remained but the steady drip of lingering raindrops sliding from the trees into the river, he closed his eyes.

If he was going to get them all out of this mess and have any hope of building a future with Anola, he was going to need a plan.

But for the life of him, he had no idea where to start. The only thing he knew for sure was that, this time, he wouldn't let Jacob get the better of him.

Emmett rose before the sun, having hardly slept during the five hours he'd tossed in his bunk. Worries that Jacob would smuggle who knew what aboard had made him jump at every sound, and twice he'd considered camping outside his brother's door to be certain he stayed put. But with the entire crew locked away, what could Jacob really do?

Unless of course Jacob used everyone thinking the entire crew was contained as a cover. Emmett rubbed his temples. If Jacob had orchestrated that level of deception, then he was far craftier than Emmett had given him credit for. The notion didn't help the state of his stomach. He laced his boots and headed out into the predawn light.

He found the bar removed from outside the dining room door. He hesitated. Surely they hadn't allowed people to be sick all over themselves all night. He must have misunderstood what had happened. No sane person would create such torture. Not for those sick or those who needed to clean it. He held his breath and eased the door open.

The captain and Stephen both stood at the rear, watching the crew members. Their eyes looked sharp enough to shave with. As soon as Emmett widened the door, both men noticed him. Stephen dipped a greeting nod, then went back to observing the crew. A crew which, Emmett had to say, didn't look like people who'd eaten bad food. For one thing, many of them ate their early breakfast with gusto, and most of them were smiling and laughing. A couple appeared pale and tired, but Emmett would guess at least eight of the ten men present had recovered from their ailment.

So why did Stephen and the captain maintain such a rigid observational post? He strode over battered wooden flooring to the men. "Everything all right?"

The captain huffed. "Be at least another day before we can pull out of here. I wouldn't even trust old Tom to be of any use today."

"I suppose talking to them won't do much good either, but we're going to spend the day trying." Stephen harrumphed. "Everyone cleared is to go look for the missing crate."

Anola's crate? Emmett edged closer to Stephen and lowered his voice. "What happened while I was in Memphis?"

Silence lingered for so long Emmett almost thought Stephen wouldn't answer. "The bag of 'herbs' Anola gave Cook weren't herbs at all. Made a fine mess of my crew."

"I wondered about that." As soon as the words escaped his lips, both men's eyes widened, and they snapped their heads in his direction. Emmett turned out his palms. "I wasn't sure what it was, but it seemed suspicious. Had I known she'd kept out one of the bags, I would have said something. I thought it had all disappeared." He met each man's gaze. "I had nothing to do with any of it, in case you are wondering."

Father and son studied him before Stephen nodded, and the captain bobbed his head. Not sure what else to do, Emmett settled beside them. "So, I'm guessing Cook added it to the food—food you didn't eat because of Anola's supper—and the crew started showing strange symptoms about an hour or so later."

It sounded a lot like that New Orleans article he'd read about making muggles illegal. From what he remembered, people smoked the plant rather than eating it, but the effects were likely the same.

"That's the right of it."

Nearby, Billy shoved an entire biscuit into his mouth.

"I'm guessing Cook didn't eat as much. That, or she's hardier than this lot." The captain tapped his nose. "She is Irish, after all. Anyway, she seems fine now. The woman had already made dozens of biscuits and platters of fried ham by the time we unlocked the door."

At least the symptoms didn't last long. What if the entire crew had been poisoned? Emmett clenched his fists. Poor Anola. She would blame herself.

For the next two hours, they questioned every man in the room. Mostly the captain spoke, with Stephen asking a clarifying question. Emmett's only part was to listen and help them remember what each man had said. None of the men admitted to knowing anything about the crate of "herbs," and every man said he had told Anola the same when she'd asked before. He was no detective, but he believed them. They all seemed too surprised to find out there'd been a mind-altering substance aboard. A few, especially Tom, were angry over how it had affected them.

After the final man had nothing more to offer, the three convened near the door.

"Well?" The captain jammed his thumbs into his suspenders and rocked off his toes.

Stephen turned his back to the men, a tick twitching at his taut jaw. "I pride myself on being able to read the character of a man, but I can't tell if any of them are lying."

"Me either." The captain grunted, slamming down onto his heels.

"What about the actors?" Emmett suggested. "Could any of them be to blame?"

The other two men shared a glance.

"Where were they, anyway?" Emmett nodded to the kitchen. Why hadn't he already thought of that? "Cook usually feeds them as well, right?"

"Shore leave," the captain replied.

Stephen snorted. "This isn't the navy. But yes, we did let the troupe go into town about an hour or so after you left. We didn't have a production yesterday, and Anola wanted a family affair. So Paul and Ben headed into town to do something with a little from their grouch bag, and Henry and Sue took the opportunity for a supper out at a nice restaurant."

Grouch bag had to mean their wallets. Why'd they call it that? Didn't matter. That accounted for the entire crew of actors, save the family. "None of the actors were around last night? Why didn't the crew also go to shore?"

"Because they get their time off opposite the actors." This from the captain.

"So the actors would have come back on the boat last night."

"What are you getting at, lad?" Stephen stroked his mustache. "You think one of the troupe, who has worked here for nigh on five years now, would have tried to ferry an entire crate of that...that nasty plant on our boat?"

That was what he was suggesting, but after one look at Stephen's face, Emmett clamped his jaw tight to keep the obvious answer to himself.

For his part, the captain appeared thoughtful. The two men shared a weighted look.

Stephen rolled his shoulders. "I suppose it's on to questioning the cast."

They left the crew inside with instructions to take the day off, which gained a rousing cheer. Then they stepped outside to a sunny day.

"This is turning into a sour stew." The captain tugged his fedora low over his brows. "We don't know who is up to what, and nothing about this season is normal." He lifted his eyebrows at Emmett. "What are you going to do about Jacob?"

With any luck, he'd still be sleeping. "I'd appreciate advice."

"I'm liking you better by the day, lad." Stephen smirked at the captain. "We've got a notion around here that what cures a man of whiskey is work."

Emmett couldn't help the curve of his lips. "Coal duty?"

"Nothing shows a man's merit better. Besides, that makes him too tired at the end of the day to miss the hooch." Stephen tapped a playful elbow into Emmett's side. "What say you we rouse him for duty?"

The smile creeping into place bloomed into a grin.

Jacob would be sorely surprised about what he'd signed up for.

20

Well, this was rather odd. Anola stood on *The River Queen*'s deck as Emmett and his brother held an animated conversation over on the *Blue Belle*. Emmett gestured with almost staged arm movements, matched in intensity by his brother.

Anola bumped Mam's shoulder to draw her attention away from whatever she kept looking at on shore. "What do you think they're talking about?"

"Huh? Oh. I have no idea." Her brows dipped. "But they do seem to be passionate about it, whatever it is."

The thump of boots across the deck announced the captain's presence. He leaned over the rail to see what the women were looking at and chuckled. "Guess he's not interested in today's work."

"What work?"

On the other boat, Jacob threw up his hands and stalked away from Emmett. Emmett clenched his fists at his sides but didn't follow.

"Shoveling coal."

163

"Isn't that the job you always give to the new fellows? Testing their merit or some such?" Before he could answer, Mam held up a gloved finger. "We can't afford another new crew member. We are stretched thin as it is."

She smoothed the freshly pressed front of her pleated emerald skirt, oddly interested in the fabric.

"Best you take that up with your husband." After a playful flick to disturb Mam's matching cloche—which earned the intended gasp—he cast Anola a wink. "Suppose I better get down there and see what I can do about that hotheaded lad."

She hurried to his side. "Shall I accompany you? Women do tend to have cooler heads."

He stopped short. Laughter rumbled through him as deep and rich as a foghorn. What had come over him? He grasped the rail, guffawing. She spun back to Mam for any sort of explanation, but she'd already disappeared.

"Who..." He pressed his palm into his side. "Who told you such a fool thing?"

Anola lifted her chin. "What do you mean, fool thing? Everyone knows women are far more logical than men. A man will rush off in a fit of fury to war or spout off things he doesn't mean when his pride's been ruffled." She gave a little sniff. "Women are peacekeepers."

Tears leaked from his eyes as he got his laughter under control. "Is that what Lady Marie told you?"

She opened her mouth to confirm she had indeed been the one to pass on that wisdom, but he didn't give her the opportunity.

"The same woman who can change moods like a pair of stockings and turn the most ordinary of circumstances into a melodrama fit for the stage?"

Anola clamped her lips shut. When he put it that way...

He wrapped an arm around her shoulder. "Male or female has nothing to do with being levelheaded, lass. We all lose our tempers at times, and it's always easier to be logical when you aren't the one getting your nerves rubbed raw or your emotions frayed."

He had a point. "You are wise, Captain."

"Comes with age, they say." He flicked his eyebrows Emmett's direction and lowered his voice as they neared. "Younger men are still working on it."

Emmett turned, his countenance crestfallen. "He'll have none of it."

"If he's not interested in such labor, then this isn't the place for him."

Although the captain spoke without judgment, the simple truth seemed to fluster Emmett more. "Is there anything else he can do?"

"You mean assign him an easy job when he hasn't worked his way up like the rest of them?"

Emmett had spent days covered in coal dust. Did the fact that he'd done the job without complaint—at least to her knowledge—mean he had earned her father's and grandfather's respect?

"This is a disaster." Emmett tugged at his already open collar on the front of the sturdy wrinkled work shirt.

She offered him an encouraging smile to show her peacekeeping skills. "Perhaps he isn't feeling well today."

Emmett snorted. "No less than he deserves."

She blinked. Stars and sunrise, what did *that* mean?

"What will we do with him, then?" The captain's gaze trailed the graceful arc of a red-tailed hawk until it dove into the white cloud of a passing steamer's pipes. "He has to work, or he can't stay."

Emmett brightened. "I'll work off his passage to Vicksburg. We can leave him there." He slapped a hand against his thigh. "That's the solution. How soon can we pull out? The sooner the better."

She shared a look with the captain. He spoke first. "Not until tomorrow, remember? The crew?"

Emmett's shoulders deflated. "Right. What will we be doing today?"

The captain pursed his lips. "Have you forgotten already?"

"What? Oh. Right. The muggles."

"Pardon?" Anola wiggled her fingers to get Emmett's attention. "Did you say 'muggles'?"

"Muggles. Mexican Marijuana. Let's see. What did that article say?" He snapped his fingers. "Oh yes. A doctor first raised the alarm on marijuana in New Orleans about two years ago. The newspaper reported there needed to be a law to stop muggleheads from selling and smoking marijuana. A law they did indeed pass not too long ago, if I remember correctly."

The captain stroked his mustache, apparently having no comment.

Understanding dawned. "So this plant is illegal, just like alcohol. And it was on our boat. When I discovered it, it disappeared." She crossed her arms. "Was no one going to tell me about this?"

"Just figured it out ourselves, my gem."

Emmett rubbed his forehead. "Best we not let anyone on or off the boat."

The captain's eyes narrowed. "We'll pull the plank. Then you can take watch."

He would take watch. The irony of the captain's statement stabbed through Emmett's gut. The very man they trusted to watch their boat happened to be the man criminals planned to use to ferry illegal substances downriver. His muscles twitched as he scanned the riverbank, vigilant for any signs of something suspicious.

Not that he could tell if there were. The busy dock swarmed with people. Men in workmen's clothes and hats slung low on their brows hefted crates and barrels onto broad shoulders. Boys ducked between them, running from one errand to another. Voices filled the morning with shouts and greetings. The city smells carried on the air. Faint wisps of stovepipe smoke mingled with the odor of animals, refuse, and sweaty workers.

All sensations he'd grown up around, having spent his life in St. Louis.

So why did he find all the noise annoying? When had he started to miss the buzz of cicadas and the croak of bullfrogs?

The humidity clung to his skin, growing thicker by the moment. The people on the dock hardly seemed to notice as activity increased. At least none of those men would be able to sneak on board. He might not be able to pick a criminal out of the crowd, but he could stop any man from boarding.

Feminine laughter separated itself from the sounds, and he stilled. He tilted his head, following the sound. Another laugh, deep and masculine melded with the first. His fists clenched. Jacob.

But Emmett couldn't leave this post. Not while Stephen and the captain counted on him. He forced his attention on the dock. The wooden walkway stood not far from the edge of the boat. How hard would it be to transport cargo even without the connecting plank?

The laughter came again, and he ground his teeth. No one would attempt to load cargo in the middle of the morning. When the voices rose in pitch, he pivoted from his position. Thirty seconds to remove Anola from Jacob's presence. Nobody could deliver cargo in thirty seconds.

He rounded the front of the boat near the ticket office and found his brother leaning too close to Anola. Jacob pulled a slow smile that raised Emmett's hackles. Anola wasn't a woman in a speakeasy. Jacob should know better.

167

Emmett stepped up to them and took her elbow. "Come with me."

She startled and pulled her arm away, her fiery brows knitting together. "Why?"

He opened his mouth to say because he said so, but snapped his teeth back together before stupidity could win. He opted for a different tactic. "I need your advice on something urgent."

"Oh." Her features softened. She dipped her chin to Jacob, who was now glowering at Emmett. "If you'll excuse me."

Jacob hooked his thumbs into his suspenders. "I'd be glad to come along to help."

"No." The word shot out of Emmett's mouth like a bullet. "Thank you. I believe you have work to do." He added weight to his words. "Mr. Flynn only allows men who work to remain on board."

Jacob raked an assessing gaze over Emmett. When Anola didn't refute Emmett's claim, Jacob pushed a fake curve onto his lips. "Of course. I'll see what the crew is up to today and join them in whatever they are doing." The smile twisted into a smirk before he sauntered away.

"See? Better already." Anola swung away from him, seeming pleased with herself.

A torrent of annoyance surged through him, and he had to force it down. Anola didn't seem to notice.

She hooked her hand through his arm. "Aren't you supposed to be watching the dock?" Before he could answer, she quickened her steps. "Oh. Is that what you needed me for? Has something happened?" She tugged him forward.

Something had happened all right. Just not what she thought. Emmett breathed in deeply and let the air out slowly, hoping the raging jealousy would subside. He couldn't let her know how much her laughing with his brother had socked him in the gut.

They came to the closed railing where they usually lowered the plank. She scanned the dock. "What am I looking for?"

"Anything suspicious."

Anola used her ungloved fingers to shield her eyes. Mundane women would have worn a hat outdoors, but she'd let her loose locks catch fire in the sunlight. "What did you need my advice for? Don't you know what looks suspicious and what doesn't?"

"Don't you?" The words were out before he could catch them. Of course she wouldn't know what a snake his brother could be. How charming and deceptive. She hadn't done anything wrong. He cleared his throat. "I'm sorry. That was unkind."

She crossed her arms over a green blouse fashioned to look like...fish scales? "Because I didn't know what those herbs were so I won't be able to recognize the unscrupulous sort, is that it?" She huffed before he could respond. Then she wrinkled her nose in her adorable way, and his annoyance melted. "I am a fair bit better with people than plants, Emmett."

"Of that, I have no doubt." He plucked one of her hands and placed a kiss across her knuckles. As he'd hoped, her eyes sparkled.

Warmth spread through him, and he yielded to the desire to rest his forehead on hers.

"While I certainly wouldn't mind a repeat of that day in the rain, this public place isn't the best idea."

He straightened, and the tension in his shoulders eased. "You are good for me, Anola Flynn. I want to be the same for you."

Her smile turned tender. "That is the heart of it then, isn't it? Two people wanting to be the best they can for one another?"

She may have left the "it" undefined, but the meaning couldn't be clearer. Being the best you could for one another, serving one another, that was the heart of love. Could this deepening affection he felt for the fascinating woman before him be love?

She smiled up at him, those vibrant eyes sparkling with life. A life he wanted nothing more than to share, to shelter, to cherish. He swallowed hard and rubbed at his chest.

A line formed between her delicate brows. "Are you all right?"

"Never been better."

"That so?" She patted his cheek. "My, but you have been swapping moods faster than Lady Marie today. I'll have to let the captain know our research on the matter of peacemakers is not yet over."

"What?"

She shooed the question away. "Oh, never mind." She wiggled her lower lip through her teeth, drawing his attention to her mouth. How inappropriate would it be to kiss her right now? "Do you think one of our crew is a criminal?"

The question jarred him out of his wandering thoughts. He looked back to the dock where the crowd remained the same. "I hope not."

Not a lie. He did hope that, even though he knew better.

"I just can't imagine who it would be. And why? Why bring that stuff on our boat?"

"Because it's worth a lot of money. And now that there's a law against it, there's more risk to bring it into the city. More risk means more money."

"How do you know about all this stuff?"

"I like to read. I subscribe to different newspapers."

"Hmm." She bumped her shoulder against him. "You're smart. You know that, don't you?"

Images of his father and brother leaving him out of business dealings flashed through his mind unbidden. They'd never once said he didn't have the head for it, but he'd always felt it had been implied.

"Thank you." A smile twitched at his mouth. "My father and brother never thought so. I appreciate hearing it from you. I always worked hard in school to prove myself."

"Well, I'd say you've accomplished that." They watched the dock men a while longer before she spoke again. "I have no idea what we're looking for, despite what I said about being able to recognize the unscrupulous sort."

"Me either." Unless Mickey or a man carrying a crate tried to board, he felt useless.

"I'm not sure if you've noticed, but standing still is a challenge for me." She bobbed in place. "Is there something else we can do?"

"I'm supposed to watch."

She huffed. "What about searching? Da mentioned that."

He didn't want her searching alone. Nor did he want to give Jacob the opportunity to offer his services. "Why don't you go ask the captain to take my shift? Tell him I'll bring him that chair he likes so much on Lady Marie's porch and he can be productive right here with his chair and his pipe."

Anola smirked. "Why, Mr. Carter, I do believe you have already figured out my family." She lifted onto her toes and pecked his cheek with a sweet kiss. "I'll be right back."

And just like that, he knew he'd be spending the rest of his life on a boat.

21

They'd never find anything in this mess. Emmett tucked a finger under his nose to stifle the sneeze tickling his nostrils. There had to be at least five years' worth of discarded props in this room. Anola tugged on a box of whatnots and dislodged another puff of dust.

"All this searching is useless." The way she cocked her hands on her hips made him smile. "What?" She tipped her head at whatever expression she saw on his face. "You don't think so?"

"You're probably right." He nudged a sack of what looked to be silk flowers with his toe. "Finding the crate now won't do us much good, I suppose, except we'd be able to turn a dangerous substance over to the law. Besides, it has to be here somewhere. If the crate of muggles is worth as much as I think it is, then no one threw it overboard."

She scrunched her nose. "Maybe you're right, but we've looked in every—"

A whistle cut her off. Eyes rounding, she hooked his elbow and tugged him from the tiny closet. He rolled his shoulders. Cramped places squeezed the air from his lungs.

"Come on." She tugged harder, pulling him through the theater and toward the exit.

The boat shifted beneath him.

"Are we really pulling out?"

"That's what the horn means, yes." She squeezed his hand, her tone a mixture of exasperation and amusement.

They burst through the doors and out into the evening air. The work on the dock had slowed as men went home for the day. The city's smell, however, hadn't improved. The ropes no longer connected them to shore. "But I thought we wouldn't be leaving until at least tomorrow."

"So did I." She released his hand and bolted forward, forcing him to pick up his pace.

They hurried down the showboat's railed edges and toward the steamer at the rear. Sure enough, the steering lines had been connected, and the two boats moved in tandem out into the water.

Three short blasts rent the air. A responding one sounded from the tiny steering house atop *The River Queen*.

The actors emerged from their cabins out onto *Blue Belle*'s decks, their confused expressions indicating they hadn't expected to be leaving today either. Emmett slowed to study them. Had Stephen finished questioning them all? If any of them were guilty, their faces gave nothing away.

Anola had already climbed halfway up the ladder on *The River Queen*'s stern when Emmett caught her. He lowered his gaze from where she scrambled up—thankfully in a pair of linen knickers and knee-high socks rather than a skirt and hose. Once he heard her feet scramble over the roof, he grasped the first rung.

The last thing he wanted was to tumble into the river. They should have a higher railing up here. By the time he reached the windowed room in the center of the showboat's flat roof, Anola had already ducked inside.

"...said the crew wasn't fit to work today," Anola was saying as he closed the door behind him, more than a little relieved to have made it across the top of a moving vessel.

"Old Tom said he was fine," Stephen responded. He gripped the massive steering wheel, controlling their direction while the steamer provided the power. Then he pulled a string that dropped through a hole above his head and let out a long, shrill whistle.

Anola tapped her foot. "If he's fine, then why are you using the signals? I haven't heard you do that in ages."

Stephen never took his focus from the churning water. "A bit of caution never hurt anyone, my gem. Did you find the crate?"

"No, sir." Emmett edged closer to the wheel. "If the box is on this boat, we're going to have to start tearing something apart to find it."

"Da?" The caution her father advised had lodged in Anola's voice, something Emmett had never heard from her. "We didn't search anyone's cabin, but..."

Stephen let out a long breath. "I've talked to every soul aboard, and each denied knowing anything. I want to believe them, but someone has to be lying."

The muddy river swirled in eddies and currents, looking unsettled. If it bothered Stephen, he gave no outward sign. They moved in the center of the river and took up a swift pace. Other boats navigated the water, everything from dwarfed tugs to decrepit paddle wheels. The air, thick with moisture, coated his lungs with each intake.

"I don't understand." Anola plopped down on a stool. "Nothing like this has happened before."

"I've half a mind to put out everyone but a skeleton crew and cancel the remainder of the season."

The words hung heavy between them. Anola pressed her lips into a tight line, her face crumpling.

What Emmett needed to say pained him. "That's for the best. The sooner we can settle this matter, the better." At both Flynns' raised brows, Emmett cleared his throat. "We need to leave Jacob in Vicksburg. It wouldn't be bad for others to disembark there as well. And the more people who come aboard for shows, the more we risk further smuggling. The crowds are too unpredictable."

"See, Da!" Anola hoisted her chin. "I told you, it couldn't have been one of our people. It was likely someone who came for a show."

"That could be true." Stephen pressed on the wheel spokes and shifted the boat left into deeper waters. "But someone here had to know about it. None of the visitors would have been in the closet on the *Blue Belle* without notice. Someone had to show them the spot or take the crate there for them. And no visitor would have known you found it to hide it again."

"Lots of people moving on and off makes it easier to go unnoticed," Emmett agreed. He wanted to tell them about Jacob's crew and the dangers they presented, but that would only worry them. As long as they kept people off the boat, then they robbed the criminals of opportunity.

"But the rest of the season, Da?" Her voice cracked. "My *last* one?"

She stiffened her spine and gripped the edges of the stool, her knuckles turning white. "All of this to-do for one crate of dried plants? Canceling the season is an overreaction."

"Maybe delay it instead?" An idea formed, and Emmett straightened shoulders that had started to droop. "What if we don't go to New Orleans? What if we go back to St. Louis, regroup, and then take a run at the tributaries?"

Her eyes shone, and her smile stirred him.

Stephen kept his attention on a passing passenger boat. "I can't do that. I've already given my word to the buyer."

"But, Da—"

He held up a hand, then repositioned his grip on the wheel when it tilted to the left. "This will require some thought, prayer, and a family meeting. We'll discuss it tomorrow."

Anola opened her mouth to speak but then shot Emmett a look.

He wagged his head.

She returned a tiny nod. She'd understood. Best not to push.

"How far are you going to travel?" she asked instead.

"The current is swift. If we use the generator for extra light, we can make it into Mississippi before it gets too dark. We'll find a spot to lower the anchors for the rest of the night."

Anola scrunched her brow, but she placed a kiss on her father's cheek with a plea to be careful, then started toward the door. Emmett followed her but stopped when Stephen called his name.

He paused in the doorway. "Yes, sir?"

"By your suggestion, I take it you've made your decision."

No question what decision he meant. Beyond the open door, Anola strolled across the top of the boat, stopped, and lifted her face to the sky. Electricity zipped through his chest, creating a warm glow that seeped into his words. "Yes, sir. I believe I have."

"I have debts, lad. We need the buyer in New Orleans."

It didn't matter. Financial challenges held no weight against the prospect of spending his life without her. He toggled a button on his collar. "I have some private savings. Maybe we can discuss the numbers for a joint venture."

A smile twitched under Stephen's mustache.

"Of course"—Emmett stuffed his fidgeting hand into his trouser pocket—"we can discuss all of that at our family meeting."

The smile widened and Stephen laughed. "Lad, you'll make a good Flynn yet."

Emmett thanked him and closed the door, hope thawing some of his fears for their future.

The air moved over her skin and tangled in her hair, carrying with it the smells of life. Anola breathed them in, her shoulders relaxing. She'd grown restless, and the sounds of the river moving and the beckoning of a new location loosened a tightness within her. Memphis faded behind them. Emmett had seemed to share her relief at taking to the water.

Dear Emmett. His idea was perfect. No need to go all the way back to St. Louis, of course. Well, not unless they changed the troupe. Or the crew. No, she wouldn't think of that now. As long as they got rid of the box and didn't go to New Orleans, they could pretend the entire affair had never happened and forgive one of their people for the mistake of succumbing to financial temptations. Then they could take one of the river branches. The L'Annguille wasn't far. They could follow it to the Arkansas. Or they could turn back upriver and catch the Ohio or Tennessee.

Arms wrapped around her waist, startling her from her thoughts. Warmth and the pleasing scents of Emmett's lye soap and aftershave enveloped her. She released her remaining tension and relaxed against the strength of his chest. "It's a good idea. Thank you for thinking of it."

He pressed a kiss on her temple. "There will be a lot to discuss. And we need to plan."

She pulled his arms tighter. "But it's a chance."

"Anola, I…"

She gave him time, sensing whatever came next would be important.

"…care deeply for you. I promise I will do everything in my power to protect you."

Unease slithered through her. What did she need protection from? She pushed the feeling aside and focused on his other words. "You haven't known me long." She tried to keep her tone light, but failed. "Are you sure?"

He chuckled. "It only takes meeting you, Anola Flynn, to realize you are the type of woman any man dreams of." His breath washed across the curve of her neck, bringing a delighted shiver. "Every moment of getting to know you after only proved it true."

Her throat thickened. She'd been praying for God to show her the way. Her heart tugged toward Emmett, but if he wasn't the one for her, she didn't want to find herself heartbroken. He rested his chin on her head, not seeming anxious for a response. Peace drifted through her.

"I wonder if I love you." The words came unbidden, and heat flooded her face. Thank goodness he couldn't see her. Stars and sunrise, she needed to take better care.

A laugh rumbled through his chest, feeling nice against her back. "I've been wondering the same."

She twisted to look up at him. "You've also been wondering if I love you?"

A grin made his lips twitch. "Well, yes, that too. But I've been wondering if this overwhelming thing I've been feeling is love."

"For me?" She hated to ask, but Lady Marie always said clarity banished misunderstandings.

"Yes, you." His lips brushed her forehead. "There could never be another who could hold a candle to your sunshine."

They stood in silence, enjoying the breeze. Sadness crept into the evening's perfection. "Emmett, I need you to understand. I don't want to leave the river. It's all I've ever known. I've tried to tell myself the unknown could be an adventure but..." She shook her head, unable to figure out the words to explain how she felt.

"It's a part of you. It's made you who you are."

He understood after all.

"Let's not worry about that right now, all right? My mother always said God has a plan, and if we are following it, then he makes a way."

"But what if I don't like his plan?" Oh dear. She shouldn't have said that. What would he think?

Instead of admonishing her lack of faith, Emmett brushed his lips across her cheekbone. "That's possible. But I believe he works out all things to our good. We may not like the circumstances we find ourselves in, but at some point, we will see it was always for our good."

The ache in her heart swelled. What was she supposed to do with this tangled knot of feelings? She didn't want to leave the river. But she also wanted to trust God and his plan. Her stomach clenched. Would his plan leave her landlocked?

Emmett hugged her, the day's growth of whiskers prickly against her face. "We'll talk about it more at the family meeting."

The way he spoke felt like he'd already become one of them. Could that be possible in so short a time? Mam and Da had done the same, sure. But despite the hopes she'd always held, she never expected to become taken with a man so quickly.

"If I stay on the river," she whispered, "will you stay with me?"

"I'll go where you go." There was no hesitation.

His words buried into her heart and tried to find purchase. But despite her best efforts, worry clawed for a stronghold.

He said that now, but... She wanted to believe she could keep Emmett, her family, and the showboat on the river. But in a matter of weeks, her life had twisted and turned like a leaf caught in the current. Would she feel this way for him if she had to live her life on shore? Would he feel the same for her if their family troubles proved more of a burden than he wanted to carry?

He cared for her now, but what if—

Tightness clogged her throat. Emmett snuggled her closer, but the gesture didn't dispel the nagging unease. She searched for the carefree girl who always flowed with whatever the day brought, but she'd disappeared. Replaced by a wiser woman who knew girlhood fairy tales couldn't last forever.

Trouble came for them, and it could well tear her family apart. What would happen to them then?

T here had to be an accounting. Consequences paid for choices made. Emmett ignored the sourness creeping up his throat and refused to be swayed by his brother's silvered tongue. Not this time. Not when Anola and the Flynns depended on him.

"You've lost your mind." Jacob scowled at Emmett as they squared off in Jacob's cabin.

"It's a sensible solution." Emmett crossed his arms to keep from stopping his brother's ridiculous pacing.

Jacob snorted. "You have no idea what you're talking about."

"Then enlighten me."

He jabbed his fingers through his already mussed hair. "They can't just stop in the middle of the river."

"They can." At least his words remained calm.

"You were supposed to keep them in Memphis another few days."

"Someone brought a crate of Mexican muggles onto the boat, and the crew ate it. That debacle has the family on edge."

Jacob blinked and then burst out laughing.

Emmett scowled. Nothing about this situation warranted humor.

The boat dipped, and Jacob threw a hand against the wall to steady himself. Funny, Emmett had barely noticed. Maybe he'd developed something akin to what sailors called sea legs.

"That must have been a sight. Never heard of people *eating* it." Jacob hooted with laughter. "No wonder they had the day off."

Emmett forced down his ire and declined to comment on his brother's disregard for the situation. "Tell me who brought it on board."

Jacob grew serious again. "I don't know."

Fists clenching, Emmett stepped closer. "I don't have the patience for your games or your schemes. When we were in the Blind Bat, you said you already had a man on this boat. I need to know who it is. Now."

His brother cocked his head as though truly seeing Emmett for the first time. "I said what I needed to."

"What does that mean?"

"It means I knew enough to figure out Mickey had a man on one of the showboats. I pieced together what you said and what I'd heard to realize this was the boat they'd been talking about. But I don't know who their man is. I don't think he's one of the gang. Just someone they paid off."

A man agreeing to a suspicious deal for a lot of money sounded a sight better than a hardened criminal living among them. "Crew or one of the actors?"

Jacob shrugged. "Could be either."

That didn't help. "Doesn't change anything. Soon as we get to Vicksburg, you're getting off this boat."

One side of Jacob's mouth twisted into a sneer. "Since when do you think you can boss me, baby brother? Have you forgotten what's at stake here?"

"What's at stake is why I'm getting you out of here. No one expects you to disembark at Vicksburg. You can slip away. Get free of those men. Take a train out West. Start over. Maybe even go to Europe."

"Are you hearing yourself?" Jacob stuck his hands in his pockets and nodded toward the door. "Is there any booze on this puritan boat?"

Emmett ignored the question. "I'm hearing clearly. Are you? This is your chance to get away."

"With what? The clothes on my back and a friendly smile?" Jacob spread out his hands, his crooked grin forming beneath their father's hazel eyes. "Just trust me, will you? It'll be worth it if you give me more time to get some things together."

Emmett closed his eyes and forced his clenched jaw to relax. "So you really did lose everything from our inheritance? You weren't just saying that to get me to join in on your next hare-brained get-rich scheme?"

The silence gave answer enough.

"I guess you'll need to figure that out on your own." Jacob barely kept a growl from his voice. Then he thumbed to the door behind him. "You're sentencing me to death. You and all of them."

"We don't have the gang's cargo. So nothing is lost." Emmett almost asked what was so important that they needed to ferry it on a showboat, but it was better if he didn't know.

"You don't understand anything."

"I understand enough. Once we reach Vicksburg, find your own way." He edged around his brother, feeling a pang of loss for the friends they should have been, and opened the door.

Jacob's next words left him cold. "This won't end well for you."

The next morning, Anola found Emmett in the hallway waiting outside her grandparents' door with a pot of fragrant coffee. She sidled up to him. "I see you've brought a family bribe."

One side of his mouth curved, but the gesture didn't lighten the intensity in his chocolate eyes. "It was a late night. I figured we could all use a little coffee to fortify ourselves for our meeting."

She tucked a stray curl behind her ear. "The meeting will have to wait. Da is already in the steering house. We'll be moving again soon."

Emmett looked dejectedly at the pot, so she added, "But you're welcome to join Mam, Lady Marie, and me as we discuss today's menu. Lady Marie, as I am sure you can understand, is determined to keep a close eye on poor Cook and manage every detail of meal preparations."

His gaze shifted around, and his lips twitched sideways. He appeared as eager to participate in menu planning as the captain had been.

"Or I suppose you could join Da in the—"

"Yes! I'd like to learn more about how he manages to steer this large of a vessel. The calculations he employs are quite fascinating."

When she chuckled, he leaned down and pecked her on the cheek. "I'll be here for the meeting."

"Wait!" Anola called as he turned to go.

He paused.

"The coffee?" She tilted an eyebrow.

With a grin, he transferred the brew and dashed off.

A sense of rightness warmed her. This was what she wanted. A good man who helped Da and her family with their livelihood and made her heart strain to the brim with affection. They could share a happy life here, simple and yet filled with adventure. Why couldn't they just—

The door swung open, and Lady Marie spotted her. "What are you doing out there, lass?" Her eyes widened. "Oh, good. You brought coffee. Smart girl."

Anola stepped into the suite. "This was Emmett's doing. But he's gone to help Da now."

"Well and good. We women have things to discuss and don't need men interjecting." The words could have been mean, but as her grandmother delivered them with such affectionate amusement, Anola could only smile. Her grandparents' banter carried on even when the other wasn't about.

"There you are." Mam placed a tray of Cook's biscuits on George Washington's table and flicked her skirt to settle into her usual seat. "We need to talk."

Why did that make her feel uneasy? And why did Mam look unusually formal? Dressed in her slim skirt and crisp blouse with her toffee hair coiled and tucked, she resembled a society lady. Like one of those well-to-dos who had turned their noses up at Anola in Kimmswick.

Strange. Lady Marie had the same manner of dress. Anola hadn't noticed at first, but those subdued grays spoke volumes. She swallowed a lump in her throat as she scooted into her place at the table.

Lady Marie wasted no time in pretense. "Something is afoot, and we need to get to the bottom of it."

"They already questioned all of the cast and crew. We didn't find out anything." Anola shifted. "Emmett suggested we dismiss the cast."

Both women nodded.

"We will have one more show in Vicksburg to send them off with as much of their season earnings as we can," Mam said.

"And leave them at a decent city where they can get passage or other jobs," Lady Marie added.

Silence stretched until Anola couldn't stand it any longer. "Then what?"

Lady Marie seemed to remember the coffee pot she'd left on a trivet. She bustled to the side table and busied herself pouring three cups of the rich liquid, fussing over their lack of cream.

Mam laced her fingers together on the table. "That's another part of what we need to talk about."

Lady Marie served the three cups and regained her seat, then twitched a ringed finger to Mam to continue.

"We've been discussing continuing to New Orleans or returning upriver to St. Louis."

"St. Louis," Anola blurted. "That's the best choice."

Mam curled her fingers around one of Lady Marie's best china teacups. "Even if we return to St. Louis"—cup halfway to her mouth, she spoke with the patient tone she'd used on Anola as a child—"we will still need to sell *The River Queen* to cover our debts."

"Debts?" Anola's teacup clattered against her saucer. She settled both on George Washington's table. She'd known they were having troubles, but she didn't realize they needed to sell in order to pay any loans.

"Your father took out a large sum from the bank last year to purchase all the new set equipment we needed. We'd hoped we would earn enough this season to pay off a portion of the loan so when we sold the boat someday we'd still have enough to purchase a modest home."

Anola tapped her chin in thought. "Can we put off the loan a little longer? If we run the tributaries, we can extend the show because of the warmer weather farther south, earn as much as we can this season, and then finish paying off the rest next year." She brightened. "What if we continue winter shows while we are docked? It might be too cold in St. Louis, but we could dock In New Orleans, right? It's warmer there, and we could stay open longer."

"What about the cast?" Lady Marie's quiet words sliced into Anola's growing jubilation.

"We keep them. I'm sure whoever brought the stuff on board didn't know what they were doing. We can forgive them and forget about this entire mess." How she wanted to shove all their troubles under a rug and pretend none of it mattered.

Mam held the cup just under her nose, closing her eyes as she breathed in the rich aroma. "What about your grandparents?"

Anola scooted forward in her seat, resting her hand atop Lady Marie's. "I don't understand."

Lady Marie grimaced and slid her veined hand free, then patted Anola's fingers. "It breaks my heart to admit it, my gem." Her eyes watered, and she paused for a slow breath. "But the captain and I aren't the young adventurers we once were. Maybe it's time we slowed down."

"You can sit in your rockers right here with the rest of the family, can't you?" Anola pressed her cup to her lips, pleased her hand didn't tremble. She sipped slowly to gather her thoughts. The bitter taste awakened her senses. "The showboat was your dream. Are you saying you don't want to be here anymore?"

"It's not that we don't want to be here," Lady Marie soothed. "Or with you. But the pace of the river becomes difficult with aching joints. Years ago, I promised my husband we would one day trade my adventure for his. I'm sorry to say I put it off for far too long."

Lady Marie never spoke of growing old. Of graying hair or tired bones. She'd waged war against aging with the courage of a gladiator. Had the battle grown too fierce?

What promise? Anola lowered her cup with as much calm refinement as she could muster, as the regal Mrs. Withersby would have done in their production of *Summer Rain* four years prior. Drops of her coffee splashed on the table.

She'd never known the captain to want to be anywhere but on the river. Just like the rest of them. What was happening to her family? "I still don't understand."

"I know, my gem." Mam offered a smile that seemed too sad to count. "Your father and I are at fault. We wanted to create a beautiful world for our only child. A place of magic apart from the troubles the rest of the world faced. For a long time, we achieved our goal. But you are a grown woman now, and it's long past time we stopped shielding you from every trouble that comes our way."

The coffee droplets merged and pooled in a worn divot, as out of place in a wooden world as she would be anchored to a stale patch of earth.

"So you are all agreed? You want to sell and live on land?" She drizzled a little of Mrs. Withersby's assurance into her words even as her throat attempted to defy her. "What will you and Da do? What will I do?"

Whatever realities they had thought to shield her from, she needed the truth. Even if she didn't want it.

Mam staunched the spill. "We are trying to discuss that."

Anola swallowed. Right. They were trying to include her in a difficult decision, and she was behaving like a spoiled girl.

Please, Lord, I could use some wisdom.

Lady Marie refreshed their cups. "I promised the captain he could have a little farm someday. Lord knows that man knows nothing about farming. But then, he didn't know anything about show business either. He has in his mind a quaint farmhouse, some chickens in the yard, and maybe some great-grandchildren to come play with the horses and goats." She waved with the coffeepot. "Goats. Can you imagine such a thing?"

"And where would this farm be?"

She plunked the pot back on its trivet before reclaiming her chair. "Somewhere on the river, of course."

A sad chuckle bubbled through Anola. At least, they'd still be able to see the water.

"We know you want to continue with the showboat." Mam clinked her cup onto the saucer and straightened her already perfect posture. "So we have a proposition for you."

A proposition?

"If we continue to New Orleans and sell *The River Queen* to the buyer we have waiting, then we will use the remainder to purchase a smaller vessel to take down the tributaries."

Yes! Exactly as she had suggested. A perfection solution that would—

Mam held up a hand before Anola's exuberance breached its moors.

"It won't be as fancy, and it won't hold as many as we can here. It would be something more like the boat your grandparents started out with."

"The *Flynns' Floating Theater*." The captain and Lady Marie had grown from there. She could as well.

"Something like that, yes."

Give up *The River Queen*? The only home she'd ever known? Anola hated the thought. But her parents were trying. They were offering her all they had.

"But what will you use to buy a house for Lady Marie and the captain?"

"We'll make that work, lass." Her grandmother exaggerated an impish wink. "The captain and I are resourceful if that's escaped your notice."

She squirmed at a sudden chill. "What about you and Da? Are you ready for a life on land too?"

She wouldn't let her own wants dictate their lives. She could figure out how to run a showboat on her own. Somehow. And Emmett. What would he think?

"Your father and I would be happy with a few more years on the river before we are ready to spend our days playing with goats." She saluted Anola with her teacup, and the mirth broke some of the tension.

Anola worried her lower lip between her teeth. "I'll need to talk to Emmett."

Oddly, that made both women beam. Lady Marie wiggled her eyebrows. "That is a grand idea. I agree."

The two women shared a loaded look. What? Had she missed something? Before she could ask, the conversation turned to Emmett and her courtship.

A strange fluttering started in her stomach. "I...think I might love him." She shifted in her seat. "How do you know for certain?"

Lady Marie tapped the end of her nose with a knowing twinkle in her eyes. "You just do, lass."

Well, that was hardly helpful.

Mam's fingernail clicked on the table. "Do you think about what would be best for him? Do your thoughts never stray far from him? Does the mere sight of him make your heart skip?"

Scooting her chair closer, Lady Marie joined in. "Have you asked God and feel like this man could be a match for your heart? Where the two of you can love and serve him together? Do you think you can spend all your days with him until one of you departs this life?"

Anola flattened her hands on George Washington's table, at a loss with the torrent of questions. The pulse in her heated palms thrummed against the cool surface.

Gracious and stars above.

She might not remember all of what they said, but her heart beat in a steady rhythm of one simple truth. A tingling warmth crept over her, matching the mirth of the women across the table.

"Yes."

H ad Emmett just said...? Anola gripped the edge of the couch she'd perched upon, the faded green upholstery sturdy beneath her fingertips. She cut a glance at Da, but he didn't appear surprised.

Evening light filtered through the windows, a slight drizzle keeping the family inside for their supper rather than out on the porch. They'd shared a simple meal of cornbread, beans, and ham brought over from Cook, then settled down in the living space of her grandparents' rooms for coffee and their family meeting.

"I have money in savings. We'll use that and have equal shares in the new showboat." Anola replayed his words. He wanted to go into business with them. And with what he'd said last night...

Her mind whirled. He spoke again, forcing her to abandon her contemplations for another time or risk missing what he said next.

"It's a good thing I maintain my own account, given that my brother drained every bit of our inheritance from the one we shared." His fist clenched. He noticed and relaxed his fingers with a nervous glance her way. "It's not much. A few thousand

191

dollars I stashed away. The simple life of a bachelor accountant didn't cost much. I saved most of my earnings."

And he'd be willing to spend those earnings on a new showboat? Affection swelled. If she hadn't been sure before if she loved this man, she was now.

"We'll need to account for the current expenses," Emmett continued, "and decide how much will be allotted for the captain and Lady Marie's house and then assess what we can afford."

No wonder God had sent them a man with a head for numbers. Satisfaction unfurled within her chest. He was exactly what they needed.

Da nodded along, and the conversation turned to what they could expect each item to cost. The numbers meant little to Anola, as she had limited experience with purchasing things other than supplies for the boat.

"You'll need to pay the cast, of course." Lady Marie drummed her fingers on the armrest from her place next to the captain in their matching chairs. "It's not their fault they don't have a job for the remainder of the season."

Mam's lip curled. "It could be one of their faults."

Da's eyebrows rose. Mam usually didn't respond with a bite in her tone. Still, the culprit had been given ample time to be forthright. The elders of her family started talking over one another as they shared their opinions. Her gaze drifted to Emmett, and she found him looking at her thoughtfully.

She infused as much of her gratitude into her smile as she could, hoping he could read the emotion. The corners of his mouth curved, though his eyes remained serious.

He cleared his throat and pushed to his feet. "If I may?"

The room grew quiet as they focused on Emmett. Anola sat settled against the cushions.

"We can tally up the numbers for what they are usually paid, but we should be fair. Some compensation is warranted for the unexpected circumstances, but as they have time to obtain other work, a full season's pay for less than half of a season's work is unjustified."

The others exchanged glances. Then Da and Mam nodded, and the captain grunted his consent.

Lady Marie made a dismissive motion. "Yes, fair enough." She swept her gaze over Emmett. "We'll leave the figuring part up to you, of course."

Emmett bent at the waist, a slight bow that made Lady Marie's blue eyes dance and the captain's mustache twitch.

"So we have a plan, then?" Anola clasped her hands. "Compensate the cast, have them disembark at Vicksburg, continue to New Orleans, sell"—her throat caught, and she had to clear the emotion before garnering her resolve and continuing—"sell *The River Queen*, buy the captain and Lady Marie a house on the river where they can have goats, purchase a new smaller showboat, and take her back up the Mississippi and onto some of the tributaries, possibly travel the Ohio?" She drew a long breath after the torrent of words. How would they ever accomplish all of that and still have time to hire a new cast and crew, ready them for a production, and get back to work?

"More or less. I think." Da rubbed his jaw, then winked. "You talked so fast, lass, that I doubt any of us heard half of what you said. But you got the heart of it."

"What about the crew?" All eyes swung to the captain as he poked a finger into his empty pipe bowl, frowned at it, and then tapped it on the knee of his knickers. "If we can be tossin' aside the cast because none of them would come clean about the crate, then how come we are keeping the crew?"

Da steepled his fingers. "We can travel to New Orleans without a cast, but not without the crew."

The captain wedged the pipe under his mustache and chewed the end. "I reckon that's true. But what if we let good people go who have been working for us for years while keeping the culprit on board?"

"If the person responsible had told the truth, we wouldn't be in this predicament." Lady Marie scoffed. "I do despise falsehoods."

"How many of the crew are vital?" Emmett deftly steered the conversation back on track.

He had a way of doing that, getting everyone on course when they veered off. Another thing to admire. Funny how she'd never noticed the meandering course their conversations took.

"Most of them." Da's tone thickened with meaning. "Only a few on board aren't necessary."

"My brother will be departing at Vicksburg." Emmett's jaw flexed. Whatever went on between the brothers had him riled.

The evening's meeting concluded with the finalizations of their plans, and a sense of peace settled on Anola. This wasn't the route she would have chosen, but it offered new opportunities and hopes. She suppressed a smirk. At least she wouldn't have to work as a laundress.

They said their good nights, and Emmett offered to walk her to her door. The idea was foolish since her room stood two doors away, but she happily accepted. Any reason for a few moments alone with him would do.

They stepped out into the quiet hallway. He stuffed his hands in his pockets, his gaze landing everywhere but on her. Unease wormed through the peace she'd so recently found.

"What's wrong?"

He plastered on an unconvincing smile. "Just thinking." He took her hand and ambled toward her door. "So, this plan..."

"Is generous of you." She stopped, staring up at him in earnest. "And you're sure? It's a big commitment." And it implied other, more personal commitments as well. Didn't it? Surely he didn't see this as merely a business venture. "And you don't like boats."

"They are growing on me." He squeezed her fingers. "Besides, I get the feeling it's time for a new adventure." He brushed a chaste kiss on her cheek. "Good night, Anola."

Wait. That was it? Before her frown could form, he turned on his heel and strode down the hall, leaving her with a tangle of confusion.

Emmett paced *The River Queen*'s deck, his thoughts in a jumble. He was making the right choice. He'd prayed and looked at his options from every fathomable angle. Joining the Flynn family on the tributaries, bringing joy to farm and mining communities... Well, it wasn't what he'd ever pictured for his life, but it felt right.

That had everything to do with Anola. He wanted to create a good life for her. But first, he had to deal with Jacob, Mickey, and the mess his brother had landed them in.

He made another trip around the deck, ignoring the mist hanging in the air and clinging to his clothes. They'd docked close to shore, but nothing other than trees stood on the riverbanks. As far as he knew, no towns were nearby. That brought some measure of comfort. At least he didn't have to worry about Jacob sneaking anything on board.

"Thought I'd find you slinking around." Jacob's voice snatched Emmett from his thoughts. He wrenched a flat cap low over his brow.

"Where have you been holed up?"

Jacob hooked his thumbs through his suspenders, the shirt underneath rumpled and in need of a wash. "There's always a good card game and a bit of fun to be had if you know where to look."

Emmett didn't like the sound of that, but he ignored the comment. He wouldn't get dragged into another argument. "What do you know about what happened to the *Good Tidings*? I want to hear every detail from the moment you decided to buy the steamer, to why you swindled me into being the one to take it to New Orleans, and what you know about the gang who stole it."

Jacob batted at the thick air. "How about we go somewhere drier first?"

Not wanting to be stuffed into one of the cabins again, Emmett led his brother into the covered hallway that opened to the theater, stopping by the ticket booth. "Here is good enough."

"Not much by way of privacy." Jacob leaned against the wall and crossed his feet at his ankles. Emmett could barely read his smug expression in the gloom.

"It's good enough. Now answer my questions."

"Since when did you get a backbone, baby brother?" A sound too hard to be quite a chuckle as such slipped between his cracked lips. "Well, it's about time, I reckon."

Emmett waited.

After a few moments, Jacob sucked his teeth. "It's like this. I got word of a good deal happening—a cut of a *hundred thousand dollars* kind of deal."

As Jacob let the words settle, Emmett's throat dried. What job could bring in such an outrageous sum?

"I knew the investment of the boat would be worth it. So I got the nod to haul the goods. But then those no-good Durkins must have caught wind of it and taken you for an easy target."

Emmett clenched his fists. "*You* should have been on the boat with your...your... What were you hauling anyway?"

"Sure you want to know?"

He didn't, actually, but he should—shouldn't he? Being in the dark when it came to Jacob was never a good thing. "Spill."

"Mickey's crew knocked over the Mercantile. Cleaned out the vaults and came away with just shy of a hundred thousand." He whistled low. "My cut woulda been twenty percent of that for hauling it downriver. I was going to turn the five thousand we spent on the steamer into twenty, baby brother. Now you go on and tell me that wasn't a wise investment."

They'd robbed the largest bank in St. Louis? And gotten away with it? He scoured his mind, but couldn't remember any write-ups in the paper about a robbery. "You mean excepting the fact that you were moving stolen goods, being paid with stolen money, and risking having your stolen goods stolen from you, leaving you with nothing?" Each time he said the word *stolen*, he emphasized it a little more.

Jacob didn't seem to notice. "Would have been a good haul if it weren't for those rats."

Emmett had no sympathy for one criminal being robbed by another. There was no use in pointing out how he'd reported the loss of legitimate goods to the bank. And the police. Would he be arrested for fraud?

"Why did you send me instead of going yourself?"

Jacob snorted. "If you got boarded, you would have handed them forged paperwork and never batted an eye. No copper is going to expect a flat tire to be a runner." He spread out his hands. "I woulda told you, baby brother, after it was all squared away. Then I would have given you a share of—"

"Stop calling me that. I'm not a baby." Emmett wasn't even sure he wanted to be the man's brother.

One side of his mouth quirking, Jacob wagged a finger at him. "There goes that backbone again. All right. Makes no difference what we call you. Mickey knows you as Joe, and it would be in your best interest to keep it that way. He's pretty tangled up over losing his haul, and my neck is in the shadow of the noose until we get it back."

"How do you even think that's going to be possible?"

"I have my ways." He pushed off the wall and started to walk away. "Don't worry about it. All you have to do is trust me."

"I don't want anything to do with your schemes."

With a glance over his shoulder, Jacob studied him. "Are you sure?"

"Quite."

"Remember you made your choice, then. All you have to do is get this boat to New Orleans and keep the family in the dark. I'll do the rest." He sauntered out of the hallway and into the drizzling rain.

Emmett stood there, watching the water droplets in the silvery moonlight. Jacob refused to be reasonable. He'd made it clear he wouldn't take the opportunity Emmett had provided for him to skip out on the justice he deserved. Letting him go in Vicksburg would only leave the door open for him to cause more trouble.

Emmett pulled in the damp air and released it, praying he'd have the strength to figure out a way to send his only remaining family to jail.

One last show in the world she'd always known. Anola's fingers twitched on the heavy velvet curtain as she peeked through, watching a good-sized Vicksburg crowd filter in. Behind her, the cast hurried through their preshow routines with their normal joviality, oblivious to the upcoming difficult conversation.

An ache settled in her chest. She swallowed it down. She would do *The River Queen* proud. She thrust open the curtains and took the stage in her peacock costume. Murmurs started when people noticed her. Normally, she waited until most had found their seats. But not tonight. Tonight must be special.

Stopping center stage, Anola hoisted her hands and tilted her head back. Her voice came softly at first, then strengthened into the soulful strands of "The Mermaid's Song." The melody carried in swells and tides as it drifted over the audience. It poured through her, a part of her. She forgot the people watching and closed her eyes, letting the melody take her.

The theater amplified her song, containing and shaping it in just the right way. She sang until her tears mingled with her melody and she let them both go. When at last the ache inside became one with the song and left her, she lowered her hands and raised her eyes.

The theater erupted in applause. People stood in the aisles, having never found their seats as they'd stopped to stare. Her heart swelled with their appreciation, and she dipped into a curtsy. Her mermaid's song. A farewell to the theater she'd loved her entire life. An ending to her girlhood and the magic of *The River Queen* with a melody carrying the truest depths of her heart. Something words could never capture.

She rose from her deep curtsy to find Emmett at the front of the stage, a brilliant yellow rose in his hand. A ray of sunshine encased in a fragrant bloom. Where had he found that?

His gentle smile nearly undid her. He understood. She accepted his offering, tears pooling anew. Then holding the flower to her heart, she sang her welcome song for the final time.

"Welcome, welcome,
All my friends,
Welcome, welcome,
This is where the story begins,
Bring your sorrows,
Bring your joy,
Every man, woman, girl, and boy,
Welcome, welcome,
To *The River Queen*,
Where every moment is but a dream."

And it had been. A dream she'd loved and now must let go. She savored Emmett's endearing gaze before whispering her thank you and slipping behind the curtain.

Dread landed like a mule kick to Emmett's gut
Mickey.

He couldn't be here. It was impossible. Emmett edged into the shadows at the back of the theater, his focus locked on wide shoulders in a striped tailored suit. He willed his breathing to steady. Mickey lumbered down the aisle, choosing an end seat midtheater.

Emmett clenched his fists and moved along the back wall to the door. He dashed down the hallway, gaining a few annoyed looks from women with coifed hair. He didn't take time to apologize. He had to find Jacob.

He knew this last show had been a bad idea. But the Flynns would not be swayed from gathering as much money as possible to pay their cast before telling them their season had been cut short. And without revealing his reasons, he couldn't convince them of the dangers.

He banged on Jacob's cabin door with three short raps, then shouldered it open. Empty. He might have known. He thrust his hands through his hair. He had to think. Would the plan he'd constructed still work? He couldn't stop Jacob and his lowlifes on his own. He'd have to tell the law. But he had little evidence.

It didn't matter. He had to let the authorities know what Jacob planned. Tell them about the robbery in St. Louis and the danger Mickey represented. Mind made up, he closed the cabin door and stalked down the *Blue Belle*'s deck.

Something caught his collar and yanked him backward. He hollered and swung his fist, connecting with another man's gut. The man grunted but held tight, yanking Emmett down the steep steps onto the steamer's main deck and into the engine room. The smells of grease and coal assaulted him even with the wall separating them from the boiler room.

Rough hands shoved him toward one of the arms powering the paddle, and Emmett stumbled. He twisted to face his assailant in the gloomy room.

A burly man he'd never seen before stood between him and the door. He regarded Emmett with eyes that could have turned the humid air to frost before he seemed to come to some kind of decision. Thick lips curled back from surprisingly white teeth. "Got a message fer ya, Joe."

His stomach clenched. One of Mickey's men.

"Mickey says Scissors vouched for you, but he's got his ways of smellin' rats." The man lifted meaty hands. "So he sent me as a bit of...insurance." The friendliness in the man's tone warred with the cruelty in his blue eyes, and the grin tugging at his mouth dried Emmett's throat.

"Not goin' to ask?" The man shrugged. "I'll tell ya anyway. We're loadin' the cargo. You get any funny ideas, and Mickey is willin' to let this boat and them that occupies it go up in flames."

"But wouldn't..." Emmett cleared his throat. "Wouldn't that ruin your cargo?"

Another shrug. "Better that than the other, yeah?"

He didn't ask what the man meant by "the other." His mind scrambled. "Tell Mickey this boat is being sold in New Orleans. This is the last show, and they are dismissing the cast and all unnecessary crew here in Vicksburg." A shadow crossed the man's face, so Emmett hurried on. "Which is good, right? Because we will get to New Orleans sooner than expected."

The man cocked his head and picked at something in his teeth with a long fingernail. "This your doin'?"

Would it help or hurt if he said it was? God help him, he'd go with as much of the truth as he could. "The family is under financial strain and planned on selling the boat. I convinced them to hurry on to New Orleans without all the stops for shows so they could sell and get the money faster."

"Uh-huh. And when are ya plannin' on dockin'?"

Hmm. At five miles per hour and roughly two hundred miles, taking into account stopping at night... "About five days."

The man's eyebrows tugged together.

"Much faster, right? It would have taken weeks with them stopping every few miles. This gets your cargo there and everyone paid faster." His pulse drummed in his ears. If he couldn't stop them from loading the cargo, maybe he could get them caught red-handed unloading it.

A wicked smile bunched the man's full cheeks under his cold eyes. "Ya might be slicker than I thought. Mickey will be pleased we are movin' faster and might overlook his dislike for ya—long as ya don't cause no trouble." The disturbing grin widened. "Then we'll have to see each other again."

He tugged a knife from his pocket and flipped open the blade, inspecting it. "Won't let you burn, of course. You and Scissors will be comin' with us, and you can listen to their screams from the shore." He snapped the knife closed. "I see you understand the nature of our partnership."

Emmett's stomach convulsed even as his fists tightened.

The gangster opened the door and strode out into the evening's deepening shadows. Emmett remained rooted in the engine room, his mind whirling. He had five days to set up a way to catch Mickey's gang, keep the Flynns safe, and pray they didn't all end up at the bottom of the Mississippi.

Either the rest of the cast had caught Anola's nervous energy or they'd been buoyed by the increased crowd. A murmur of anticipation had permeated the backstage area, forcing her to find solace. Her heart squeezed. What a shame to have one's spirits soaring only to finish the night with them scattered to the wind. She fingered a curl, her thoughts too distracted to worry with the details of her costume change.

"Did you see the crowd?" Mam bustled into the green room, her face flushed. "I had no idea we'd have so many."

Lady Marie squeezed past Mam and dropped into her dressing chair for one last dab of lip rouge. "So many men too.

Without wives and children, no less. Why, the theater is half full of them."

Anola shimmied out of the full skirt of her peacock dress and tugged on the simple pioneer frock for Miss Edith Cole, the character she would portray in the second act this evening. "Have either of you seen Emmett?"

The women's conversation paused, and Mam turned to her. "He was in the theater earlier, wasn't he?"

"I didn't see him when the first act started, and he wasn't out there selling candy with the captain and Freddie."

Lady Marie batted her lashes. "Ah, new love. Lass, you don't have to keep track of a man every moment. I'm sure he's off on some errand or other for the captain."

Probably true.

Mam encased her in a warm embrace. "Are you all right?"

Tears stung, but Anola forced them away. "A bit melancholy if I'm being honest, but making the most of our last show."

"It's not your last show." Lady Marie rose and joined them. "Soon, you'll have to start off on your own and make your own way. That's the cycle of life, my gem. Parents raise their children to be independent and send them out into the world to fly." She took Anola's shoulders and looked her in the eyes. "You will soar. Do not see this as the end of your story, but rather the start of a new adventure."

A sad smile struggled to find purchase. "I will try."

"Change is hard," Mam said. "But if we trust the God who formed the rivers and the oceans to direct our course, we will end up where we need to go. I know you didn't want or expect this to happen, but God's timing puts us in the places he intended us to be."

Anola swiped a tear as the door to the green room banged open and Sue burst inside, face stricken. "Hurry! You must come now!" She dashed back out of the room, leaving the other women to scramble after the actress.

They wound through the backstage, the vaudeville sounds still coming from the stage. Paul plucked at his banjo and crooned to a girl in the audience while they clapped along. The women rounded the set table backstage stacked with Western props for *The Sheriff's Folly* to find Henry lying on the floor.

Ben, his ankle wrapped and a crutch under his arm, peered at his friend with concern. Sue cradled her husband's head. He twisted in her arms, mumbling.

Mam dropped down beside Sue. "What happened?"

"I don't know. He came backstage at the end of his scene looking pale and then got dizzy. He fell down and..." She patted his cheek without response. "He seems confused and keeps mumbling."

Mam frowned. "Marie, see if you can locate a doctor in the audience. Anola, find the captain. Sue, stay with him while I tell Stephen we must end the show. Thank goodness it was nearly over."

Voices erupted around them, Sue's wail making any individual words indiscernible. Anola shot a prayer heavenward for Henry and then dashed from the room to follow her mother's instructions. Then Paul's song came to an abrupt halt, and Lady Marie's clear voice called out for a doctor.

Rather than cut through the theater and cause more of a panic, Anola rushed to the ladder behind the green room, climbed to the second floor, and dashed down the upper hallway. She descended the main stairs and scampered to the ticket booth.

The captain exited the room, candy tray hung on his shoulders. "What's happening?"

"Henry is unwell, and Mam says we have to cancel the rest of the show. She sent me after you."

The theater doors opened, and several men exited. She expected them to stop at the booth and demand their money back, but their gazes slid over her and the captain as they filed past.

Anola ushered the captain toward the theater. "Mam said to fetch you."

"I ain't a doctor, lass. Don't know what I can do." Nevertheless, his feet started in that direction.

They wove through the departing crowd, up the steps to the stage, and behind the drawn curtain. Henry still lay on the floor with Sue cradling his head. A man near ninety crouched next to him, peering at Henry through thick spectacles.

The man nodded. "Apoplexy."

Sue paled further, though it hadn't seemed possible. Her skin appeared ghostly against her dark hair. "What can we do?"

The aged doctor spread out venous hands. "In my experience, the body needs to heal on its own. He needs a good bed and lots of rest."

Anola gripped her fingers and shared a look with Mam just as Da joined them. He took in the situation with one glance and a crestfallen expression. He put a gentle hand on Sue's shoulder. "Let's get him moved to your room until you can get a place to stay in Vicksburg."

"Stay?" She blinked rapidly and Da winced. "What do you mean, stay? He'll be fine in a few days—I'm sure of it."

Ben hobbled closer. "My leg's getting better. I'll take his roles for the next shows until Henry gets back on his feet."

Da pressed his lips into a line, and Anola's heart wrenched. She stepped forward and set her shoulders. "We were waiting until after the show to make this announcement, but given the misfortunes continuing to come upon us, now will have to do. We'll be dividing everything we made this evening among you four as well as offering you a stipend for the train fare home."

Confused questions jumbled together, and voices rose. Da crossed to her side and squeezed her hand.

"I had hoped to finish out the season," he said, his voice solemn. "But circumstances outside our control have made it so that will be impossible. We are selling *The River Queen* once we reach New Orleans."

Stunned silence lasted for only a heartbeat before the chorus of voices started up again.

"Enough!" Everyone froze at the captain's shout. "We need to get Henry off the floor and into a room. Then you all can come up to my apartment, and we'll explain."

The statement sent everyone into a flurry, and soon they had fashioned a stretcher from two stilt poles and a sheet. With as little jostling as possible, the able-bodied men got Henry situated. Paul took the end by Henry's head while Da lifted the foot, and they trudged through the curtains and down the steps into the empty theater.

Anola followed the somber procession halfway through the auditorium before a thought struck her.

Where was Emmett?

The night air threatened to choke him. Though in truth, neither the scented breeze nor the thick humidity had anything to do with Emmett's inability to breathe. After leaving the engine room, he walked out to find men who must belong to Mickey's gang strolling in the private areas of both the showboat and steamer.

Three times, he passed crew members trying to direct a fellow off the *Blue Belle*. In each instance, the crew member was refuted with a turn of the subject, feigned confusion, or an abundance of unnecessary questions. He skirted old Tom as he bellowed at a young man a foot taller than he was. The lanky fellow merely smirked with his hands in his pockets. None seemed to be doing anything in particular other than being a nuisance.

Mickey had outsmarted him. This ruse was some kind of distraction.

Think!

Emmett forced the anxiety swirling within him to calm. He checked the moon for an indication of the time, but couldn't tell with the scattering of clouds. But the show couldn't have finished already.

He crossed to *The River Queen* and kept his back to the showboat's flat side. Not that any attempt at stealth would do much good. The Flynns lit this place up like a blazing sun with the generator they used on show nights.

He crouched behind the railing and scanned the shoreline. They were docked just south of Vicksburg, on the city outskirts. Far enough out of town not to be pressed up against other boats jockeying for docking space, but not so far as to be out of the way of paying customers.

Turned out to be a perfect location for whatever the gangsters had in mind, judging by the activity. Finally, he spotted something moving among the shadows.

A skiff separated itself from the shore and snaked along the bank. He kept his back pressed against the wall as the vessel eased around the *Blue Belle*'s stern. Keeping to the shadows as much as possible, he worked his way back the way he'd come.

He made it onto the main deck when Jacob appeared in his path.

"Figured I'd find you slinking around."

Emmett ignored his brother and moved to step around. Jacob blocked him. "I'd only go that way if I'd changed my mind and were planning to help."

He hadn't been planning on anything other than observation and something to report to the authorities. "Get out of my way."

"See, I got a lot riding on this, Joe," Jacob said. "So either you're all in or you're in the way."

Emmett didn't see anyone else in this darker section. The crew must be on the other side of the boat dealing with the men sent to distract them. Yet someone had to be lurking nearby for Jacob to have called him Joe.

When Emmett still didn't answer, Jacob eased closer, his voice lowering. "It's almost done. Best you know as little about it as possible, right?"

Emmett needed to see what was happening. But then, could knowing too much cause him more trouble? He hesitated, then shook his head. "I'm going to see for myself what you are loading on this boat."

Jacob spread his hands. "In for a penny, in for a pound, as they say. Right, Joe?"

"Mother would be ashamed of you." Emmett hadn't meant to say it, but the words sprang free of their own accord and reached out to slap his brother.

Jacob drew back a fraction, a flash of pain in his eyes. But it disappeared as quickly as it had come, and he sneered. "What do you know of my mother, Joe? It's not like you ever saw how she treated me."

What did he mean?

"Hey, Scissors, you got trouble?" A skinny man separated himself from the gloom clinging to the aft deck's far back corner.

"Trouble out of old Weaselly Joe?" Jacob scoffed. "He's a slick one, sure, but he ain't got the guts to cause any actual harm. He just likes to slink around and stick his nose where it isn't wanted."

The other man narrowed his eyes at Emmett, sniffed, and turned his back to address Jacob. "Boss wants to talk to you."

"I'm watching to make sure the cargo's loaded."

"That's what I'm here for." The skinny man spit a stream of amber liquid that splattered on the deck.

Jacob lowered his voice to say something more Emmett couldn't hear, but he wasn't sticking around to find out. He eased away, then hurried off before Jacob could call out. What real reason could he give for not letting Emmett pass if he wanted to continue this ruse?

Only the muted conversations of the flustered crew and the lap of water disturbed the night. Had he missed the loading? Emmett peered over the aft railing but didn't see anything other than the massive paddle wheel.

His mind scrambled for a way to stop them without getting himself killed or putting the others in danger. Where was

Stephen? No doubt Anola's father could disperse the loitering men. With the distractions gone, would one of the crew notice the criminals? Would the thugs act in violence if they were spotted?

Coldness seeped through him. Had something happened to the Flynns? He wouldn't put it past Mickey to—

Muffled scrapes drew his attention to the water. The skiff had tucked itself alongside the paddle wheel. As far as he knew, there weren't any storage areas inside the cavern housing the paddle mechanism. But the space would make a clever hiding spot if they'd managed to create a secret compartment. Something that would have had to have been crafted well before now.

The implications further soured his stomach. No way he could handle this level of corruption on his own, and he had no idea who to trust. There'd be only one way forward. Seeing all he needed to for now, he backed away to find out what had happened to the Flynns.

Stars above, what were all these people doing? Anola whisked her way down *The River Queen*'s upper deck, over the connection planks, and onto the *Blue Belle*'s bow. About halfway toward the stern, she found Billy standing on the boiler deck with his arms crossed and his face reddening as he addressed a man in a suit.

Oh dear. Best she cool whatever situation had unfolded here. She mustered up a sweet smile and stepped up to the two men. "Good evening. Is everything all right?"

Billy's stance loosened, and his arms swung to his sides. "These fellows have been told to get off the *Belle*, but they are being right stubborn about it. I'm about to start chucking men into the water if they refuse to listen to sense."

The suited man stood a few inches taller than she was, well short of Billy. He had combed his brown hair with pomade and donned a lazy smile. But something about his eyes... She'd spent her entire life with actors, and she could tell when mannerisms didn't match the thoughts churning behind the eyes.

She gestured back toward the showboat. "Now, Billy. I'm sure this good fellow has merely gotten lost." She drawled in the sugared tone Lady Marie claimed always made men forget they were angry. "I'll show him back to the ramp down."

Billy shook his head. "No, ma'am. I don't think—"

"A fabulous idea. Thank you." The fellow, who didn't appear much older than Anola, offered her his arm.

Billy's face darkened, and Anola gave him a meaningful look. "You'll keep an eye on us, I'm sure."

The other man didn't seem to care for the statement, but despite what her parents claimed to be a sheltered life, she wasn't a fool. She ignored his proffered arm. "This way, please. We'll gather up some of your lost friends as well." She kept her tone pleasant, but something about the man unsettled her.

He followed, with Billy not far behind. As they passed the dining room door, Emmett's brother stood speaking to a man in a striped suit—a man with a farmer's wide shoulders but a banker's smooth face. She paused.

"Excuse me?"

Both men faced her, Jacob with surprise and the other man with consideration.

"This is the private area for my crew. I'm not sure why so many men are wandering around on this boat, but I'll ask that you please follow me to the exit."

While Jacob cast a nervous glance at the other man, the big fellow smiled. "This is my fault, I fear." He stepped past Jacob and out onto the deck with Anola and the young man still following her. Then he spread his fingers. "I'm so fascinated by these boats, you see, so I had to come have a look. Since I didn't get to finish the show I paid for all my coworkers to see, I figured no one would mind if we took a tour."

Anola hesitated. "Well, sir, I am sorry about the show. We had a medical emergency and couldn't finish the second act. I do hope you understand such things are out of our control." She beckoned toward the steps to the main deck. "If you would kindly follow me, please?"

The man stepped out of the shadowed recess. She let him pass her and stand with the shorter stranger.

Anola called out to Emmett's brother, who stood as still as a possum caught in the lamplight. "Jacob? I'd like you to come too, please."

His eyes widened, and she turned back to the men waiting on the deck in time to see the suited man narrow his eyes at Jacob. They must know one another. A pit formed in her stomach.

What was going on?

The men followed her without protest, and the man in the striped suit called out to the other men meandering around. Every man snapped to his command. Within moments, she'd circled the *Blue Belle*'s upper and lower decks and gathered a strange parade.

Billy strode close enough on her heels to provide comfort, and she was somewhat certain old Tom and at least two other crewmen pushed the procession along from the rear. They crossed back onto *The River Queen*, and she directed them toward the plank at the bow. "Thank you all for attending our show. I am sorry we will be unable to offer you a replacement performance, as we are leaving tomorrow."

The men filed past her without a word, many tugging down bowlers or flat caps as they exited. Fourteen in all. What had so many men been doing wandering around on the boats? And why hadn't she noticed any of them as they'd taken Henry to his cabin?

"Thank you for your hospitality, ma'am." The man in the striped suit stopped and tipped a felt hat he'd donned. She hadn't even noticed him carrying one. "We wish you great speed to New Orleans."

Before she could reply, he sauntered down the ramp.

How had he known where they were heading?

She stood there until the last of them disappeared into the shadows beyond the ramp, tension coiling inside her. What a strange night.

Her grandfather found her still anchored to the deck. "That the last of them?"

When she sidled close to his side, he ran his rough palm down her arm.

"This has been an unusual evening." She sighed. And one filled with too much strangeness to all be coincidental. "Is Henry doing all right?"

"Best we can tell. He's sleeping now, and Sue is staying with him. Your da's gathered the rest of the cast and Tom upstairs to give them the news. Thought you might like to be there."

She rubbed the gooseflesh from her arms. "And Emmett? Have you seen him?"

The captain frowned. "No, lass. Not since before the show."

"I better look for him. I didn't see him when I gathered all those men."

"Stephen probably found him and hauled him to the meeting. Best you look there first."

Perhaps. She took her grandfather's arm, and they turned toward the main staircase. Then she stilled. "Do you think we should go ahead and pull the plank?"

Catching her meaning, he patted her arm and stepped away. "Probably best. I'll go find Billy and some help and then be along shortly."

She climbed the stairs and followed the voices to her grandparents' rooms. She opened the door to a living space stuffed with fidgeting people. Her insides uncoiled as her gaze landed on the man in the corner.

Emmett.

He motioned for her to join him near the porch doors. She pressed close to his side, savoring the wisp of mingled soap and coal. "Where have you been?"

"Dealing with my brother and a bunch of men who shouldn't have been on the steamer."

The concern weighing his voice matched that swimming though her. "Something strange is going on. What were they doing there?"

"Where were you and why was the show over early?"

They spoke at the same time, neither answering the other. Before she could explain, her father spoke up, quieting everyone's anxious buzz.

"Thank you all for coming. I had hoped this evening would go differently, but that has not been the case."

Lady Marie and Mam had spent hours in the kitchen with Cook this morning baking treats that now sat untouched on George Washington's table. Da had wanted to share a second lunch with the cast, explain the financial situation, and offer each cast member their pay. With the show's abrupt end, Henry's condition, and Anola's blurted confession about their finished season, everyone's nerves had frayed. No one seemed much in the mood for the confections Lady Marie had insisted would soothe hurt feelings and sweeten bad news.

Da cleared his throat and put his hands in his pockets. "This season was to be our last on *The River Queen*."

The statement was met with grumbles, and under his breath, Ben muttered that no one had bothered to tell them that when they signed on this year.

"However," Da continued, "it's become necessary because of circumstances beyond our control to hasten my plans for selling *The River Queen* in New Orleans."

Paul shook his head in disgust while Ben scowled at the floor. Only old Tom seemed to accept the statement at face value. He'd pass the news onto the crew.

"So that's it, then?" Ben asked. "You didn't even tell us this was the last show and you planned to boot us off the boat in a random city?"

"After all these years, Flynn"—Paul rubbed the back of his neck—"I expected more of you."

Da flinched as the words bit into him, and Anola's heart pinched. She stepped away from Emmett's side. "I promise you this decision was not made without much heartache, dire necessity, and trying for the best accommodations possible. You all know Da is a fair and loyal man. He wouldn't be doing this unless he had no other choice."

Both actors had the decency to appear sheepish.

"We've evenly divided all the money from tonight's full show between you four," Mam said, moving to stand at her husband's side. "Which came out to be what you would have been able to put in your grouch bag from at least three of the types of nights we've been having lately. We are also providing you with enough for train fare to wherever you need to go next. Return home. Find a new show. The season is still young."

Ben sighed and pushed himself up to standing. "I reckon with my ankle and Henry unwell, we would have been out for a time anyway." He used his crutch and hobbled over to Da and Mam. He stuck out his palm to Da. "It's been good working with you. I'm sorry to hear of your financial troubles and wish you and your family the best."

Tears gathered in her eyes as the two actors said their good-byes to each of the family in turn and then exited the room with promises to pass the information along to Sue. They would also see to it that Henry and Sue were settled in a nice room in Vicksburg until Henry could travel again. Ben would first take Freddie back home to St. Louis before looking to sign on with another troupe.

After they left, old Tom spoke up for the first time. "I'm guessin' I'm here tonight because ya need me to cut some of the fat from the crew?"

"If we can," Da agreed. "There will be less work since we'll push downriver all day and stop only at night. No set up for the show."

The door opened and the captain entered. He headed for his chair and plucked his pipe from the side table. He jammed it between his teeth. "Plank's up and all's shutting down."

On cue, the generator rumbled to a halt, and the electric lights glowing through the windows turned the room from day to night. The lamps Lady Marie had already lit flickered cheerily.

Da and old Tom discussed the crew and what needed to be done while Mam, Lady Marie, and the captain engaged in their own conversation, leaving Anola time with Emmett.

"What aren't you telling me?"

His eyes widened. "What do you mean?"

"Something's going on with your brother. I saw him talking to a dubious fellow in the dining room."

His jaw tightened, and he took an unsteady breath. "My brother has a way of getting himself into trouble. I reminded him he is disembarking here in Vicksburg. He'll be off the boat before we head downriver."

An answer that wasn't quite an answer. Still, she was too exhausted to think about it much more tonight. What she needed now was a warm bed and a quiet time to pray. She squeezed Emmett's hand.

"Good night."

He opened his mouth to say something but must have thought better of it. His shoulders deflated. "Good night, Anola."

She did her best to push the worries from her mind as she headed toward her room. But one thought persisted.

Something wasn't right. And come tomorrow, she'd do everything in her power to uncover the truth.

L eaning over the portside, Emmett clutched *Blue Belle*'s side rail and once more prayed for forgiveness. He'd spent the entirety of yesterday avoiding Anola and her questions, using the excuse of helping pick up the slack with the skeleton crew. He could scarcely take it anymore. The sneaking around. Skirting the truth. His stomach soured.

Grant me wisdom, please, Father.

At least Jacob had kept his word. Emmett hadn't seen hide nor hair of him since they left Vicksburg. They'd reach Natchez this afternoon. He stuffed his hand into his pocket and fingered the paper there. His plan was fragile at best and useless at worst. But if he was going to go through with it, he needed evidence.

Steeling himself, he stalked down the main deck to the stern. Checking to make sure no one followed, he ducked into the room hosting the paddle wheel's mechanism. Powered by the steam belching black smoke from the two smokestacks, the wheel churned through the water and propelled them downriver.

The paddle's steady *chug, chug, chug* reverberated behind the wall. Emmett eased closer to the mechanism to which he couldn't put any names. Two chest-high cogwheels and a series of arms somehow converted the steam in the boiler into motion to spin the wheel. In turn, the wheel caught the water and propelled the steamer forward, pushing the showboat in front of it.

Emmett examined the room and the machine parts. He knew nothing about boats. How ironic his life now centered on one.

Other than the wheel's components and a wall keeping out the churning water, nothing else occupied the space. But he'd seen those men loading something back here. At least, they'd situated the skiff near the wheel. They must have had somewhere they were storing...whatever they'd put on board. Possibly more of the Mexican muggles. But with a group of men who had robbed one of St. Louis's largest banks, who knew?

He ran his hands along the engine room walls, seeking any sort of clue. The men from the skiff had never come on board. So they had to have accessed a hidden door outside. Could he find anything from here? He couldn't swim around the back of the boat once they stopped without someone noticing.

At a shuffling sound, his blood grew cold. The hairs on the back of his neck stood on end. He crept down the wall, inching toward the door.

A familiar deep voice stopped him. "Well, if it ain't Weaselly Joe."

Emmett peered through the pumping mechanism to glimpse the man who'd grabbed him the other day. "Who are you?"

"We never did have any proper introductions, did we?" His dark chuckle mingled with the machine's metallic grind. "Name's Sam."

Sam. Not "Cleaver" or "Fists" or anything ridiculous and unnerving. Though Emmett doubted it was the man's real name any more than Joe was his. "What do you want from me, Sam?"

The shadows across the room shifted. "Not much. Just thought ya could do with a reminder."

Ice settled in his stomach. He hated to ask. "A reminder of what?"

"That I'm here." The calm voice grated on Emmett's nerves. "That I can go anywhere on this vessel at any time and ya'd never know. But so long as there's no trouble from ya and ya do yer part, then there's no trouble from me."

Emmett ground his teeth. "You leave the Flynn family alone. They don't know anything about this."

"And yer goin' to keep it that way, ain't ya, Joe?" Sam laughed, the sound coming from the rear of the room. "You may be the weasel, but I'm the wolf."

What was Emmett going to do now? With this man on board, they were all in danger. Sam would be guarding whatever illegal substances they'd loaded, and Emmett didn't doubt the man would take drastic measures if he suspected anything. No way could Emmett find the items and dump them overboard.

Maybe he should tell Stephen and they could gather the crew. Overpower this gangster and—

"Shakin' in yer boots over there, little weasel?" The voice moved along the wall, accompanied by only the softest scrape of shoes. How did a man so large move so quietly? "Or are ya tryin' to scheme?"

The man made a sucking sound against his teeth. "Probably best if we don't do that. See, my orders are to light the fuse on that dynamite the moment anyone other than me gets near the cargo. So no use in wonderin' if ya can gather up enough of the crew to make a run at me, yeah?"

Dynamite? They would sooner blow up this boat and everyone on it than get caught. What kind of man would be willing to kill himself rather than go to prison?

A mad one. Or desperate.

"Best ya run on now." Sam's smiling voice raked over Emmett's frayed nerves. "Make sure we stay on course. Mickey will be waitin' on us at the docks, and he ain't one who likes to wait."

So Mickey would be there. Ideas churned. Dangerous ones. "I'll get us there," Emmett said. Good. The words came out solid and steady. "But you have to promise to stay away from the Flynns."

"Big words for a weasel. But all right. What say you keep yer nose from snoopin' and yer tongue from waggin' and I'll keep my trigger finger from itchin'. We got a deal?"

What choice did he have? "Deal."

Emmett Carter was going to give her answers whether he wanted to or not. Anola stalked down *The River Queen*'s lower deck and with a leap over the most precarious spot crossed to the *Blue Belle*. The man had been avoiding her. She was sure of it. Question was why?

Jacob had departed in Vicksburg along with the entire cast and most of their crew. The boat seemed empty now, and she itched to leave the ghostly feeling behind. She'd be taking a short trip into Natchez while Da loaded more coal and Mam, Lady Marie, and Cook procured kitchen supplies to get them to New Orleans.

She and Emmett would be traveling to the post office to send word to the buyer in New Orleans, a Mr. Horace Trafford, whom they needed to inform they would be arriving early. And while they were walking, she'd get answers. She rapped on his cabin door, only to find the room empty. He wasn't in the dining room or on the boiler deck.

So help her. If that man—

She spotted him at the stern, overlooking the paddle wheel. She reached him and touched his arm.

Emmett startled and lurched back from the rail. His head swung around, eyes intense. When he noticed her, however, the breath left him. "Anola. You startled me."

Clearly. "What has you as nervous as a worm on a hook?"

He blinked at her. "What?"

"You. I barely touched you, and you nigh on jumped out of the skin God gave you."

Emmett rubbed the back of his neck. "Sorry. I'm only..." He shook his head. "Never mind."

When he sealed his lips in that way men did when they didn't want to say more, she looped her fingers into the crook of his elbow. Women did have their ways of loosening a man's tongue. "I need you to escort me."

He straightened away from the rail. "Where are you going?"

"You and I are going into Natchez to the post office."

"What for?"

"To send a post."

She could see him eyeing her from the corner of her vision, but she adjusted the brim of her straw picture hat and hurried him along.

"Why?"

She steered him onto *The River Queen* so they could disembark from the lowered plank. Since they were near enough to the city's edge, they shouldn't have to walk too far. With the showboat and her steamer, they took up more room than most and couldn't park next to the other riverboats easily.

"Everyone has their errands today. Mine is to let the buyer know we'll be in New Orleans early." She guided him down the plank. "What were you staring at back there?"

"What?" He shaded his eyes from the sun. He'd forgotten his hat. "Oh. Nothing. Just thinking."

"About what?"

He paused. "You."

The warm breeze glided over them, ruffling his hair. The nearby city bustled with activity, but here they stood alone.

"Oh?" She arched an eyebrow. "How so?"

He pursed his lips, and red climbed up his neck.

She swatted him with her gloved fingers. "Were you thinking of kissing me, Mr. Carter?"

"No!" His eyes widened. "I mean, I do think of that, yes, but I wasn't... What I mean to say is..."

Laughing, she turned him to face the hill leading to town. "You do get flustered rather easily. I find it quite charming."

He relaxed as they resumed their stroll. He still didn't seem at ease enough to give her more than the succinct answers a man used when he didn't want to talk. Best loosen his tongue with something mundane first.

"Should we return for your hat?"

His hand rose to touch his hair. Then he shrugged. "It's fine. I've been to town looking worse."

Like how he'd been in that horrible rumpled suit when they'd met. They ascended the riverbank and a steep hill climbing into the city proper. They strolled along before the questions pressing inside her demanded release, loosened tongue or not. "What happened with your brother?"

His arm stiffened under her hand. He was quiet for so long she thought he might not answer. Then he blew out a breath. "As far as I know, he got off the boat like we agreed. We aren't on the best of terms."

"And who was the man he was talking to?"

"What man?"

Why did she get the feeling he was being evasive? "Big man. Shoulders like a farmer, face like a banker. Wore a striped suit."

A hesitation. "I'm not sure of their relationship."

"But they know one another."

"Yes."

She might as well be trying to wrestle a catfish. No matter how she tried to grab the conversation, it slipped every which kind of way. "Something strange is going on, Emmett. I want to know what it is."

223

He grunted. "So do I."

She peered up at him as they walked, his longer legs mounting the hill with greater ease. "Does this have anything to do with the crate of... What did you call it? Muggles?"

"I don't know." He noticed he was practically pulling her along and slowed his pace. "Let's just get to New Orleans, all right? I'm sure everything will work out."

What did getting to New Orleans have to do with anything?

He cleared his throat. "Why did you say we're going to the post office?"

She allowed him to redirect her with an unnecessary question, but she wouldn't skirt his inquiries the way he had hers. Even if she'd already answered this one. "Da needs us to send word down to the buyer in New Orleans, letting him know we'll be arriving early."

"Do you know where, exactly?"

"There's a wharf, I understand. I've never been there. *The River Queen* is hard to miss, however, so the man won't have trouble locating us. But since we will be there several weeks ahead of schedule, we have to send word."

"Who is the buyer?"

Why did such eagerness cling to his question? "Mr. Horace Trafford."

Emmett nodded, expression thoughtful. They continued up the hill and leveled out on a nice area with a bustling street. Automobiles sputtered down the pavement. The smell of the black smoke they emitted hung in the air.

"Do you know where the post office is?" He paused at an intersection.

"Can't be hard to find." She shrugged. "I'm sure anyone could tell us."

Emmett searched the thickening crowd.

"What are you looking for?"

His gaze darted back to her. "The post office."

Anola tugged her arm from his and tapped her foot. "Do not lie to me, Emmett Carter."

His face paled. "I'm worried. I didn't like the look of those men on the boat back in Vicksburg."

"And you think they followed us here? They were odd and more than a little suspicious, I'll grant you, but I doubt those same people would be here as well."

"You're right, of course." He offered his arm and started walking again, but his gaze never stopped bouncing over every face he encountered.

They stopped at a filling station and walked inside. Anola smiled at a young woman she passed, and Emmett approached the clerk. The blonde woman tilted her nose and then smirked at Anola's dress before making a wide berth around her and exiting.

She ran her hand over the bright-yellow skirt. Why had the woman looked at her like that? The yellow paired beautifully with her emerald blouse, and she'd attached green glass gems to the straps of her tan pumps to tie the look together. She'd even worn stockings. Anola dismissed the petty woman. What ills must someone suffer to look down her nose at another woman based on her choice of clothing? Really.

"Thank you." Emmett's voice pulled her attention from where she'd been staring at the door.

The chime rang overhead as they exited. Outside, a man in a pair of coveralls operated the pump to fuel a shiny black automobile. The snooty woman perched on the seat, applying powder to her nose. What would it be like to wear fashionable clothes she or her mother hadn't made themselves and ride around in an expensive vehicle?

"Don't you think?"

"I'm sorry." Anola focused on Emmett. "What did you say?"

"I asked if it was a good idea to hire a vehicle. The post is all the way across town."

"Walking is fine." And cheaper. She glanced back at the automobile and chided herself for it.

They walked for almost an hour, or at least what seemed like one, before arriving at a square brownstone building topped with ornate decorations. People with parcels tucked under their arms bustled in and out of the double front doors. Two light poles flanked the door, the white domes in contrast to the black poles.

Emmett held the door for her. Inside, he surveyed the customers, then leaned down to her ear. "I'll be right back. Send your letter and then stay right here and wait for me."

"Why? Where are you going?"

"I need to do something." He kissed her cheek and spun on his heel before she could say anything more.

Anola fumed.

Impossible man!

E mmett should have known Anola wouldn't wait for him. He scanned the post office once again, then scowled. But he'd better send a message of his own before going to find her. He'd already given the Natchez police as much information as he could. Sending word to Deputy Olsen wouldn't hurt. He pulled the paper from his pocket and went over the notes he'd made with every name and detail he could recall.

Then he procured a paper, pen, and envelope and wrote a letter to send back to the first lawman he'd spoken to, explaining what he understood to be the connections between his brother, the men who had stolen the *Good Tidings*, and the current situation on *The River Queen*.

It had taken a fair amount of convincing to keep the Natchez policemen from boarding *The River Queen*. Maybe the mention of the dynamite and the dangers of it exploding near their town persuaded them to send word down to New Orleans and coordinate a raid instead. Either way, they agreed their best chance of apprehending the most gangsters would be catching them in the act. Even with the dynamite on board—assuming it wasn't an idle threat Sam had used to scare Emmett—he wouldn't put it past Mickey's men to do something to harm them or the boats before they got to New Orleans if a handful of policemen tried to board *Blue Belle* now.

Emmett had considered every possible outcome. Surely the best scenario was to play along and keep everyone safe until the police could secure the boat, commandeer the illegal cargo, and catch the criminals.

If he didn't make sure they went to jail, he and the Flynns might never find peace from men seeking revenge.

Finished with the letter, he stuffed it in the envelope and paid the postage. Then he stepped back out into the warm summer day. Nothing had happened to Anola. She was simply a flighty woman who had become bored waiting on him and had found something interesting to occupy her time.

He continued to attempt to convince himself of that probable truth as he circled the block around the post office three times, but the longer he went without seeing her, the more worry clawed through his chest. Where could she have gone?

He shouldn't have left her. He should have figured out a way to get his message to the police without leaving Anola alone to—

A flash of vibrant yellow snagged his attention, and he veered left, bumping into a man in a straw hat who shook his fist at him. Emmett didn't bother to apologize. His gaze locked onto the feminine figure darting down the road.

He quickened his pace and wove through the crowd. The clomping of hooves and rumble of wagon wheels mingled with the sputter of automobiles as the old and modern worlds collided. Smells of horse manure and black smoke clogged his throat.

Where did she...? There!

With another bright spot of color, Anola reappeared on the street, hands planted on her hips and a scowl on her beautiful face. He broke into a jog. When he reached her, she lifted her eyebrows underneath her wide-brimmed hat.

"What are you doing?"

He gaped at her. "What am *I* doing? I told you to stay in the post office. What are you doing out here?"

She drew back. "Do forgive me. I'm *sure* you had a good reason for telling me to stay in the post office while you ran off to do...well, whatever it was you went to do."

Was she mocking him or...? He opened his mouth to come up with some kind of response, but she continued before he got the chance.

"Which I'm certain was important, whatever it was, even though you didn't tell me where you were going or when you might return." That fiery eyebrow arched again in a now-familiar way. "I was waiting for you to return when I thought I spotted one of the men who was on the boat last night. Since I am still confused over what that was all about, I decided I'd follow him."

Emmett's jaw slackened, and he had to snap his mouth closed. "You saw a criminal and decided to chase him?"

"A criminal? What makes you think he's a criminal?" Something in her tone said she dared him to refute her. "Turns out I was wrong and it wasn't the same man. But how interesting you think a criminal has followed us to Natchez and didn't seem at all surprised I thought I spotted one."

Cornered. How could he answer without lying? He groaned and hung his head, defeat pushing his shoulders down. He could use a little wisdom. How was he going to keep her safe when—?

A vague memory of a verse rose in his mind. Something about how two are better than one because they have a good return for their labor. And if one of them fell, the other could help them up. The last part of the verse came with stark clarity. *Woe to him that is alone when he falleth; for he hath not another to help him up.*

"Well?" Anola tapped her foot.

He winced. Every instinct told him to protect her and her family at all costs. But he'd been praying for wisdom, and perhaps this was a little of what James had been talking about in chapter three when he'd spoken about the difference between earthly and heavenly wisdom.

Emmett squeezed his eyes shut, and when he opened them again, he found Anola studying him. He pinched his lips together, then forced the words free. "I think God wants me to tell you everything. But it's dangerous, and you can't let anyone know you know."

She sucked in a quick breath, but the surprise vanished. She gave a firm nod. "If I am to be your wife, then I am to be your partner. Your danger is mine as well. Besides, two working at a problem together are better than one."

Something warm expanded in his chest. Before he could dwell on the anxiety and elation swirling inside him like a tempest, Anola snagged his hand and beckoned him into a tiny restaurant. Sunlight bathed a two-person table beneath the wide window, the room mostly empty this time of the afternoon. Good. They'd have semiprivacy.

A young woman with bobbed hair and a pleasant smile came to take their order, and he requested two slices of whatever pie they were serving today and two cups of coffee.

"Start at the beginning. You knew who all those men on the boat were, didn't you?" Anola leaned across the table, her eyes shining. This woman would take on trouble with the determination of a lawman and the experience of an infant.

Are you sure about this...?

Right. Heavenly wisdom. He clasped her hand. Lowering his voice, he started with what he'd discovered at the Blind Bat in Memphis.

Anola listened with rapt attention. He thanked the waitress when she returned with chocolate pie and coffee. Then he nodded to Anola to eat and sipped the hot brew before resuming the story. By the time he reached the part about the cargo, Sam, and the dynamite, her face blazed almost as red as her hair.

"He said *what?*" She lurched back from her chair. "I have to warn everyone. I have to—"

"Anola."

At the harsh whisper of her name, she dropped back into her seat. She shoved her half-eaten pie away. "Why didn't you tell someone? How could you have stood there and watched them load dangerous things onto my boat, things that could mean death for all of us, and do nothing about it?"

The words knifed through him. For all he'd told himself he kept secrets to protect them—and in many ways, he did—another truth had grown alongside it. He'd been unable to stop them, and admitting defeat to the woman he loved and having her look at him as she did now burned like fire.

"I didn't know." The quiet words wavered between them.

Her face softened. "I'm sure you would have done anything you could to stop them if you thought it would do any good. You were trying to protect us."

Her easy forgiveness clenched his heart. What had he ever done to find favor with a woman like this?

She tapped a finger on her chin, his failures dismissed as she moved on to the next part of the discussion. "But what are we going to do now? We can't travel all the way to New Orleans knowing we might erupt in flames at any moment."

Emmett tugged at his collar. "I do have a plan."

Now her eyes twinkled. "Of course you do. You are the smartest man I've ever met."

Her faith in him nudged out a fraction of the pain at having failed her. He would do everything in his power to live up to that faith. "I left you at the post office to go to the police station. I told them everything, including where we are going, the fact that Mickey was going to be there to unload their cargo, and what to expect about Sam. They are sending word through their connections to New Orleans."

She slid her lower lip between her teeth. "That's a pretty good plan. We can catch them in the act."

"I also sent word back up to the deputy I'd reported the stolen steamer to. I'm not sure how they are connected, but I gave him all the information I had. I did confirm his suspicions about the Durkin gang."

"So all we need to do is pretend nothing is wrong until we get to New Orleans, where a swarm of lawmen will arrive to arrest these gangsters before they can destroy our boat and murder us all." Anola flashed a smile even as he felt the blood drain from his face. "Good thing I'm an experienced actress. You did well telling me."

Despite his determination to believe otherwise, he wasn't quite so sure.

How did she do it? Anola reigned over the bow of *The River Queen*, the name more fit for her than any vessel could do justice. Her glorious hair hung down her back and danced in the wind. She tilted her face to the sun and smiled.

How could she be so content when his stomach did flips and his nerves felt frayed to breaking? Emmett stepped closer, unable to contain the question. "Is this part of your acting you mentioned?"

She opened her eyes and favored him with her sparkling gaze. "Is what part of my acting?" When he gestured up and down to indicate all of her, she frowned. "My clothes? What's wrong with my clothes?"

In her gypsy skirt and white blouse, a headband of paste gems across her temples, she looked different from any other woman, but the outfit suited her. "Not that. Your clothes are fit for a vibrant woman. I mean *you*. You seem content while I can't keep my stomach from trying to climb up in my throat."

"I've learned the secret of being content in any and every situation, whether well fed or hungry, whether living in plenty or in want."

What did...? Realization came. "Are you quoting Paul in Philippians?"

"Very good. Then you know the secret as well." She turned back to the water, the morning light gleaming off the churning surface.

I can do all this through him who gives me strength.

Yes, well, he knew that. His mother had taught him the same verses. Trouble was, he couldn't apply them in the way Anola could. "Aren't you worried about..." He motioned behind them. "All that?"

"Take therefore no thought for the morrow: for the morrow shall take thought for the things of itself. Sufficient unto the day is the evil thereof."

The "evil thereof" was the problem. He stood with her against the rail and closed his eyes, listening to the call of birds, the lap of water, the chug of the boats they passed, and the soft and soulful tune hummed by the beautiful soul next to him. Peace still eluded him. There were too many things to contend for. Too many worries to carry, too many decisions to make. Decisions that could prove fatal if he chose poorly.

"Cast all your cares on him, for he cares for you."

Emmett peeked at her from the corner of his eye, finding her peaceful face smiling again. "Do you have a Bible verse for everything?" Apparently even thoughts he hadn't voiced?

She beamed, either not noticing or not caring about his disgruntled tone. "I hope so. That's what they are there for, after all."

The statement landed like a punch to his sternum, and he had to reach up and rub the ache in his chest. How long had it been since he'd spent any time studying the Word? His prayers had become little more than half-hearted cries for help that, if he were being honest, he didn't expect to be answered. Especially given his lack of truthfulness during this entire debacle. The verses that had come to mind yesterday had been the closest he'd felt to his neglected faith in some time.

He wrapped his arm around her shoulders. "I'm thankful for you, Anola Flynn. You are a blessing."

She snuggled against him. "I'm glad to hear you say so. I have a plan."

Unease fought against the first ray of peace he'd been able to find. "What do you mean? We already *have* a plan."

"Well, yes, but out here on the water, we are on our own. If we gather up all of the men on board, we can—" Her words cut off when Emmett leaned forward against the rail. "What? What is it?"

He pointed ahead to a steamboat anchored along the shoreline. "That boat."

She followed his gaze to a steamer similar to the *Blue Belle*. "What about it?"

"Look there. At the side. Do you see any red lettering showing through the paint?"

Anola looked closer. "I see...yes! I do. I see a *G*...and an *O*. There, under that. More. Looks like...an *I* and a *D*, and then...another *G*."

His pulse spiked. "I think that's the *Good Tidings*. They painted over it. That's why no one has noticed it."

"Your boat that was stolen the night we met?"

That felt like years ago now. "Right." His grip tightened on the rail. Where were they, exactly? He'd need to report the sighting to Deputy Olsen the moment they reached the nearest town.

Anola made a strange little noise and darted away.

"Wait!" What was she doing?

She didn't stop, leaving him no choice but to dash after her.

Anola snatched her skirts when they tried to tangle around her legs and hauled the fabric up over her knees. She'd scaled *The*

235

River Queen's top ladder and dashed across the roof to Da's domain.

He spun around when she lurched inside. "What's wrong?"

She panted and pointed at the boat they were now close to passing. "That's Emmett's boat!"

He frowned at the steamer. "That packet boat there, that's the stolen one?"

"Yes. We need to stop." When he hesitated, she pointed with more insistence. "It's right there!"

"I see it, but what are we going to do about a stolen boat? Steal it back?"

The words hung between them as Emmett hurried inside. "What's happening?"

"I'm trying to get Da to stop." She reached around him to grab the chain to the whistle, but Da caught her hand.

"We can't do that."

"That's not a good idea."

Both men spoke at once, and both with equal alarm. Anola stilled. "But it's right there."

Da and Emmett exchanged a look, and Emmett's expression seemed to say her father should be the one to speak.

"The men who stole the boat are dangerous, lass. We can't go marching over there and demand they give it back. That kind of thing is for the law."

She dropped her hand. He was right, of course. Still, what a waste to let it sit *right there*. Something Emmett had said surfaced, and she shot her gaze to him.

An almost imperceptible shake of his head.

Hmm. She pressed her lips together. "Da, can we at least stop at the next town and report the boat?"

"There aren't any major towns until we reach Louisiana. Baton Rouge is still about another hundred miles out."

"Then we need to stop at a small one. Surely someone can send word down the wire even if they don't have a telephone."

Da and Emmett shared a conversation of looks. How did they do that? Was it a language all men instinctively knew?

Emmett nodded. "I do need to make a report. However we can do so."

They decided to make a stop at the first town they saw along the river's edge. This was the first time Anola had traveled so far south on the lower Mississippi. They usually only traveled to Natchez and then back up the other side of the river on the return trip to finish their season, often staying for days at a time in the larger towns.

As they neared the smaller vessel, a man emerged on the deck. He looked up at the showboat. At this distance, she could make out his rumpled blue shirt and a flat cap tugged over long blond hair. He craned his head, then threw up his hands, and raised a shout, pointing at the boat.

She couldn't distinguish his words from here, but the urgency was plenty clear. Four more men appeared, their conversation animated.

Seemed they recognized *The River Queen*, and perhaps had even identified Emmett. She couldn't help but smirk. Maybe they knew their ruse had failed and justice would soon be at hand.

29

This was madness. She knew it to be true, but Anola couldn't help herself. She took another step toward the shoreline and moved behind an oak. Her heart beat furiously. About two hours after spotting Emmett's steamer, they'd stopped a few miles downriver at a town that barely had a post office, much less anyone who would be of much help confronting a band of river pirates.

Anola moved to the next oak, her steps quiet. Despite the colorfulness of her outfit, she did her best to blend in with the undergrowth and shadows. Da and Emmett had sent her back to the boat while they tried to send word to the local lawman.

She'd done as they'd asked. Then she'd noticed the stolen steamer tucked along the curve of the bank not far behind the *Blue Belle*. Had the men followed them, or were they making the same stop? With this type, unlikely. She needed to find out what they were up to.

Voices came from ahead, and she sneaked closer. All she needed was to gather information for Emmett. See if she could learn anything useful. Then she'd hightail it back to *The River Queen* before anyone knew.

A little closer, and the voices became distinct enough to make out words.

"Should...find..."

"...no, that's not...pay for..."

She wouldn't learn anything like this. The closer she got to the shore, the more the underbrush thinned. She crouched low and scuttled to the next tree, concealed behind a prickly bush tangled around the trunk.

"I'm tellin' you. It was him." A man's voice rose to almost a shout.

"How would you know? You barely saw him before you tossed him overboard."

"Got closer than you."

Anola sucked in a breath. Were they talking about Emmett?

"I think he's right." Another man's voice joined the first two. "I've heard descriptions of Scissors, and he matches the bill. Didn't see much of him on either occasion, but I saw enough to agree with Jerry."

The voices started to move away, and Anola missed pieces again. Something about stealing...and... She strained to hear. Revenge? Her heart sputtered. Who was Scissors? What kind of a name was that, anyway? They couldn't be talking about Emmett.

She eased away from the tree. Whatever they were talking about, it wasn't good, and she needed to let her family know. They'd followed them and stopped here for a reason.

A bird let out a squawk and flew from the branches overhead, and her heart flipped. She placed a hand over it and drew a breath, chiding herself for being jumpy. She should get out of here before she did something silly like scream at a squirrel. Still crouching low, she worked her way up the bank, keeping to the trees and bushes.

Behind her, something clicked. She paused, her mind scrambling to place where the noise could have come from.

"You stop right there." A deep voice sounded behind her.

Anola dove for the ground and scrambled forward. A shout, followed by the crack of gunfire. Wind shot past the side of her head.

He was shooting at her!

She gained her feet and lunged into a run. Something smashed into her from behind and sent her flying forward. She hit the ground with a weight on her back, and all the air left her lungs. Her vision swam.

Sucking in gasps of air and dirt, she tried to gather enough in her lungs to scream. A sweaty hand clamped over her mouth, robbing her of breath again. She struggled as the man hauled her to her feet and pressed her against a wide chest. One hairy arm held tight around her middle with the other across her shoulders and his hand on her mouth.

"I don't want to kill you, girl. But I will if I have to." His voice came low, right next to her ear. "I'm going to let you breathe. But you scream, and I'll snap your neck."

Her vision began to fade.

"Understand?"

She managed a weak nod. His fingers eased away from her face. She drew air as quickly as she could, remaining still against the man, even though every instinct demanded she fight and flee. First, she had to breathe.

Once her vision cleared and her lungs eased their heaving, the man spoke again.

"I'm going to ask questions. You nod or give soft, short answers."

Anola swallowed against the grit in her throat.

"You come from the fancy showboat?"

A slow nod. What good would it do to lie?

"Does a man on board with you go by the name of Scissors?"

She shook her head.

"Hmm. Probably wouldn't have told you that." He shifted her, and a little of the pressure released from around her waist. "Did a man show up on your boat claiming to have been thrown overboard?"

They were looking for Emmett. But why? And who was Scissors?

His grip tightened again. "Did he?"

Anola clamped her lips shut. What were they planning to do to Emmett?

The man lifted his arms, pulling her body tighter against him and raising her feet off the ground. "I thought so."

She kicked her feet. He clamped his hand over her mouth again, barely leaving room under her nose for air.

"You're coming with me until we get your man's debts settled."

Her man? Did he mean Emmett? What debts? She fought against him. But his size and strength proved more than she could hope to counter, and he hauled her down the bank and to the stolen steamboat.

Another man appeared on the deck. He shot out a series of curses as the brute carried her on board. She kicked and screamed against the moist palm over her face.

She had to get free!

A door opened to a black maw of despair, and she was tossed inside.

Emmett stuffed his hands in his pockets and sent a prayer heavenward. They needed help. They'd left word with the postmaster to send the information about the *Good Tidings* to Deputy Olsen and a note to the police in Natchez about the latest development. Stephen had thought it best for Anola to return to the boat after he'd noticed her following them. She'd sputtered and shot Emmett a fierce look when he didn't speak against her father, but she'd yielded and stomped back to the boat.

Now came the hardest part.

"Mr. Flynn?"

The older man glanced back at Emmett as they made their way out of the town and to the riverbank.

"I need to tell you something important before we get back on the boat."

Stephen stopped at the graveness in Emmett's tone. "Does this have something to do with that boat that you haven't told me?"

He cringed. "Partly, yes. My brother was working with some kind of crew that robbed a bank in St. Louis. They used the *Good Tidings* to get their loot out of the city. He tricked me into going so, if we got caught, I wouldn't know anything about it and would present the false paperwork thinking it was legitimate."

Stephen narrowed his eyes. "And when did you discover this?"

"The first part I learned in Memphis when I found my brother and realized he'd gotten tangled up with a gangster ring. The rest he told me while he was on the boat."

"And you didn't know anything about it?"

"No, sir." Emmett straightened and held the man's probing gaze.

A few tense heartbeats later, the rigid lines around his mouth eased. "Thank you for telling me. It's not your fault your brother took advantage of you."

How desperately Emmett wanted to leave it at that. "But there is more that is my fault, sir." The words scraped out of him, each one wanting to stick in his throat. "Those same men came on board in Vicksburg."

Deep creases formed between Stephen's brows. "The men who stole your brother's boat or the ones he was working with?"

"The ones he was working with." Sweat broke out on Emmett's neck. He rubbed it away. "They were there to cause a distraction so others could load cargo onto the *Blue Belle*."

"What? You allowed men to put illegal cargo onto my boat? What is it? More of that opium plant? Why? Are you using us?"

Each question landed like a blow.

"No, sir." He forced himself not to withdraw from the fury in the other man's gaze.

"They threatened the safety of your family. Anola. I was trying to..." He let the excuse dissolve. "I should have told you sooner instead of trying to handle everything on my own."

Stephen's eyes softened, though his jaw remained hard.

Emmett swallowed against the grit in his throat. "It gets worse. I went looking for the cargo so I could create a report to take to the law. There's..." He forced the words out. "There's a man hiding on board who claims to have dynamite. He said that, if I spoke a word to anyone or anyone came looking for their loot, he'd blow both boats and everyone on them."

Stephen paled. "He's been there since Vicksburg? How is that even possible?"

"He's hiding in the hull, if I were to guess. The cargo is supposed to go with us to New Orleans."

Stephen's fists clenched, and he marched toward the shoreline, muttering something Emmett couldn't hear.

"I've spoken to the law in Natchez!" Emmett called after him. He quickened his steps to keep up. "The plan is to have officers waiting for us when we get there. They are going to catch the crew in the act so they can all go to jail. Otherwise, I fear we'll never have peace."

Stephen whirled on him. "And what does this have to do with you and your brother's boat?"

"I'm not sure, but I think a rival gang stole the boat my brother used to haul the bank cargo. This load is how he is making up for it. He said if I didn't go along they'd kill us both." Emmett shook his head. "I shouldn't have listened to him. If I had acted sooner, things would be different."

Stephen grunted. Then, surprisingly, he clapped a hand on his shoulder. "We have a mess to deal with, son. And you've gone and made it worse by not being forthright. If you're going to be a part of this family, that kind of thing can't happen again."

The air left his lungs. Stephen would still consider letting him be a part of the family? After all he'd done? Emotion clogged his throat. "Thank you, sir. I—"

A loud crack fired through the air.

"Was that gunfire?"

Before Stephen had finished the question, Emmett started running toward *The River Queen*. Only one thing filled his mind.

Anola.

He raced up the plank, Stephen on his heels, and onto *The River Queen* to find the decks empty. He *had* heard a gunshot. So where?

The *Blue Belle*!

They ran for the tug.

The crew milled about doing their usual chores. Emmett spotted someone on the boiler deck and shouted up to him. "Billy!"

The man leaned over the rail as Emmett and Stephen crossed onto the lower main deck. He met them at the top of the stairs.

"What's wrong?"

"Did you hear a gunshot?" Stephen demanded.

"Where's Anola?" Both men looked at Emmett then, her father's face hardening and Billy's eyes widening.

"Haven't seen her." Billy scratched at his disheveled hair. "Didn't hear a shot. Nothing's been going on here."

Stephen gestured to Emmett. "You find Anola and the rest of the family. Meet me in the theater. I'm gathering the crew, and we are going to handle this problem."

Emmett didn't dare argue. They had to take the chance and overpower Sam. Traveling as far as they had with that danger had been reckless and stupid. How had he convinced himself keeping such a secret would be helpful?

He spun on his heel and hurried back down the steps and across to the showboat. He found the captain on the bow, pipe clenched between his teeth. He glanced at Emmett as he sprinted toward him. He pointed with his pipe. "Heard gunfire from that boat there."

Boat? Emmett looked to the water, and his chest seized. "That's the *Good Tidings*. I'd thought maybe they recognized me, but then I figured they would run, not come after us."

"What are you talking about, lad?"

He'd know soon enough. "That's my boat that was stolen. Turns out my brother used it to haul a bunch of things they robbed from a bank in St. Louis and a rival gang caught me and tossed me overboard. That's how I ended up here."

The captain let out a low whistle. "My son know about this?"

"He does now." Emmett jabbed a hand through his hair. "There's more to tell, but it has to wait. Stephen told me to gather the family in the theater. He's bringing the crew. There's something we need to do." He glanced around the deck. "Have you seen Anola?"

The other man's gaze clouded. "I thought she was with you."

A nola huddled in a corner and tried not to breathe too much through her nose. The place smelled of sour sweat, oil, and something else she couldn't identify as anything other than foul. But at least she was alone and unbound.

She'd played the part of Miss Mattie Lou quite well. Mattie Lou was a shy and quiet girl she'd portrayed during her sixteen-year-old season when they'd performed *Lady in the Ozarks*. Mattie Lou was the first real "adult" role Lady Marie had given her, and Anola had been determined to do it well. Too bad Mattie Lou had been such a mousy girl. Anola had struggled getting into her character. But that work paid off now.

Pretending to be cowed, terrified, and unwilling to do anything other than huddle in the corner of this—storage space?—and covering her eyes had convinced the men to shut her in here and leave her in peace to plot an escape. Well, if she was being honest, not all of it had been an act. She had been rather scared out of her wits. But she'd kept enough of them to play the part and give herself room to think of an escape.

The men's voices came from outside the door, muffled to the point she couldn't understand anything. It didn't matter. These were bad men who thought Emmett was some fellow who went by the ridiculous name Scissors and had somehow duped them.

How, exactly, seeing as they were the ones who hijacked his boat and tossed him in the river, she had no clue. Not that she would be staying to find out. Satisfied they wouldn't be bothering her anytime soon, she rose from her corner and eased through stacks of junk. Looked like they'd stashed her in a compartment near the engine room.

Likely, these were the only two rooms on the main deck, the majority of the space having been left open for cargo. Most of the regular rooms would be on the upper deck, so she'd have limited space to work with. She slunk to the opposite wall around stacked crates and piles of discarded burlap. With the room so stuffed, she had to turn sideways to squeeze between boxes. A seam of light came from beyond a particularly tall and rather precarious pile of burlap and stacked crates.

Anola grinned. A window.

She had just enough room to squeeze past the crates to the window, but they'd have to be moved if she had any hope of exiting this way. On her tiptoes, she leaned over the crate blocking the windowsill. Using her forearm, she judged the width of the rectangular opening. It would be a tight fit for her shoulders, but doable. As long as no one stood on the port deck, she should be able to scurry outside. First, she had to make more room. She crouched, gripped the bottom of the crate, then used her legs to scoot it forward. The boxes groaned and scraped, making a terrible racket.

Oh dear.

Anola dashed back to her corner and tucked herself into a ball on the floor. An instant later, the door banged open, and light flooded over her. She whimpered and put her arm over her head. She didn't dare peek out. Whoever stood there waited, probably looking around the room, and then closed the door.

She let out a long breath. That had been close. She waited another few heartbeats and then returned to the window. She paused with her fingers on the latch. If it made another racket, they would catch on. "Father, please make them confused like you did for Gideon or strike them with blindness like you did for Elisha. Deaf ears would be good too, if you're willing."

That should do it. She pressed the window open, and it swung outward with silent hinges. *Thank you, Lord.* She stuck her head outside. No one on the port deck. They must all be above or on the other side, discussing the woman they'd captured.

She smirked. One last thing to do. She shimmied out of her gypsy skirt and rolled it into a coil, then tied it like a rope around her waist, leaving only the knee-length bottom of her chemise to tangle her legs. She couldn't swim in the long layers of the skirt, but she wasn't leaving it behind. She yanked the headband from around her temples and looped it over her wrist. Her fingers flew through a quick braid, and then she tied the length of her hair in a knot at her nape and secured it with the band. She lost a few of her gems, but they could be replaced. Better she not have hair tangling around her neck and face.

She gave one last glance around the room, then shucked her shoes. A shame to lose them, but they'd be too much trouble to take. After a moment of thought, the stockings went too. She lifted herself onto the window and then twisted around to check the length of the deck.

Voices still came from the starboard side, animated and gaining steam. Another prayer answered. God clearly had no intention of leaving her with these men.

She wriggled and forced her hips through the window and thudded to the deck. Without pausing to see if anyone noticed, she launched over the rail. She tucked her feet tight and curled herself into a ball.

She splashed into the water.

Not deep this close to shore, her toes sank into muddy silt, and she kicked herself to the surface. She sucked in a breath, caught her bearings, then ducked beneath the water, and propelled herself forward. She skimmed along with her eyes squeezed tight and her hands outstretched until her lungs began to burn. Then she surfaced again.

She emerged about fifty feet from the stolen boat. Treading in the river's deeper section, she wiped water from her eyes. Shouts came from behind her, and she dared a glance back to see the men pointing and yelling. They would never be able to catch her now.

Anola gave them a little wave, then kicked her legs, and let the Mighty Mississippi carry her downriver.

This was all his fault. Emmett paced the back of the theater, his insides on fire. Why hadn't he walked with Anola back to the boat? Or insisted she stay with them? He'd done a hundred things wrong from the moment he found his brother in the Blind Bat, and every one of them had brought them to this point.

Anola missing.

They'd searched every inch of the boats and hadn't found her anywhere. Now Stephen was gathering the crew and instructing them about going out in teams of two for search parties. Only old Tom and the captain had pistols. The rest of them would be going out armed with whatever they could find. Billy had strapped a sword to his side that appeared as sharp as a wooden block and likely came from the prop table.

"Billy," Stephen said from his place on the stage where he directed the search operation. "You stay near the engine room. I want your eyes watching for trouble."

The fellow tilted his head, then nodded. "Yes, sir."

They'd deal with telling everyone about Sam once they found Anola. Stephen paired the rest of the men and instructed his wife and mother to stay on the deck and watch the shoreline. Emmett flexed his tingling fingers. Had the early stop and their search for Anola alerted Sam something was amiss? Would he come out of hiding? Be on alert?

Questions pulsed through him, all without answers and out of his control. Stephen finished whatever instructions Emmett had been too distracted to hear and sent the men out.

He could only pray no one would find her shot somewhere.

Paired with the captain, Emmett stalked from the theater and onto the deck, his mind intent on one purpose. No matter where she was, he would find her. No matter what had happened, he would... He didn't know. He felt so out of control. Helpless.

No, there was something he could do. Something Anola had reminded him held great importance.

Help me, Lord. Please. Give me your wisdom and help me find her. Protect her, Father. We are all in your hands.

He blew out a breath and started toward the plank, and some of the weight eased from his shoulders. He had a lot to ask forgiveness for and a lot of consequences to handle, but he didn't have to face them alone. God was always with him, and he'd even given him people to stand at his side.

Emmett's boots hit the plank when shouts rose behind him. The captain pointed to something in the water. Emmett narrowed his eyes.

Was that...?

Before he could even finish the thought, Emmett raced to the bow and leapt from the railing. He hit the water feet first and pushed with all of his might toward the spot of red coming their way.

He swam for about twenty feet before he reached her. "Anola!"

She paused in the powerful stroke propelling her through the water and righted herself. She grinned. "Emmett! You're safe!"

He was safe? He closed the distance between them to gather her In his arms. He kissed the top of her head, her forehead, her temples. "I thought we lost you."

She clung to him and rested her head on his shoulder, their bodies bobbing in the water and drifting toward the showboat. "I'm sorry. I shouldn't have gone over there. I only wanted to get information."

"Gone where?"

"To your boat." She grimaced. "It wasn't wise of me, I know."

He clutched her tighter against him. His questions could wait. First, he needed to get her to safety. "We need to get you out of the water." He tried to swim with her in tow but only succeeded in making it difficult for the both of them.

"I do thank you for your help and your concern, dear Emmett, but it would be best if you let me swim on my own."

She was right, of course, and he released her. He gestured for her to go first, and she cut through the water like she'd been born to it. In a way, she had. He watched her before following.

What had happened to her shoes?

They reached the shore near the showboat, and she scrambled through the mud to the bank.

Was she...? He looked away before he could see too much of her bare legs and the thin wet fabric clinging high above her knees. Heat poured through him. If any of those men had hurt her—

He cut the thought short and focused on climbing out of the river. He could remove his shirt and give her something to cover herself with. A flash of bright fabric drew his attention and he couldn't help but glance at her.

Anola shook the water from her long gypsy skirt, swung it out, and wrapped it around her waist.

She caught him watching and winked. "Hard to swim in a thing like that, but hardly proper to walk around soaking wet without it."

Voices swarmed, and Emmett finally noticed something other than Anola. Her parents and grandmother rushed toward her, crushing her in their arms. The crew gathered in a circle around them, the conversation too jumbled to have any meaning.

The captain swiped his hat and placed it over his heart. "Answered prayers, aye, lad?"

Gratitude swelled in Emmett's center.

"She's a smart one, our gem. Can't wait to hear the story she has to tell about this adventure."

There were plenty of things to tell, and none of them would do much for his reputation with the Flynn family. When the Flynns and their crew hurried back up the plank and onto the showboat, Emmett trailed them. He didn't deserve this family. And they didn't need him causing trouble.

He tried to push the thoughts aside, but they persisted. He could only think of one thing to do.

"Help me to make it right," he prayed.

31

Anola worked her fingers through her damp braid as the family gathered on *The River Queen*'s main deck.

"This does complicate things," Da said, his frown deep enough to droop his mustache.

"They seem to think Emmett is some fellow named Scissors." She flipped the braid over her shoulder and adjusted the blanket Lady Marie insisted she needed. A few towels would have been better, but she could change later.

Emmett groaned. "That's what they call my brother."

Her mother and grandparents' expressions all held confusion, but Da's face held only resignation.

When Emmett's gaze landed on her—it never strayed far, something that warmed her insides—she gave him another encouraging smile, hoping he could see how proud she was of him.

"Your father knows," he'd whispered as they boarded the vessel.

Thank goodness. Telling her father everything couldn't have been easy for him. Now they needed to hold a family meeting and let everyone else know about the dangers.

"We need to pull out," the captain said around his pipe stem. "If these men took her and think Emmett is..." He plucked the pipe from between his lips. "Whatever kind of trouble his brother was in, it looks like they're trying to bring it here. Best we put distance between us."

"From what I understand," Emmett supplied, "Jacob was moving stolen cargo for a man named Mickey when the Durkin gang stole the *Good Tidings*. Something I was not aware of at the time."

"And they think you are him." Anola wrinkled her nose. "Who has a name like Scissors, anyway? Why would they call him that?"

Emmett's lips pinched. "I don't think I want to know."

Perhaps she didn't either.

Da turned her toward the stairs. "We need to get moving." He addressed her mother. "Take care of her while I get us back into the water."

Mam put a hand to her throat, her weighted features making her look older than Anola ever remembered. "But what if they follow us?"

Emmett's head dropped. "This is all my fault. I was trying to keep everyone safe and ended up putting you all in danger instead."

"There's an old Irish saying, lad." Da rolled the sleeve of his linen shirt up to his elbows, his fingers steady. "'A loud voice can make even the truth sound foolish.' You did what you thought you had to with the threats they used. At the heart, you wanted to protect us."

Emmett's mouth screwed tight, and Anola's heart went out to him.

"But there's another saying too," Lady Marie announced. "'Truth speaks even if the tongue is dead.' What else is going on here you two aren't telling us?"

Before Emmett could confess, Da held up his hand. "Later. We'll go over everything tonight after we get away from these men." His gaze leveled on Emmett. "There's much to discuss, and family always trusts one another enough to share the truth."

The single downward jerk of Emmett's chin indicated a determined commitment Da seemed to accept.

"Come with me." Da directed Emmett to the pilothouse.

He cast a look over his shoulder at her, the pain in his gaze cinching her heart. She sent him as much of her encouragement with her eyes as she could. She wanted to whisper that it would be all right. That she loved him. But the words stuck in her throat. A second later, he turned away, and they were gone.

The captain announced he would be watching over the crew and exited, leaving the women alone. As soon as they entered Anola's room and the door closed behind them, Lady Marie collapsed into Anola's dressing chair and fanned her face. "This has been more excitement than I've seen in all my years. We should write a play about this."

Mam rolled her eyes. "I hardly think our situation is exciting. Harrowing, more like." She moved to put her arm around Anola. "Are you all right? You can speak freely now that the men are gone."

Tension slid out of Anola's limbs like an eel from a weir. "I'm sore from where that man grabbed me and hauled me down to the boat, and I was frightened. But God had mercy on me, and I was able to get away before they had me even half an hour. If I'd stayed too long, I fear what they may have done."

"A blessing, to be sure." Lady Marie straightened the brush and perfume bottles on Anola's dressing table, arranging them in a line by the mirror.

Mam opened Anola's wardrobe and removed a simple skirt and blouse. "Let's get you into something warm."

Anola set aside the damp blanket and peeled off her wet clothing, leaving it in a pile that would need to hang on the railing to dry. But that could wait.

The boat lurched.

Lady Marie looked around as though she could see any-thing through the walls. "My heavens. That was a rough start. Stephen must be in a mighty rush."

"Can you blame him?" Mam shifted her weight and steadied herself as the showboat pushed deeper into the river.

From the window beyond her bed, Anola watched the shore-line slip by. The *Blue Belle*'s shrill whistle cut through the air.

If the men who had taken her didn't know they were leaving, they did now.

Mam moved to the window, and Anola put a hand on her shoulder. The burden to share all she knew about the depth of their dangers weighed on her.

But should she say something or wait until Emmett could speak for himself?

The hesitation lasted only a moment. No more secrets. "You need to know something else."

She started at the beginning, telling them everything Emmett had shared.

"Did you hear that?" Emmett looked out the pilothouse's rear windows. "I think I heard a gunshot."

Stephen grimaced and tugged on the whistle chain in a series of long and short bursts. A response series sounded from behind. Old Tom stood in the pilothouse between the *Blue Belle*'s billowing smokestacks. The boats lurched forward, moving faster downriver. Emmett put a hand on the wall to steady himself.

"Are you sure?"

The wind rushed through the open window, something he'd learned boat captains did so no distortion in the glass obstructed their view of the ever-changing river. The air buffed his face.

Along with the drone of an engine set at full steam, he could understand Stephen's doubt.

"I think so."

He turned the wheel. "Get down there and see about it, lad. I'm a mite busy here."

Emmett scrambled out of the pilothouse and across the flat roof. He hurried down the ladder to the *Blue Belle*, where he found Billy stationed outside of the engine room. Did he know about Sam, or had Stephen kept that a secret until they'd made a plan to oust him?

"Billy! Did you hear that?" Emmett skidded to a stop. "A gunshot?"

"Came from behind us. George said he saw a steamer coming in close. Best we can figure, a fight must have broken out and one of them shot." Billy thrust his chin behind them. "Would go and have a look, but Mr. Flynn insists I stay right here."

"I'll go." Emmett ran back to the bow and up the narrow steps to the boiler deck. He took the corridor between the staterooms at a jog, passing by the galley and dining room before coming out at the stern. He paused at the rail over the churning paddle wheel. Tingles scalded down the back of his neck. A smaller vessel moved behind them. Were they really following him in the boat they stole from him? Why? What would they do if they caught up?

No reason he could fathom sounded good. According to Anola, they thought he was his brother. And if they were coming after Jacob, then something must have happened with the cargo. Had Jacob swindled Mickey? Was the cargo missing from the boat when the Durkins took it?

Possibly. He wouldn't doubt any scheme his brother came up with. But if that was the case, then why was Jacob so afraid of Mickey? Emmett pushed from the rail. It didn't matter. All that mattered was getting to New Orleans and keeping the Flynns safe.

A plan formed. It would be risky, but it could work.

He scrambled back into *The River Queen*'s pilothouse. "It's the Durkins, sir. They are following us. Billy thinks the gunshot was aimed on board their own boat, and as far as we know, they haven't tried shooting at us. But whatever they want with me, it can't be good." He jabbed his fingers through his hair. "I have an idea that might let us get rid of two problems at once."

Stephen never took his focus from the churning eddies as the boat cut through the muddy water. He'd once said no run down the Mississippi was ever the same, the sandbanks and towheads always changing, ready to waylay the unsuspecting. "Let's have it, then."

"Sam claimed he had dynamite. We can use that to throw behind us. Churn up the water and scare them off while we put some distance between us. Might even get the local law to come looking."

Stephen's fists tightened on the wheel. "You want to wrestle dynamite from an armed man hiding in the hull and toss it at a boat full of gangsters?"

It did sound ridiculous when he said it like that. "Yes, sir."

The dark chuckle from Stephen's chest surprised him. "And how do you plan on accomplishing that?"

There had to be a way. "If we gather enough of the crew and take him by surprise..."

"Which you aren't going to do midday going downriver. Best chance is when he's sleeping."

"With the engines going full steam like we are, he won't notice anyone taking his dynamite until it's too late."

Stephen cut a glance over his shoulder. "I'll be here needing to steer, and Tom has to operate the *Belle*. That puts you down two men."

"Still leaves me, the captain, Billy, Pat, John, and George. Five men should be able to take down one."

"But without any of you getting shot?"

What could he say? It would be dangerous.

"Make sure my father has his pistol."

"Yes, sir." Emmett turned to go.

"And, son?"

He paused. "Yes, sir?"

"We are all counting on you."

His stomach lurched. That's what he was afraid of.

Oh no he didn't. There would be no dashing off without includ-ing her in whatever mad plan he had going.

Anola caught Emmett's arm. "What did you say?"

He paused, but his gaze darted every which way. "I need the captain...and his pistol."

Lady Marie took the bottom stair and joined them on the deck. "What now? A pistol? Why? Is someone shooting at us? Are you trying to shoot back?"

"No, not exactly." Emmett scanned the deck. "Where is your grandfather?"

Anola pointed a finger at him. "Have you learned nothing at all, Emmett Carter?"

He drew back and focused on her. "What do you mean?"

"Here you are going off to do something—probably danger-ous, I might add—and you're once again attempting to do so without telling me what's going on. I am a forgiving sort, but I'm becoming rather annoyed."

He blinked, confliction in his eyes. "I discussed it with your father. The men are going to find Sam and confront him and take the dynamite if we can."

Her father approved this? "You mean while we're moving downriver?"

"Yes."

Mam came down the last of the stairs, and she and Lady Marie spoke at the same time.

"Did you say dynamite?"

"Dynamite!"

Red colored Emmett's ears.

Anola had started to tangle up the details about who knew what aspects of this debacle. How had she forgotten to mention the man in the hull with the dynamite?

"This is why we tell everyone everything." She pinned him with a stern look. "Always."

She addressed her mother and grandmother. "Da is already aware. Emmett told him earlier. We were planning to discuss this situation with everyone, but we were distracted when we found Emmett's boat. A man's in the *Blue Belle*'s hull with the cargo I told you about. He claims he has dynamite and has threatened to explode it should anyone attempt to reach the cargo."

Both women's mouths fell open. Lady Marie fanned herself.

Mam recovered first and narrowed her eyes at Emmett. "How long has this man been on board?"

"Since Vicksburg."

Mam's brows dove toward her nose, and her eyes took on lightning.

Oh dear. Anola stepped between them before tempers could flair. Mam still had a little of the feisty Irish blood in her. It rarely came out, but when it did, she could snap better than any alligator.

"Mam." Anola held out a hand. "Emmett knows he should have said something sooner, but he was trying to keep us safe. He did tell Da. But then I was taken by those men and..." She shook her head to dislodge the memory and stood taller. "He will not keep secrets from us again."

Mam spoke through clenched teeth. "Will you?"

"You have my word."

The two older women eyed him while Anola patted his arm. "Now, what is going on?"

"I told you. I'm going to gather the men, except for your father and the engineer, and we're going to catch Sam by surprise."

"Then what?"

His lips compressed. "Then we're going to throw the dynamite at the boat behind us to dissuade them from following."

"And my father agrees with this?"

A jerk of his chin was his only answer.

Lady Marie began to bluster while Mam gathered air in her lungs to protest.

Before either of them could voice their disapproval, Anola announced, "We'll need to assist—and put on pants so we aren't burdened by skirts."

"Oh no." He snagged her hand before she could slip back to the stairs. "You need to stay here where it's safe."

"Safe?" Which of them had been captured by bad men and escaped? True, she'd been given a massive dose of divine help, but still. She crossed her arms. "We can help. We will not cower and wait to see what happens like a lot of helpless damsels."

He gaped, but when his gaze landed on the other two women, their features determined, he snapped his teeth together. Perhaps she'd been mistaken when she'd thought the others were going to disagree.

"I don't know what you can do," he ground out. "We're taking five men into an already tight space. And surely you don't think you're going in there to fight. That man is dangerous."

Mam twisted her lips to one side. "We won't fight," she said before Anola could respond. "But we can do something else to help."

A sly smile crept over her mother's lips, and Anola couldn't help but grin.

32

This was a bad idea. Emmett stopped at the engine room and prayed for steady nerves. They were going into a bottleneck against an armed man capable of causing massive destruction, and here he stood at the head of a determined, but odd, squadron of volunteers.

The captain had followed close on his heels, with an ancient pistol Emmett wasn't sure would fire. The remaining crew members crowded close. Men who they still didn't know for sure weren't somehow a part of the scheme. Emmett looked over each of them. Billy's wide face was set with determination. Pat and John both appeared nervous, but Emmett likely did too.

Only George, the thin man who usually jumped into the river to secure the deadman anchor held himself with ease. Did nervousness or placidity point to guilt in this case? Best not leave anyone a chance to box them in.

He leaned close to the captain and spoke so only he could hear. "Still don't know if we can trust all of the crew. Maybe you should cover our backs, just in case."

The older man's mustache twitched, and he scooted behind the group. If the move bothered any of the other men, they didn't show it.

"You all stand guard. If anyone you don't know comes out, disable him."

He'd waited for this to see if any of the men gave a hint they knew Sam hid in the hull. None of them did. Maybe the culprit had been one of the actors after all. "Spread out around the room. We're looking for a hidden compartment."

This brought more confused looks, and John spoke up. "I've been working in the engine room for two years. There's no compartment."

"There's also been a man hiding in there with a stash of illegal cargo since we left Vicksburg."

John snorted. "Impossible."

"Lad speaks truth," the captain said from behind them. "Do as he says."

Despite their disbelieving expressions, the men shuffled their feet and made themselves ready. Emmett was just about to grab the doorknob when another figure bustled toward them.

What in the...Cook?

The stout woman strode over with determination on her reddened face and a frying pan in her hand. What did she think she was going to do?

Cook joined them, her focus landing on the captain. "I'm agoin' to help, and not a one of ye is goin' to stop me."

The captain grunted. Emmett met her gaze and let the woman be. More scurrying steps made his fingers twitch. Would the Flynn women come armed with spoons and forks?

Worse.

Each woman held a lidded kettle with the handle wrapped in cloth. And all three wore an Old-West-type bandana over the lower part of her face and aviation goggles. He looked to the captain for explanation, but the older man's eyes lit before he gave the women a nod. Emmett withheld a groan.

Please, God, don't let me get us all killed.

Anola held her breath as Emmett eased the engine room door open. At full steam ahead, the chug of the cogs muted any sound of their entrance.

Sweat popped up on her forehead. Had Emmett deciphered their plan, or should she go tell him? Given the look in his eyes, she had best move to the front. Keeping her smoldering kettle away from her, she passed through the door. The men fanned out, covering any hope of escape Sam might find.

Her gaze sought Mam's, and reading her unspoken question, Mam gestured with her chin toward Emmett. Anola slipped between the crew members and to his side. When he glanced down at her, she nodded to her kettle.

He stared at her blankly.

Oh stars and sunrise. She held out the heavy kettle with one hand and lifted the lid just enough for a tendril of thick black smoke to escape. Emmett's brow furrowed before realization took hold. He pursed his lips, then gave her a nod.

She stepped back to wait. Holding a burning kettle, she couldn't be much help looking for the hidden compartment. But she did know boats better than most, having spent all of her curious childhood years on board. She studied the rear wall. Something wasn't right, but she couldn't place what.

Then it hit her. This wall was too close. There had been more room between the engine and the wall separating the paddle wheel. She was sure of it now. But how could that be? She thought back to a conversation she'd nearly forgotten at the start of the season. Something old Tom had said about the *Blue Belle* undergoing repairs. Had their engineer constructed a compartment for smuggling?

Her skin pimpled despite the heat. Right now, it didn't matter. They had to find Sam and keep him from exploding dynamite on their boat. This close to the combustible, none of them were likely to survive its detonation.

She needed to focus. Think. If they added an extra wall, then there had to be a way to access the space behind it. Emmett had said Sam surprised him in the engine room. No one else had seen him in here or seen him anywhere on the boat. The wallboards formed an interlocking pattern with the seams of one row of boards falling in the middle section of the board beneath it. She checked the floor too but didn't see anything like a door a man could fit through.

Emmett grunted, and she turned from her study to find him sticking his fingers into a space between the boards at about waist height. She moved closer. He tugged, and the board moved, revealing a crack of an opening blending seamlessly with the overlapping wood pattern. She nudged him with her elbow, her eyes telling him to wait.

Emmett hesitated, his body tense. He looked over her head and gestured for the captain. Mam and Lady Marie noticed, and by the time the captain and his pistol reached him, so had they.

He pulled in a deep breath and snatched open a "door" little more than a section of wall without hinges. Before he could do something stupid like rush inside, all three women crowded the opening.

The oversized kettles used for heating water and cooking soups for a full crew suited their purposes today. They set the three in a row along the opening's base, removed the lids, and fanned with the dishrags. The smoldering concoction of coal, grease fat, and some kind of viscous substance she'd snagged from the crewmen's storage closet caught flame. Thick black smoke churned like a fabled witch's brew and began to rise. Cook appeared behind them, and the wind increased twofold.

Anola grinned. Cook used her apron and flapped it with vigor. The smoke billowed out of the kettles and poured into the dark opening.

Coughing came from inside.

"Stand back," Emmett growled.

Their part complete, the women moved away, leaving the kettles to continue smoking.

Oh no.

Now that they stopped fanning, smoke began to fill the entire room. Emmett's and the crew's eyes watered, and someone behind her started coughing. She needed to cover—

A form lurched from the opening. Between one breath and the next, the figure sprang toward her. Anola scrambled away. The indistinct shadow tripped on the kettles, and an unholy howl ripped through the air as his body lurched. Flailing arms swung at her.

A gunshot cracked.

Someone screamed.

Anola sucked in smoky air, and everything around her erupted into chaos. The men were in a pile on the floor. With the pitching and rolling around, she couldn't distinguish whose legs belonged to whom in the melee of fists, shouts, and curses.

"The fire!"

Lady Marie's shout had Anola moving. The kettles! They had to get the kettles out. She lunged past the pile of fighting men and snatched one overturned kettle. Even with the wooden grip on the handle, her palm heated. She grasped it anyway and ran for the door. Not knowing what else to do, she flung the burning kettle filled with coal into the river.

Behind her, Mam and Lady Marie hurried to do the same. Mam's splashed into the water. Lady Marie grunted under the weight, and Mam reached to help her. She yelped when her fingers brushed the hot metal, but they heaved the kettles overboard.

"Find a blanket or something. Some of the coals spilled!" Mam shouted as she rushed toward the stairs. Anola sprinted the other direction, toward the paddle wheel. Billy kept a bucket back there to dip mop water.

The paddles slapped into the river, the churning wheel creating a dull roar as mist coated her skin. She skidded along the damp surface and grabbed the bucket. She hauled up a load of water and unhooked the clasp. She lost half on her dash back to the engine room, but she still had enough to fling at the spilled coals burning at the rear.

They hissed and steamed while the flames died. If the fire had gotten too close to the engine or the boilers, they'd have been done for. Not to mention reaching the hidden dynamite. She coughed as the greasy smoke settled in her lungs. The plan had worked, but it could have been a disaster.

The immediate danger quelled, she focused on the men. While she'd been busy with the kettles, the crew had subdued the stowaway. Though it hadn't been an easy task.

Billy and John secured a bound man between them. When had they gotten rope? The captain aimed a gun level with the man's broad chest, though he'd never use it. The man's glazed eyes, however, proved he believed otherwise. He coughed, his watering, enraged gaze fixed on the captain. He bled from a cut over his eyebrow. One of his pant legs had been burned through, and the skin underneath had blistered red. He'd need a salve.

As for the crewmen, George's crooked and clearly broken nose bled while John sported cuts and what would soon be a black eye. Pat fared no better. While she couldn't see any visible cuts or bruises, he leaned against the wall clutching his stomach. Apparently, Sam had put up quite a fight. A bloodied dagger lay nearby.

Where was Emmett?

His voice coming from the opening throttled the pulse pounding in her veins. "Anyone have a light?"

We're all safe. Thank you, Lord.

The captain appeared with one of the lanterns they'd stationed around the boats and had the lamp lit by the time he reached the secret opening. He thrust the light in front of him and ducked down to step through.

Without waiting for permission, Anola followed him.

How had anyone managed this? Anola stepped through the opening and down three steep steps into the hull. The thump of the paddle wheel echoed through the space, and everything felt damp. There had to be another opening in the outer hull somewhere. Lamplight jumped off the walls, illuminating stacks of crates and burlap-wrapped items.

A pallet lay on the floor near the steps with a rumpled blanket, canteens, and cans of foodstuff. She put her fingers under her nose. Where had he done his personal business?

"What's in there?" Lady Marie's voice came from behind them. After a muffled reply, her voice rose. "I'll go in if I want to."

Anola rolled her eyes. Emmett must have thought to discourage Lady Marie. He was probably annoyed she'd ducked in ahead of him.

The captain lifted the lantern. "Lad, you best come see this."

Emmett scooted past Anola at the bottom of the steps. His boots landed on the rumpled blanket, and he brushed aside a discarded sardine can. Lady Marie appeared right behind him, but she and Mam were unable to get any farther into the opening

269

than hovering on the steps. Emmett ducked, his head brushing the short ceiling.

Her grandmother put both hands on Anola's shoulders to keep her balance and peered past her. "What's in those boxes?"

Anola shrugged. "No idea. Maybe more of those foul little herbs."

While the captain held up the light, Emmett unwrapped a burlap bundle. Three bottles of amber liquid. Without comment, he set them aside. The next bundle contained more of the same, with the bottles varying in size and shape but all likely containing alcohol. They were using her boat for bootlegging?

Made sense, actually. The showboats moved freely downriver and made a lot of stops. If someone wanted to ferry illegal substances, it would be easier in a hidden boat compartment than by land where law officers assigned the task of catching bootlegging trippers patrolled the motorcars.

Emmett grabbed one of the crates and pulled on the top. "It's nailed shut."

Without wasting a second, Mam called out over her shoulder, "Someone get me something to pry open a crate!"

Less than a minute later, a long-handled screwdriver passed from her mother to grandmother and into her hand. Anola held it out to Emmett.

He kept her gaze. "Whatever is in here could be dangerous."

If he and her family stood here in the midst of danger, he could hardly expect her to flee. Reading her determination, he set his jaw and focused on the crate.

Emmett wedged the screwdriver's flat metal end between the lid and the wooden box and pushed the handle down. The creaking grated on her ears, and she cringed. He repeated the motion around all four sides until the lid popped free.

The captain stepped in front of her, his form blocking her view, and peered into the opened crate. Neither he nor Emmett spoke.

Anola huffed and wriggled to look around her grandfather. "What? What's in there? Is it the dynamite?"

"No..." The captain drew the word out. He scratched at his chin. "Can't say I was expecting this."

"What?" Lady Marie drooped so far over Anola's shoulder that Anola had to shift her feet to keep her balance.

"Grandmother!" Anola reached for the wall to steady herself. "You're going to make me fall."

Lady Marie eased her weight off Anola's back, grumbling about not being able to see a thing.

"Why go through all that trouble to hide boxes of canned fish?" The captain plucked a tin from the box that matched the discarded sardine container on the sleeping mat.

Emmett tossed several cans on the floor. He continued to rummage, throwing out more until he grunted in satisfaction.

"False bottom." He dumped the sardines and hoisted a flat wooden plank.

Anola shifted, trying to get a better look.

"What's in there?" Lady Marie whispered in her ear.

"I don't know," Anola whispered back. "I can't see past your husband."

The captain let out a long, low whistle. "Now this is more what I'd expect those pirates of yours to be after." He chuckled. "Think of the story for this kind of booty."

"This must be the loot from the bank robbery." Emmett rubbed the stubble on his chin Anola hadn't noticed.

He did look rather handsome with that bit of dark scruff. Her mind snapped back to what he'd said. "Bank robbery? Isn't that what you discovered Jacob had on the *Good Tidings*?" She craned her neck around her grandfather, but whatever remained in the crate was too deep down.

"That's what he said." Emmett still stood staring into the box. "I wonder if that's what's in all of these crates."

Something darted around in the back of Anola's mind, trying to find purchase. "When I was captured on the boat," she said, her thoughts churning, "they had a lot of discarded burlap and empty crates. Whatever cargo they'd had was already gone. But they kept saying something about Scissors duping them. They were upset about it."

"There's got to be a reason they are following us," the captain agreed. "I don't suppose it matters why so much as we need to stop them."

"Right." Emmett plopped the lid back on the box and scooted it away as much as he could in the tight space. "Sam would have had to keep the dynamite nearby. He wouldn't have sealed it in one of these crates. Too hard to access."

The two men checked between the crates, around the wall, and in every spot they could, but didn't find any explosives.

Mam fingered her collar. "Do you think he lied about having it to scare us?"

"Could be." The captain replaced one of the lids and stepped around a crate. "I'll ask him."

He squeezed past Lady Marie and Mam, who both hurried Anola further inside as soon as there was room.

Mam surveyed the area from the bottom step. "What I want to know is who built this hideaway."

A good question. Anola pursed her lips while Emmett pried into another box. "What did old Tom say? Something about repairs...?" She thought back to a vague conversation early in their season.

"He said they did maintenance and repairs on the *Belle*," Lady Marie supplied. "He said his son helped him with the costs by some of his friends helping with the work." Fire edged into her tone. "I best go have a talk with that sour old coot."

Mam's hand shot out and grabbed her mother-in-law's arm. "Probably not the best idea right now."

The women argued in hushed tones, but Anola ignored them. She was far more interested in seeing what Emmett uncovered. He popped the lid from a second crate and deposited it onto Sam's pallet.

"More sardines." He scooped out the cans and added them to the growing pile around his feet. "And another false bottom." He stuck his finger in a hole at the corner and popped the board free.

Anola gasped. Gold coins, jewelry, and pearls glistened on the base—at least three inches thick. She reached inside and lifted a hefty diamond necklace.

"I wonder who this all belonged to?" After counting eight more crates, she looked back to Emmett as she laid the necklace down. "If the rest are like these two, there's a fortune down here."

Lady Marie and Mam crowded Anola and peered into the box. Mam put her hand to her throat.

"Can you believe this?" Lady Marie fanned her face. "Why, the captain will have a tale to add to his collection for sure. We haven't seen adventure like this in ages."

When had they ever had an adventure involving stolen jewelry and gangsters?

Emmett replaced the false bottom and scooped up the discarded sardine cans to deposit them inside. "We need to keep this as quiet as possible. Too much temptation."

Anola shared a look with her mother. Someone had created a hidden room in their boat. Someone working with the gang of men who'd come aboard in Vicksburg. Emmett's brother had a hand in the scheme as well, though she hadn't figured out how the *Good Tidings* fit into the puzzle. Not to mention the crate of Mexican muggles the crew had accidentally sampled.

"So what do we do now?" Mam asked the question floating around in Anola's mind.

"We seal this room back up and place a man we can trust on guard duty." Emmett wiped his hands on his trousers.

"Tom is going to give an accounting." Lady Marie punctuated each word with a jab of her finger. "He must have known about this compartment."

"Then why not hide the box of muggles down here?" Anola asked. "I found the crate in the storage room. If whoever did that had known about this room, wouldn't they have stashed it here instead?"

"Good point." Emmett rubbed at his scruff again. "I have a feeling my brother has the answers. What I don't understand is how he would've known I'd end up on *The River Queen*."

He gestured at the space, shoved his sleeves up his arms, and jammed his hands on his hips. "There must be a connection here we aren't seeing. There must've been a plan to use the *Blue Belle* long before the Durkin gang took the *Good Tidings*."

"And off to Tom we go." Lady Marie shooed Mam up the steps.

Emmett rocked back on his toes. "I should report all of this to your father before we do anything more."

"And I need to keep my grandmother from running off to confront the engineer on her own."

He caught her hand before she could dart out. "Thank you."

She paused. "For what?"

The depths of his brown eyes drank her in. "You could have blamed me for all of this. I showed up on your boat one day with a wild story, and you've had nothing but trouble since."

Doubt wiggled through her. Now that he said it—no. She shook the thought off. "I believe you're a good man. Whatever is happening here, I don't think it's your fault." She squeezed his fingers. "I trust you."

His expression softened, and he gave her fingers a return squeeze before releasing them. She exited the room and found her grandparents in deep discussion.

The captain spread his hands, the pistol wavering. Did he have it loaded?

"Now look here, my lovely bride. I say this man lied." He wagged the pistol in Sam's direction. "There's no dynamite down there."

Anola wasn't sure if she should feel upset or relieved. Throwing dynamite at a bunch of river pirates did have an adventurous ring to it. But it was also dangerous, and discovering they weren't carrying around explosives that could detonate at any time was a good thing.

"We need to do something with Sam." She plucked a burlap fiber from Lady Marie's disheveled hair. "We have to inform Da what's happening, and someone needs to guard this room."

After a rather heated discussion where everyone voiced their opinions, they decided how to proceed. Billy and George would guard the engine room. Sam would be tied to the railing on the main deck so he could be seen at all times—guarded by John who could also clearly be seen. The family would hold a meeting on *The River Queen*'s roof where they could oversee as much as possible while Da steered. From there, they would all watch Tom in *Blue Belle*'s pilothouse.

A risky plan when they still weren't sure whom to trust, but it was the best they could do.

They were gone. Emmett stared at the churning water behind them. The missing steamer no longer chasing them had to be a good thing. So why did his nerves catch fire and send anxious tingles through him? At least he didn't need to throw dynamite at anyone. He could only imagine what the police would have thought.

He continued to scan the water. Didn't the police have patrol boats? Maybe they'd gotten lucky—no, blessed—and the Durkin gang had seen a police patrol and either been arrested or taken a different course. He couldn't let himself think they'd somehow passed them and were lying in wait for an ambush.

"Still have eyes on him?" The captain's words cut into Emmett's thoughts.

He shifted his gaze from the Mississippi to the man tied to the railing. "Yes, sir. Doesn't seem John has any inclination of letting him out of sight."

"So long as he doesn't have any notions of letting him go, either." The captain twitched his mustache. "Doesn't sit right, not knowing who among us we can trust."

Emmett's stomach knotted. Did they count him as one they didn't know they could trust? He wouldn't blame them if they did. "I'm sorry I didn't tell you everything from the start. You have my word, for what it's worth to you, that I have only this family's best interest at heart."

The captain grunted. "I should hope so, lad, seeing as you have it in your head to join this lot of fanciful Irish actors." He cut him a glance. "Are you still thinking about marrying my gem?"

"Yes, sir," Emmett replied without hesitation. "That is, if she will have me and you and her father give us your blessings."

The older man patted his shoulder. "Good answer, lad. Soon as we get things settled, we'll have that conversation."

It was the best he could hope for. "Yes, sir." He steered the topic back to more pressing matters. "Where's your wife? I thought the women were coming up here for us to have a meeting."

"Lady Marie operates on her own sense of time. She's likely down there giving poor Jocelyn and Cook a tongue-lashing because three of those kettles went into the water." The captain shrugged, then pointed. "There's Anola now."

Anola climbed the ladder to the showboat's roof, her flaming hair doing its usual dance with the wind. Emmett's chest tightened. How had he come to care so deeply for this woman in such a short amount of time? Her gaze found his, and she smiled, increasing the pressure across his rib cage. He'd done nothing at all to warrant her faith in him. But her belief only made him want even more to be the type of man she deserved.

"Cook and Lady Marie are"—she glanced at the captain as she hesitated—"discussing what to do about new kettles. I told them we have far more important things to worry about. But she insisted that since Sam is captured and there isn't any dynamite, then figuring out the kettle problem could be left to her and Mam."

A knowing look entered the captain's eyes. He gave a nod. Perhaps this was his wife's way of leaving the more dangerous issue to her husband to handle. That surprised Emmett in some ways, and yet made sense in others. Lady Marie was a spitfire, yet she also held her husband in high regard and, from what Emmett had been able to tell, didn't chafe at following his leadership.

They walked closer to the pilothouse, and Anola stepped inside. Stephen exited a moment later, leaving Anola to steer the boats. Emmett wouldn't have thought she'd be one to miss this conversation. Apparently sensing his study of her, she looked over her shoulder, saw him watching her, and cast him a wink. Was she doing the same thing as Lady Marie or...?

Before he had too much time to think, Stephen took control of the conversation.

"Big fellow." Stephen thrust his chin toward Sam. "But no dynamite, you say?"

The captain nodded, obviously having shared that information while Emmett had once again been captivated by the fair river queen.

"We did find crates of what we think are stolen valuables from the bank robbery in St. Louis," Emmett added. "All hidden underneath false bottoms and stacks of sardine cans."

"I don't understand." Stephen tipped his cap back to reveal a furrowed brow. "I thought you said your brother had the bank robbery loot on the *Good Tidings*."

"I thought so too. Anola said there were empty crates and discarded burlap, but she thinks whatever cargo they had before was gone."

The captain scrubbed a hand down his face. "Did Jacob have the cargo moved from the *Good Tidings* to the *Blue Belle*? Why?"

"And who created the storage place?" Stephen asked. "That required planning."

Both men looked to Emmett, and the air knotted in his throat. "I don't know how Jacob would have known I'd be on *The River Queen* or how it factored into whatever they are doing. All I know is I called my brother from Kimmswick and he sounded like he was in trouble. There were angry voices in the background. Then I met him in Memphis, and he said he had to get a boat for Mickey or he'd be dead. Probably me too. Then he knew about the showboat and said you all would be in danger as well." He sucked in a breath after the rush of words.

"What was it Tom said about those repairs before the season?" Stephen asked the captain.

The captain's shoulders sloped as he rubbed at his forehead. A low rumbling sound escaped before he spoke. "Said his boy helped him out. Had some friends do a lot of the work, and they did it for cheap."

Emmett mentally turned the puzzle pieces, seeking a reasonable fit. "Do you think his son had something to do with the muggles?"

"If he did, why not hide it in the compartment?" Stephen crossed his arms, his mustache drooping. "And, if they were moving stolen goods from St. Louis, why not hide them in the *Belle* before we departed for the season? Why load them in Vicksburg?"

"And if they had the jewelry from the bank robbery, then what did we have on the *Good Tidings*?" Emmett rubbed the tight muscles in the back of his neck.

None of them had any answers to the others' host of questions.

"I suppose I shouldn't have sent Jacob away." Emmett's chest throbbed, and he rubbed at the offending place. "He could've told us what is going on."

The captain snorted. "Lad, if that fellow had wanted to tell you the truth, he would've done so long ago. Seems to me whatever happened on the *Good Tidings*, he set you up for the fall."

Ice solidified in Emmett's center. His brother wouldn't, would he? Yet hearing it from someone else's mouth made the probability freeze through him with more certainty than he cared to admit.

"We aren't going to puzzle the answers out here." Stephen set his shoulders, the fabric stretching against taut muscles. "What we need to do now is come up with a plan for how we are going to handle the problem on board."

"First, we need to talk to Tom." The captain peered toward the pilothouse on the other boat, though they could see little more than the engineer's form.

"I doubt he knew anything about it." Stephen removed his cap and ran his hand over his hair. "I'm guessing he was duped along with the rest of us. They probably thought no one would find the compartment and they would be able to smuggle their cargo up and down the river. They wouldn't have known this would be our last season or that we would be going to New Orleans."

"Where hopefully the law will be waiting to catch those involved," Emmett interjected before they could devolve into more scenarios and speculations on what the builders of the secret compartment planned to do with it. "But since we have Sam, I don't know how we're going to pretend everything is going according to their plans so they can be caught in the act."

Stephen mashed his hat back into place. "We can always keep him hidden."

"Or throw him overboard." The captain's eyebrows lifted at Stephen's frown. "What? I'm sure he can swim."

"Right to somewhere to warn the others." Stephen's head-shake jostled the abused hat. "We have to keep him. But we still don't know if any of our crew is a part of their gang."

This conversation was starting to go in circles. Time to redirect. "Is there somewhere secure you can keep him where we three can post guard?"

"The green room doesn't have any exits and is right under our rooms where we can hear a commotion." The captain jammed his hands in his pockets, his shoulders further hunching beneath his tweed. "We could store him in there."

Emmett tried to ignore the odd choice of words about storing a man like one would a pair of old shoes. "And we'll need to ensure everyone stays on board at all times. We can't give anyone an opportunity to get a message out."

The other two men agreed.

"Then we push to New Orleans as fast as we can." Stephen widened his stance. "The sooner the better."

"Except I sent word we would be there in three days, which is when the police will be looking for us."

They stood there in tense silence until the captain huffed out a long sigh. "Well, lads, looks like it's going to be a long few days."

Anola locked her gaze on the jack staff, afraid to let her attention drift from the showboat's prow. As fast as they were moving, her fledgling skills at reading the river might get them in trouble if she didn't focus. Still, she tried to listen to the men's conversation.

She could catch only snatches of words. The open front window channeled the breeze through the pilothouse and pushed it out behind her. Their voices carried with the flowing breeze toward the *Blue Belle*. But it sounded like they had a plan to keep everyone safe. Hopefully.

A hundred questions swarmed her, but all she could do was pray God would get them through to the other side.

Warm hands slid over her shoulders, and she started. "Oh, Emmett. It's you." His clean scent of lye soap mixed with smoke and something pleasingly manly that must come from his pomade or aftershave announced his presence. That and the uncanny sense she felt every time he came near. "Did you decide what to do?"

His palms glided down her arms to rest on her hands where she clutched the wheel, leaving tingles in their wake. How did he do that? He spoke close to her ear, which caused more delightful flutters.

"We are going to *store*"—he put extra emphasis on the word—"Sam in the green room and continue with the original plan you and I had. We go to New Orleans and wait for the police to capture the gang in the act of unloading their illegal cargo. We'll keep everyone close until then."

She nodded along, trying to focus on his words and not on the way his closeness made her feel more alive than the time she'd jumped from a high bank into the river.

He kissed her temple. "We are doing everything we can to keep us all safe."

"I have no doubt."

His breath came in a warm wave over her cheek. "You are far better than I deserve, Anola Flynn. I have little to offer you other than my love and undying devotion, but I willingly give you all I have." His embrace tightened, and his voice deepened. "Will you do me the honor of becoming my wife?"

Her heart fluttered. This wasn't the way she'd pictured being proposed to. Something more like a grand romantic gesture with dramatic flair had always sprung to mind. A ring, perhaps. And yet, standing here steering *The River Queen* on her final voyage with the wind in her face and the arms of the man she loved wrapped around her... Well, perhaps this was nothing short of perfect after all. It fit her and Emmett. Unexpected and unconventional.

He tensed, and his arms started to move away. "I still need your family's blessing, and you need to make sure I am who I say I am and not involved in—"

"Oh, you dear man." She laughed and risked pulling one hand off the wheel to grab him before he could put distance between them. "Of course I will marry you. I'm sorry I hesitated too long. I was thinking about how perfect we are together and forgot you'd need to hear the yes singing in my heart as a word spoken out loud."

He relaxed behind her and placed his cheek against her temple. "You are a fascinating woman. Do you know that?"

"I might have an inkling." She nuzzled her face into his. "We will have an exciting story to tell our children and grandchildren someday."

"Ah, yes. We'll regale them with tales of how we met when dastardly pirates threw me into the Wicked River and their dashing grandmother with flaming hair rushed to my rescue."

A deep laugh erupted from her full heart. "If that's how you want to tell it, who am I to stop you?"

They drifted into silence, watching the shoreline pass by. Peace at odds with the worries hanging over them settled in her heart. Whatever dangers awaited them, she could thank God for the blessing of facing them with Emmett by her side.

Only ten more miles. Emmett grasped the rail on *The River Queen*'s lower port deck and watched each boat they passed. The traffic thickened the closer they got to New Orleans. Everything from passenger ferries to tugs and flat-bottomed dinghies he'd never take out into these waters pressed together as they flowed toward the major city.

The warm breeze gathered up the steam puffing from the smokestacks on the steamboats, whisking the vapor away before it could paint the cloudless sky. Anola joined him, her countenance thoughtful. These past days had been stressful. They'd not slept much as the men kept guard over Sam and the women worried. But even with smudges of dark skin under her eyes, Anola was beautiful. She'd dressed in a long flowing emerald skirt he'd never seen before paired with a crisp white blouse embroidered with green vines along the draped sleeves hanging at her elbows.

He had no idea what era the fashion had come from or if it was another element of Anola's own style, but it suited her. As did the wind playing with her long loose hair and the sunshine caressing her pale cheeks. He wrapped his arm around her, and she leaned into him.

"Today will likely be a trying one." She placed her head on his shoulder. "Would you pray for us?"

"I have been." He rubbed a piece of her silky hair between his fingers. "In fact, I've been praying quite a bit more since meeting you than I have in a long time. One of the many benefits you have brought to my life."

"That's good." She smiled up at him, her eyes bright. "But I mean here. Together."

A pang of conviction nipped him, followed by a sense of rightful duty. She looked to him to lead them in prayer as a husband ought. A privilege he would gladly carry. He kissed her forehead and closed his eyes as he gathered his future bride close.

"Lord, I thank you for this beautiful soul who has brought me joy and has guided me closer to you and for her family who I hope to soon call my own as well. Thank you for your protection as we have faced many dangerous circumstances. We don't know what the future will hold, but we know you are a good father and we can trust in you. If you are willing, Lord, we ask that you would keep us safe, that you would bring these men to justice, and that you will allow for the stolen goods to be returned to their owners. Please be with us each step of the way today. In Jesus's name, amen."

Anola echoed his amen, and a profound sense of peace swept through him.

"There now." She straightened. "We are armed and equipped for whatever may come."

How he admired her faith. It bolstered his own. "Yes. But let's not look for danger, shall we?"

"What makes you think I would?"

Facing such wide-eyed innocence, he nearly faltered.

Then she winked. "I promise, future husband, I will not put myself or others at undue risk."

Before he could ask for clarification on what sort of things she'd consider an acceptable risk, Lady Marie and Jocelyn approached.

"The time has come upon us," Lady Marie announced in true thespian fashion.

Jocelyn rolled her eyes. "Really, must you be so dramatic?"

The other woman smirked. "If today isn't one for drama, then when is? Here we have pirate loot, our boat's final voyage, new love, and soon courageous officers will sweep in and save the day." She spread her jeweled fingers. "Quite the tale, I say."

God help them.

Emmett hoped the women didn't find the dangers of their situation something to make light of. This wasn't one of their plays.

"We are doing what is right to the best of our ability and have coated the situation in prayer." Lady Marie patted her dyed-brown hair. "There is no harm in pointing out how it will make for an interesting story."

Interesting might not be the word Emmett would choose. Distressing, more like.

The port at New Orleans was unlike any other Anola had seen. While large cities were not new to her, something was different about this one. The buildings huddled close to the water, teeming with people of every type. A host of smells from roasting meats to rotting garbage assaulted her senses. She stayed at the rail, determined to experience every moment.

Would policemen be waiting nearby? Would they be hiding? Had the gangsters already spotted them? Would they know something was wrong because Sam should have sent a signal?

Her palms grew slick with sweat. An hour later, *The River Queen* settled into an open section of the wharf. Then Da, Emmett, Lady Marie, and Mam joined her on the deck. Normally, they would lower the plank. But not today.

"Ready?" Da asked.

They'd agreed not to confront Tom until they reached New Orleans because they couldn't risk losing their engineer before making port. Keeping an eye on all of their people had been an emotional and mental drain, but wondering about Tom had been especially hard for Da.

The family followed his sure footsteps across to the *Blue Belle*, where Da called out orders to the crew to gather in the dining room. Then he left Emmett and Cook in charge of keeping them there while he and the others went to speak with Tom.

They found the old engineer in his pilothouse, fingers smoothing the polished wood of the wheel.

"A man thinks he knows how he will feel when his last day behind the wheel comes, but turns out, he couldn't ever truly be prepared."

Something about the way he spoke brought both suspicion and sadness. Anola gripped the doorframe and hung back at the threshold, allowing her parents and her grandmother to fill in the space inside.

"Did you know, Tom?" Da asked.

"Not at first." Tom gave the wheel a fond pat. "Wasn't around much. My fault. Maybe Phillip would've made different choices if he'd had a pa who spent more time with him." He straightened, the quiet assurance of a riverboat captain cloaking every inch of his stout frame. "When Phillip asked me if he could store something in the closet and get it when we reached Vicksburg, I didn't think anything of it."

Anola tilted her head. "But I asked everyone, even you, if they knew what happened to that crate when it disappeared. You said you didn't know anything about it."

Tom shifted his feet. "Sorry, miss. Something seemed off, so I took the box and unpacked all those little bags. I stuffed them down behind a loose board in the wall, and then I tossed the crate so, when we reached Vicksburg, I could make sure Phillip talked to me before he retrieved anything. Figured there was no harm in that."

Silence settled. Then Tom cleared his throat.

"But then we ate that soup." He rubbed the creases furrowing between his brows. "And you all started asking a lot of questions." Those deep lines shifted to regret. "I'm sorry my boy used my *Belle* to transport something he shouldn't have."

Da and Mam exchanged glances. "And the spot in the engine room?"

Resignation tautened into stony resolve. "I didn't know nothing about that, Jocelyn. I swear it on my hat."

"And, Sam, the man we found in the hull?" Mam's soft voice made Tom's mouth twitch.

"Never seen the fellow before. Been wondering when you'd come ask, and given what happened with Phillip and what I'm guessing he did to my *Belle*..." Tom slid his cap from gray hair and crushed it between his thick fingers. "I can see why you would wonder. But I give you my word I didn't know nothing about the hidden space nor the man they put in it."

The strain stretching his words beckoned Anola to believe him.

"But I did know my Phillip put that crate on board, and I never did say. Figured after it was discovered, there was no point. I'd deal with him."

Da's voice sharpened. "And did you?"

Tom's knuckles whitened on his cap. "While we were in Vicksburg, I met him. Told him you'd found what he had hidden and what it did to me and the crew. He was right mad when I told him I'd dumped the rest of it in the river soon as I got the chance."

Well, that explained what had happened to the Mexican muggles.

"You should have told us." Lady Marie wagged her head. "We would've understood."

"Figured there was no harm done since I got rid of the rest of it." Tom sighed. "I didn't know he'd been involved in more. When he offered to help me and get us a deal on the repairs, I had no idea he'd betray me like this."

He cleared emotion from his throat, working his hands around the hat brim and refusing to look up. "I thought he was wanting to take his place here. Finally work the river with his father. Turns out he only wanted to use *Belle* right under my nose."

An ache tightened her throat, and she stepped into the room. She touched Tom's arm. "Thank you for telling us. I'm sorry how this has hurt you."

He turned shining eyes on her. "Thank you, miss. You've always had a kind heart."

After they let Tom gather himself, Da spoke again. "Do you think Phillip is connected with the gang of men who came aboard in Vicksburg?"

"Seems likely. If he had the hidden compartment built, then he would've been able to show them. He was in Vicksburg that night."

So how did Jacob play into all of that? "What about Emmett's brother? Had you seen him before?"

"No, miss. Never saw that boy before he was on board doing his best to avoid work."

"Well..." Da trailed a finger along a piece of driftwood Tom displayed on the windowsill. "That probably means the rest of our crew didn't know anything either. Might as well tell Emmett to let the crew out of the dining room."

He extended a hand to Tom. "I've enjoyed working with you these past seven years."

"Same here, sir." Tom gave Da's hand a firm shake, then settled his cap back in place. "I'm sorry we have to depart on these terms."

"I hate to be the one to ask." Mam laced her fingers together. "But if Phillip is in the same group of men as Jacob..."

Her sentence drifted away as she and Da shared a loaded look.

Then Phillip would likely be among those arrested. If they let Tom go now, he might try to warn him. He'd already tried to save his son from trouble by dumping out the muggles.

Tom's eyes widened, his weathered features going slack. "Law's coming, then?"

He tugged his cap low onto his brows. "Well, then, I guess it's time to steer into the storm."

E vening shadows crept over the water and wrapped tendrils of darkness around the boats. Emmett paced *Blue Belle*'s portside deck, nerves on fire. They should have been here by now. Tom and the crew waited in the dining room with the captain. After confessing to hiding the muggles and lying to the Flynns, Tom had taken to shore. Emmett didn't know what the man would do now.

A figure emerged underneath a nearby streetlight, and Emmett's breath caught.

Mickey.

Emmett met the man on the dock, careful not to look around too much and give away the fact that he prayed the police were somewhere nearby.

"Well, now." Mickey hooked his thumbs in his pockets. "Looks like the weasel came through."

Emmett's molars welded together. Why had his brother started calling him the weasel? He forced his words to come out with confidence. "Let's get this over with. Your cargo is here as agreed."

Mickey sucked his teeth and pulled something from inside his jacket. The light glinted off the barrel of a long revolver. "We need to settle a few things first."

Fighting to keep his face passive, Emmett refused to look at the weapon.

"I'm not the kind of man who takes well to being double-crossed." Mickey toyed with the gunstock.

How could he know they'd captured Sam and the law was on the way? "What are you talking about?" Emmett gestured toward the boat. "Your cargo is all there. The agreement was you'd leave the Flynn family alone and call it even with my...uh, friend."

"You mean your brother, Jacob?" Mickey snorted as Emmett reeled back. "You don't get as far in this life as I have without knowing a few things, *Emmett Carter*."

Emmett's dry tongue cleaved to the roof of his mouth.

"See, I suspected Jacob would try to dupe me. Old Scissors isn't as sharp as he likes to think, though, so I set men to watch him and follow *Good Tidings*. Imagine my disappointment when a rival of mine knew when and where to relieve me of what was mine."

"Jacob meant for the boat to be robbed?" Fury unfurled in Emmett's center. "They could have killed me." He mumbled the last part more to himself than to the other man. His own brother.

Mickey shrugged. "According to my sources, Scissors told Durkin he was switching gangs. Tipped him off to where to find the boat and, best I can tell, told him not to kill the men on board. It wasn't a bad plan, really, if he'd been able to pull it off."

That didn't make any sense. Unless... "I'm guessing the Durkins discovered they'd been had and there wasn't anything valuable on board."

Mickey gave a confirming tilt of his head. "Good thing I figured out before I went through with killing him. After I caught him sending Durkin to steal my loot, I realized the part you had to play in all of this." He waved the gun at Emmett. "And of course, you did make good leverage. I kept him close and let him believe I thought Durkin had my money."

Emmett let his gaze drift to the weapon and took a step back. They must've been the ones in the room when he'd called Jacob. "I didn't know about any of that."

A wicked smile creased Mickey's face. "You think I'm a fool too, do you?" Before Emmett could respond, Mickey sneered. "So I'm to take it as pure luck that you swim from the *Good Tidings* and onto the steamer I had outfitted for hauling?"

Emmett tried to move back another step as Mickey raised the gun. He turned out his palms. "I went on *Good Tidings* because my brother asked me to. Then I met him in Memphis, and he was afraid for his life. He comes on the boat and tells me to keep quiet about some cargo that is going to be loaded. Your men load cargo in Vicksburg into a hidden compartment in *Blue Belle*. That's all I know."

"You let him escape."

"What? He was there when you were loading the...cargo." He almost said too much and revealed he knew what was in those crates. He dared a look around, but still no men in uniform. What if they didn't come? He'd have to try to keep Mickey talking. "Who is Phillip?"

Something malicious flashed in his eyes. "Just some kid we paid to make sure the boat was outfitted. Why do you ask?"

So maybe Tom's son wasn't in the gang. Had the box of muggles been something Phillip did on his own unrelated to Mickey's schemes? "But then how did you know *The River Queen* was taking its last run and would be going to New Orleans?"

"Stop trying to distract me from talking about your part in this. Where is Scissors?"

"I don't know. He got off in Vicksburg, and I haven't heard from him since. I thought he went with you."

"I know what we found wasn't all of it. Figured either he or Durkin would lead me to the rest, but looks like the weasel let him slip off. You're going to take me to him and the rest of my stash."

So they'd created a cargo space in the *Blue Belle* before any of this happened. Something Mickey had said earlier took hold. He'd said he let Jacob believe he thought the money was gone. Clearly, he'd loaded at least part of it in Vicksburg.

Jacob must have hidden the real cargo instead of putting it on the *Good Tidings*. Probably planning for Mickey and Durkin to fight one another while he took off with the loot. Then Mickey caught him before he had the chance and kept him close. Until he got off at Vicksburg. But the jewelry from the bank was in *Blue Belle*'s hold. So when had Mickey gotten it back, and what had happened to Jacob?

"Now see, that's a shame." Mickey motioned with the gun, snapping Emmett out of his rapidly firing thoughts. "Looks like you'll have to go the way of Henry after all."

"You killed Henry?" Emmett had wondered about the timing of the actor having a heart condition in Vicksburg and conveniently creating the distraction. Ice collected in his stomach. Henry must have been feeding Mickey information. The man had been alive when they'd left them in Vicksburg, but who knew if he'd pulled through.

"Look, I don't know where Jacob is. I promise. We're here in New Orleans. You have your cargo of muggles. We can go our separate ways now, right?"

Nothing flickered in Mickey's eyes when Emmett mentioned the wrong cargo. Instead of answering, he motioned with the gun. "Lead the way."

Anola's heart pounded so fiercely she feared it would call out like a siren. Everything in her strained to rush down to the dock and give that man what-for. But she'd have to bide her time.

Please, Lord, let Emmett's warnings have reached the right men. Let them make it to us in time.

Emmett crossed the plank back onto the *Blue Belle*, Mickey behind him with his gun trained on Emmett's back. Where were the others? Surely they'd have the rest of the gang nearby to unload their cargo. With her back pressed to *The River Queen*'s wall, Anola eased her way around the aft deck to keep an eye on Emmett as he approached the engine room. What would happen when Mickey discovered Sam gone?

She had to do something. If only she could see where the rest of her family hid on the *Blue Belle* and signal them. Da waited in the engine room with the captain's pistol. The captain and Lady Marie remained in the pilothouse, prepared to pull the whistles or ready the steamer to escape if they needed to.

She and Mam had kept watch to signal any policemen. So far, none could be seen. The men boarded and crossed the main deck.

There.

A figure emerged from the shadowed dock, followed by four more. Were those policemen or Mickey's crew? Each man wore a wide-brimmed hat and a long dark coat despite the heat. How she hated not knowing if they were friend or foe. She shifted her gaze back to the steamer, but Emmett and Mickey were gone.

Every muscle in her body tensed. She couldn't just stand here, could she? On fleet feet, she crossed to the other boat and darted to the engine room unseen. She hoped.

The door stood open, and voices came from inside. She hovered at the frame, back pressed against the wall, and listened.

"Think you are clever, eh, Weasel?"

Weasel? Why would Mickey call Emmett that? He couldn't be one of them. Claws sank into her stomach. They'd trusted him. Believed he'd been protecting them and had sent word to the law.

But what if he hadn't? What if it had been a ruse and she'd been as gullible as a new lamb?

"It's all there. Just like we agreed."

Agreed? That word from Emmett's lips sent a knife through her chest, and her throat clogged. No. It couldn't be true.

Help us, Father. Let the truth be known and justice prevail.

But what if that justice included Emmett? What would she do if her hopes for a future with him were nothing but a ruse to keep her content and her family doing what the gang wanted?

The sound of feet shifting tempted her into peeking around the corner. Her knees trembled. Da. His shadow moved across the doorframe, and then he was behind Mickey.

"Stop right there!" Da's voice boomed through the engine room.

Anola slipped inside.

Emmett dove away as Mickey turned. Rage contorted the man's face. He swung his own gun.

He wouldn't care if Da held a pistol to him. He would shoot. Before her mind could catch up with her body, she dove.

Her body slammed into Da's as a gunshot split the air.

E verything exploded into chaos. Emmett's heart froze mid-beat and then pounded against his rib cage. Behind Mickey, Stephen shouted. Mickey pivoted, gun at the ready. Emmett lurched forward when a flash of vibrant color vaulted through the air.

A shot fired, but he didn't know if it came from Mickey's or Stephen's gun. Anola and her father hit the ground in a tumble while Emmett collided with Mickey's larger frame. The man grunted and stumbled, but kept his balance. Emmett struggled to keep Mickey's gun arm lowered even as his gaze desperately sought the others. Were they shot? Injured?

Voices came from outside, but he couldn't focus on anything more than the desperate struggle. Mickey pushed against him, easily outmatching Emmett. He shoved Emmett against the wall, pinned him with his forearm, and leveled the pistol at Emmett's nose.

Mickey spat to the side. "Never would've thought a weasel would best my wolf, but this here ends the last of your scheming. Now tell me where Scissors is, or I off the gal first and make you watch."

"I don't know. I swear it!" Emmett shifted against Mickey's arm, but the man held fast, any hope of wrestling the gun from him futile.

"If you think you'll be able to continue your plan of making off with my goods you're mistaken." He waved the gun in Emmett's face. "Best you can hope for now is to save this nice family and die quickly."

Did that mean once Jacob had left in Vicksburg he'd headed straight to where he'd hidden the loot, thinking he'd conned both gangs? Emmett's stomach soured as things his brother said resurfaced. Trust him. He had a plan. It would all be worth it.

Jacob mustn't know Mickey had discovered at least some of the haul. But if Mickey was still looking for him, had Jacob gotten away? Maybe he'd stashed the loot in several places so he didn't return to the hiding place Mickey must be watching.

Shots fired outside.

Mickey's attention wavered.

Movement separated from the shadows behind him.

No. Not—

Something metallic swung through the air and connected to Mickey's head with a sickening crack. The man blinked. Swayed. His weight moved forward, and his arm slid up Emmett's chest to his throat.

Pressure increased at the base of his neck, arresting his air. Emmett surged against him, fighting for freedom. Mickey's eyes rolled back in his head, and the pressure released. He thudded to the ground.

Emmett sucked air into his aching throat. Where was...?

The breath left him in a rush. There.

Anola stood over Mickey, massive wrench in hand. Stephen took a place next to her, one hand gripping his bleeding upper arm while still holding an unwavering pistol aimed at the downed gangster.

"Nobody move!"

At the shout, Emmett turned to the doorway to find a man dressed in the finest attire he could imagine. A policeman's uniform.

"Oh, thank heavens." Anola puffed her cheeks. "I had begun to fear you'd never arrive."

The policeman swept his gaze over the three of them and then to the man on the floor before landing back on Anola. "Step outside, please, miss."

She opened her mouth, and Emmett thought she might protest. Instead, she handed the wrench to the policeman and exited with all the regal air of a queen leaving her throne room. And how he loved her for it.

The officer gestured to Stephen with the wrench. "Drop the weapon."

Stephen complied, and the antique pistol clattered to the deck. Without being asked, he pushed it out of Mickey's reach with his toe. Then he addressed the officer. "I'm Stephen Flynn, owner of *The River Queen*." A nod to Emmett. "This is my future son-in-law, the man who sent word ahead of us."

The man's brown gaze slid to Emmett. "Emmett Carter?"

"Yes, sir."

After an assessing look, the officer knelt to handcuff Mickey. "What took him down?"

Mickey groaned as the officer tugged his arms behind him and secured the restraints.

Stephen's chest puffed. "My girl."

The officer's eyebrows arched before settling into professionalism again.

Emmett motioned to the rear wall. "The hidden compartment is back there with the items stolen from the Mercantile Bank in St. Louis, and we've been keeping another member of the gang tied up in the dining room."

If he wasn't mistaken, he'd think the slight curve of the officer's lip said he was impressed. "Very good. My men have arrested five more. We had them surrounded, so once they all boarded, we made our move."

He called for another officer, and a dark-haired man in a matching uniform appeared. "Let's get this cargo unloaded." He turned back to Stephen. "You and your family stay close. I have a lot of questions."

Emmett shared a look with Stephen, and the man gave him a nod. "You go to her. I'll handle things here."

With a grateful tip of his head, Emmett slipped out to find Anola.

Stars and sunrise. That had been close. Anola held her palm against her fluttering heart. Moonlight trickled over the water and illuminated the wave of officers doling out justice.

"I'm telling you," Lady Marie said with a dramatic sweep of her arm. "*This* is the play they should do next season." Her grandmother motioned at Anola. "It has everything you want, my gem. Mystery, intrigue, adventure, and romance. What's not to love?"

Anola let out a shaky laugh. "Let's finish living it first and see how it ends, shall we?"

Lady Marie balked. "All good plays end happily."

That may be true. But life wasn't a play, and sometimes things ended in tragedy. The only permanent happy ending came in heaven. She rolled her neck to release some of the tension in her shoulders.

Emmett emerged from the engine room, concerned gaze seeking hers. When he spotted her across the deck, he hurried to her and wrapped her in his arms.

He clung to her, kissing the top of her head. "You were so brave."

She relaxed into him, then eased back, searching his eyes. "What happened? All of the truth, Emmett. Hold nothing back from me."

Confusion, followed by a flash of hurt, crossed his face before understanding settled in his gaze. "Mickey must think I was working with my brother and helped him escape. Best I can figure, Jacob tried to double-cross Mickey but Mickey found out and stole back at least part of his loot without Jacob realizing it. I guess he thought he would smuggle the loot along with his bootlegging down to New Orleans, then find out where Jacob hid the rest of it after the heat in St. Louis died down. But Jacob must have given him the slip in Vicksburg. I don't know if Mickey's men caught him or if he escaped with a load of cash."

"What does any of that have to do with the muggles?"

"Maybe Phillip did that on his own. He might not have wanted to risk revealing Mickey's secret room for one crate, but he could still use the cover of Mickey's operation to do a little smuggling of his own. I'm sure he didn't expect anyone to find the box in the storage room."

"And you had nothing to do with any of these plans?"

He cupped her cheeks and made sure she held his gaze. "My guilt lies in not telling you and your family about the dangers I allowed on your boat and in thinking I could handle things on my own. I also should have made sure my brother was arrested, instead of letting him slip away. It was wrong of me to suggest he disappear, but at the time, I thought he was only escaping some bad men. Turns out I have allowed him to escape justice as well."

She chafed at doubting him, but she had to be sure. "So, you think Jacob loaded fake cargo onto the *Good Tidings* to double-cross Mickey and then the Durkin gang stole the boat."

What a tangled net. She pressed her hands against her middle. "That would explain why they had all of those empty boxes and burlap and why they kept talking about getting revenge against you. They thought you were your brother."

301

Emmett wrapped one arm around her shoulders and steered her farther down the deck, away from where Mam and Lady Marie were holding an animated conversation about which of them would be tending to Da's wounded arm. Thankfully, the bullet had only grazed him. He would need stitching, though.

"That's my theory." Emmett settled against the rail. "Based on the things we've learned and what I heard both Mickey and Jacob say, I think Jacob bought the *Good Tidings* planning to haul the cargo for Mickey for a cut of the profits. At some point, he decided to hide the loot instead and put fake cargo on the boat. He then tipped off the Durkin gang, telling them he would switch sides if they gave him a bigger cut. He sent me downriver while he hid the real cargo. Problem was, Mickey suspected him. I'm guessing they caught Jacob at our house before he could get to the loot."

"But then you were the one on the boat when the gang took the *Good Tidings*, and they threw you overboard." She fingered the collar at her throat. "It's a miracle they didn't kill you."

"Part of the deal with my brother and perhaps the only evidence he still holds any brotherly love for me." Emmett gripped the rail at *Blue Belle*'s bow. "By the time the Durkin gang figured out they'd been tricked, I was already gone downriver with you. Mickey must have kept Jacob close and threatened him if he didn't get the cargo back or make it up to him. So when I met Jacob in Memphis, he was trying to put together another job for Mickey. He said it was luck I happened to be on one of the boats Mickey had already been outfitting. I'm not sure how much Mickey orchestrated and how much of it was seizing an opportunity."

Anola pursed her lips. "So Mickey had Phillip create a hidden cargo place long before your steamer was stolen."

"Right. Which means they were planning to use it to smuggle other things. Maybe the muggles, maybe liquor, maybe other stolen goods. I don't know."

She snuggled into his side. "So then what happened to Jacob?"

"I'm guessing since Mickey found Jacob's hiding place and stole the loot back, he was planning on confronting Jacob in Vicksburg after it was loaded."

"I did see him speaking with Jacob in the dining room when I gathered up all of the men and we escorted them off of the boat."

Emmett nodded. "Mickey believed Jacob and I were in on the scheme together and planned to escape with the loot and let him and the Durkin gang fight over it. He didn't know we'd already discovered the bank loot, and I'm pretty sure the only reason he didn't shoot me on sight was because he thought I knew where my brother went."

"Thank goodness. And once the Durkin gang hears about Mickey's arrest on *The River Queen* and the confiscation of the goods, they won't have any reason to come after us again."

They stood in silence while the policemen filed out of the engine room with crates and stacked them along the deck.

After the last crate joined the others, Anola released the words churning inside. "For a moment, I did doubt you. I wasn't sure when you told Mickey the cargo was in New Orleans as planned if you had been a part of it all along." Emotion thickened her voice. "I'm afraid I let myself get carried away worrying about all of the what-ifs."

He kissed the top of her head. "You've nothing to apologize for. I kept secrets from you and was less than honest. Anyone could understand your hesitation."

"So you forgive me?"

A chuckle rumbled from his chest. "How could I not when you have so often and so easily forgiven me?"

She nudged his ribs. "Well, then, as long as we agree we will both always be honest and forgive one another, I suppose we shall make it just fine."

His hand cupped her cheek, and his warm gaze sent lightning bugs dancing through her. "You, my river queen, have to be my favorite of God's creations."

STEPHENIA H. MCGEE

She tugged her lips into a playful grin. "I think you're working your way to that place of affection for me as well."

He laughed. "After the river?"

She pretended to think. "A close second."

"I'll take it." He tipped her back, the starlight dancing over their heads.

He kissed her then, sweet and tender with a promise of all of their tomorrows filled with love, life, and adventure.

"There it is." Anola squeezed Emmett's fingers as they looked at the tiny showboat from the St. Louis shore.

A swarm of tiny dancers tapped through her middle. This would be fun!

Emmett frowned at the peeling paint and the missing section of railing, his features crestfallen. The only boats they could afford were a far cry from what *The River Queen* had been. "I'm sure we can find something else."

And take more money away from her grandparents' farm? She settled her cloak around her shoulders to dispel the hint of coming winter. "Come. Let's have a look. She needs a little work, of course, but that's all right."

Still appearing dubious, Emmett followed her onto a show-boat about half the size of *The River Queen* and shook hands with Mr. Elroy Tipton. While the men talked, Anola took the liberty of exploring.

First, the theater. The boat Mr. Tipton had named the *Bella Notte* followed much the same floor plan as *The River Queen*. She descended a short hallway, past the ticket booth, and through open doors to a theater ready to seat a hundred new friends. She ran her fingers along the dusty seat backs. Twelve would require new upholstery.

And the stage. Anola spared a glance for the cramped orchestra pit and climbed to the planked surface. It would need a good sanding and several coats of polish. She tapped her finger on her chin. As an older boat of the first showboat era, it didn't come equipped with electric lighting. She'd need to ask Emmett if they could afford the expense.

She inspected the curtains in surprisingly good shape, the levers and pulleys, and the green room in the back. A good cleaning would do wonders. And they'd need new furniture and props of course, though they'd been able to keep as many of the costumes as she'd wanted.

She settled in the middle of the stage and crossed her feet underneath her. A feeling welled in her center and worked its way around her heart. Bittersweet. A tangle of eagerness for a new adventure and a melancholy over the loss of her beautiful home. Selling *The River Queen* had been difficult, and unloading George Washington's table had been quite the feat, resulting in more than one dockhand despising them. Then hauling all of the stuff they didn't sell onto a ferry and traveling like homeless people back up the river had drained her. If not for Emmett and his steady presence, she may well have crumbled.

"I figured I'd find you here." Emmett entered the theater and sauntered down the aisle, seeming not to notice the torn seat backs or the worn stage. His focus remained on her, his eyes filled with a new light. "Have you inspected every nook and cranny?"

She patted the stage next to her. "Not yet. I've only made it as far as the theater and the green room, I'm afraid."

He intertwined his fingers with hers. "There may be hope for this boat yet. But first, I have some news. I'd been waiting to tell you until I was certain, but now seems like a good time."

"Oh?"

His face grew serious. "If you'd like, your father and I have worked out a deal for *Blue Belle.*"

What? Her pulse skittered. "I thought Da sold it along with *The River Queen.*"

"In a way, he did. Turns out old Tom fancies a run up the Ohio as well. He offered to purchase the boat, and he's going to hire out to us, if we will have him."

The idea brought a shimmer to her eyes. "Of course we'll have him." She pointed her finger. "But we will be getting rid of the storage hole."

Emmett held out his palms. "Already done, according to Tom." He wrapped his arm around her. "He hasn't heard from his son since Mickey's men were arrested. Tears him up, and staying with people he considers family would be good for him."

As it should be. "The familiarity would be good for me as well."

"Glad to hear you say that since I've also hired Cook, Billy, and George."

Her heart swelled. "A fine start to a crew."

Dear Emmett. He knew her well. After discussing what Cook would think about life on the Ohio, Anola steered the conversation to the others who wouldn't be joining them. "Have you heard anything yet?"

"No. Your father said he checked this morning."

"He's here?"

"Yes, he and your mother arrived minutes ago. Stephen is in a...shall we say, *animated* discussion with Mr. Tipton about his price." Emmett gave her a squeeze. "There's been no word from Henry and Sue."

They'd told the police everything, including what had happened with Henry and his heart in Vicksburg and the part he'd played in informing Mickey, but no one had been able to locate them. They still weren't sure how much the couple had been involved with the gang's activities. "You don't think he..." She couldn't bring herself to finish the sentence and ask if the man who had worked for her family had died at the hands of a cruel criminal.

"I'm not sure, my love. It's in God's hands."

"As is Jacob."

His arm around her tightened. "Since the police say the majority of the stolen jewels were recovered, it's doubtful he escaped with much. But then, a lot of the money's missing. Maybe Mickey had it, or maybe Jacob made off with some. Jacob kept telling me he had a plan and that, if I would trust him, everything would work out."

"We'll keep praying for them."

Emmett kissed her temple and lifted her to her feet. "That we shall. But for now, I want to show you something."

They exited the theater and mounted the staircase to the upper floor. Emmett motioned to a set of doors on their right. "In here."

She swept inside a room filled with light. "Oh my stars and sunrise."

No wonder he'd looked far more pleased when he'd come into the theater. This room must have changed his mind about *Bella Notte*.

With a grin, he led her deeper into the sun-washed area. An entire wall of windows opened onto a sweeping porch, letting in a wide view of the river. She put a hand to her throat. "What an amazing view."

"I thought you'd like it." He stepped up behind her and encircled his arms around her waist. "We'd have plenty of room on the porch for night lunches and rocking chairs." He turned her in a slow circle. "And look, a coal fireplace. Over there, we can put a table for the family and a seating area here."

"Will this be Da and Mam's rooms?"

He spoke as though this would be the primary residence on the boat, like the captain and Lady Marie's suite had been on *The River Queen*.

He chuckled against the top of her hair. "No, my love. These rooms will be ours. Your parents will take the second smaller set. Your father insisted they wouldn't need the bigger suite since they wouldn't be the ones who might expect children."

The peeling wallpaper and paneling in need of repair couldn't diminish its perfection. "I love it, Emmett."

He showed her a bedroom that even had a space for a nursery, and then they toured the other rooms on the floor. An apartment with a bedroom and sitting area and another single bedroom were situated across the narrow hallway.

"One more thing special thing I want to show you about this boat, and then we'll need to decide if we want to make Mr. Tipton an offer." He rolled his eyes in mock annoyance, but his amused tone gave him away. "That is, of course, if your father hasn't already either finished the deal or flustered the man to the point of tossing us overboard."

They exited the perfect guest room for when her grand-parents wanted to visit and stepped into the hallway.

This boat was the one for her. Those windows! A new home to decorate and run as she and Emmett decided together? It was perfect.

She entwined her fingers with his and let out a little laugh. "And I thought I was going to have to be a laundress. I should've known better than to doubt when God promises he will do more than we could ever think or imagine."

"I have to agree." Emmett gave her a little twirl, eliciting another laugh. Her man may dance yet. "When I landed in the muddy Mississippi, I couldn't have imagined it would turn out to be the best day of my life."

She scrunched her nose. "That was your best day?"

The dashing man winked at her. "Of course. It was the day I met you."

Anola dropped into a deep curtsy. "Glad to know I charmed you."

"That and more, my love." He led her outside to the upper deck and around to the stern, where the shipbuilder had put in a rear porch.

Anola surveyed the space. "You could hold a dance back here!"

"Or a wedding."

Rows of chairs, a preacher, and Emmett in a suit filled her vision. "Oh yes. It will be enchanting."

"I was thinking an evening wedding and a short honeymoon tour as we take our maiden voyage. Then we'll pick up the cast and be ready to start *The River Gem*'s first season." His eyes burned bright with joy, and her heart vaulted.

"I can think of nothing in the world I'd like better." The other part of what he'd said took hold. "*The River Gem?*"

"Rather fitting, don't you think?"

Words weren't enough. Instead, she looped her arms around Emmett's neck and pulled him close. Her heart swelled with gratitude for all she'd been blessed with, and a new song filled her mind.

Welcome, welcome,

From far and near,

Join us, join us,

For the magic here.

Adventure, beauty, and romance unfold,

A story for the young and the old.

Welcome, welcome,

Step through these gates,

On *The River Gem*, a new beginning awaits.

The Ohio / Mississippi River split

May 14, 1924

Nothing about this day could be any more perfect. Emmett checked the final details of the suite of rooms he would soon share with his bride. She'd somehow managed to make the space as unique as the lady herself, and it already felt like home. Vibrant blue curtains lined the windows and matched the bedspread in the other room. The Flynn women had spent the winter months sewing and creating while the men had stripped, painted, and repaired.

He ran his fingers over the table in their little dining space and adjusted the vase of yellow roses he'd set in the center. His gaze slid to the clock over their mantel.

Five. Finally.

He adjusted his tie one last time and stepped into the hallway, his focus jumping to the door across the hall. Feminine laughter filtered through, and he lingered to enjoy it, his pulse quickening at his bride's jubilance.

"Ready, lad?"

He started at the captain's voice. How did that man always manage to sneak up on him? "Do you practice stealth?"

The older man chortled. "Not hard to surprise a fellow struck moon-eyed, lad." He fiddled with his green bow tie. "Let's get you where you need to be."

They strode to the party deck on the stern where the chairs had been set in two neat rows and Anola had decorated each one with a shiny green ribbon. The pastor from the nearby town of Cairo, Ohio, smiled at him from his place stationed by the rail, which the Flynn women had tied with fluttering green ribbons and bows.

The captain gripped his shoulder, halting him before he could join the preacher. "She might be takin' your name, lad." His voice thickened, increasing his Irish brogue. "But you're about to become a Flynn. Are you sure you're ready?"

Emmett gave him a wry smile. "I was ready nine months ago."

"I reckon you were." The captain's laugh rumbled in his chest. "But now you're ready to start life together. *The River Gem* is perfect for my gem, and so are you, lad. We are glad to call you our own."

Emmett's throat tightened. "Thank you, sir. I consider it a great honor to be a part of this family."

"Of course you do. What's not to love about this lot?" The captain gave Emmett another pat and then sauntered off to meet the guests gathering on the deck.

Theirs was to be a simple affair, attended by those they cared about the most. The captain and Lady Marie took their seats on the first row. Old Tom, Billy, George, and two new crew members, Alex and Jerry, settled behind them. Even Cook had dressed for the occasion. He'd never seen the woman in a gown before with her hair styled. She spotted him and waved, and he returned the gesture.

They'd taken on a few actors to round out the traditional allotment to complete the cast. A heavy, to play the villain, a comic, a character man, a character woman, and a lead actress. The family had even convinced him he could play "general business" roles, which meant he'd be someone's friend or brother, and he'd have very few lines. As long as he didn't have to dance.

He greeted Eric, their new comic, and his wife, Ellen, who would play a villainess or character role. Abe would be the heavy opposite of the character man Stephen would play. It would be a small cast, and they'd have to perform doubles. But Anola was thrilled. She, of course, would always be the leading lady. Starting with playing the daring heroine in a dashing tale about river pirates and stolen treasure.

The people settled into their seats, and the minister called for their attention. He nodded to Jocelyn, who sat at a pianoforte moved up from the orchestra pit for the occasion. She beamed at Emmett as her fingers flew over the keys.

He locked his eyes on the corner where Anola would appear. The evening sunlight glittered on the white paint, and a breeze ruffled over the witnesses. He breathed a short prayer of thanksgiving despite the pinch in his heart that he had no family of his own to share this moment.

She emerged, and he couldn't help the grin that split his face.

Anola Flynn made a stunning bride. White beaded lace swooped over her shoulders and overlaid creamy white silk. The fabric fell in soft layers to the floor, leaving just enough space at the bottom for the toes of vibrant green shoes to peek out. She'd gathered her long fiery hair into a mass of curls atop her head, secured with emerald gems in a band. Reminiscent of the first day he'd met her, a plume of peacock feathers crowned her. A delicate white net dipped down over her forehead. He shifted his feet as her father brought her down the short aisle and to his side. Emmett took her gloved fingers. "My beautiful river queen."

They spoke their vows and pledged themselves before God and family, and then he swept her up into his arms.

He kissed her soundly before the preacher even announced his right to do so. The audience hooted and cheered. He righted her, delighted when she blinked at him.

Then he took a deep bow and waved to the crowd. Anola laughed and dipped into a curtsy.

She snaked her arm through his elbow. "I might make a stage man out of you yet, Husband."

How he delighted in the sound of that word from her lips. "Perhaps, my fair lady wife. Perhaps you shall."

"Presenting Mr. and Mrs. Carter, pride of *The River Gem*!" The preacher's voice rang out over the evening air, and the people's cheers renewed.

Emmett led Anola through her family and friends while a boisterous Irish tune danced from Jocelyn's fingers on the pianoforte and Stephen Flynn dipped his captain's hat.

The river churned around them, waiting to whisk them away on a new adventure. He breathed in the smells of life and beauty, then turned his bride into a spin for an impromptu dance.

She twirled, her face radiant. As they danced across the deck, her radiant soul filled his heart, and her song filled his mind.

Adventure, beauty, and romance unfold...

I had so much fun researching this story. I found all of the riverboat and showboat history fascinating. One thing stood out, and I believe it's important to note that there were two distinct showboat eras. The first and primary era happened before the Civil War. This is the main time frame most people would expect a showboat story. However, in the early nineteen hundreds, a secondary showboat trend arrived. Unfortunately, this era didn't last long, and by the mid-to-late 1920s, the showboat era drifted away. The years in between felt perfect for Anola and *The River Queen*.

Many scenes in this book are inspired by the real-life escapades of Betty Bryant, who gave a detailed account of her childhood on a showboat in the early 1920s in her book *Here Comes the Showboat!* She shows what life was like on the *Bryant's Showboat*, giving descriptions of the boat, the acting troupe, the family's schedule, and information on the crew from her life on the river. *Bryant's Showboat* traveled the Ohio River while *The River Queen* traversed the Mississippi, and while I took inspiration from Betty's fun stories, I used them in my own way for the book.

Another point to note is that the Montesano Springs Park mentioned in the book closed in 1918 for the war and never reopened. However, it was an interesting place and in such a perfect location for the book that I took creative license and pretended it stayed open long enough for Emmett and Anola to visit.

The term "muggles" and the start of illegal marijuana distribution in New Orleans and along the Mississippi River began around the same time as the story. On February 18, 1922, the New Orleans *Times-Picayune* announced a new drug habit was growing in the city. The newspaper reported the "passage of a drastic law to curb the constantly growing practice of selling and smoking marijuana, also known as muggles, will be sought at the next session of the Legislature." On May 29, the council prohibited the possession and sale of marijuana in New Orleans, with violations punishable by a fine of up to twenty-five dollars and thirty days of imprisonment. So by the time we reach the story in June of 1923, it is plausible gangs would have been smuggling marijuana along with the bootleg liquor they would have already been moving up and down the Mississippi.

While I did my best to stay true to the times, I did take liberties with the era in terms of Anola's personal sense of style and her unique childhood.

Thank you for taking time to read!

Moonlight on the
Mississippi

River Romances Book Two

T his fella had lost his sunbaked mind beneath that striking mop of smoky-brown hair. Camilla Lockhart stifled
a smirk as she propped her hip on the *Alma May*'s wheel.
"You'll need to explain why you think *this*"—she slapped one
of the spokes and a splinter jabbed her palm—"old gal will
help you find a boat at the bottom of the Mississippi."

He opened his mouth, then pressed his lips together.

Why the confusion? If he couldn't see the *Alma May* had
sputtered ten years past her useable life and was being held
together with a handful of prayers and buckets of tar, then
she couldn't help him. They did their best, but they could
only do so much for a ramshackle tugboat.

And if he thought she would ever get involved with treasure seekers again, then her first estimation on the nature of
his wits had been too generous.

The man—not much older than her own twenty-six years
if she didn't miss her guess—tipped his hat back in a roguish
way that made her heart give a traitorous tremble. By her
boots, Lula rumbled a growl. Exactly. Too handsome for
anyone's good.

317

"You run a scavenger boat, right?" He rubbed a day's worth of dark scruff and then shoved his hands into the pockets of clean but worn britches.

Camilla snorted. "Who told you that?" She'd wallop them for sure for stirring up old rumors better left buried.

"Look, Miss—"

"Captain."

He blinked. To his credit, the surprise vanished quickly. "Captain Lockhart. I promise this will be a trip worth your while. The pay is good."

A sweltering August breeze poked through the windows and attempted to cool the sweat from her brow. What a mess she must look. Though to be fair, she hadn't planned on receiving company when she'd docked in Natchez. Least of all the handsome sort. She ran a hand down her trousers and hoped there weren't any grease stains.

Lula pawed at her knee, waiting to be picked up. When Camilla scooped up her furry companion and settled the black-and-white terrier on her hip, Lula swayed toward the man, sniffing.

The fellow's face softened, and an endearing tip curved his lips.

Handsome and turned a kind eye on her pup? Something in her chest pinched. She needed to get this man off her boat before he could cause all sorts of trouble. Like muddling her senses.

She cocked an eyebrow at his near-threadbare shirt and put her mind back on topic. "I don't indulge fool's errands."

His cheeks tinged pink, and he straightened broad shoulders. "I don't have the money yet, but as soon as we find that treasure—"

"You mean if. *If* we find this supposed treasure." She blew out a breath and gestured toward the exit. Whoever had let this man into her pilothouse deserved three extra shifts moping the deck where Lula did her personal business. Camilla turned sideways to squeeze past him and escape.

"Please. You're my only hope."

Maybe it was the note of desperation in his voice. Or perhaps it had something to do with the arresting quality of those emerald-green eyes that seemed to hold a century's worth of life. A girl could get lost in eyes like those. Dangerous waters, that.

Whatever the reason, she and Lula paused at the door. "Mr..." She twisted her lips. "What did you say your name was?"

"Gray." He thrust out his hand, and she slid her palm against his calloused one. "Daniel Gray."

His gaze latched onto hers and held. Snakes and salt water. This man could convince a common field mouse she was a warhorse, and she'd follow him into battle.

Camilla extracted herself from his grip. "Sorry, Mr. Gray. I wish I could help you."

She'd barely made it three steps from the pilothouse, that unnerving fellow on her heels, when a shout came from the deck.

"Trouble ho!"

Great. What else could go wrong today?

Read *Moonlight on the Mississippi*, River Romances book two.

Stephenia H. McGee is a multi-published author of stories of faith, hope, and healing set in the Deep South. She lives in Mississippi, where she is a mom of two rambunctious boys, writer, dreamer, and husband spoiler. Her novel *The Cedar Key* was a 2021 Faith, Hope, and Love Readers' Choice award winner. A member of the ACFW (American Christian Fiction Writers) and the DAR (Daughters of the American Revolution), she loves all things books and history. Stephenia also loves connecting with readers and can often be found having fun with her Faithful Readers Team on Facebook. For more on books and upcoming events and to connect with Stephenia, visit her at www.StepheniaMcGee.com

Be sure to sign up for my newsletter to get sneak peeks, behind the scenes fun, recipes, and special giveaways!

Sign up using this link and get a free eBook!
https://newsletter.stepheniamcgee.com/u9qdt7amwv

Stephenia H. McGee, Christian Fiction Author

stepheniahmcgee

Stephenia H. McGee

Buy direct from the author's online bookshop!
Support the author and find great deals.

Shop.stepheniamcgee.com

Books by Stephenia H. McGee

Ironwood Family Saga
The Whistle Walk
Heir of Hope
Missing Mercy

The Accidental Spy Series
*Previously published as The Liberator Series
An Accidental Spy
A Dangerous Performance
A Daring Pursuit

Stand Alone Titles
In His Eyes
Eternity Between Us
The Cedar Key
The Secrets of Emberwild
The Swindler's Daughter

Time Travel
Her Place in Time
(Stand alone, but ties to Rosswood from The Accidental Spy Series)
The Hope of Christmas Past
(Stand alone, but ties to Belmont from In His Eyes)
The Back Inn Time Series
(Stand alone books that can be read in any order)

Novellas
The Heart of Home
The Hope of Christmas Past

Buy direct from the author's online bookshop!
Support the author and find great deals.

https://shop.stepheniamcgee.com

"Be warmed. You won't be able to put this book down."
-**Patricia Bradley,** USA today bestselling author of the
Natchez Trace Park Ranger Series

She pretends to be a widow to save a child.
Until he comes home to a wife he didn't marry.

When Ella Whitaker rescues a newborn baby, they take
refuge at Belmont — but will Union Major Westley
Remington take kindly to discovering his home is being run
by a fiery and independent woman—one many believe to be
his wife?

"A whirlwind adventure full of action, secrets, plots, romance, family drama and more!"
- InD'Tale Magazine

Captured and mistaken as a spy, can she unravel a conspiracy before her secrets cost a man his life?

Once a privileged heiress, Annabelle Ross is now struggling to hold her home and her life together through the devastation of the War Between the States. But with a forced marriage and a desolate future on the horizon, her hopes are beginning to dwindle. When she discovers an encrypted note on a dying soldier, she seizes the opportunity to use it to deliver a message of her own. Instead, she's mistaken for a spy and captured. Now her only chance to escape is the handsome soldier in charge of discovering her secrets.

★ The Accidental Spy series is a 2020 rewrite of the previously published Liberator Series (Leveraging Lincoln, Losing Lincoln, Labeling Lincoln)

★ Please note these books must be read in order and that while each book has a complete storyline, the overall plot is completed throughout the trilogy.

It was just one night at a B&B. Until she woke up in 1857.

Have you ever wondered what it would be like to visit the eras you love to read about?

The Back Inn Time series books are fun, faith-filled stories of what it might be like to suddenly experience life in a different time. These clean historical romances are packed with humor and adventure, and answer the question every historical fiction fan wonders—what would it be like if I went back to that time? Come visit a seaside Victorian inn where you can "step back inn time and leave your troubles behind!"

Sign up for my author's newsletter for behind the scenes, early sneak peeks, writing fun, giveaways, deals and more. As my thank you, you'll receive a free eBook (digital book) copy of *The Heart of Home*.
https://newsletter.stepheniamcgee.com/u9qdt7amwv

He asked if he could die on her porch...but instead he brought hope for new life.

Once a wistful romantic, Opal Martin now simply aspires to scrub the remnants of the War Between the States from her tattered life. But when a nearly drowned soldier appears and asks if he can die on her porch, she must guard against the sudden revival of her heart's hope for love.

Fans of *In His Eyes* will also enjoy seeing Ella and Westley again in Opal's story.

Printed in the USA
CPSIA information can be obtained
at www.ICGtesting.com
BVHW032016300823
668992BV00001B/3